PRAISE FOR
PATRICIA A. MCKILLIP

"A popular fantasy writer casts her spell again."—*The Washington Post Book World*

"McKillip tells an intricate, beautiful . . . tale with her usual cool elegance."
—*Chicago Sun-Times*

"McKillip conjures a world of secrets and ambiguities, where the magical and the mundane constantly intersect." —*The Boston Globe*

"[McKillip] skillfully weaves together two eras and two sets of believable characters to create a single spellbinding story that brilliantly modernizes a beautiful old formula." —*Publishers Weekly* (starred review)

"The author's graceful prose and remarkable depth of characterization bring to life a tale of love and loyalty that transcends time and space."
—*Library Journal* (starred review)

"This is McKillip at close to the height of her powers, which is to say close to the highest pinnacle in contemporary fantasy." —*Booklist*

"McKillip has once again proven herself a master in the field." —*SF Site*

"Mesmerizing and unforgettable—a true flowering of a major talent."
—*Kirkus Reviews*

"Her unique brand of prose magic splendidly repays your attention."
—*Locus*

"Her tales are invariably charming." —*Analog*

Ace books by Patricia A. McKillip

THE FORGOTTEN BEASTS OF ELD
THE SORCERESS AND THE CYGNET
THE CYGNET AND THE FIREBIRD
THE BOOK OF ATRIX WOLFE
WINTER ROSE
SONG FOR THE BASILISK
RIDDLE-MASTER: THE COMPLETE TRILOGY
THE TOWER AT STONY WOOD
OMBRIA IN SHADOW
IN THE FORESTS OF SERRE
ALPHABET OF THORN
OD MAGIC
HARROWING THE DRAGON
SOLSTICE WOOD

Collected Works

CYGNET

Cygnet

PATRICIA A. McKILLIP

ACE BOOKS, NEW YORK

THE BERKLEY PUBLISHING GROUP
Published by the Penguin Group
Penguin Group (USA) Inc.
375 Hudson Street, New York, New York 10014, USA
Penguin Group (Canada), 90 Eglinton Avenue East, Suite 700, Toronto, Ontario M4P 2Y3, Canada
(a division of Pearson Penguin Canada Inc.)
Penguin Books Ltd., 80 Strand, London WC2R 0RL, England
Penguin Group Ireland, 25 St. Stephen's Green, Dublin 2, Ireland (a division of Penguin Books Ltd.)
Penguin Group (Australia), 250 Camberwell Road, Camberwell, Victoria 3124, Australia
(a division of Pearson Australia Group Pty. Ltd.)
Penguin Books India Pvt. Ltd., 11 Community Centre, Panchsheel Park, New Delhi—110 017, India
Penguin Group (NZ), 67 Apollo Drive, Mairangi Bay, Auckland 1311, New Zealand
(a division of Pearson New Zealand Ltd.)
Penguin Books (South Africa) (Pty.) Ltd., 24 Sturdee Avenue, Rosebank, Johannesburg 2196,
South Africa

Penguin Books Ltd., Registered Offices: 80 Strand, London WC2R 0RL, England

This is a work of fiction. Names, characters, places, and incidents either are the product of the author's imagination or are used fictitiously, and any resemblance to actual persons, living or dead, business establishments, events, or locales is entirely coincidental. The publisher does not have any control over and does not assume any responsibility for author or third-party websites or their content.

PRINTING HISTORY
The Sorceress and the Cygnet, Ace hardcover edition / May 1991
The Sorceress and the Cygnet, Ace mass-market edition / January 1992
The Cygnet and the Firebird, Ace hardcover edition / September 1993
The Cygnet and the Firebird, Ace mass-market edition / September 1995
Ace trade paperback collected edition / March 2007

Library of Congress Cataloging-in-Publication Data

McKillip, Patricia A.
   [Sorceress and the cygnet]
   Cygnet / by Patricia A. McKillip.
      p. cm.
   ISBN-13 978-0-441-01483-5
   1. Magic—Fiction. I. McKillip, Patricia A. Cygnet and the firebird. II. Title.

   PS3563.C38S67 2007
   813'.54—dc22

                                                              2006047653

PRINTED IN THE UNITED STATES OF AMERICA

10 9 8 7 6 5 4 3 2

Contents

The Sorceress
and the Cygnet

PART ONE

RIDER
IN THE
CORN

ONE

HE was a child of the horned moon. That much Corleu's great-gran told him after, pipe between her last few teeth, she washed the mud out of his old man's hair and stood him between her knees to dry it.

"You have your granda's hair," she said.

"Tell him take it back." A thin, wiry child, brown as dirt otherwise, he stood tensely, still trembling with the indignity of being crowned with mud, tied up with Venn's granny's holey stockings and left in the sun to dry.

"I can't. He's dead now. His hair sprouts into dandelion seed. Moon seed." She smelled of smoke like a wood fire, he thought, leaning into her, and lavender and something dank but not unpleasant, like a cow barn. She was talking again, telling story as she stroked his hair with the cloth. Her own hair, proper dark, not moon hair, had a few white seedlings here and there. There were seedlings above her upper lip, and a mole like a black moon, which fascinated him, so the story he had to take out and examine later—years later—to understand it fully.

"He rode between the rows of corn on his great dark horse, and all I could think was: His hair is white like the corn silk in my hand. I thought how it might feel, under my hand. Hot from the hot sun, and damp from his sweat. I stood there in the corn, thinking those things for the first time. Everything grew farther away, closer he came. His eyes were green, he wore green. I never saw green the same way, after. Everything was singing: My mam, a row away, was singing 'the little dark house falling, falling. . . .'"

"I know that," Corleu said, finding a place in the story to stand, a stone rising up in a river while the quick blurred water spun past.

"Everyone knows. Dark house falls to everyone. But that day it sounded like a love song. Even the corn was singing, under hot sun, leaves quiet like they never learned how to whisper secrets, but whirring and buzzing from their shadows like blood flowed in them. I held the ripe corn heavy in my skirt, and the one in my hand I pulled leaf and silk aside with my teeth and bit into, sweet and hard and full of sun. . . . He rode up to me and stopped."

She stopped, too, suddenly; Corleu gazed up at her, feeling as if the river had stopped.

"Go on. Tell story."

"Nothing much more," she said. There was more: He saw it in her eyes. "Only how all the corn leaves pushed together to hide us, and made the sky turn green. . . . And then he rode away. And I had your granda. With his hair." She pulled Corleu straight, scrubbed at his hair with the cloth. "He could fore-see in a bucket of still water, your granda. He could see with his feet, they said. He could find anything in woods, any herb, mushroom, flower."

"Who was he?" Corleu asked. "Who was rider in the corn?"

She made a sound in her nose, in the back of her throat, like a laugh, but she wasn't smiling. "So many asked me that so many times. But how was I to know? I never asked, he never spoke. 'Corn,' I told your granda. 'Corn was your father and sun your grandfather.'" She smiled then, her lined face rip-pling like pond water. She touched his chin. "And old horned moon his grandmother, who turned to see him just as he opened his eyes first time, to see her. So all her power spilled out of her horns into his eyes. Likely you looked at her, too, with that hair. But you haven't learned to look in other ways. My son was reading petals by your age. He could see the simple things: weather, birth. He learned to fight young, too, like you. No place for the white raven among the dark." She stroked his damp hair flat. "And all Way-folk are dark-haired."

"Why?"

"Because long ago we wandered down out of the stars, that's how restless the Wayfolk are. Looking for new ways and roads and paths. We still carry night in our hair." She lifted his face between her fingers. "And eyes. Even though you stared at moon, you're one of us, with night in your eyes. And that's why women always put a braid in their hair, so the night and Wayfolk past won't flow out of it at sunrise."

"Tiel doesn't braid," he said, thinking of her dark, straight, glossy hair.

She chuckled, hauled to her feet, and said something else it would take years for him to understand. "She will, one day. She'll braid, like all of us. But whose name will she braid into her hair?"

For all those years to understanding, it seemed to him that all else he inherited from his granda—or great-gran, more likely—was a gift for getting into trouble. "Moonbrain," he heard endlessly. "Corleu fell off moon. Limehair. Catch a cuckoo in Corleu's hair." Fists would fly, a small brawl erupt among the colorful wagons, always with the lank, corn-silk hair at the center of it, until someone's mam waded in with soup ladle or a pan of dishwater. He could turn even a simple game hobble-nobble. It might begin peacefully enough: all the dark-eyed, barefoot, raw-kneed smallfolk in a circle, holding hands and moving around the moonbrat, who held his hands over his eyes, in a game as old as memory.

"In a wooden ring," the circle chanted,
"Find a stone circle.
In the stone ring
Find a silver circle.
In the silver ring
Find a peacock's eye.
Lady come, lady come,
Find my eyes, find my eyes.
Circle, circle . . . Blind can see!"

The circle jostled to a sudden halt; the blind dropped his hands. In front of him: Jagger, a stocky child with coarse straight hair and an eye for trouble. By rule of the game, Corleu must do whatever Jagger ordered, to get himself out of the circle. They stared at one another, mute, challenging, while the other children whispered and grinned.

Jagger gave his command at last. He pointed a grubby finger toward Venn's parents' wagon and said, "Go stick your head in that bucket of milk. Milkhead."

When the older children finally peeled the pile apart, there Corleu was on the bottom, with his hair rubbed so full of dirt he looked almost one of them. His nose was running, his eye wild, his fists clenched; Sorrel, receiving him into the wagon, sighed worriedly, for her fey son hardly looked human.

She cleaned him up and sat him down at the tiny painted table. She emptied a basket of dried flowers in front of him: wild rose, lavender, verbena, dandelion, hawthorn. "Pick the stalks out," she instructed. "And the leaves. Only leave the petals." She was a tall woman, with lovely almond eyes and a soothing, husky voice. She wore bright ribbons braided in her long black hair; that and the songs she sang had entranced Corleu since he was old enough to uncross his eyes. They had also entranced Tul Ross, a stolid, hard-working man who had fallen in love with her as she sang in the fields. Un-afraid of her peculiar father and her own odd gifts, he had married her and had only said resignedly, when the past echoed in her newborn's hair:

"That's out of the way. Likely you'll have the dark ones now."

But she never did. She watched her son sniffing and picking at the petals, so gently they barely stirred under his hands. As he had watched her do, he blew over them, winnowed them with his breath, so that colors formed patterns on the wood. He sat silently again.

"What do you see?" she asked at last, curiously. He looked up at her, his eyes huge, shadowed.

"Face."

"Whose face?"

"Table's."

"What?"

He showed her with his finger: two knotholes and a scowling crack. She shook her head, baffled, and gave him one of his granda's books to read, for he had an odd, useless gift for that.

As smallfolk became halflings, they ceased tormenting Corleu and began trailing after him, for he also had inherited his great-gran's tongue. He told them the tale of the Rider in the Corn many different ways, always feeling his way closer to the truth of it, until one day they all stumbled into under-standing, and the tale took off in wild variations. The Rider was a lord from Withy Hold. The Rider was an evil mage from Berg Hold. The Rider was a cowherd on a borrowed horse. There never was a Rider, only his great-gran's fancy, and the warm, sweet, singing corn. One of Wayfolk boys had fathered the bastard and Corleu's great-gran had looked at a white goat under the full moon, that's why his hair. Since by then, great-gran was dead, they couldn't go to her for the true story. He told them other tales, collected from Granda's books, or from listening silently in the dark while the oldfolk talked around fires on mild winter days in the deserts of Hunter Hold, where they met with other Wayfolk companies for the season, or in the barns and stables and cider houses on the sweeping farms of Withy Hold. One sum-mer, he learned to take more than tales from the cider house.

He lay with Jagger and Venn and a crock of cider on hay they had piled, one hot midsummer night when they were all pushing into adulthood several directions at once, and all of them in the dark. Early in the morning, tales took a turn from fathers, girls and ghosts, to the stars above them, thick as sheep in a shearing pen. Living between earth and sky, little escaped their notice underfoot or overhead. Corleu, who was racing Jagger for height, but was yet all scrawny wire and muscle, took a swallow, slapped a mosquito on his cheek, and said,

"There's Peacock."

It was hardest to see: a spray of glittering eyes clustered near the almost perfect Ring. Venn grunted.

"I see it." He grunted again. "I see two Rings."

Jagger burped. "Where's the Blind Lady?"

"There is no Blind Lady," Corleu said.

"Blind Lady wears the Ring of Time," Jagger argued. "She sees out of the Peacock's tail." Venn giggled, was ignored. "So where is she?"

"In stories. In the sky you only see her Ring."

"How come she's blind?" Venn asked. From farmhands, shepherds, they all knew bits and pieces of the silent shapes of fire and shadow that haunted the night. Corleu said dreamily, hugging the crock against his chest:

"The Cygnet tricked her. If she looks straight at you, you die, because the end of time is in her eyes. So the Cygnet, when they were all fighting, tricked her into looking at her reflection in the full moon. So she went blind. Now she sees out of the Peacock's eyes."

Venn juggled his arm. "You'll split your tongue with book lies. Pass crock."

"I'm not! It's not lies, it's stories."

"It's stories," Jagger said. His voice was deeper, his jaw was shadowed, he held a weight of authority. "Pass the crock over."

"Stars don't fight," Venn muttered.

"These did," Corleu said. A dog barked somewhere, catching wind of them, then subsided. He shifted on the hay, an intimation of dawn creeping over him: Tul's furious face; haying under a blazing sun with the headache oozing out of his pores. But for now, night seemed on the verge of forever. "They fought the Cygnet. The Gold King. The Dancer. The Warlock. The Lady."

"For what?"

"For Ro Holding."

"Who won?" Venn asked fuzzily. Jagger nudged him with a beefy elbow; cider splashed out of the crock onto Corleu.

"You mucker, watch my hair—"

Venn snickered. "Been watching it, it's still white as bird shit."

Jagger's arm weighed across Corleu's chest as he started to sit up. "Don't brawl in the hay," he warned. "Bad enough we're drinking in it. Get on with story, I want to hear. Venn, you say another word I'll take your teeth for my sling."

"It's the cider in my tongue," Venn said meekly.

"It's a talkative cider," Corleu said darkly.

"Go on. Who won the star fight?"

"The Cygnet of course, you loon, it's the Holding Sign of Ro Holding. The others are only Hold Signs."

"Gold King is," Jagger said after a moment, calculating. "Sign of Hunter Hold. But not the others. Not the Dancer or the Warlock or the Lady. Hold Signs are the Blood Fox and the Fire Bear—"

"And the Ring," Venn said, catching up. "The Ring of Withy Hold."

"It's the Lady's Ring," Corleu said.

"What of Blood Fox, then?"

"Cygnet broke the Warlock into pieces and trapped him in the Blood Star. His shadow fell to earth, into the Delta, into Blood Fox's shadow. That's why they say: Beware the Blood Fox with a human shadow."

They were silent a little; the thick, blazing stars had edged closer, it seemed, to listen to Corleu's tales. The Cygnet, its broad wings spanning the sky at an angle, gazed with a frosty eye over its realm. Winking, the Warlock shifted, stars limning his shadow, which, oddly enough, was both in the sky and in the Delta, attached to a Blood Fox's pads.

Jagger said, "Fire Bear."

"Fire Bear chased Cygnet all over the sky, roaring fire at it, protecting Dancer. But the Cygnet stayed just ahead, until Fire Bear held no more fire, only that one last red star in its belly. Cygnet trapped the Dancer in ice on the top of the world. Fire Bear guards her. But there's no more fire left in the Fire Bear to melt the ice. So the Dancer stays frozen."

Jagger yawned. "Pass crock. There's Gold King, still."

"You've got the crock under your arm, crockbrain."

"Get on with Gold King. Then we throw Venn in the sheep dip."

"Gold King is trapped." Corleu yawned, too, hugely, trying to suck stars into his breath and bones. "The Cygnet trapped the Gold King in the Dark House. There it is, above the farmhouse. The black house with the lintel of gold and roof of gold."

"Cygnet trapped them all," Venn said drowsily.

"All."

"They're angry up there, likely. Being trapped so long."

Hay rustled as Jagger rolled suddenly, peered over the stack. "They're not the only things angry," he muttered. "My granny sleeps like a stump, but your da had an eye to your empty bed, Venn, and so did Corleu's. Your mam's out there, too, Venn."

Venn groaned, trying to crawl deeper into the hay. Corleu took a final swallow, passed the crock to Jagger. "Summer," he said, meaning the still, green-soaked air, the vast, glowing sky, the tales and touches that seemed to tremble constantly on lip and fingertip. Jagger grunted and toasted the moon.

Withy Hold for sowing and harvest, Hunter Hold for winter, and back again . . . and again . . . and then one year the wind changed direction, or the stars shifted a hair's-breadth, or some such, for two things happened, only one of which Corleu's mother had foreseen. Venn's younger sister, Tiel, crossed the camp one day carrying a bucket of water from the stream, and Corleu, chopping wood, glanced up to find that in the interim between her going to the stream and returning, the world had transformed itself under his nose. The wooden ax handle was of a finer grain; the ground her bare feet touched had never been walked on before. Even the air was different: too shallow to breathe, so that she seemed to sparkle as she moved through the morning. She glanced up at his staring. For a moment their eyes clung. Then she looked down quickly, the water trembling in her bucket, and for the first time in his life, he cursed his great-gran and the rider in the corn, for no one, he felt, of such dark, sweet, mysterious Wayfolk beauty, could love a head of hair like his.

He had reached his full growth by then; with his father's shoulders and his startling corn-silk hair and something of the stranger in the slanted cast of his face, he drew attention. But, giving and taking pleasure now and then with young women from farms or other companies, he had thoughts only for Tiel. He watched her, and realized that all the young men in their company were falling all over each other watching her. Then someone spoke a word that, for a little, drove even the thought of Tiel into the back of his mind.

Delta.

No one ever remembered who first spoke the word—maybe it had travelled with them from Hunter Hold—but there was talk of going south to the warm, misty Delta for the season instead of to Hunter Hold. Tul snorted; Sorrel foresaw and was baffled by her seeing. "Something falls," she could only say, and, used to water, leaves, seeds, something always falling out of the sky, no one paid mind. Talk grew stronger through harvest, swept from morning fire to night fire, until autumn, when nights began to chill and old bones began to ache, and suddenly it was true, they were turning south for the winter, toward the country of the blood fox and the sea and the ancient house of the rulers of Ro Holding.

Corleu was as amazed as everyone when his parents decided to leave the company. He was still whittling away at Tul's arguments the evening before their paths forked between known and unknown.

"Withy Hold in spring, Hunter Hold in autumn and back again," Tul said, "that's what's done and what's to be done. I never liked change. Swamps and bog lilies, that's all you'll find down there. Beetles big as your hand. Damp air like steam from a kettle, smelling of rot. That's no place for us. We follow sun and stars. You should come with us, not chase after some butterfly future."

Corleu shook his head. "Past is here," he said. They sat in the wagon Tul had helped him build. The back was open to dark and fire and tender songs yearning under wanderers' fingers for times and places that never existed. On his tiny table, Sorrel had spread her petals; scents of lavender, white lilac, violet, wove into the smell of burning applewood. Corleu picked out a harebell leaf absently, twirled it between finger and thumb, his eyes, intent and implacable, on his father's face. "You can't leave past behind you like a holey boot. We're all family and ghosts of family. You'll be without shadow, in Hunter Hold."

"I'll be without son, is what," Tul retorted. "Your place is with us, to feed us and drive our wagon when we get feeble and toothless. You come with us."

"I'm going south."

"Your mother has only you. What will she do for the little folk if you marry elsewhere?"

Corleu snorted. "Likely I'll have to wait till I'm bald to marry. Who in any company would want to wake to this head of hair every morning? It's got questionable past in it."

"Your granda married," Sorrel reminded him. "And in this company."

"My gran was fey to begin with. I'm going south. I want to see Ro City."

"What for?" Tul asked in astonishment. "Walls, stones, straight lines, roofs—why city, of all?"

Corleu shifted slightly, his eyes falling away from his father. "It's old," he said to the harebell leaf. "It's got past running straight back to the beginning of Ro Holding. It casts a long shadow."

"You're Wayfolk. What has a city's past of any kind to do with you?"

"I don't know." He dropped the leaf, ran his hand through his hair. "Stories, maybe. Old stories, Old words. Books, maybe, like Granda's."

"You have books here."

"I've read."

"Well, what more reading do you need? What more can books give you?"

"I don't know," he said again, hoving against the chair he straddled until it creaked. "It's a fair question," he admitted.

"There's no work we're used to, in cities."

"I know."

"Then what are you using your head for, besides to hang your ears on? You can't eat story, or wear it, or bed it. Best come with us."

"I'm going south."

"It's your hair," Tul said recklessly, but Corleu only nodded.

"Likely, for once. The rider in the corn gave me an unnatural taste for words. But you have them all twisted. It's not me leaving you, it's you leaving me, for something done and done until it's a wonder we don't meet ourselves coming back on the road to Hunter Hold. You might like change; you never tried it."

"I never needed it," Tul said. "None of you knows what lies south in the Delta, and here's even your mother seeing against it. Change is for weather and geese and worn-out trousers. You stay with us."

"I can't."

"Won't. Stubborn as an old root ball, you always were. Your place is with us, not by sea or swamp or whatever unfurrowed place this company muddles across. You come with us."

Corleu started to answer, then did not. His eyes were hidden; the lamplight overhead drew stray shadows beneath the bones of his face, giving it a smudge-eyed, secretive cast. Sorrel gave him an opaque glance. She sifted petals through her fingers; a pattern of colors formed on the wood. "It's you being stubborn," she said to Tul. "And blind as a harrow after a hare. He's in love."

Corleu stirred suddenly, as if he had left a splinter or two in the chair he straddled. He could feel Tul's stare like a flush of fire over his face; he refused to look up. Tul found his voice finally:

"What's that to do with the time of day or the price of a turnip? You've been in love before."

"No."

"The world is full of pretty faces."

"No."

"So you'll stay," Tul said a trifle sharply, "and go south with the geese, to mope after some girl who will show you the back of her head while she smiles at true Wayfolk—"

"I am true Wayfolk," Corleu snapped, goaded into staring back at Tul. "I walked Wayfolk paths my whole life."

"You're looking to cross thresholds in Ro City. Wayfolk shy at doorposts. My da had to drink his way through doors."

"I can't help it. It's not the doors or straight roads or high walls or lintels I want—it's the past that built the city."

"How do you expect any Wayfolk woman to understand that?"

His hands closed on the chair back. "I don't know," he said tightly, holding the chair as if Tul were about to toss it and him into deep water. "I just want. Both."

"You're besotted."

"Likely. Likely that's a word for it. Wayfolk word would be 'moonbrained.' "

Sorrel breathed softly across the petals; they drifted across the wood, changing pattern, colors hidden, colors revealed. She studied them a moment, brows pursed; then she gave notice to the tension in the air.

"Tul." Her deep voice, half imperious, half pleading, eased them both. "It's our last night."

Tul muttered softly, yielding; Corleu slumped against the chair back. Three haunting notes from a reed flute caught his ear; then he named the song and could let it go.

"My lady walks on the moon's road,
Shod, she is, in peacock feathers,
All eyes, she is, all eyes . . ."

"Besotted," he sighed. "If that's to have your head so full of one face you don't even remember whose feet you're walking on."

"Have you said so to her?" Sorrel asked practically.

"I'm biding my time."

"Till when?" Tul inquired. "Till her hair is the color of yours?"

Corleu glared at him, then dropped his face into the crook of his arm. "Till I can drag my voice back out of my boots when I try to talk to her."

"Ask now. Tonight. If she says no, you can come—"

"Tul," Sorrel murmured, and then to Corleu, "You've only spoken to her all her life." Both men looked at her in surprise. She patted Corleu's shoulder. "Nothing's secret around here. Except to your father."

"She's different now," Corleu said, gazing at the swirl of petals. "Like she went somewhere without us and came back. She makes me forget words." He cast a warning glance at Tul, waiting for abuse. But his father only blinked down at the petals as if he finally saw the pattern in them.

"I don't want you to leave us," he said gruffly. "That's the all and that's the end."

"Then come. Come with us."

"No. Not to Delta."

"Why? It's only a Hold, not another world. By the sound of you, we're travelling toward some place outside Ro Holding, not held by Lauro Ro, beyond even the Cygnet's eye."

"How can the Cygnet see anything under that bog mist?" Tul retorted. Corleu, wordless, met Sorrel's eyes and saw the end of their lives together. He stared wide-eyed at the table. She gave him no comfort; she had seen it coming since he was born.

"Well," she said softly, intent on the petals, her voice snagging here and there on a word. "You'll always know where we are. Withy Hold, Hunter Hold and back. When you need us." Then she was still, not even breathing, so still that both men drew toward her. Her hands went out, staying them, before they disturbed her pattern.

"Strange," she whispered. "Strange . . ."

Corleu studied the breath-blown petals. Troubled, he only saw in every delicate, circling path, an ending.

Two

SO the Wayfolk came down from the heart of Ro Holding to the Delta. Corleu, plodding through days, one eye to the road past his mare's rump, the other to the strange, dark, tangled horizon, never knew exactly when they left the clear, endless blue of Withy Hold sky behind and passed into the Delta mists. There the sun was invisible by day; at evening it hovered, huge and blood-red, above silvery, delicate forests. The rich, steamy, scented air clung to everything, even time, it seemed, until it moved like the slow, indolent water moved, deep and secret. The bog mists, the great red sun, the lovely green drugged the eye. The final, glowing moments of sunsets, trees like black fire against a backdrop of fire, burned into memory; Withy Hold paled, ghostlike, into past.

Tul had guessed it: In the Delta, the Cygnet was invisible. In the Delta were low, sultry skies, smells of mud, still water, the sound of hidden water, the sound of a great river breaking up into roads and trails and ruts of water, black pools and backwashes, before it drained into Wolfe Sea. Huge, shy, graceful birds—yellow, rose, teal—cried at night in throaty, urgent voices. Flowers of burning colors floated on dark water, left their imprint on the eye like the sun. Like the old river road they followed, Wayfolk were drawn from wonder to wonder toward what lay beyond the mists. But the mists never parted and the road ran endlessly into them.

Corleu, driving at the end of the line, eating the dust Jagger's wagon kicked up, felt a thought move, slow and fishlike, in his swampy brain. A warm weight sat on his head, his eyelids; sat on his thoughts, too, like hot light on water. The thought surfaced finally, making him lift his head, blink. The scythe-like, silvery leaves danced above his head, not a touch of autumn on them. We have been travelling forever, he thought surprisedly. Then the drowsy, sweating, perfumed air filled his veins again. The slow wagon ahead of him, with Jagger's gran peering out the back, and the dogs trotting behind it, grew smaller and smaller. He drifted in and out of a dream of blue sky. "Limehead," he heard someone call in the dream. "Catch a cuckoo in Corleu's hair." A bird had spoken, or the river. "Moonbrain. Corleu fell off the moon." He was on the haystack again, with Jagger and Venn, pointing to the Blood Fox prowling, huge, silent, dangerous, along the horizon, dragging the star-limned shadow of the Warlock behind it. "Delta fought Cygnet under the Hold Sign of the Blood Fox . . . Milkhead. Stick your head in a bucket of milk."

He raised his head, groggy, astonished at what he was hearing. A great blood fox flowed silently out of the shadows across the road under his horse's nose. The horse reared, jolting Corleu awake; hooves pounded down on the blood fox's shadow. Corleu, staring at the shadow's human hands, nearly lost the reins when his horse bolted.

He pulled at them, shouting; horse and wagon careened across spongy, shifting ground toward a broad, lily-choked swamp. Water loomed closer; the wagon reeled, nearly throwing him; he wondered if he should jump. Then both he and the horse saw something at the water's edge. The mare veered sharply away from it. The wagon groaned on its axle; things tumbled and smacked the floor. He got the wagon turned, its back wheel laying track within an inch of water, and he harried the mare back across the trembling ground to the road. He set the brake and jumped down, shaking, his head jerking back at the swamp where he had had a confused image of the blood fox's shadow, standing upright, black as the inside of nowhere, juggling stars in its hands.

He saw no one, nothing but the lilies, little burning crowns of light on the dark water, all of them just opened that morning, it looked, or maybe the moment before he saw them. He heard a noise behind him and spun; it was Jagger, loping down road.

"Gran said you tried to drive on water," he said. He had grown into a burly young man, grim, lately, a dark, puzzling force in the world, pent-up like a beer crock and apt to blow for no reason.

"Blood fox came out of nowhere," Corleu said, and saw again its human shadow across the dust. "Ran under the mare's nose, scared her."

Jagger grunted. "Would scare me. I'll send Gran to ride with you. She pinches if you fall asleep."

"I wasn't asleep."

"She said you were drifting."

"Maybe." He shivered suddenly, breaking out of a dream. "Likely that's all it was."

"What was?"

"Just a daydream."

"What? Blood fox?"

Corleu looked at him, then away, picking through shadow at the swamp's edge. The perfect lilies teased him again, irritating, like the whine of an unseen insect. "No. Thought I saw something, is all. It scared me. Jagger, how long ago did we cross over from Withy Hold?"

Jagger shrugged. "Days. Week or two maybe."

"A month?"

"Maybe."

"Two?"

"Why?" There was sweat on Jagger's face, dust on his shoulders; he did not want to tally time. "Do you have urgent business in the city?"

"Look around you."

"What of it?" Jagger demanded, not moving.

"Just look! We left Withy Hold in autumn! Where's the dead leaves, the birds flying south overhead, the flowers withering away? Where's the season? Feels like we've travelled into winter, but nothing dies here. Nothing dies," he said again, with a curious prickling of fear, but Jagger only looked annoyed.

"Winter's gentler in the Delta," he said brusquely. Corleu snorted.

"So gentle here that death tiptoes past the flowers. And where," he added, "is everyone in this wonderland? Could harvest all year long, here, if you drain a field or two. Yet we meet no one."

"Too far from the city."

Corleu eyed him askew. "You don't find it peculiar?"

"You've never been to Delta before, why should you find it one way or another? It's Delta, nothing we're used to—"

"It's Ro Holding, not the backside of the world! Winter travels, just like Wayfolk. It should have caught up with us by now."

"Winter." Jagger squinted at him. "A week or two out of Withy Hold—"

"Or a month or two—"

"We've been slow in this heat!"

"It shouldn't be this hot!"

"You've never been here before."

"No one has!"

"There's old road under your feet——"

"Road to where? We've been nowhere but here, days, weeks——the same sky, same trees, same flowers that always look like they bloomed just a moment ago when your back was turned. Just exactly where are we, here?"

"Delta," Jagger exploded. "You cob-haired gawp, where do you think? We've found a road leads out of the world? Have you been sitting back here with your face in the cider?"

"Don't call me cob-haired." His fists were clenched; he heard himself, the edge in his voice, the idiotic words, in sudden wonder. He and Jagger hadn't brawled in years. But there was something between them, like air tense with storm, and Corleu couldn't put a name to it. He eased his hands open, said more calmly, "It feels strange here to me, is all. Something does."

Jagger kicked at a clump of grass, blinking. "My brain's melting in this heat," he muttered. He added with an effort at thinking, "I forget you can't see moon changes under this mist. Women must know, though, they keep track of days. Except my gran." A corner of his mouth went up. "She thinks we're still in Withy Hold." Then someone stepped between them and his face went dark again. Corleu breathed in the scent of hair rinsed with lavender water.

"Da sent me to ride with you."

Tiel's hair fell past her waist; behind its darkness, and her sun-polished skin, the pale swamp flowers grew, thickly clustered, carved of ivory, without a bruise of time on them. Corleu drew breath, feeling Jagger's eyes boring at him. Someone else pushed among them, clung to Tiel's skirt.

"And me," said Tiel's youngest sister, her face and hands grubby from the bread and honey she was eating. Tiel, her face suddenly averted, lifted her up. The stiff, bulky line of Jagger's shoulders eased; he grinned fleetingly.

"Shall I send my gran, too?"

"Why not." Corleu took the child from Tiel, swung her onto the wagon seat. "Send the dogs, too." He added abruptly, as Jagger turned, "It was you, then, calling me."

"What?"

"You calling me names before the horse bolted. To wake me."

"I wasn't calling you names," Jagger said. "You didn't give me time."

Corleu was struck mute for a time by the bone in Tiel's bare ankle, by the gentle, light bird-gestures of her brown hands. The child did most of the talking. Tiel stirred now and then; the threads of her skirt dragging over wood grain seemed loud as language. She said little. Corleu felt the brief, dark, wordless glances she gave him, but she never let him meet her eyes. He wished another language would startle out of him, in the shape of small birds or pearls, for his head was as vacant of words as the sky. It's my hair, he thought hopelessly, remembering his father's warning. No one could love a head of hair like this. We could talk, once. What happened?

That was north.

"Shadow fox, fox shadow," the child chanted, and Corleu tensed, his eyes flickering across the road. But it was only a rhyme for a hiding game. "Hide your fox, hide your shadow—"

"Hide your face, hide your shadow," Tiel corrected. Corleu glanced at her. She leaned toward the child; the long, dark, heavy line of her hair hid all but the brown curve of her cheek. "Go on. Red star, blood star . . ."

"Find your eyes and see."

Find your voice and talk, you gabblehead, Corleu thought. The tall, graceful trees, thick with vine and moss, cleared ahead, gave him a glimpse of the wagons strung along the overgrown track, meadow feverishly green with dank, dark water beyond it, more trees.

"It's so empty," he breathed. "We've seen no one since we left Withy Hold. Not a traveller, a trapper, a boat—you can't walk a mile in Withy Hold without running into a field wall or stepping in a cow pile. Something hinting at people."

Tiel turned her head, let him meet her eyes a moment then; the dark, flickering glance dragged the breath out of him. "Strange," she agreed, but nothing in her voice truly considered the word. She was content, her eyes seeking colors. Her hair rustled against her back as her head turned. "It's so beautiful, it is odd no one has stopped here, of those who like stopping in one spot."

Corleu, watching her speak, almost stopped the wagon, wanting to taste and swallow the words coming one by one out of her full mouth. A wheel bumped over a stone; the child, climbing into Tiel's lap, clutched at Corleu's wrist with sticky fingers, dragged him back to earth.

"Dancer danced to a dancer dancing,
"Dance! said the dancing dancer,
"Dance the dancer dancing—"

"No," Tiel said, laughing. "Dancing, the dancer danced—

"Dancing dancer danced—"

"Dancer danced—ah, my tongue's muddled. Dancing the dancer—You say, Corleu."

"Dancing, dancer danced the dance."

"And danced," they all chanted. *"And danced. And danced."*

"Tell story," the child demanded, and Corleu's tongue went on without them:

"She danced on a hill, she danced in a rill,
She danced on a moonbeam, danced in a dream,
Danced on a star, danced very far,
Danced in a bear's den, danced home again."

"What bear?" Tiel demanded, smiling, her eyes full on his face. They were the proper color for the sky, he thought, not blue, but deep, warm, shadowy brown, for day, for night. He shook his head, smiling back at her.

"Fire Bear, likely. I only tell them, I don't make them."

"Yes, you do. I've heard you make them, with Venn and Jagger." Her face flushed suddenly, was hidden behind her hair. But she finished, "When you would sit by the fire late, behind our wagon. You thought everyone was asleep. But I listened."

He felt his own face warm. "They weren't meant for you. Only for our potato ears and sheep brains."

"I know," she said. Her face came out of her hair, composed again. "Goat brains, more like. Bat-wing ears. But I liked—I like how you say things. How you see. Even asleep, I'd hear your voice." She was gone again, bird-quick. He swallowed, a blink away from letting the reins slide out of his hands, touch a strand of her hair with his fingertips, shift it aside to find her.

He said unsteadily, for he had never put it to words before, "All stories seem old to me, even the ones born in my brain. Likely it's because words are so old. Story words, that is. They carry bits of older tales with them. Like Dancer. She could be you, dancing. Or she could be the star Dancer, who brings you dreams from both the fair side and the terrible side of morning." He paused. "It's what I think I want to do."

"What?"

"Go to Ro City and learn more words." His mouth crooked. "Sounds silly. More stories, maybe. Something."

"But what would you do with them?"

"I don't know." He flicked a fly off the mare's rump with a rein. "Keep saying and keep saying them until I get all the way back to the first thing they mean." He glanced at her, wondering if she wondered what murky waters lay between his ears. But she only asked thoughtfully:

"Can you do the things your granda could? Or your mother? Foresee in water, in petals?"

"Me? No. I only got his hair." He slid it back between his fingers, to cool his face. "My mother tried to teach me petals, but all I ever saw in them was color, never any—never—" He faltered, his mind filling with petals then: dried roses, verbena, lavender . . . the pattern they had made under his mother's breath, paths circling, circling. . . .

Something—an echo—made him realize she had spoken again. "What?" he asked, then knew he had made no sound. He had gone away again, to some place chill, lonely, terrifying. "What?" he said again, and came back to the pale, heavy misty sky, the long afternoon. He shivered suddenly in the heat. His eyes searched sky, trees, water, for some sign—any sign—of change: a hill, a different kind of tree, even a wild swan or a stork flying south for winter. "I think," he said tightly, "I know where we travelled to."

"Where?"

"Trouble."

But she did not seem to notice the word. The child sat drowsing in her arms; her eyes had strayed from Corleu to a long tumble of orange and yellow blossoms, all fully opened, he noticed, all perfect, not one too young or too old for the moment he saw them.

"My mother foresaw this," he breathed.

"What?"

"This place. Day after day circling under this grey sky, no true sky for stars to point the way, no moon, no sun . . ."

"Yes, there's sun. Look. It's about to set."

The evening fire was beginning, the slow kindling of the horizon into gold, then red, then deep, deep purple before the black, starless night poured over them again. Tiel's eyes filled with the sunset; her face held the smooth blankness of a dreamer. She had forgotten Corleu.

It's this place, he thought, terrified. This place.

They made a loose circle of the wagons in a meadow. Children of all ages broke out of the small colored rolling houses, flickered like night sprites in and out of the twilight. "Corleu," a boy called, and then a girl: "Corleu." In the dusk their faces blurred past him; their changing voices were unfamiliar.

Surely there were not so many smallfolk in the company, he thought. There were too many voices, echoes of the past, as if they had carried even his own, Jagger's, Tiel's childhood ghosts down from the north. Then he saw Tiel, chasing after one of the smallfolk, laughing, her hair rising in a slow, dark wave, then settling as she ran. The world went simple again, everything in its place, no mysteries beyond the mystery of Tiel's hair, rising darkly and falling. Then a girl said, "Corleu" behind him and laughed. He turned quickly, for that voice, that laugh, was long past and far behind. Someone circled behind him silently; he felt a long skirt whirl and fall against him, a brush of long fine bones: hands, back, shoulders against his shoulders. He turned to face her, saw only Tiel, walking away from him as she carried the child across the camp.

He drew a deep breath, moving through the still, heavy dusk as if it were thick with ghosts. He took the ax from inside the wagon, walked down the stream to cut wood. The underbrush rustled, as if someone walked beside him. The slow water murmured his name. He felt the hair rise on the back of his neck. "Corleu," a girl whispered: the young, flaxen-haired lord's daughter who had stopped him in a field one day. He smelled again the crush they had made of grasses, of wildflowers, mingling with the scent of her body. A flower or a finger brushed his mouth. He turned, felt again the quick, light touches of someone's body, circling him as he turned. Skirt wrapped around his ankles, a hip touched his. He dropped the ax, reached out with both hands to catch the dancer. No one was there. Leaves rustled, farther down the stream.

He came back under full night. Around the camp fires, he saw faces that bewildered him with their sullenness. *Where did you go, Corleu?* eyes asked. *Who have you been with?* They gazed at him without smiling, without moving, their bodies shadowed, only their expressions molded in both dark and fire. *You* their faces said, with envy, longing, mistrust. *You.*

He concentrated the next day, as intent on moving into one simple moment after the next as if he were piecing his way step by step across a bog. The reins in his hands. The string of wagons—blue, yellow, white, red— with drying clothes flapping and children's brown faces peering out the backs. A woman singing behind him. The song stirred his memories. The deadly, silver smiles of scythes among the ripe wheat, the dry *hwick* of their work. Women bent, bundling the wheat; he and Tiel, Jagger and Venn, and Lark, their hands almost too small, picking up the bundles, leaning them together in threes. He, then Tiel, then Jagger. When Tiel's hands slowed, brought her closer to Corleu, then Jagger's movements would slow, until she

was centered between them, then closer to Jagger. All afternoon, sun soaking
into them; the whirling glint of metal; a baby crying; the smells of wheat,
earth, wild flowers; their joking; Sorrel ahead, singing as she bound up the
stalks. Singing of . . . what?

A baby's rhyme, a nonsense tale about a little black hut with a gold roof
and a lintel of gold that tumbled out of the sky, and how you must never
pass beneath the lintel, for if you do, you will see it is not a hut at all, but—

Corleu!

His head jerked. The world built around him again: mist, pale green, and
the feverish colors of the flowers. His throat swelled with a silent protest. He
felt the sweat on his face. Luckily the horses were still plodding in line. He
thought of calling Jagger, but what could he say? *I was dreaming again. You
gawp.* He concentrated. The reins in his hands . . . The little hut with the
gold roof, falling, falling out of the sky . . .

He was still concentrating at the end of the day, so hard he had all but
forgotten how to speak. Stop wagon. Feed and water horse . . . The water in
the skins was low, so he slung them over his shoulders, walked through the
camp as through a company of shadows, ignoring all claims on his name.
Find flowing water, kneel. Open skins . . . Then, at the bottom of the shallow
stream, he saw jewels flash. He stared at them, and finally recognized what he
had not seen since Withy Hold: stars, reflected in the water, so clearly he
might have picked them out like pebbles. If he looked away from them, they
would vanish, something warned. So he knelt on the bank without moving,
gazing at the ring of stars the Blind Lady wore on her finger. The water darkened; the stars grew bright, luminous, fire-white. They held all time, those
stars, and he watched, his lips parted, scarcely breathing, for it seemed that
any moment the dark within the stars would open, show what lay beyond the
endless night.

Something struck him so hard he sprawled with a grunt on the muddy
bank. Someone straddled him, gripped his shirt at the throat. His head rattled a few times against the ground before his eyes adjusted to the milky light
that the moon shed behind the mists. He cried sharply, astonished, "Jagger!"

The weight shifted off him. Jagger was breathing heavily, a dark, ag-
grieved presence in the dark.

"Do you know," he demanded, "how long you've sat there? Just sat, like a
rabbit cross-eyed under the moon?"

"I just got here, you muckerhead! I just came for—"

"It's full night!"

Corleu's breath stopped. He sat up; his eyes went back to the water. But the stars were gone; they never could have been there. He made some sound Jagger took as argument.

"You go off," he continued doggedly, "you're gone hours, you come back looking like you've been some secret place, with your ax but no wood, or your skins—" He picked them out of the mud, flattened by Corleu's back. "Empty. I had to follow you, to see where you go when you go."

Corleu rolled to his feet wordlessly; Jagger caught his wrist, nearly sent him into the water. Down the bank a blood fox's eyes caught some stray swamp light, flared amber red at them.

"It's this place," Corleu said. He was breathing so shallowly he could hardly speak. "This place. It's bewitched. I tried to tell you—"

"Not this place, it's you!"

"No—"

"You look at us all like a stranger, like something is swallowing you from inside. You barely talk anymore, even to her; you don't see us, not even her—"

"Who?" He jerked at the suddenly painful hold. "Who?" he said through gritted teeth. Jagger hauled him closer.

"Who. You blind owl. We watch her, she watches you, and you walk past her like she's smoke. It's you her eyes follow. And you don't—you don't even—you sit here staring at water while Reed and Dawl and Steof and me, we have to fight to lie in her path for her to walk across while she watches you—they all do. Watch you. You with that hair the color of—"

Corleu wrenched free. "Bird-shit. Slug-slime. I've heard all the white words there are by now. I can't believe you're standing there throwing your tongue around the color of my hair while you're knee-deep in trouble and sinking fast. Can't you see it? We blundered onto a road to nowhere; we drove our wagons outside time into a haunted place. Things are strange here. Things are dangerous."

"Something is," Jagger said tightly. "And it's you in danger. You've got us all smoldering and you're too spellbound to see—"

"It's not me!"

"It's you wandered out of the world, not us. Someone twisted your path for you, and if you don't find who, you'll keep on reeling through your days, trapped inside your head. I'd say most likely Steof, his mother knows things."

"No." He gripped Jagger's shoulders. "It's none of us! Jagger, I've seen Blood Fox with the human shadow here. I felt the Dancer dance circles around me. Tonight you stopped me falling headfirst into the Ring of Time at the bottom of the water. It's a dream world we wandered into, and it scares my blood thin. We think we're heading south through Delta, but we're only circling and circling, that's why we never meet anyone, and why we never reach the sea, because there is no sea, there is no south, no north, we've travelled outside Ro Holding and not even the Cygnet itself can see into this land."

"You're babbling," Jagger breathed. "You're moonstruck."

"But what moon?" Corleu shook him furiously, rocking him off balance half a step. "We left moon and stars in Withy Hold!"

"You don't even care."

"Of course I care. Why do you think I'm shouting myself blind, you stump-headed—"

"You don't even ask what I'm talking about."

"What?"

"You just ramble. You don't care who."

Corleu was silent, baffled by the mist in Jagger's head. He closed his eyes wearily, looking for words, and saw Tiel behind them, her hair so straight and heavy that when she swung her head it fanned the air and fell strand by strand back into place. He swallowed. "That's why." He opened his eyes to Jagger's night-hollowed eyes. "That's why you're angry at me. Because I followed her here, instead of taking my moonhead to Hunter Hold, out of her sight. But can't you see for once it's not Tiel matters, what matters is this place we—"

The night exploded in his eyes; he found himself trying to finish with his face under water. I should have gone to Hunter Hold, he thought bleakly. He felt Jagger's hands hauling at him. He turned and kicked hard; there was a cry and a massive splash. He waded out, dripping and coughing, saw again the chilling, red-washed stare of blood-fox eyes.

He woke near dawn, and, still half-dreaming, had all the horses loose and wandering off into the trees. Then he walked aimlessly across slow branch water, through perfumed woods—in circles, he thought likely—but he kept moving, until heat and weariness wore him down. He rested under a cascade of lilies flowing down tree branches into a small, deep pool. He sat shredding the perfect flowers, listening to the furious, distant shouting. "Corleu!" they called; gathering up the horses, they would blunder across him eventually. "Corleu!" He picked another flower, tossed it into the pool. It floated, turning delicately on an invisible current.

"Corleu."

Tiel stood beside the tumble of lilies. He stared at her; she looked like something the morning had just fashioned out of shadow and light and the mysterious, silvery green leaves. "Corleu," she said again, softly, when he didn't speak. "They're all angry with you. Jagger says you've gone moon mad."

"There's no moon," he said. But there was, he realized; she had brought it with her: moon and stars, the memory of the green-scented summer nights.

"Everyone is looking for you. Jagger says you should go back to Withy Hold, the Delta mists are driving you loony."

He shook his head. "This road goes one way only, and where, none of us knows yet." He barely heard himself; he wanted only to sit and look at her, in the bewitched morning, while the world turned circles around them.

"Delta," she reminded him, but there was the shadow of a question in her voice.

"No."

She paused, perplexed. Their eyes held in the silence. She swallowed. "Corleu," she said, and, surprised, he felt as if no one had ever spoken his true name before. "What—what's to be done, then? If this is not true Delta, then where do we find it?"

"I don't know. But I can't just go on blind; there must be something to point, someone to say why all this, why this place that never changes, why . . ." But under her gaze he was forgetting why he cared, why they should not circle forever in that changeless, sultry, scented air. Her body had pulled back from him a little, disturbed at his words. But her eyes clung. Within them he watched doors open, one after another, revealing things he had never seen in her before. Her voice sank, barely more than a whisper.

"Maybe if you—if you come back with me and try to explain—Maybe, Corleu, maybe if—" She faltered into silence. They stared at one another, lost, he felt, in a dream within a dream.

He wanted to put his cheek against her long eyelashes to feel them brush his skin. He wanted to gather all her long, heavy hair into his hands until they overflowed with darkness. He wanted to circle her bare ankles with his fingers, her bare neck with his hands. He wanted to fall into her eyes with all the opening chambers in them, and keep falling and keep falling. . . . He whispered, "Tiel." And then she fell toward him, seemingly from a long distance, and as she fell, he felt himself yearn toward her as if a wind had pushed him.

The block of night across the small pool finally caught his eye. It had been dragging at him for some time: a square of black between his hand and her breast, a flick of dark over her closed eyelids, hidden within the braid his busy fingers had unwoven. He raised his head, one of her bodice laces between his teeth, blinking at strands of her hair that clung to his eyelashes. There it was, fallen out of nowhere: the tiny house. Four black walls, the gold roof, the lintel of gold. Standing without sound or movement in a riffle of mist.

He was still, so still that Tiel, fingers tangled in his hair, finally opened her eyes. She turned her head. Her lips moved silently, as if they were remembering a song. Then she sat up in horror, tugging at her bodice as if the lintel were an eye. "What is it?" she breathed.

Four stars its walls, one star its roof, one star its lintel, and the blue star its latch, so he had heard the lord's daughter describe it, in formal language, as she lay beside him, her ringed hand pointing out stars in a warm night tumbling with wind. The Hold Sign of Hunter Hold: seven stars that trapped the golden warrior's face of the sun.

The little dark house that falls from the sky . . .

He shuddered, feeling the cold tighten his skin, the bone-bare chill of recognition.

"Corleu!"

He dropped his face, kissed her numbly. "My mother saw it. Something falling. And she saw our path in her petals circling, circling. . . ."

"But it wasn't here when we came!"

"It was always here. It's the dream we're in." Still holding her tightly, he eased to her side, his eyes intent on the house. He breathed, "And there's the door."

"What door?"

"The door out of the dream."

She stared at him. "How do you know? How can you say that's the way out, just looking at it?"

"It's a door. It's the only door we've come across anywhere for weeks. You come in a door, you go out."

"No." She pushed against him suddenly, her face in his neck, hands gripping his shirt. "No. Wayfolk don't cross under doorways."

"Listen to me."

"No! I'm not listening!"

He kissed her hair, her jaw, found her lips again. "Listen," he whispered, and she stopped him speaking, plundering his words until he fell back, inarticulate. A stone, intruding between soft ground and his head, made him remember how to talk. "Listen to me," he said, blinking, hoisting to his elbow. "Listen. We're all spellbound in this dream country. Nowhere is where we're going. There's a door out. It's here, to be opened now—now, or we may be left here on our own in a world where nothing lives as easily as in one where nothing dies."

"Find Venn's mam, she knows things—"

"No. What if it goes? What if it's our only way and it disappears? My da was right. Not even the Cygnet can see through this mist. The only one can see in it and around it and beyond it is trapped in that little ancient house. . . ."

"What are you saying? Whose house is it? Who is trapped?"

"And he trapped us. . . ."

"Who?"

He had made the first movements away from her without realizing it: pulling up, beginning to rise. She grasped at him in horror, and he felt the blood lurch out of his face, at where his next steps would take him.

"I'll be back," he said, pulling her to her feet as he rose.

"No! Corleu, no!"

"I will." He pulled her against him, hard, and even then he felt the cold slide shadowlike between them. "Wait for me."

"How can you leave me?" she cried, as he loosed her, and, stepping away, he felt his whole body pull toward her. He caught his breath, dazed, her face and the house and all the colors of that enchanted world blurring together in his eyes.

"I don't know, I don't know, I don't know, I love you, I love you."

"Corleu!"

"I'll bring you back the stars. . . ."

He was running, half-blind, along the edge of the pool, when he heard her scream at him again.

"Corleu! It's the house! It's the black house with the roof of gold that falls from the sky! Don't go into it! Don't! It's the house you'll never leave!"

He ran faster. In another country, he heard oars in an oarlock, water stroked and lifted, words. He left all his thoughts behind, ran under the gold lintel, into the dark.

He stood with his eyes shut, waiting.

THREE

 THERE was a smell of fish cooking.

Startled, he opened his eyes. He was instantly sorry. Inside, the small house stretched endlessly; the dark around him shimmered with vague colors, forms that he almost recognized until he stared straight at them, and then they dissolved, washed away by some invisible, lightless tide. He made the mistake of looking down.

All the stars in the night sky hung beneath his feet, as if he had stepped through the Ring to stand outside of time. He closed his eyes again, felt his whole body cry out, though his voice was frozen and made no sound. He began to fall back into the black, shining waters of time. Stars flowed past him like the bubbles of his final breath.

He smelled grass. He opened his eyes, lifted his head groggily. Sunlight he had not seen in weeks struck his face. Through the misty gold he saw Tiel again. He stretched his hand to her, tears of relief filling his eyes that he had fallen through all the worlds there were to find himself with her again.

Darkness fell between them before he could touch her. The filigreed dome of night rose over him, with its vast humans and prowling animals. The Dark House hung above the Cygnet's outstretched wing: the four stars marking its walls, one star its peaked roof, one star its lintel, the seventh the door latch that Corleu had opened. Within the dark house . . .

Within the dark house . . .

Within the dark house he opened his eyes and saw the shrunken, dusty floorboards. Beyond the door he had flung open, perfect lilies tumbled from the tree-bough, down toward the pool.

There was the smell of fish cooking.

Within the Dark House he opened his eyes and saw beyond the open door the black, black night and the huge, northernmost star of the Cygnet's outstretched wing.

Someone was singing. It was a smallfolk rhyme, about a dark house falling, falling out of the sky, and how you must never enter it, for having entered, you will never leave. . . . He lay listening, his skin prickling with horror, because the door was open, he could have touched the dusty sill with his hand, but he could not move; he had leaped beyond the world into a child's song, into the story behind the song.

There was the smell of fish cooking.

He opened his eyes. He no longer saw the black walls, but he knew the Dark House rose all around him, beyond the mists, its four walls the night, its shining lintel the star that was the world's lintel.

There was the smell of fish cooking.

He sat up so abruptly that stars flecked his vision; he blinked fire into shape, water, a face.

A shaggy-haired man cooked over a fire beside the pool; from his battered pan came the smell of fish. Corleu's eyes flickered across the pool. The lilies cascaded endlessly; the petals he had shredded still circled slowly in the water. He could not see Tiel. He turned quickly, looking for the house, in a desperate hope that he had only leaped into a dream and knocked his head against truth so hard he saw stars. . . . A tinker's wagon stood where the house had been. The black horse that drew it was stone-still in harness, not even blinking; its hooves and mane were shaggy as the tinker's hair. Corleu could not take his eyes off the wagon. It was a tiny, rolling house, shadow-dark, with a peaked yellow roof and a yellow lintel; black stairs ran up into the open door. Painted in weathered yellow on the door was an ancient Hold Sign: the Gold King, with his furious, sun-round face and fiery petals of hair, imprisoned by the seven stars that formed the Dark House.

Corleu dragged his eyes from it finally to the face beside the fire.

It was a lean, swarthy face, with astonishing eyes of such light hazel they looked yellow. They smiled a little at Corleu; for a moment the smile was unfathomable. Then, in a shift of light, it was simply friendly. The tinker stirred the fish in the pan, cocked a dark brow at Corleu.

"Fish?" He ticked his fork against the side of the pan as Corleu stared at him. "Have a bite. Fish improves the mind. They say."

"Fish." His voice barely sounded.

"They say. Though," he added, "those swamp fish are ghostly things. Sweet, mind you, but pallid, as if they've been down in that pool for several hundred years. They might do for the brain, but they do nothing to improve the eye."

Corleu said nothing. He felt as ancient and pallid as the fish in the pool, something washed out of time's backwaters, without much brain to speak of, for he had been caught, it seemed, on a tinker's hook. Or had he? He cast a glance at the tiny, wheeled house; the Gold King glared fiercely at him, dusty and peeling. He swallowed drily. The tinker was filling his patched plate. His clothes were patched as well, with motley at neck and knee and elbow. He wore gold in one ear; a thin gold chain around his neck disappeared into his shirt. Words tossed crazily in Corleu's head. Tinker or King? King or tinker? He said finally, since the tinker had handed him a fish to deal with:

"Mist might do that to them."

"Mist?"

"Make them pale. For lack of sun. There is no sun under these mists. Except that on your wagon."

The tinker's mouth went up a fraction. "Likely you've hit upon the problem."

"Could cut these mists with a knife."

"To be sure. But," he added, raising the knife he cooked and ate with, "knife is not what's needed here."

"No?"

"No. Besides, you haven't got one. I noticed, as you slept. Not a knife or horse nor pot to your name."

"Not here. Wherever here is."

"A damp, muggy, empty place it is. Pretty, though. Smells nice."

"It wasn't empty—" His hands had closed; he kept his voice calm with an effort. "It wasn't empty. It had all my Wayfolk company in it."

"Ah. Wayfolk, are you? You wandered off the road a bit."

"Far off. So far off I don't know anymore where I am."

"You're between earth and sky like the rest of us, walking from morning until the fall of night like all folk." He worked a fishbone out of his mouth. "Going from here to there, in one door, out the other, one place to—"

"Door." His voice shook as it seized the word. "In one door. What other door?"

The tinker crooked a brow. "It's a saying. An expression, so to speak. Are you sure you won't have a—"

"No. In one door, out the other, you said. A way in, a way out. That's what you said."

The yellow eyes, catching light, seemed to smile again. "You're a quick one, taking words up as fast as they fall. But, glancing around, I don't much see there's an in or an out here, unless maybe to the world itself."

"There's one," Corleu said. He was as tense as if he were poised to run for his life: A flower hitting the pool in the silence that followed his words would have sprung him piecemeal all over the ground.

The tinker glanced at the door, surprised. "So there is. But that's only my wagon with the one door in and out."

"It's a door. It's here."

"You're welcome to it. I'll be here waiting," he added, as Corleu got to his feet, "when you come back out."

Corleu paused. The dark house stood, weathered and tantalizing, a dream within a dream. He had yet to enter it, he had already entered it. It rose all around him, invisibly. Beyond it, there was Tiel, inside . . . another dark house, with perhaps inside it another dark house. . . .

And another . . . He was shivering in the warm air, as if the icy stare of the Cygnet's eye had rimed his bones as he fell past. He slid his hands over his face, murmuring, uncertain that Tiel would be anywhere in any of those houses, no matter how many he entered. He dropped his hands. The door was still there, beyond the tinker, who was still picking at his fish. He walked toward it. The tinker smiled; creases ran down his brown, stubbled cheeks, imprisoning his smile.

"Where are you going, Master Corleu?"

He felt his heart pound at the sound of his name. He did not dare look back. "To undo what I just did."

"Ah. Doing and undoing." Something in the tinker's voice caught Corleu mid-step, as if he had reached out long, clever fingers and gripped him. "You can't do and undo through the same door." Corleu turned slowly, the cold sweat gathering at his hairline. "You know that. Under that hair."

Corleu was silent, staring at the tinker behind the flames, with the gold in his ear and the flecks of gold in his eyes. Smoke billowed at Corleu; he blinked away tears, trying to see clearly through the harsh mist. He felt words push out of him, the last thing he wanted to say, the only thing he had left to say.

"That house," he whispered.

"My wagon?"

"Your dark house with the yellow lintel and the yellow roof."

"It's my house."

"It's the house of the Gold King."

"It's my house."

His heart beat raggedly; the colors of leaf and lily were suddenly too vivid. "Then you are the Gold King."

The tinker's smile did not change. He spat out a fishbone and said, "The dark house is a child's song. One of those songs Wayfolk brats are endlessly singing. If I were King would I live in such a tiny, dark, windowless house?"

"Not if you could find a door out."

"The Gold King is a moldy old shepherd's tale, one of those silly stories that get passed around the world like air, only if they were dreams and smoke they wouldn't be keeping such as the Gold King alive, would they, listening to his spoken name? Yes or no, Master Corleu?"

"Yes." Sweat, mingling with tears from the smoke, ran down his face. "No."

"If I were the Gold King, if I just happened to be him, eating fish in your company, how would I free myself?" He chewed a bite, regarding Corleu, knife pointed at him to invite answer. "How would I, do you think?"

"I don't—I don't know—"

"Think."

He licked dry lips. "You would likely find a door."

"I have a door."

"Then you would—you would—" He closed his eyes, finished in the dark. "You would likely find a moonbrained fool muckerheaded enough to enter your house, and get him to do what you can't."

"Ah. A muckerheaded fool who thinks, is it? Good, Corleu. And think this over: What, likely, would I ask you to do?"

If he closed his eyes tightly enough, to shut out every splinter of light, he could see Tiel again, under a tumble of green leaves and lilies, her hair unbraided, her bodice loosened over her soft, nut-brown breasts. If he closed his eyes still tighter, he could see her eyes smiling, he could see his smiling reflection in her eyes. If he shut out all light, maybe he could slip through the dark, back into memory. There he could linger forever as he had been, in some distant, former life, too stupid to do. There in that private green memory, he could bury himself instead of asking the question that was forcing itself like breath out of his mouth.

He opened his eyes; they were burning; his throat burned. "I don't know. What would you ask me to do?"

The tinker, finished with his fish, gazed at his reflection in the round tin plate. "Most likely just a small thing. Very small. Maybe I would . . . Yes. Maybe I would ask you to find something for me."

"What thing?"

"A little thing." He tapped the knife against his teeth, musing to himself. "A very small thing . . ."

"Where?"

"That's just it." He raised his head to smile at Corleu. "It's possible, Corleu, that I don't know where this small thing is. I've mislaid it, lost track of it, it went its way through time without me. It's entirely likely that you'll have to find it for me, as a clever young man who found his way through my door could do."

"Where?" Corleu whispered.

"Back, ahead, before, behind. It may be hidden in a stone, a star, another child's song. I have a few friends who might have glimpsed it, might have heard, might know exactly where. For instance, you might ask the Blind Lady. You've seen her silver ring. If you had something in trade, something she might wish for, as I have wished for this thing . . . For instance, you might give her what's on the peacock's feather. That's all we're in the business of here, you understand, Corleu. Trade. A bit of labor for me, a return to you of what I'm keeping of yours. A little something for us all."

"What is it you want?"

The tin plate in the tinker's hands was beginning to glow; light reflecting off it turned his face gold. His eyes, contemplating Corleu, were gold as coins. For a long time he looked at Corleu without answering, only smiling his tight smile, while the light crept over fire, water, lilies, even the black horse, coloring them gold.

"A small thing, Corleu. Just a small thing."

"But what—" He had to struggle to find air. "Tell me what—"

The circle in the tinker's hands was acquiring a face. The tinker covered his face with it like a mask. The gold light spilled over his hair. The eyes in the circle opened, blazing gold, tempestuous. The hot light flared into Corleu's eyes. He flinched away from it, crying out, "I don't know what you want!"

"Find it. . . ."

The world flooded with light. He threw his arms over his eyes, feeling the sun drench him, close around him like the hot, heavy, clinging embrace of the summer days he remembered. A voice blasted at him like a roaring furnace. He dropped his arms, trembling, feeling oddly scorched.

He stood in a vast hall of pure gold, no other color; the light cast no shadows. Upon a gold dais sat a gold throne; upon the gold throne sat the Gold King. Lip, eyelash, fingernail, he could have been melted and stamped for coins. His face was a mingling of tinker's face and the sun-face in the Hold Sign of Hunter Hold: wide-boned, wide-eyed, crowned with wild locks of gold hair. He wore a massive sword and armor spiked with points of gold at neck and wrist, knee and elbow. He was chained by one ankle to his throne.

Corleu stared at him, stunned.

"Don't fret, Corleu. You'll find it." The tinker-king moved restively, testing his chain, pulling it after him as he paced. "A quick young man like you, who can see through dreams and shadow-lands. Who knows? If you find this for me, I might see my way to rewarding you with other things you might have seen and coveted, along your way." He held up a gold-armored hand as Corleu opened his mouth. "Now, don't be hasty. I know all you want now is your love beside you, and an open road through the Delta to the sea. I'll give you that, don't fear. But, as you search for this, you may begin to think a little, about what else you might ask for. I can listen, I'm prepared to be accommodating."

"Why?" he asked, his voice raw with bitterness and terror for Tiel. "Of every sheep-brained fool in Ro Holding, why did you pick my life to fall into?"

The tinker-king laughed, swinging his heavy chain with an effort. "You were easiest to spot, with that hair. You were always saying our names, stargazing, never thinking who might be listening. Why did you go into my house? You knew what it was. Everything you ever heard about that dark house said: 'Do Not Enter.' And what do you do? You get a little weary of looking at mists, of not seeing the sun or the stars that turn time in their cogs, so you throw yourself headlong against the oldest warning of all. Look at you, standing here while your love wanders in an empty garden without you. Who else would have left her there at such a moment? Who else in Ro Holding would have been that moonbrained?" A sound came out of Corleu, half sob, half wordless agreement. "Ah, I told you, don't fret. I need you, so I took you."

"If you—if you harm her, any of them—"

"You'll what? Stop the dark house from falling? Stop the sun from rising?" He turned again, grimacing slightly as he dragged his chain. "It's a simple business, Corleu. You'll see. If you give me what I want, I'll give you what you want. But you must never tell. Listen to me. Don't speak. You must never tell anyone what you are looking for. Because, then, even if you find it for me, you will never find, either awake or dreaming, anywhere in your life, this little misty, timeless garden you have abandoned."

"I don't know what you want!"

The cry echoed off gold walls, splintered in corners where lines of gold melted to a single point. Corleu, his unanswered plea bouncing all around him, felt himself fall again, the endless falling within dreams. Eyes watched him: the Peacock's tail, the Blood Fox's yellow star, the Fire Bear's ice-blue stare. He heard his younger voice, telling a story. . . .

The tinker sat beside his fire, roasting something small on a twig. Overhead the mists were darkening; the curve of gold in the chain around the tinker's neck caught, from somewhere, a stray spark of light.

"Bite?" he asked genially. The small thing on the stick was charred. Corleu's throat knotted at the smell. He shook his head, his eyes gritty from the harsh smoke roiling up from the spattering flames. He had fallen on his knees, supplicant to a tinker-king, but he had torn his voice raw with his last cry. He could barely whisper, as the thing on the stick dripped into the fire and the heat and the smoke billowed over him.

"Just. Tell me. What you want."

The tinker lifted the twig from the fire, slid the small, bloody, burned thing off and bit into it.

"The heart of the Cygnet."

FOUR

CORLEU opened his eyes.

His face was in a puddle, one foot was in a stream, and the water in both places was freezing—that much he realized before several hands heaved him up and tossed him like a hay bale into the bottom of a boat. His head cracked against an oar; the breath was knocked out of him. Stunned, he could not move. The boat rocked under him; a pair of boots settled next to his ear.

"That's it. That's the last of it." The boat wallowed away from the bank. Current caught it. The oarlocks rattled and creaked.

"Petrified blood-fox spoor, she said," a younger voice objected. "She wanted that, she said."

"She may want what she wants, but nothing petrifies here. Things molder or get eaten here." The boot near Corleu's ear lifted, tapped his cheek. "This one is fresh dead. His skin is still on his bones."

"He never came out of the bog," the second voice protested. "Bones buried in the bog, she said."

"Where'd he come from, then? Fallen out of the sky?"

"We could toss him over, let a bog-hole chew on him, then pull him out again. He'd be authentic then. A true bog man."

Corleu caught his breath at the idea. There was a sudden silence; even the oarlocks were silent. "He's alive." A hand pulled his hair, tugged his head up. "He's breathing. He's bleeding quick blood."

"Well, how were we to know? What was he doing lying alive in this sour mire?"

"Throw me rope. Quick!"

Corleu moved dizzily, futilely. His hands were caught, knotted behind his back. When he opened his mouth to protest, a cloth smelling of old fish was jammed between his teeth. He was rolled onto his back. He blinked the faces above him clear against the misty dawn.

"He's not a bog man," a heavy-set, one-eyed man pronounced finally. "Nor marsh bones. Nor even dead."

"Toss him down the next sinkhole," a skinny young man with a wispy beard suggested. "Then we'd have it: dead bones out of the marsh."

The one-eyed man considered Corleu dispassionately. He shifted a twig from one side of his teeth to the other. "She won't pay for murder. I'm not climbing those stairs for nothing."

"She'll never know!"

"She'll know. I gave her murdered bones once, and she said they did nothing in her fire but weep and complain at her until she stopped and buried them. None of my fault, they never complained to me, so how was I to know? But she knew. Things talk to her."

"Then what will we do with this one? Heave him back on shore?"

"He'll be annoyed by now, likely. I'm too old for dealing with him if we untie him, and you're too puny. If we leave him here tied in this wild, that will be murder. Turtles would eat him if blood fox didn't."

Corleu chewed ineffectually at the cloth in his mouth. A grey-brown world slid past him. Tall trees with pale trunks rose out of the water, their long scythe-like leaves long fallen; the boat tacked unhurriedly around them. Carpets of rotting lily pads sent a bitter smell along the breeze. The dawn world rustled and cried with hunger. A snake, draped in deep blue scallops along a branch, straightened like a whip and dropped into the water, narrowly missing the boat. An oar slapped at it. Water flecked Corleu's face. A thought was reeling crazily into his head: that this was the true Delta, of snakes and slow cold murky water and trees that had not only left summer behind but autumn as well. The boat passed vines cascading down from a rotten bough into the water. They hung limply, leafless, shrivelled with cold. He had a sudden vision of Tiel sitting under them, growing pale, drawn with despair, fading away like a ghost in a fading dream world. He pulled at the rope, gave a muffled groan of such fear and frustration and bewilderment that the eyes above him became almost human.

"Should we let him talk? Ask him what left him here?"

"No," the one-eyed man said. "Let her ask. She might find a use."

The boat meandered endlessly under the colorless sky. Great white birds cried hoarsely overhead, their wings rattling like old bones as they flew. Now and then a blood fox barked in the distance. They were travelling south, Corleu saw, with an eye on the current. Deeper into the Delta. Shivering with cold, he dreamed the sun, a fuming, hot-eyed, petal-haired face busy eating day and stars, the world, time. It fixed its furious gaze on him, said his name: *Corleu*. He jerked himself awake, heard a bird cry mournfully: *Corleu*.

The trees thinned; water shunted into a slow side channel and from there bled into a wide lagoon. They passed a great, dark tangled cave of tree roots where a huge tortoise older than Ro Holding, it looked, slowly blinked at them as it turned itself into stone. Its neck protruded from a shell ruffled with white agate; its jaws could have enclosed Corleu's face. Its eyes, velvety with age, pondered him and narrowed into slits of night.

The boat slipped through lazy shallows, among a grove of statues: old, worn, silvery stumps still rooted in the water, that some passing artist had whittled into shapes. A huge, long-legged egret gazed upward, its beak open as if to nibble at the sun. A squat toad sat on the water, its rolled tongue about to snap and snag the boat. A child, pulling her skirt above her knees, waded through dead lily pads; a lily trailed from her long hair. A naked man with the bunched, bulky shoulders and pointed teeth of a blood fox smiled at Corleu. He started; human blood fox became tree again, its shoulders molded of broken boughs, one eye a dark stain of pitch.

"Blood fox," the young man said, and Corleu turned his head. A huge one gazed at them from the shore; the young man stared back at it, an odd mix of hate and wonder in his eyes. "Big. Look at its eyes. Evil. Beware the blood fox casts a human shadow."

"That's a worn old tale. Blood fox isn't evil."

"It kills. I saw it kill a hunter once."

"What was hunter hunting?"

"Blood fox."

"So, then. Bad luck to kill a blood fox."

"They're bad luck. Look at its eyes. Blood fire in them. Look at it. How it's watching. How it's watching."

"Delta belongs to the blood fox," the one-eyed man said. "It laid claim long before us. Long before any Ro held Ro Holding."

"It hates us. We took the Delta from it. We kill it, with long knives and nets for sport."

"It doesn't hate us, any more than the little-boned animals it eats hate it. Things are killed. Things kill."

Corleu shifted, trying to make himself smaller against the cold. Shadow darkened over his closed eyes. He smelled damp earth, roots that snaked over the banks to slide deep into the water, weaving, in their ancient courses, doors, windows, pathways for the small animals. He smelled water everywhere. He opened his eyes. Moss hung like women's hair from the tree boughs, the only color to be seen; the sky seemed very far away. Something swam after the oars, grabbed one; there was a tussle between rower and water before whatever it was sank away.

"One of hers?"

"No. Old stone-back tortoise."

"Did you see its eyes? Old as Ro Holding."

"Older."

Hours later, the boat eased toward a dock. For an eye-blink, Corleu saw a luminous woman, all in weedy white lace, sitting in the prow of a long, graceful boat; the woman she spoke to, all in black, lifted a pale face toward the passing boat. Then the bright ghost vanished. A lamp hung on a mooring stump spilled light across the dark; moths as big as birds flickered around it. The men made for the light. On the hillside above the water, Corleu saw a house; one thick, smoky window burned red as a fox's eye. The men pulled him to his feet. He stumbled onto the dock and fell, half frozen and dizzy with hunger. They hauled him up again, pushed him toward the rickety wooden stairway that curved up to the house. Before they could begin the climb, the woman, still sitting shadowlike in the long boat, spoke.

"You're late," she said coldly. "You took all day."

They all started. The one-eyed man said breathlessly, "Thought you were the ghost herself—"

"We've been talking." She stepped forward into the moth-stippled light. Her face, it seemed to Corleu—spare, proud, untamed—might have been the face of the dark, secretive woodfox, perhaps, or the beautiful, imperious wild swan. Her eyes, so pale they seemed to hold no color, went to Corleu's face. "What's this?" she said sharply.

The one-eyed man sighed hopelessly and was silent. The young one said brashly, "Bones, ma'am."

"Bones."

"You said bones out of the swamp. We found them lying, so we took them."

She gave an exasperated hiss, like an old swamp tortoise that just missed its prey. "You bubble-fish, I told you bones!"

"Yes, ma'am. We—"

"He's not even dead! Or is it just my eyesight going, too? Is he a ghost over his bones?"

"No, ma'am. He—"

"Are you?" She reached out, pulled the cloth from Corleu's mouth. He took a deep breath that did not smell of fish. Her eyes caught at him again; he kept looking for color in them. "Are you dead?"

He shook his head, though not with absolute certainty. "I'm Wayfolk."

"With that hair?"

Then he knew he was among the living. "With this hair."

"What would Wayfolk be doing in the Delta swamp in midwinter? Catching butterflies?"

He was silent. Her strange eyes were pulling his thoughts off balance, and suddenly he realized why. "They're like the mist we travelled in," he breathed. "As if you looked in at us."

"What?"

"It was never winter there. I thought it should have come, but it was always warm. It wasn't Delta, where I was."

"Well, then, where was it?"

"I don't know. I kept falling. Sky, maybe."

"You fell out of the sky."

"Swamp gas ate his brain," the young man suggested, grinning. The woman ignored him.

"And what," she asked softly, "were you doing in the sky?"

"Talking to the sun."

She pulled her eyes from him abruptly; he swayed as if the world had shifted. "Bring him. He is obviously a lunatic, a runaway, most likely. No one will miss him. I might as well keep him to clean my hearth. Did you get everything else? Blind-fish? The roots of bog lilies? Canaries?"

"There was the blood-fox spoor," the one-eyed man said heavily, and she glared at him. "Petrified. Things don't linger here to petrify."

"Tortoises do," she snapped, and he sighed. "Get the spoor. And bones. Old bones. I need old eyes to see out of. Do you understand?"

His head ducked turtle-like into his thick neck. They followed the woman up steps that hung together on a promise. The porch slanted crazily over the water; the windows sagged in their frames, looking neither in nor out, curiously opaque. The men deposited Corleu and the squirming sacks at the open door, then retreated to the top of the stairs. The woman heaved the sacks over the threshold herself. She turned to the men, who were eyeing Corleu with a morbid, fascinated speculation.

"Go," she said sharply, and they did so, old rails groaning under their feet. She touched Corleu gently. "What's your name?"

"Corleu Ross."

"Corleu. Come in. You didn't fall out of the sky dressed for winter, did you? Did they give you anything to eat?"

"Only that fish-blown cloth." He felt an odd resistance at her threshold, shadows dragging at him like water, and he stopped, finding the same resistance in his thoughts. But she put her fingers lightly on his wrist, coaxing him forward.

"Never mind them."

"I have trouble with houses, is all. What are they?"

"Just my doorkeepers. My house wards." Dragging sacks behind her, she led him through a short hallway, into a dark room that smelled, he thought, like cider gone bad. She snapped her fingers. Fat candles in fantastic holders lit themselves. Chairs, small tables, books, seemed to arrange themselves hastily, as if in the dark they had been wandering around. Corleu stopped again, not knowing if his head or the room were shifting. Walls had been torn away to make one huge room of oddly vague dimensions. In the middle of the room was a fire pit, open on all sides, with an enormous chimney straddling it. Several large tables stood around the fire pit, cluttered with stones, knives, glass pipes, crystals, nuggets of silver and gold, books, feathers, clothes, jewels cut and uncut, small bones, bottles full of tinted liquids and salts, jars with things floating in them—shadowy, withered and half-formed things that brought Corleu out of weariness and hunger and memory to stand prickling with horror, wondering what trouble he had just carelessly walked into.

The woman watched him silently. She was younger than Corleu had guessed, a scant handful of years older than he. Her hair, bound hastily at her neck with a gold clip, was long and fine and so dark it reminded him of another such night he had buried his face in. He whirled, to escape into the Delta night again. But instead of the hallway between workroom and porch, he found only a musty room full of doves sleeping in the rafters.

He turned back, bewildered, beginning to panic. The young woman gazed down at the sack by her feet, ignoring him. The string untangled itself, fell to the floor. Corleu, his heart pounding sluggishly, watched the sack crawl like something living. Birds fluttered out of the opening: yellow canaries, and tiny, iridescent hummingbirds beating eerie, frantic, silent circles around the room. They made no noise.

"Their tongues are in here somewhere," the woman said. "I also need their wings. You will see to that."

Corleu flung a side door open. The room beyond it had no windows, no other doors; it held a small black boat with a broken mast and the constellation forming another improbable house painted on its bow.

He slammed the door again, leaned against it. His heart seemed to be circling above him with the desperate birds. The woman was watching him expressionlessly.

"You can't leave," she said. "This house has a hundred doors into itself. If you do what I tell you, I'll feed you and give you a bed. In the morning you can tell me what you were doing in the sky talking to the sun. Or if you are simply demented. If you don't do as I bid, you can starve. Suit yourself. They're only birds."

Corleu ran down the hallway again. A door rose before him; he threw it open and ran on, one arm raised to ward off whatever might come at him. He came to another door, opened it, ran down a longer hallway. Another door rose before him; he passed through it, found himself back in the workroom.

He sagged against a table, spilling things, sobbing for breath, and found that all the birds had come to perch on his hair, his shoulders. He shook them into the air.

"Tear them apart yourself," he said furiously. "I'll starve."

She rummaged in the sack. Somewhere in the shadows a clock ticked. The small birds fluttered down to rest in his hair again.

She did not feed him for two days; he did not speak to her for three. By then she had her bones and spoor and had taken the bird wings herself. Slumped on her floor, growing numb to both hunger and horror, Corleu watched her build her spell step by step. She made a fire of dogwood and willow and hard black gallwood. Tiny gold suns snapped toward the ceiling, gold lintels, a sun-king's golden face. . . . The fire turned strange colors and shapes as it ate her gleanings from the swamp. The shadows in the room were tinted blue and purple; curtains and paintings shifted uneasily. When she had fed the fire the last bone from the marsh, it turned grey-white and shaped a skull without eyes. The skull said one word and collapsed. The woman left Corleu lying in the haunted dark and went to bed.

The next evening, tired of walking around him, she relented and fed him.

She guided him out of the workroom, deeper into the rambling house and gave him a bed. The next day, while she sat reading beside a normal fire, Corleu searched the house for the one door that would undo. Rooms opened into rooms in her house, none holding anything predictable. In one, all the chairs in the house had gathered except the one the woman was sitting in. Another room, with white walls and white curtains, held nothing but a stuffed white peacock. One room seemed blown out of glass. Frozen flowers tumbled around Corleu as he stood in it. Delicate green ivy grew up the walls, soft purple lilac hung overhead. He could smell lilac. Wondering, he closed the door, then opened it again. Old tapestries hung from the walls now; a glass vase the color of lilac held a faded branch of lilac. He walked on, down silent carpeted hallways, opened another door at random. This room, for some reason, was filled from top to bottom with goose feathers. He sneezed. Pinfeathers startled into the air, drifted down like snow. He found a staircase and mounted it. At the top of the stairs he found a door with a sign on it that said "Do Not Enter."

He opened a door into memory. The tinker sat in the waning light, cooking something small over his fire. . . . Falling, falling through endless stars, he came up against another door. But which was this? In? Or out? He touched it, hands flat against the wood, as if he could feel a secret, trembling heartbeat within it. He was shaking at what might be within: the gold, armored king pacing the length of his chain, the smell of fish cooking . . . worse than either, what he had to find. But there was no undoing without doing. His hand slid to the latch; he opened the door.

Inside, the woman sat in her chair, reading. Her feet were bare; she nibbled a strand of hair as she read. She looked at Corleu; her pale eyes were as expressionless as water.

He spoke to her, for the first time in three days. "What are you?"

She shrugged a little. "I have been called everything from sorceress to bog hag. I know a great many things but never enough. Never enough. I know the great swamp of night, and sometimes I do things for pay if it interests me."

"And if—and if they can't pay?"

Her eyes narrowed slightly. "Are you bargaining with me?"

He swallowed. "Sorry. It's Wayfolk habit."

"But for what? You loathe what I do. What could you want from me?"

"It's—you know things. You have so many books. You must know other than burning owl bones. My grandfather knew a little. Country magic. But all I know is stories, and all they've done is get me into trouble."

She studied him curiously, as if he were a rare kind of tree frog that maybe she could use in her fire. She had a fine lady's sunless skin and slender fingers, though hers had chipped nails and blisters from the fire. Swathed in some black shapeless dress, all her thoughts hidden away in her lovely, cold face, she gave him again an illusion of someone who prowled or flew by day, and only walked, wept, spoke, in the darkest hour of night. She said finally, "You fell out of the sky. You talked to the sun. You ran all the way out of the world, it sounds like."

"Yes." His hands clenched, opened again. "I went into the wrong door."

"In this house?"

"Likely here, too. But even before they found me in the swamp. It was another house that said 'Do Not Enter,' plain as if it had shouted at me."

"Do you always open doors that say that?"

"I'm getting in the habit of it. So I went in, and now I must find something."

"What? Where?"

"I don't know where. It could be anywhere. So if a door like this one bothers to talk at all, even to warn, that's a door I need to open, to see if what it warns of can help me at all. Even you."

Her brows went up. She said drily, "Even the likes of me."

"I didn't mean—" He held his breath a moment, under that colorless, speculative gaze. "I'm used to a harmless magic. You know some terrible things. But you do know, and I'm short of knowing anything besides my name. I'll sweep for you, I'll clean your hearth. I'll do anything but kill for you, except for what you need to live. I'll cut wood, I know herbs and flowers, I can even mend your stairs. If you'll only help me, even only tell me where to begin—"

She shook her head, her fine hair sliding laxly over one shoulder. "I like my stairs that way," she said shortly. "They discourage company. I don't understand you. Begin what?"

"To look for what I have to find."

"And what might that be?"

"It's—just a small thing." His hands had clenched again; his eyes flicked past her as if shadows of his memories moved on the wall behind her. "A small thing. He said to ask the Blind Lady."

"What blind lady?"

"The Blind Lady of Withy Hold. He said to give her a gift."

She shifted, impatient, bewildered. "What gift? What small thing? What 'he' said you must find it?"

"The sun."

She made an unladylike noise. "You," she said, "may be too demented to be useful."

"No—"

"Demented people talk to suns."

"And to old burned bones that answer back." His retort left her wordless; he pleaded quickly, "You brought me in here. Likely you thought you could stand a few lunatic ravings."

"Or likely not—"

"I have no place to go, no one else to ask. Please. If you could only listen. Only that. Please." Her face promised him no indulgence. But she didn't stop him. "We travelled south this year from Withy Hold, instead of going to Hunter Hold, like always. We were bound for Delta, but somewhere we took a wrong turn."

"We."

"My Wayfolk company. Except my true kin—they went on to Hunter Hold."

"Get on with it," she said with some asperity. "I don't want details about all your barefoot siblings."

"I—my parents went to Hunter Hold instead, because my mother saw something in her petals, something falling out of the sky, and all our paths twisting and turning and going nowhere—"

"Like your tale," she muttered.

"It was a beautiful place we came to," he said, skipping over the endless roads. "Nothing like the true Delta. Nothing. It was like the days in spring when you find everything has flowered and nothing has begun to die, so it seems that's the way the world must go on: always just breaking into blossom, and the air full of soft, sweet smells, and colors to wring your heart, after all the white and grey of winter. That's what this place was. Day after day after day. Nothing ever died. But once we left Withy Hold, we never saw sky, nor star, nor sun . . . just those colorless mists." His face was blanched beneath its color: he was sweating lightly, as if the warm, sultry air clung to him again. "We kept driving, driving, never counting days, never seeing sunlight except when it turned red at sundown, and then one day I saw it—how we must have driven past autumn into the dead of winter, and still we never reached city or sea, and still nothing in that land died. . . . I tried to tell them, but they were content there, they saw no harm. . . . Then I found a way out and I took it. Alone. They're still all there. I can free them, he said. If I find the thing he wants."

"How did you escape?" she asked, groping for a thread in the tangled skein. "The color of your hair?"

"Something like," he whispered, so deep in the memory he scarcely saw her. "There's a song."

"I might have guessed."

"One of those you're born knowing, you never remember learning. The little dark house that falls out of the sky."

She nodded, impatient again and mystified. "I know it."

"You must not enter it."

"It's the house you'll never leave."

"Everyone knows it. But no one pays mind to it. I never did either, until it fell." Her fingernail, ticking at the chair arm, missed a beat. "There was no other door I could see. No other way out of the dream world. Only that black house, with the roof of gold and the lintel of gold. So"—he drew breath raggedly—"I went into it."

She was motionless, in a way he associated with animals fading into their surroundings at a scent, at something barely glimpsed. "You did." Her voice was devoid of expression. "And what did you find, in that little dark house that falls from the sky?"

"The Gold King."

He had closed his eyes at the memory. He could not hear her breathing, and he wondered suddenly if, exasperated, she had taken her book and walked through a wall. But she was still there, gazing at him without blinking, spellbound, it seemed to him, sculpted out of air and painted.

"The Gold King is a Hold Sign." She picked words carefully, as she might have picked a path across a marsh.

"Yes."

"The yellow star its lintel, the yellow star its roof, the four stars of red and pale marking its walls, the blue star marking its doorlatch . . . The Hold Sign of Hunter Hold."

"Yes."

"It is a banner, a constellation, an ancient war sign. A song. How could you walk into it?"

"Who am I to know that?" he asked her. "The likes of me? How did the Cygnet get into the sky? How did the Gold King's house get into a song? Maybe it was us put them there. Or maybe they're the ones whispered to us that they were there. Or something was there, hiding behind Cygnet, behind sun's face. Something dark and powerful and terrible, that we hung faces on to make them less terrible. The house fell. I went into it. How is what I could break my mind over till I die. What matters is that, standing here in front of you, I'm still in that house. What I need is how to get out of it."

Her face was so pale it reminded him of the waxen dream-lilies. Her eyes were wide on his face; he saw color in them finally, the palest trace of lavender. "That house," she whispered. "Here. In the Delta."

"In a dream."

"Why you? Why would the Gold King fall out of the sky into your life?"

He swallowed, his throat burning. "I asked him. He said no one else in Ro Holding would have been muckerhead enough to enter his house."

She drew breath, moving finally. Shadows moved and melted on the walls around them; he wondered, eerily, if they were her suddenly busy thoughts.

"The Gold King wants you to find something for him. In return for your people. What? Some treasure?"

"A small thing, he said. Being trapped, he can't look for it."

"A small thing."

"Something only he still values, after all this time, he said."

"The Gold King did." She slammed her heavy book suddenly, so hard he started. She caught his eyes in her unsettling way. "A small thing. Corleu Ross, you may be a muckerhead, but what kind of idiot do you think I am? The Gold King would not tumble out of the sky in his ancient house to send you on a goose chase for some bauble of sentimental value. I would guess that what he wants you to find is powerful enough to rattle Ro Holding like a weathercock in a storm. Tell me what it is or I will not help you."

"I cannot," he whispered. "I cannot. I will never see them again, he said. Never in the true world."

"But you do know what it is."

"Yes. I know."

She held him still under her scrutiny, as if she were trying to see the mystery inside his head. But not even she could do that, or wanted to; the intensity of her gaze lessened; he could move again. She nibbled a thumbnail; shadows shifted like smoke behind her. "This thing," she said. "Would you want it for yourself if you could find a way to keep it?"

His face twisted, as if he smelled smoke again from the tinker's spattering fire. He shook his head.

"Then, if I take it from the Gold King after he frees your people, you wouldn't fight me for it? Think. You might change your mind once it's in your hand."

"No," he said, brusque with horror. "It's a terrible thing. Likely even you won't want it."

She smiled a little, thinly. "Likely I will, if it's anything of power. In return for you finding this thing for me, I will help you with all my power. Which," she added, "is considerable, and not confined to this moldering backwater. I have taken it from all over Ro Holding."

"Are you Wayfolk?" he asked bewilderedly, for lords' daughters seldom rambled the length and breadth of Ro Holding, or took to living like a cuckoo in an untidy, haunted nest in a swamp.

She shook her head absently, already conjecturing. Her answer took his breath away. "Of course not. I am Nyx Ro."

FIVE

HE could not stop staring at her. Even though the door had moved and there was a hallway where he remembered stairs, and all the portraits hanging along the mauve walls were upside down, his eyes kept returning to her face, for never in his life had he thought he might be close enough to touch one of the three daughters of the Holder of Ro Holding. She ignored his staring, as well as all the white, closed doors they passed, until she came to one that had, maybe, one more grain of dust on it than the others, or it cast a slanted shadow. She opened it and they stepped back into her workroom.

"You never get lost?" he asked.

"No."

"You made this house, then?"

She shook her head. "I found it." She went to the fire; its embers glowed like a multi-eyed beast in the shadows. "It's quite old and full of memories, dreams, thoughts, reflections of time. But it's addled with age. It can't remember what's real and what's memory, or where it puts things; that's why they constantly shift." She reached for wood, then changed her mind before she touched it. "Make up the fire, Corleu. Use pear and coralwood, that will clear the air."

He was getting used to the stenches that came out of her fires, but this last had been formidable. "It smells like the dead were dancing in here," he muttered, raking the embers. "Why do you live like this?"

"Like what?" She was at a worktable, sorting through a pile of books that smelled of smoke and leather and ancient ink, and that flickered sometimes in the candlelight like star-fire and jewelled salamander tongues.

"Like this," he said recklessly. "Barefoot in a rickety house, summoning hobgoblins out of your fire, when you could be——"

"Shod in velvet, wearing pearls in my hair in the Holder's house by the sea?" She lifted her eyes; again he saw the faint wash of color in them, and then her narrow-eyed, sardonic smile. "I came here to learn what the swamp had to teach me. To look out of the stone-tortoise's ancient eyes and see what it has seen."

"But why?" he asked, thinking of the tongueless, fluttering birds. "It's a twisted power you get out of all this slow, deep running water, all these bog pools layered with dead things."

"Power is power. It's neither good nor evil, it's simply there to be used, either way. It's like fire. If you feed it silver it will shine like a summer's day and speak to you as fairly, and if you feed it gallwood, it will turn black and stink like the dead, and prophesy sickness, storm, misfortune. All that matters is what you put into it."

He dropped pearwood onto the grate with a clatter. "Bird skulls," he said tersely. "The beating hearts of fish."

"There's power in the living and the dead. Power in the bird's eye and in the eyeless skull. Not all knowledge is clean, innocent. I came here to learn, I don't choose what to be taught. If there is knowledge to be taken from the heart of a fish, I take it."

"Is that all you know? This mean, bloody kind of power?"

She was silent, absorbed in her reading, he guessed; he wondered if she had heard his rough question. She answered it finally, her eyes on the pages of her book, as if she were reading a tale from it. "In Hunter Hold, I lived among the desert witches, who are dedicated to the Ring of Time. Their lives are exemplary. I slept on bare ground, I wove my own garments, I ate nothing that possessed an eye or a heart. I learned how time is layered like tree rings, and how, with dedication and proper stillness in mind and body, you can see beyond the ring you circle at the moment. In Berg Hold, I studied with the oldest mage in Ro Holding, the last descendant of Chrysom."

"Who?" He was kneeling with his hands full of wood, entranced by the double vision of her: half unscrupulous bog witch, half the Holder's daughter, with all the history of Ro Holding in her name.

Her eyes flickered at him; her expression gave him a glimpse into his ignorance. "Chrysom was the great mage in the court of Moro Ro, who was the first ruler of Ro Holding—"

"I know that."

"I'm overwhelmed. Chrysom built the house on the Delta coast, during the Hold Wars, where the Holders have lived for a thousand years."

"The house that flew."

"The house that flew."

"The air," he commented, "must have been thick with houses once."

"Don't take all day with the fire. Can you read?"

"Yes. My granda got into the habit. It was a place to get away from being teased about being a moon-haired bastard. My mother kept his books."

"So you got his hair. He had some power, you said?"

"I didn't get that."

"How do you know?"

He glanced at her, surprised. "I'd know by now, likely. I can't foresee in small ways, in dreams or petals, like he could. He could float herbs on water and forecast from their shadows. My mother could do those things. I never could."

"You brought the Gold King's attention to you somehow."

"I kept using his name in stories," he sighed. "How was I to know he was listening?"

"What was he like?"

"A tinker," he said tersely. Since there was no help forthcoming from Nyx Ro, he lit the fire himself with one of the fat candles that never seemed to burn down. The flame danced along the coralwood, spicing the air with a resin that smelled of oranges. He gazed into it, seeing again the brilliant, bitter gold face.

"A tinker," she repeated curiously.

"And a king made of gold, chained to his own throne."

She glanced at him, startled, catching a glimpse of something, then losing it. "How strange," she breathed. She went back to her reading. He watched her, as he tended the fire. Books piled up around her, threatening to topple as she worried at them, pulling them from mid-pile, flipping pages, then heaving them shut with massive thuds that sent dust flying and books swaying. Her hairclip was sliding down her back; her full sleeves kept tangling in her fingers; she would push them impatiently up one arm or the other, where they would slowly creep back down. He wondered suddenly at the power trapped in her, behind her intent, dispassionate gaze. He straightened; as if he had disturbed some delicate tension in the air, a pile of books sagged precariously.

"What are you looking for?" he asked tentatively, and got the sharp edge of her tongue.

"What do you think I'm looking for? I'm trying to find a gift for the Blind Lady."

"Oh." He slid his hand through his hair, blinking, and found a blood-fox skull gazing back at him from a shelf. "The Gold King said a peacock feather."

Nyx Ro lifted her head, looked at him with as much expression as the skull behind her. She slammed her book, then glared at a pile threatening to topple. "Why didn't you tell me?"

"I didn't know what you were doing."

"Do I have to tell you everything?"

"It's easier," he said steadily, "if you do. That way you won't have to shout at me."

"I'm not used to explaining things. Nothing around here asks."

"Nothing around here has a tongue to." He added, at her silence, "Likely I won't either, much longer."

"Likely."

"There's a stuffed peacock around here somewhere, could get a feather from that."

She folded her arms, still frowning at him, but no longer in irritation. "A peacock feather. Are you sure he said that?"

"Yes."

"Think. Remember the words."

He did then. "I'm wrong. He said: 'Offer her what's on the peacock's feather.'"

"Ah," she said softly. "That's clear enough."

"Is it?"

"You tell me. What is on a peacock's feather that a Blind Lady might want?"

He stared at her, his eyes widening. He shifted closer to the fire, feeling the old house shunt a breath of winter up from the cellar. He said after a moment, "The dark house of Hunter Hold fell in the Delta. Will I find the Blind Lady here, too, or do I go back up to Withy Hold in mid-winter?"

She was still searching among her books, slowly now, absently, as if she knew what she looked for but had misplaced it and memory might find it before her hands did. She paused, favored him with a long, dispassionate gaze. "That's a good question," she said. "What do Wayfolk say about the Blind Lady?"

"What all folk say, likely. She wears the Ring of Time. She dealt death with her eyes until the Cygnet tricked her into gazing at her reflection in the full moon and she blinded herself. The Peacock guides her across the night sky with all its eyes. In Withy Hold, they say she weaves the threads of lives, meetings, partings, marriages, births, such. She weaves out of the dark and light of days."

"To the witches of Hunter Hold, she is only a tale. Time is not woven, they say, of threads that can be broken."

"In Withy Hold, they gave her gifts, long ago. To coax her into weaving fortune. One farm I worked had a giving place: a little ring of trees with a stone in it, where things were brought to her. The lord who owned the farm plowed around the trees, even though no one comes there now. He said it was a ring of time."

"You went into it," she said with sudden insight. He nodded.

"I wanted to stand inside time."

"What happened?"

"Nothing. What would? It was only story."

She bent over her books, found what she wanted at last, it seemed, for she read silently a long time, while Corleu kept the fire going and watched for a shift of light beyond the windows. But whether it was night or day, he could not tell, for all any of them gave was a reflection of the room. Nyx Ro closed her book finally. She stood silently, her arms folded, musing on something in the dusky shadows that hid the room's true dimensions. She said abruptly:

"Where did your grandfather get his hair?"

Surprised, he told her the tale of the Rider in the Corn, as he had re-membered his great-gran telling.

"She died," he said, "before I was old enough to understand it, or ask her more. Something must have caught her eye about him besides his hair. But she was old, and years might have changed him from stableboy on a nag to a corn-lord on a stallion."

"Perhaps." She was still eyeing him, in a meditative measuring way that made him uneasy. "For someone who just came face to face with a story, you're far too ready to dismiss them. The Gold King's eye fell on you because you were looking at him, apparently, and what made you bring him to life is a mystery that may well have begun among the corn. Maybe you have some gifts, maybe not, but the Gold King summoned one of Wayfolk to find this treasure for him, not a powerful sorceress who might take too much interest in it. So. My hand must be on none of the work that may need doing for this. Everything must be done by you. Your hand on the wood the fire burns, your hand on the making and unmaking. Will you try?"

He shrugged. "I'll try anything. But you must keep in mind I'm still an ignorant gawp under this hair, and not even you with all your power can make a fish gallop."

"Don't be too sure," she murmured. She left her book lying open, came to the fire. "Find some warmer clothes around this house. You're going to Withy Hold tomorrow."

He nodded, not pleased but unsurprised. "I'll need a horse," he said. "Will there be one roaming somewhere in the house?"

"You won't need a horse," she said. "You'll bring Withy Hold to the Delta."

He stared at her. "How?" His voice had lost all sound.

"You will make a Ring of Time."

He wandered in and out of rooms the next morning, found clothes finally, in a trunk sitting strapped and ready for a journey in an empty room. He pulled out wool and leather and linen, hardly seeing what he put on, feeling, even after he had dressed, that there was something he had forgotten. But there were good boots on his feet and a heavy cloak over one arm, and a list in his head of all he would need for a long, hard journey north into winter. It would take more than the color of his hair to shorten the road to Withy Hold, and he expected to be hunting up a horse somewhere along the river by evening. The faint, melancholy sound of a reed pipe accompanied him as he left the room.

He found Nyx Ro brooding over a book beside her fire. He stood watching her pale, still, secret face; the way her long, unruly hair slid over her shoulder; the way she picked at things with her fine, callused fingers—a bead, a button, a loose stitch—as she read. Her coloring reminded him of Tiel, yet she was unlike in every way: She was lonely, fearless, wild and powerful, and her knowledge was a vast country he scarcely knew existed.

She lifted her eyes, caught him watching. She said only, rising, "I thought you were a ghost, in those clothes." She went to one of her tables, cleared of all but a round bubble of a bottle and an odd assortment of things around it. "Come here, Corleu. This is where you will make your ring." He joined her silently. All the oddments around the jar were labelled in some painstaking, flowery, antique script. He read a label.

"Is that real?"

"Of course."

He stared at her. "Is this going to work?"

"Even," she said, "for the likes of you." She shifted, watched him from the far side of the table. He drew breath, feeling a wintry chill in his bones, as if by accident, moon-blinded eyes had met his eyes. "All you must do now is lay a fire within the jar from the things as I have placed them. Begin at the top of the circle, with the flaked moonstone, and go to the left from there."

He reached for it; as though it lay within a charmed circle, it seemed too far to touch. His hand fell, empty, on the wood. "I'm afraid," he said, not looking at her. "Of this, of the Blind Lady, of being in this house, of leaving this house. I'd go through this ring and run and keep running, likely, leave them all there in that summer place, if not for leaving Tiel there, too—"

"Tiel."

He looked at her then, wanting to swallow the name, put it back into his heart where it was hidden even from Nyx's strange, clear eyes. But her eyes asked, relentlessly.

"I left her," he said softly. "Tiel."

"Ah."

"For that house."

"I see." She seemed to: as if the green, peaceful private world had formed in the air between them. "Tiel," she said again, musing, curious; and at the reminder, or the rare gentleness in her voice, his hands eased open. He reached for the moonstone.

"The Ring of Time is a circle of stars, a silver ring on the Blind Lady's finger," she said as he worked. "The Ring has no beginning, no ending. Meddling with time, past and future, is a sorcery I have little skill in. But this Ring you are making is very simple; your hands do the work, not your mind. It opens only to the present, in another place. There are more complex rings, that open to remembered past. Two or three mages even wrote of Rings into the future. But they left no spell for that; if they returned at all to write about the future, they did not recommend it. They say little about their journeys, they seem to have lived brief lives afterwards . . . or perhaps they made the Ring a final time and stepped through it forever.

"For you, it will simply be a door opening there, and then back here."

Corleu, listening, was laying the strangest fire he had ever made in his life: a tiny thing inside a squat glass bottle that was so round he thought his breath might unbalance it. Into its narrow mouth he dropped filings of gold, of black dragon's bone, purple-green scales from the wings of a flying lizard, half a silver ring, a crushed pearl, twists of paper that held the dried tears of a weeper-owl, a single eye from the tail feather of a peacock, a long, silver hair.

"Do I drop myself in there last?" he murmured. "Or does time come out of the bottle?"

He added a bone button and a bit of amber enclosing a drop of wizard's blood that was the color of tarnished silver. He paused then, gazing at the fragment of amber, and wondering at the slow seep of time out of the tree that had enclosed and frozen a pearl of wizard's blood . . . and how time, too, had slowed within that magic drop of blood so that it had waited for the tear of amber to slowly weep around it.

"Time passes," Nyx Ro said, "in as many overlapping lengths as notes in a song."

He thought of Tiel then, caught in such a motionless pool of time. Dried, crumbled lily petals fluttered from his fingers down into the jar; he almost saw her there, a tiny young woman with petals in her hair and a lizard's scale beside her for a pool. But it was only an odd reflection in the glass.

"Could I walk through this Ring to Tiel?"

"She doesn't exist in any time you or I know. She is like a thought in the mind of the Gold King. You would never reach her through this Ring. You might see her reflected off a moment of time, like an image in a mirror, but only that."

He shook pale fragrant powder of the hoof of the extinct blue horse into the jar, and, finally, black dust from the obsidian deserts in the barren southern regions of Hunter Hold, which had been formed out of layer upon layer of volcanic fires.

"Breathe into it," Nyx said. Corleu leaned over the jar; gold, obsidian, petals, swirled in his breath; the round glass misted. "Now pick up the fire."

He reached for the fingernail of frozen silver fire that lay like a dead leaf on a silver plate. Quiescent as it was, it burned his fingers slightly, though with heat or cold he wasn't sure.

"The only thing complex about building this Ring is gathering the ma-

terials for it. That alone could take a lifetime. Sorcerers have died squab-
bling over a drop of spell-steeped blood in amber. I was fortunate: I took
mine from Chrysom's tower, though it took me years to recognize it for
what it was. Put the jar there on the floor, in that silver circle. When you
drop the flame into it, step back quickly, or you will become part of the
Ring. Which may be an interesting fate itself, but you probably would not
appreciate it."

The fire that kindled and exploded out of the bottle licked the rafters: a
flowing, changing loop of pure silver. It gave little more warmth than something held for a long time in a closed hand. Corleu could have stepped
through it easily, though at this point, he would only have travelled as far as
Nyx's untidy table.

As he watched, mute with wonder, night dropped like a filmy eyelid
down over the center of the circle. He could no longer see Nyx; she stood
somewhere on the other side of darkness.

"It is complete."

He drew breath, watching silver fall like water through the air, cast its
glow on stone and wood and the threadbare velvet on a chair. Nyx stepped
from behind it; for a moment her eyes were the same color as the falling silver.

"Good," she said, with as much expression, Corleu thought, as if he had
just made a broom handle. "Now, Corleu, you must envision where you are
going, on the other side of this door. Think of the place in the field you
stood in, long ago, where people left weavings, or fine thread for the Blind
Lady to weave into their good fortune. It will be a silent place, bare now,
stripped by winter, an odd lonely place where no one ever comes except those
of us who felt her presence once. To others it's only a little ring of trees, and
an old stone, once flat, but hollowed slowly through centuries by the weight
of those gifts, by the touch of hands. You may have to move the wild grasses
to see the stone. When you see it you will know. And in that place you will
summon the Blind Lady. You will summon. You will summon... Go
now...."

He stepped forward into the Ring, and remembered, too late, what he
had forgotten. "I have no gift!" he cried. Nyx Ro's words followed him
through time.

"Offer her your eyes."

He stepped onto a field he had harvested.

The clouds hung heavy over it; he smelled snow in the air. The trees lin-
ing the edge of the field seemed to lift the cloud away from the earth with

their bare branches. A crow, picking among the ice-rimed furrows, eyed him and startled away. In the distance, between gentle slopes of field, he saw the prosperous stone farmhouse, chimneys smoking, animals secured, gates shut. In late summer, the Wayfolk camped under the grove of trees behind the house. He could have walked there, found their wagon ruts, traces of their nightly fires. Then memory pulled his eyes to the crest of a hill a couple of fields away. The hill was plowed but for a small tangle of trees, brambles, underbrush on the top. The snowy furrows circled away from the little wood, ring after ring spiralling down from the top of the hill until it sloped away into other fields. Corleu began walking toward it.

In his memory the place was green, sun-soaked, still as a stone with heavy, late summer heat. He had gone in there years ago, looking for something. Someone? Tiel, maybe, though that long ago it would never have been her, luring him in there. Perhaps it had only been the thought of a few moments in the shade that took him away from his work, to fight through berry brambles and wild roses, long grasses, vines hanging from the trees in walls of leaves, encircling the place. The trees, he noticed then, grew in a circle.

He had been surprised at the silence, he remembered. He had stood there a long time without realizing time was passing, for it seemed that in the next moment whoever or whatever he had sought, or had summoned him, seemed about to move, to speak. But always in the next moment, never now . . . He heard his name shouted, in a world so far away the voice was like an insect's. And then he realized there were no insects in that hot, sweet-smelling place; there were no birds. Nothing rustled, nothing made a sound. . . .

Turning in sudden panic, he had tripped over something half buried in the grass.

Now, the vines and brambles were a brown weave that hid nothing. They did not give way easily, even then; he had to fight his way among them, old as they were, and so closely knit that rose twined with berry or grape indiscriminately. Emerging finally into the ring, he was battle-scarred, almost warm. A light, icy snow began to fall, whispering softly against the branches, the first noise he had ever heard in that place.

He went to the center of the circle. He found what he had tripped over so long ago, and he knelt down to uncover it, pulling the frozen weeds and grasses from it until he could see it: a dark round stone, slightly hollowed in the center, where over the centuries, gifts laid there had gradually worn away the stone.

You will summon, Nyx had said. *You will summon . . .*

"But how?" he whispered. "I have no gift."

Offer her your eyes. . . .

Then he remembered, from so many past years that it seemed another life: a dozen grubby children clinging to one another, hand to hand in a circle spinning faster and faster around someone—Tiel?—who had covered her eyes with her hands, and was herself spinning dizzily as they chanted at the tops of their voices:

Lady come, lady come,
Find my eyes, find my eyes,
Circle, circle . . . the blind can see!

Breathless, still kneeling among the weeds, he put his hand on the stone. He heard the rhyme he spoke as if the grass had spoken it, or the snow, or the distant voices of children:

In a wooden ring
Find a stone circle . . .

Stone, trees, fields vanished in a fiery blaze of summer night. He saw her: the Blind Lady, who wore the Ring of Time and saw out of the eyes on the Peacock's tail. The Peacock's tail was a spray of white fire against the dark; its head was turned toward the Blind Lady, its visible eye was sapphire. The Lady herself had hair the color of the moon; strands of starlight wove from the Ring on her hand. She was beautiful and terrible, with her blind face and the constantly weaving strands of light between her fingers. Her head moving slightly from side to side, she seemed to search a darkness she could not see.

"Who summons me?"

The voice came from the stars, but the footsteps breaking the icy grass were behind Corleu. He turned on his knees, startled out of his vision, falling back against the stone. The face he saw struck him dumb.

It was an old woman's strong, fleshy, lumpy face. Her eyelids had sunk over her eyes; her face itself seemed to peer from side to side as if to smell Corleu or hear his breathing. She wore layers of old wool and linen—skirts and shifts and shirts, shawls and aprons of all colors, all faded, dirty. Frayed threads hung from every hem and sleeve, every seam, cuff and collar. She was big, shapeless, her hands gnarled and swollen with age. As she listened for answer, she gathered threads absently from a frayed vest, began to pull them, weave them. On one forefinger she wore a tarnished silver ring.

"Who summons?" she demanded again; her voice was deep, brusque. Her shoes, Corleu saw, were sewn of peacock feathers.

He found his voice finally. "I summoned you." He shifted hastily out of her way, when it seemed she would walk over him or through him. She kicked at the ground until she found the stone. She settled herself down on it with a sigh, and felt at her threads again.

"Corleu. Of the Wayfolk."

His heart hammered. He stared at the frail, colored threads between her twisting fingers; he wanted to touch her hands, beg her to be gentle.

"Well?" she said. "You summoned."

"I came—I—The Gold King sent me to you."

Her pale, shaggy brows lifted; her sunken eyelids twitched, trying to open. "He! Why?"

"I must find something for him," he said. "He doesn't know where it is; he said you might. He said offer you what's on a peacock feather and you might help me."

She dropped her threads, groped toward him. "Let me feel you. For all I know of humans, you're all made of thread or light." Her hands roved over his hair, bumped against his cheekbone, his jaw. He felt the silver ring against his throat, cold or hot, like the silver fire he had dropped into the jar. "No, flesh and blood as ever. You came here once before, I remember."

"Yes."

"No one comes here. They used to, they brought me gifts to turn my weaving their way. Sometimes they moved me. They praised me, they called me beautiful." He felt her shake with silent laughter. "Was I or was I? I never knew. Why did you come here so long ago?"

"I don't know why. I thought the tree ring hid a secret. I wanted to know what. I was of that age, when everything seems to say something, even an old stone."

"And did it speak?"

"Nothing spoke. The silence spoke. I ran." The sleet had turned to snow, drifting down in another ageless silence. "I never forgot the sound of this place."

"It was me you heard, weaving."

"Likely."

"And you came back and brought me a gift. I can't see you, but that King had his eye on you. Well, where is it?"

"What?"

"My peacock feather."

He drew breath, his eyes flickering across the tangled ring around him. He caught one of her gnarled hands before it went back to its endless work. He held her fingers lightly against his eyes.

A quick wind shivered through the bare trees. "So . . . the King found a way to make you desperate, did he? Something you want badly enough to give me sight?"

"Yes," he said, and felt the snow slide like an icy sweat down his face.

"Tell me what the King seeks."

"What the Cygnet is hiding."

He heard her breath, a harsh, wordless sound. Her fingers twitched, as if to weave his eyelashes. "Yes . . . Oh, yes. He's been thinking, in that little black house of his. He's been thinking. . . . And he reached out and trapped you to do his bidding. You're trapped like him, like we all, or you'd be running like a hare by now back into the daylight."

"Do you know where?"

"No." He shifted, murmuring with despair, and her hand tightened across his eyes. "Hush, now, let me think. It wouldn't be lying around like a pebble, would it? Would it?"

"No."

"It's hidden too well even for my seeing eyes. But I hear thoughts and whispers along my threads now and then, from those who have guarded it through the centuries. Let me remember them. . . . There's a secret within a secret. . . . A web. There's a secret at the center of a web. Above that web the Cygnet flies night and day."

"A web—"

"That's as it comes to me, in broken words and memories. A web in darkness. It's not there, what you seek."

"Not—"

"No."

"Then what—"

"The secret of where to look is there."

"A web under the Cygnet," he repeated, bewildered, reaching toward her hand so he could see.

"Not yet, not yet, these are my eyes still."

"But you must tell more! I can't go looking at every spider web spun under the Cygnet's stars. You must know something more, something clear—"

"It's from my eyes that small thing is hidden. Not only from innocent Wayfolk eyes, but from such as fought the Cygnet. It's layered in secrets like an onion, not like a hazelnut you can crack with one blow. However"—she pulled his head back against her knee, her fingers weaving in his hair—"if you're this desperate, you may want to ask the Dancer. She sees into dreams, she may have seen more than I. Yes. Wake the Dancer at the top of the world. Offer fire to her Fire Bear and it will leave you alone. She may know. It's all I can give now, but when you find what the Gold King seeks, then none of us will refuse you. Whatever your Wayfolk heart desires . . . or whatever heart you have by then. Find my eyes, find my eyes. . . . The blind can see."

SIX

SCREAMING, he fell into a room full of mirrors.

Raising his head, gathering breath again with his throat raw from his last cry, he opened his eyes and saw, all around him, within mirrors ancient and ornate, framed plainly in wood or silver, oval, square, diamond, hexagonal, vast mirrors too heavy to lift propped against the wall with smaller mirrors strewn against them: crouching figures in torn silk and muddy leather lifting thorn-scarred faces, staring with black, empty eyes. For a moment he did not recognize himself.

The breath left him in a long, shaking sigh, with a sound to it like an unshaped word. He got to his feet; so did his reflections. He had an eerie feeling that even at his back his reflection was gazing at him. As he turned to look, all the images vanished.

He stood like a ghost in a room full of mirrors that took no notice of him.

"I'm dead," he said, startled. He heard Nyx Ro calling his name. Her voice sounded sharp, bewildered. He looked around for a door, saw only mirrors crowding the walls, a few hanging bannerlike from the ceiling, their faces blank as the Delta sky. He touched one; he could not even cast a shadow.

In sudden panic, he spoke Nyx Ro's name.

She appeared in one of the ornate mirrors. "I couldn't find you." she said tightly. "I heard you scream. I couldn't find you."

"I can't find a door." He turned again, searching, and caught his breath at the sight of Nyx multiplied, in threadbare blue velvet, her face waxen, a smudge of ash across one cheekbone. "I can't see myself at all. Only you."

"I can only see you," she said. Her arms were folded tightly; she was frowning, at once disturbed and curious. "I thought I knew every room in this house. Why didn't you come back through the Ring?"

"I did," he said tersely.

Her eyes widened. She said, "Corleu. Can you touch my hand?" She held it out to him; his fingers were stopped by cold glass.

"Am I some place out of time? Is that why I can't see myself? Should I break a mirror?"

"No," she said quickly. "Mirrors hold your image; they should be treated with care."

"These don't. They're all ignoring me. I saw myself in all of them, and then I vanished, as if an eye blinked somewhere, or they stopped thinking of me."

For a moment, even she stopped thinking of him. "How strange," she breathed. "How strange . . . A secret room within a house full of a thousand secrets. I wonder what it sees when no one is here?"

"If you wait long enough, no one will be here, and then you can find out, likely."

She held out her hand again. "I don't know why you're still standing there complaining. One of me is real. Find me."

He circled the room, touched her glassy hand in every glass. Finally, in a small mirror ringed in tarnished silver, he felt her hand close on his. He stepped forward. The mirror widened into a ring of motionless, icy fire. He stepped through it into her workroom.

The ring dwindled swiftly until there was nothing left of it but a tiny circle of silver that dropped back into the round glass jar. Nyx left it sitting within the circle painted on the floor. She looked for chairs; they had all gone elsewhere. Impatiently, she pulled a couple out of the floorboards, great, shapeless things smelling like mushrooms from the cellar. Corleu sat down gratefully; his eyes closed.

He was on his feet in an instant, pulling away from a glimpse of the Ring he had fallen into. Nyx watched him dispassionately.

"Why did you scream? Did she try to harm you?"

"No." He wheeled at her abruptly. "You tricked me. I had nothing to give her but my eyes."

She shrugged. "It worked, didn't it? What did she give you in return?"

"Not much."

"Did you tell her what you were looking for? Did she recognize it? As something valuable? Something of power?"

"She recognized it, yes. A toad in a hole would recognize it."

"But she didn't—"

"No."

"Did she help at all? Was she angry with you? Did she not want you to find it?"

"Oh, she does want me to find it." He found a wall in front of him and paced back. "She does."

"Did she make any suggestions?" Nyx asked patiently.

"She said there is a web . . . a secret at the center of the web. The Cygnet flies over it day and night."

"And that's where it is?"

"No. That's where the secret of finding this thing is."

"A web . . ." She was silent a little, her brows puckered, a fingernail between her teeth. He looked at her in the candlelight, Lauro Ro's daughter, with her cold, curious eyes that, for all their look into power, had never glimpsed what there was to fear.

"It's not just story," he said harshly. Her eyes rose to his face.

"I guessed that much."

"If I give the Gold King what he wants, he won't just vanish back into words. Nor will she. Likely that's where the stories will end, because now they wear them like rags and tatters, but they'll grow too big, too powerful for us to keep them trapped in words."

She was gazing at him, motionless. "Are you warning me?"

"You don't know what it is I'm trying to find. I do."

"Well, Corleu, what use is there fretting until I do know? Are you going to stop looking for it? Leave your Tiel sitting there forever in a dream?" He was silent, trapped. "That's why I want this thing. I can use it against them, if need be. Was that all she said? A web?"

"She said to ask the Dancer."

She was still then, her eyes narrowed; he stood tense, waiting for her to catch a glimpse of what he sought. But she said only, "Sit down. Tell me a story, of Corleu and the Blind Lady. Maybe then you won't be afraid of the dark."

He sat. He dropped his face in his hands. "She was like . . . she was like this house. Old, rambling, crazed, untidy, like a beggar woman you might see at a crossroads, mumbling to herself, her fingers moving always, weaving,

weaving . . . At the end, she made me look at her weaving. She threads even the stars into it. I saw the Ring of Time she makes, where all the threads there are flow together and you can't see one life, one star, from another, and outside that Ring there is nothing." He raised his head. "That's the Ring I fell through. I thought I would fall into that nothing."

She mused over that, twisting a pearl button. "Yet even she is trapped, Corleu. Even she. And what you saw is only another story, of the Weaver of Withy Hold. The Cygnet holds her powerless."

"And even that is only another story."

"Well, story or no, the thing you are looking for is real enough. Isn't it?"

"Likely," he said after a moment.

"So you move from tale to tale to get it." She studied the pearl, as if the light shifting across it wove a pattern. "A web . . . beneath the Cygnet flying day and night. Why does that tease my memories? Something I read when I was little, something I saw . . ."

"In your books, maybe."

"Then again, maybe I dreamed it." She drew herself up. "You'd do best to go ask the Dancer."

"I'd sooner find the web than wake the Dancer."

"Why?" she asked, surprised. "All the Dancer does is dream, beneath the ice."

"I'll have to carry fire to face the Fire Bear. And I'd sooner find the web than travel to the top of the world and wake someone who dreams sometimes like what appears in your fires."

"You find the web, then," she said, turning. "Meanwhile, I'll find what fire you must take to the Fire Bear."

"I'm not going there."

"You'll go."

"I won't need to."

"You'll go," she said, and there was a flicker of something deep in her eyes, another glimpse into his seeking. "That's what they want."

Wordless, he watched her cross the room. She turned at the door. "There's food in the kitchen. I baked bread. Someone will come to the door tonight. My doorkeepers will give him what he has come for. If you stay in here, you may see one or two of them. Don't look directly at them; they take offense. Good night."

The kitchen, he had discovered, never moved. It could be found at the bottom of some stone steps, which sometimes moved, but never far from what they were attached to. Corleu carried books down with him, roamed through them for a web as he ate fresh bread and goat cheese and cold smoked river trout. The only web he found was cobweb. Wandering upstairs hours later for more books, he was startled by voices. Something vague and bulky in the shadows that looked like a misshapen hand or a forked root turned a pale eye at him and hissed. He stopped staring hastily, built up the fire and settled beside it with more books.

He woke in the morning, face-down in a book. Nyx was stirring the fire.

"You should never sleep between two spells," she commented.

He raised his head, blinked at the ancient writing in blue and gold and black inks. *Chrysom*, it said, at the bottom of each page, like a warning.

"I was looking for the web."

"You won't find it in there, that's spells only." She tossed fragrant wood on the fire and sat beside him on the floor, leafing through the pages of one of the books lying open. He watched her sleepily. She wore a long dress of stiff green cloth that rippled with light when she moved. Its top button was missing; he could see the ivory skin at the hollow of her throat, and the thumbnail of shadow below that. Her eyes were on him suddenly, chilly, colorless, like a winter sky, like a slap of cold water.

"Corleu. I know the fire you must bring to the Fire Bear, but I haven't found yet where the Dancer sleeps."

He sat up, groggy and stiff from the floorboards. "I'm not waking the Dancer. She sleeps in ice beneath the Fire Bear."

"Meaning what?"

"She's under the constellation."

"So is all of Berg Hold. And all of Ro Holding, nearly. Where will you step to, if you go through that ring to Berg Hold? What do Wayfolk say of the Dancer?"

"If you think of her at the fair side of midnight, you'll have good dreams; at the dark side, you'll have foul dreams. If a woman's braid is undone during sleep, Dancer can draw memory away. If you sleep with fresh lavender on your pillow for her, she'll tell you who you will marry. If the lavender is withered, she'll tell you who will die. If she dances hooded in your dreams, your life will change. If you see her face in your dreams, you will die. The Cygnet trapped her in ice so she could not dance. Freed, she never stops. Fire Bear would free her, but it has no fire left in it, after pursuing the Cygnet. So it guards her."

"But where?"

"At the top of the world . . ." He paused, then shook his head. "That's all I know. At the top of the world. You never saw a likely place in your wanderings?"

She mused, remembering. "In Berg Hold I visited the northern witches. I sat around their fires in the dead of winter in their tiny dark huts smelling of tanned hides and smoke and bitter herbs, and I learned how to foretell from the forked horns of snow deer, and how to braid strips of leather into safe paths through the snow, and how to understand the language of the white crows, who gossip of bad weather, travellers, deer herds, death. The witches made do with what they had against storm, hunger, fever. They used to dance to invoke dreams of foreseeing. To them, the Dancer came alive in those dreams; where she slept in the ice was of no importance, that was only a tale. I also studied with the mage Diu, who is the last living descendant of Chrysom. He is very old; he went to Berg Hold to live in peace, he said. But he taught me what I wanted to know, anyway, for Chrysom's descendants have always spent time serving Ro Holding. He made nothing of the Dancer, for he slept little. He only knew what Chrysom had written. The Dancer was a folk tale. A constellation. Inconsequential." She turned a page, leaving Corleu to wonder at her down-turned, secret face.

"You were curious," he ventured. "That's why you went there. To Berg Hold, to live close to earth in the dead of winter. Just curious."

She lifted her head, gave him for the first time a true smile. "Yes."

"Were you always this way?"

Her eyes were clear again, expressionless, but not, he thought, offended. "I like to use my mind," she said.

"Does—does the Holder—" The mist in her eyes seemed to chill into frost then, but he persisted. "Does she wonder—does she know—"

"Does she know that I'm in the Delta torturing small animals?"

"I wondered," he confessed, and she shrugged slightly.

"Oh, yes. She knows. After this, she may not want to see much of me again, but I think she will always know where I am."

"How could she not want to see you?" he protested. "You're her daughter."

"She has Iris and Calyx. And she has Rush Yarr, who is not her son but might as well be. And she has Meguet. She can spare me." Her voice was dry, dispassionate. Corleu, feeling as if he had blundered into some complex, bewildering and totally unfamiliar country, said:

"You're like a story to us. The Holder of Ro Holding and her children: three daughters who wouldn't recognize their fathers from three fence posts, because that's the Holder's business and that's the way it is in your world. Once I saw a procession crossing Withy Hold when I was harvesting. We all stopped to watch it: long lines of riders in black, with other riders in fine, airy colors between them, and the Cygnet on a pennant as long as a furrow, flying like a black flame over them all. That's all I've seen of the Holder. Is she so cold or cruel or stupid that you ran away from her?"

The Holder's daughter shook her head, surprised. "My mother is none of those things. Maybe if she were, I could have lived in the same house with her." She added abruptly, frowning, when Corleu opened his mouth, "Enough. I don't like answering to her, why should I want to answer to some Wayfolk man who fell out of the sky?"

"Likely," he suggested, rising, "because of how I got there."

He wandered away to wash and change his clothes, torn by the thorns and stained by the fields he had known in some distant, lost life. When he returned, dressed in odd, rich, mismatched clothes, combing his wet hair with his fingers, he found her in the same place, beside her fire, so immersed in what she read that she seemed only an illusion of herself.

But she raised her head after a moment. "I have work to do this morning. You won't want to watch it. Take what books you want with you. I'll find you when I'm done."

Chilled, he took himself and an armload of books far enough away, he thought, that not even the anguished bellow of a swamp tortoise could reach him. In a small room containing an old velvet couch, an empty chest, an empty bird cage, he searched for a web until he fell asleep himself and dreamed of Tiel within a fall of vines within the bird cage. He woke and saw the sorceress's face above him.

He started, confusing himself, cages, small wingless birds. Then he drew a breath, leaned back again. He lifted the book that sprawled opened across his chest and said, "I found the Dancer."

"Where?"

" 'On the top of the world,' " he read.
" 'On the top of the mountain,
On the top of a cliff,
On the top of a stone,
Beneath the night,
Beneath the moon,
Beneath the snow,
Beneath the ice:
The Dancer sleeps.
In her breath,
The last breath of winter,
The breath of prophecy.' "

He closed the heavy book and sat up. "It's someone's—I don't know— scraps of sayings, tales, bits of history, even recipes. Riddles. Accounts, where wild herbs were found. Such like that."

She took it from him. "Rydel. She was head gardener for Timor Ro. She knew some herb magic. Chrysom's grandson wrote of her. He thought highly of her. He wrote that she held secret powers of a kind not even Chrysom knew of, or would have understood. So I read whatever I could find that she wrote, or was written of her. But all her other writings are of herb lore, and no one else attributed such great mysterious powers to her. I have read these lines about the Dancer. I didn't remember them."

"Is there only one mountain in Berg Hold?"

"There is one peak much higher than the rest. There are many tales about what lies under its mists: ice spirits, the ghosts of travellers, the palace of the north wind, a real fire bear. I should have remembered that the Dancer and the Fire Bear are always together, even in tales. It's a grey barren peak in late summer, and by autumn you can no longer see it."

Corleu was silent, weighing the impulse to step out of the Delta onto the frozen peak of the world, to free the Dancer and ask her a question that might end his search, and then, with Tiel safe, to close his eyes and hope that the heart of the Cygnet and the heart of Ro Holding had no more to do with one another than a random pattern of stars had to do with a smallfolk rhyme. Impulse turned to desire; desire was nearly overwhelming. He said, his voice shaking, hearing the rustle of leaves in a place where there was no wind, "And if she doesn't know? You know where she will send me."

The green in his eyes resolved into the watery sheen of the sorceress's skirt, rustling as she shifted. She said only, "And if she knows?"

"And if she doesn't?" He closed his eyes, counted recklessly, deliberately. "Gold King, Silver Ring, Fire Bear—it's not only tales I'm stirring up. It's Hold Signs."

She was silent. He looked up; her eyes caught his, absolutely colorless. She made no movement, no sound. Suddenly terrified under that chill gaze, he thought she must have seen straight through his thoughts to the place where he had hidden his secret, and that, child born under the Cygnet's dark wing, she would kill him before he shook apart Ro Holding.

But she moved finally. Her fingers closed tightly on her arms; her face, always pale, seemed ghostly in that pale room. "How complex and fascinat- ing," she breathed. "This is a power like no other power I have ever encoun- tered. If in the end I must fight it, then I must understand it. And I can only do that if I see it unmasked, open, not skulking behind poetry and folk myths. If you don't finish this, the Gold King will find someone else who will, someone who may not fall into my hands as tidily as you did."

"You'd risk Ro Holding out of curiosity," he challenged her, miserable and desperate. Her brows went up. Behind her, in the frame that had been empty, he saw the night sky in miniature, the constellations of the Holds—the Gold King, the Silver Ring, the Fire Bear, the Blood Fox—circling the Cygnet in its flight. Circling among them were the lesser stars: the Peacock leading the Blind Lady, the Mage shadowing the Blood Fox, the Dark House, the Dancer guarded by the Fire Bear.

"Of course I'm curious," Nyx Ro said. "What else would I be?"

"Likely if you're that powerful you don't have to be afraid."

"Not until you tell me what it is you want me to fear."

He looked away from her steady eyes, back to the night sky. The frame was empty again. "If I knew exactly," he sighed. "I could say. They're just tales, how could there be danger? Just stars our eyes picked out and made into patterns so the night would be less lonely with faces looking back at us. But because of stars and smallfolk rhyme, I've lost everything I ever knew."

"It's only a step through time from here to there, from Delta to Berg Hold, Corleu. From not knowing to knowing. And only at the cost of fire. Will you wake the Dancer?"

Fire rippled inside the picture frame: a Fire Bear's soundless roar, a tinker's fire. He saw the tinker's face in the fire, his yellow eyes, his narrow, side-long smile. He stared back at it, trapped and shaken with sudden fury at his helplessness. He said abruptly, "No."

"No? Corleu, it might take a lifetime to find the web, if that's what you're thinking."

"What I'm thinking is that likely I'll have to give the tinker what he asked for, but there's no reason to give him the world and stars besides. I don't have to bring the Dancer to life for him. All I must do is ask a question."

"So—"

"So." He met her cool, misty, slightly bemused eyes. "I'll wait for the last day of winter. She'll answer me truly and then she'll dream like always, and none of us will have to see her waking face."

Nyx was silent, studying him. Her head bent slightly; she turned, closed a couple of tomes and picked them up. She said only, "The work I do here might well drive you to Berg Hold long before the end of winter."

"I'll chance it." He heaved books into his arms. "If you'll let me stay."

"Only yesterday you would have given the world and stars to get out of here."

"That was yesterday." He waited for her to open the door, for she would find the workroom behind it, while he would find only another memory. "I can search for the web. If I find what that is, I won't need to ask the Dancer anything."

"You won't last here till winter's end," she predicted, and opened the door.

"I'll last," he said.

There was a woman leaning against a cauldron in the workroom.

Nyx stopped so abruptly in front of Corleu, he nearly dropped books on her; it was a moment before she spoke. The woman waited, her face composed. She wore black silk and leather; the Cygnet, limned and ringed in silver, flew in the hollow of her left shoulder. She was slender, broad-shouldered, tall enough to wear the long blade at her belt. Swans swirled up the metal sheath and over the hilt of the sword; one tried to soar out of the pommel. Her braided hair was pale ivory. Her face, broadboned, sun-colored, reminded Corleu at first glance of the easily smiling daughters of the wealthy lords of Withy Hold. In the next moment she reminded him of no one he had ever met in his life, and he guessed where she must have come from.

"Meguet," Nyx breathed.

"The Holder sent me." She did not look at Corleu; her still, intent gaze was for Nyx. Nyx moved finally, to a table, and set her books down. She folded her arms. Corleu, following, saw her face as she turned. It looked bloodless in the candlelight; she was frowning deeply.

"Is the Holder well?"

"The Holder, both your sisters and Rush Yarr are all well." The woman's voice, low and slightly husky, was quite calm under the stares of Nyx's assortment of skulls.

"I didn't ask about Rush Yarr."

"So you didn't." She detached herself from the cauldron with the grace of one intimately acquainted with movement. Her curious glance fell here, there; she picked up a bird skull, examined its clean, delicate lines, its empty eyes, as if searching for the magic in it. Nyx opened her mouth to protest, closed it again. Meguet put the skull down. "So you didn't," she said again. "I'll tell him that if you want. He'll ask."

"After all this time?" Nyx asked sharply. "Nine years?"

"He won't listen to reason." She touched a book or two, paced back to the cauldron, her movements light, quick, restive, like one troubled by walls, Corleu thought, or more likely only these, full of bones and smells. "He still loves you."

"What for?" Nyx said, astonished. The woman's eyes flickered at her; in the pallid light, Corleu caught a hint of their color.

"You must ask him to know. If it's important at all." She glanced into the cauldron. "You have a toad in your cauldron. A big, bloated moon of a toad."

"It's an albino," Nyx said crossly. "You've known Rush as long as I have. Tell him to stop. Tell him I said to."

"I will tell him. Does it jump?"

"It jumps out of everything but that."

"It looks too fat to jump."

"It jumps."

"Its eyes are sapphire. . . . He would have come with me, had he known."

"He should have come," Nyx said dourly. "This house would have opened his eyes."

"Perhaps. What do you do with an albino toad?"

"You feed it to an albino fire."

"Ah," the woman said softly. She reached into the cauldron with one hand, did something that made the toad give a deep, lazy grunt. "It speaks."

"As it will in the fire," Nyx said implacably. "If you are finished playing with my toad, perhaps you will tell me why my mother sent you."

"The Holder sent me to remind you that you will have been away from home for three years in spring."

"Three—" Looking surprised, she calculated, from dust motes apparently. "Two years in the desert, last spring here . . . so it will be three years."

"In spring. The Holder asks that you remember your promise to return for the Holding Council."

Nyx was silent. She went to the fire, tossed a handful of wood chips from a bowl beside it onto the embers, and the harsh, charred smell in the air subsided. "Of course I'll come home," she said reluctantly. "I did promise. But I would think, under the circumstances, she would rather not see me in the company of all the Hold Councils."

"You think she should wait until you are doing something less disturbing and all the disgusting rumors of you have died down?"

Nyx met her level gaze. "You could put it like that."

"I just did. You're overlooking one thing. Your mother misses you."

Nyx's fingers found a strand of hair to worry. "I can't think why."

"She hoped you would come back with me."

"She must be getting tired of hearing comments about my life."

"That would be the only reason she wants to see you."

Nyx sighed. "If I go back now, we'll only quarrel."

"You've been here nearly a year. Is there that much to learn in this soggy backwater?"

"There are a few things left. Tell my mother I will come home in spring."

Meguet inclined her head without comment. Nyx studied her a moment, the look in her pale eyes unfathomable. She asked, "Is that the only reason you have come, Meguet? All this way through the swamp, up my rickety stairs? The Holder could have sent a message upriver; it would have reached me, my reputation what it is."

Meguet did not reply immediately; she seemed to hear a question beneath that question. "Your mother holds you in more regard than that. Even now. As for your stairs, I would think anyone as powerful as you could mend a stair."

"It discourages visitors."

"So it must. There are two morose trappers waiting for me in a boat at your dock, who almost refused to bring me here. They said you wouldn't want company."

"They were right."

Meguet's calm gaze did not falter. "Then I will leave you," she said softly. "It's getting dark and the trappers may not wait for me."

"How do you know it's getting dark?"

"What?"

"You can't see out of these windows."

"It was dusk when I came in," Meguet said surprisedly. She picked a heavy black cloak off a chair and swung it over her shoulders. The Cygnet, black and silver within a ring of silver, flew around her and settled at her back. She stepped into candlelight; the fire turned her pale hair silk, and Corleu shifted. A memory nagged him, a tale. Her face looked pale now; the things half-hidden in the shadows wore at her, or the odd sharpness in Nyx's questions. Nyx said more easily:

"I forget sometimes whether it's day or night when I work. Tell my mother I will see her in spring."

"I will."

"And tell the trappers to come back here in the morning; I will have work for them."

"I will tell them," Meguet said evenly. She held Nyx's eyes. "They say you are ensorcelled by this swamp. But, now and then, I think I actually see why you are here, why you burn albino toads. I may be wrong. I know so little of magic. But I do wonder, if any of us knew as much as you, where we would make the choice to stop learning."

A little color rose in Nyx's face. She did not answer, but words gathered in the air between them. Before she turned to go Meguet looked at Corleu. He saw the color of her eyes. And then he saw the corn rows standing in the summer light, the cool secret, shadowy world they hid between their leaves. He blinked but he could not separate her from the tale: corn-silk hair and eyes as deeply green as his great-gran's green-drenched memory.

He swallowed drily, motionless under her gaze, not knowing how long they stood there silently, not knowing, from her expressionless face, what she thought. She turned suddenly, and almost dragged at him to take a step and follow her. Nyx stayed silent, listening to the fading footsteps on the porch. She looked as grim as Corleu had ever seen her. He asked tentatively,

"Who is she?"

"She is a far-flung cousin, Meguet Vervaine. She lost her family early; my mother took her in, raised her with us. She has a penchant for weapons and for wandering. She goes where the Holder sends her, and she is the only person in all of Ro Holding permitted to enter armed into Ro House. She is a descendant of Astor Ro, Moro Ro's wife, who in a thousand years produced some varied and eccentric descendants."

"Does she have power? Like yours?"

She gave him a brooding, searching look. "She has never shown signs of it. Why?"

"Just—how she looked at me, before she left. At me, into me, and out the nether side. As if—as if she might know me, but couldn't remember . . . Something like you're looking at me now, only it's not me troubles you, it's her."

"She was in my house." Her fingers tightened on her arms; she stared at the dark empty hallway as if to see her cousin's shadow there. "My door-keepers could keep even Chrysom out, and Meguet walked through them twice as if she did not even realize they exist."

PART TWO

THE
GUARDIAN

ONE

MEGUET Vervaine sat silently in the trappers' boat, to their three eyes wrapped in authority and glacially calm; in truth she was deeply troubled and sitting in a puddle. Expressions haunted her: Nyx's, seeing her; the face of the young man, whom she had never seen in her life, and yet who nagged at her, called her back the farther the river took her away. He was no one, she thought; Wayfolk, or part, with that odd hair; wanderer, who had found his way to Nyx's doorstep. Or, more likely, since Wayfolk were rare in the Delta, he had trailed Nyx across Ro Holding, promising this and that in exchange for . . . what? What could he have that she might want, enough to keep him with her? Mute, maybe; he had not spoken but with his eyes. If she kept him to bed, she would not have to listen to him in the morning. But he looked troubled, haggard, ensorcelled maybe, but by Nyx—who had run out of Chrysom's tower and out of Ro House and out of her own life in pursuit of freedom? It seemed unlikely she would extend her dark sorcery to humans just because for one year out of nine she had chosen to live in a swamp.

Meguet shifted; the trappers glanced uneasily at one another, unnerved by her as they were by the woman she had visited. The darkening water caught her eye; it went the wrong direction, she felt: away. The man's face had pulled at her, his dark eyes clinging to hers, stunned by something she could not see. She touched her pale hair, thinking of his hair. Wayfolk did not live within walls or in swamps, nor did they know those expressions, or have that hair. Nor had Wayfolk ever disturbed her before, hung in her thoughts clear and hard-lined as the moon over Wolfe Sea, tugged at her, like the moon tugged the sea, so strongly she said sharply:

"Stop."

The trappers eyed one another, wondering, obviously, how to stop the river. The one-eyed man asked gruffly, "Shall we turn to shore, Lady?"

"Turn back."

"Will cost," the younger man said timidly, and the older shoved at him.

"Will cost nothing," he said hastily, "to the Cygnet. But, Lady, how far back? Not to the house again?"

She nodded. "To the house."

The younger slumped over the oars. "It's not for the likes of you," he protested, "that witch's house. She's demented."

Meguet smiled thinly. "She is my cousin." They were silent then, rowing quickly, lest she reveal an arcane kindred power and find some unpleasant, peculiar use for parts of them.

They left her at the dock, gazing up at the opaque, dragonfly lights in the windows. What Nyx would say if she found Meguet spying on her was something Meguet chose not to contemplate. She heard a sigh behind her and turned, startled; the beautiful river-ghost in her water-stained tumble of lace sat in the prow of her boat and gazed mournfully mid-river. Meguet turned back and a blood fox's eyes flared in the mooring light on the bank. She grew still, not touching her sword, for the blood fox, like the swan, was of an ancient lineage, and had known the Delta before humans. To Delta folk of old family it was not so much bad luck as bad manners to harm their neighbor. When the red-washed eyes vanished, she went up the stairs.

She passed the odd shadows clinging batlike to the walls of the entryway; they were alive, she sensed, but did not consider her worth peeling themselves off the walls to challenge her. No one was in the workroom. She crossed it, under the empty stares of owl and goat and muskrat. She heard voices near, and froze. A few murmured words, silence. She heard no steps. They were together, Nyx and the stranger, nearby. She saw a door in the far wall and opened it a crack. The room beyond was empty. She slipped noiselessly into it. If Nyx found her, she could protest that she was only wandering through the house searching for her to talk further, to reason, to argue. It sounded innocent enough: They had been friends once. The walls of the room were blood red; a stuffed white owl watched her from its perch, looking alarmed, ready to ask its question. The room offered her eight closed doors to choose from. She opened one at random, bewildered, and felt, eerily, as she passed into a dense silence, that somehow she had gone too far: Nyx was not only in some other room, but in some other time. The room she entered was a twilight place, everything in it—candlesticks and chairs and heavy curtains—mauve; it offered her only one door. She pulled it open, expecting the owl room again, but found another room with a great canopied bed and one shoe set neatly next to it.

The door closed behind her; already, she guessed, the twilight room was changing. She stood blinking, bewildered, feeling more lost than she had ever been anywhere in the wilds of Ro Holding. The old house would ramble forever in its memories, like some fey old woman rummaging through her past. She would wander with it until she was forced to call Nyx's name for rescue. She closed her eyes, touched them with cold fingers, concentrated. After a moment, the Cygnet moved across her mind, the black swan flying against a circle of white. Instinct, and experience with that odd, secret habit, made her follow its direction. Eyes still closed she opened the door she had just come through and stepped into the room beyond.

Opening her eyes, she saw a hundred black swans flying around her. The vision lasted only a moment, and then the mirrors the swans had flown through were blank as sky. They changed again as she stood motionless, were suddenly busy with impressions. She saw herself in a small round mirror framed in silver, hung high on a wall. The big mirror beneath it reflected a room full of opened chests and wardrobes, rich clothes tumbling out of all of them. An ornate, square mirror propped against that revealed a room blown entirely, it seemed, out of glass. On every wall, in every corner, high and low, mirrors of every size framed the house's memories, some changing now and then, as if there were not enough mirrors, while at another moment it seemed that, as she stood there, mirrors were coming into existence around her, as if the house were baring its heart to one who could see.

Stunned, she could only stare, her eyes snagged by every peculiar revelation; not even growing up with Nyx's astonishing gifts inured her to this. She was able to move finally, a slight, unguarded sound coming out of her, when she saw Nyx herself, in an oval, wood-framed mirror on the floor. She knelt down in front of it. Nyx and the young man were in a kitchen; ovens and spits and blackened hearths lined the stone wall behind them. They sat at a vast wooden table surrounded by books, nuts, torn loaves of bread, smoked fish, apples, cheese, onions, pitchers of water and wine. Nyx, holding a half-eaten apple between her teeth, was flipping rapidly through a huge book. The young man was reading, his lips moving noiselessly, a frown, intent and anxious, between his brows. Wayfolk he certainly was, with his brown skin and black eyes; that he could read at all was curious. That he wanted to read buried deep in a maze of walls in the middle of the sunless Delta was astonishing. He was, Meguet decided, in dire need of a spell. Or someone he knew was. She leaned toward the mirror, studying him, feeling something cold, dispassionate, ruthless in the scrutiny.

The man lifted his head; for a moment he seemed to gaze back at Meguet, puzzled, uneasy, as if the mirror were water between them and he caught a strange shadow in its depths. Nyx removed the apple from her mouth and chewed a bite.

"What is it?" she asked. "Did you find something?"

"Just a dead spider between pages." He rubbed absently at the pale stubble on his chin. Nyx still watched him, not, it seemed, with a lover's attention, but with a rather detached interest, as if he might, if coaxed right, predict, but then again he might not. "Nothing anywhere about a web. Not even in a rhyme for curing warts or jumping stooks."

"Jumping stooks?"

"In a wheat field. It's a smallfolk game."

"Oh."

He closed the books wearily, rubbed his eyes. "We'd get beaten for it when they caught us, but that was part of the game almost."

Nyx, uninterested in stooks, pushed her book aside, pulled another from the pile. "I thought you Wayfolk had a rhyme for everything."

"So did I." He poured water, drank it. There was dust all over his hands; Nyx had a streak on her face. They had, judging from the crumbs on the table, been at this mystery for some time. "It's a secret," the Wayfolk man suggested. "This web. So secret it's nowhere in these books. So it wouldn't likely be in a rhyme smallfolk gabble at each other."

"Nothing in this world is that secret."

The man's eyes flickered to her lowered head. He raised his hands to his face again, linking his fingers across his eyes. Meguet stopped breathing. She leaned forward, touched the cold face in the mirror, as if to draw his hands away, see what he was seeing.

Something is, she thought. *You know something that secret.*

His hands dropped. Nyx leaned back, contemplating him as Meguet was herself, so close to the mirror that her breath misted the cracked painted walls of the kitchen. Finally, Nyx spoke the young man's name.

"You can still change your mind, Corleu. You can wake the Dancer now, if you're fretting."

Meguet, repeating his name silently, felt something stir deep inside her, like the Dancer herself might have stirred, in her cocoon of ice, at the sound of her name.

"No." His hands closed; he said again, not looking up, "No."

"You're not fretting."

He raised his head at the bait; Meguet heard his breath. Then he came close to smiling, a taut smile that barely grew past his eyes. "No. I don't care anymore. The swamp is full of women trapped in mists, waiting for me. They can all wait till winter's end."

"Tell me," Nyx said curiously, "what she is like. Tiel."

He looked at her. "You wouldn't even see her face, likely, if you passed her," he said simply. "You'd see her dark skin and her dark hair and that would be all; your eye would say: She is Wayfolk. She—I could hardly see her face, when I—before I lost her. What it is like truly. She was like the world, like sky, like leaves, like night. Her face was my face. When that dark house fell and I ran into it, I never left her. I'm still there in that mist, like that ghost on the dock, like the Warlock's shadow in the stars. I'm outside my heart, looking for the way back in." He added bitterly, after a pause, "It was easy enough to leave. I only had to go through a door."

Nyx was still, in a way that Meguet remembered: so still the watery sheen on the fabric of her gown seemed painted; no light trembled on the gold clip in her hair. Then her hand moved, fell across the open pages, close to Corleu's hand. If she had straightened a forefinger, she could have touched him.

"You had no choice."

"I should have stayed with her. I could have."

"Then there would have been no mist trapping your company, no falling house, no spellbound love, no timely meeting with a bog witch—just a straight road through the Delta to the sea, because if you were a man who could not recognize that house, or had been warned by it, it would never have fallen into your life. Though," she added, "that can't be a flea's worth of comfort."

"Not even that," he sighed, and dragged at another book on the heap.

Meguet watched, unblinking, scarcely breathing. It sounded simple
enough: the Wayfolk man in trouble, needing a spell; Nyx helping precisely
because it wasn't simple, and all her life Nyx had loved nothing better than a
challenge. That was all. Yet she could not move; she held the mirror with both
hands, her eyes on the haunted Wayfolk face, learning every line and hollow
of it, for the words he spoke were illuminating, like lightning shedding
glimpses of a traveller's road, some dark, ancient landscape within her mind.

The words almost came together, the landscape was almost revealed.

The dark falling house . . .

The Dancer . . .

The Warlock . . .

The web . . .

For a moment, as she concentrated, every mirror in the room showed her
face: pale, intent, motionless, her green eyes narrowed, alert as a hunting animal after a scent. Then the road went dark again, the words fell apart, mean-
ingless. She dropped her face against the mirror, wondering at herself, drawn
upriver into a room full of mirrors by a Wayfolk man with no power, just a
problem that, compared with Nyx's usual swamp sorcery, sounded remarkably innocent.

Yet she stayed, her eyes rarely moving from him, and bored herself into a
stupor while they read. They spoke little more, finally closed their books with
weary thuds, and Meguet slipped away, through the workroom before Nyx
returned to it. She borrowed the ghost's boat and the dock lamp, and rowed
herself downriver to the ramshackle inn where she had left her horse. The
next morning, she sent the boat back upriver and rode out of the swamplands
down to the sea.

She followed a narrow trail along the river, which widened and eventually
became a road, a tavern at the point where it widened. Another half mile, and
she caught a glimpse of Wolfe Sea, a line of deep grey running into the
cloudy sky. The low swamp mists changed into a stormy winter sky over the
city. The road beneath her crossed other roads now, fronted houses, buildings, boat docks. The river was growing broad, fanning out to mingle with
the tides; sea birds and swamp birds wove overhead, with an eye to what the
receding tide was leaving in the mud flats.

The road skirted wide around them; houses, shops, guild halls, ware-
houses, sprouted cheek by jowl, eye to eye across the road. The road itself was
cobbled here, and in the late afternoon, crowded. Presently, the buildings
yielded to a high stone wall that rambled along the road; ancient trees leaned
over the wall, their bare boughs chattering together in the wind, like a private

conversation between many very old friends. In the distance Meguet saw the sea again.

She heard it finally; the road wound around a curve in the wall and brought her to the gate of Ro House. It was late by then; the sea was very dark. A single red star broke through the clouds, hung low on the horizon: the Blood Star. The gate faced the sea; the waves turned sluggishly along the pale sand, broke with a frail, lacy line of silver that teased the eye and vanished. Beyond it, night fishers, their bows lamp-lit, flickered like fireflies on the vast restless dark.

The Cygnet flew diagonally across the gate, lit by torches on either side. Meguet rode up to it and dismounted. The Gatekeeper, who had seen her coming from his high perch on the wall, was already opening it.

"Lady Meguet," he greeted her, and swung the gate wide. "Welcome."

The house that the mage Chrysom had built on the curving shore of Wolfe Sea was a great, shining wheel of seven towers circling the high black tower above which the Cygnet flew on a pennant furling and unfurling, by day and night. The towers were built of granite and marble cut in Hunter Hold, of pale wood from the Delta and dark polished wood from Berg Hold and delicate glass blown in Withy Hold. A miniature city rambled around the tower walls, of stables, smithies, barns, kennels, hen coops, forges, tanneries, workshops, cottages with gardens in front of their doors. Some of the household and cottagers could trace their families back a thousand years to Moro Ro's time. Behind the towers the outer walls sprawled out of sight, for Chrysom had made room for fields, ponds, pastures, a small lake around which ancient oak mingled with the vast, dark firs he had taken as saplings from Berg Hold. Legend had it that he had built the house to move from Hold to Hold, eluding siege like a flea eludes a hound's tooth. At the end of the Hold Wars, the warlords had come to the Delta to pledge fealty to Moro Ro, in his house by the sea, and there it had stood since.

Meguet dismounted tiredly just inside the gate; the Gatekeeper held her horse while the stable girls ran across the yard. She lingered to talk to him. He was tall, muscular, with short, muddy sun-streaked hair, and eyes as silvery green as the scythe-shaped leaves on the swamp trees. He was a reticent man, with a clever, unerring eye, discreet despite the household gossip that found its way to him like water found holes in a sieve. He had opened the gate to Meguet for the ten years she had worn the Cygnet on Holder's business. Though he was swamp-born, as far as she knew, he always guessed where she had been when she returned.

"Has the house been quiet?" she asked him. A corner of his thin mouth slanted upward.

"In a manner of speaking." He wore the Cygnet at both wrists and over his heart, though on him they were apt to fly haphazardly, rucked up over his forearms, or half-hidden under a sheepskin vest. "I opened the gate a dozen times to the sons and daughters of the Delta lords. Most are still here."

"To see Rush?" Meguet guessed. "Or Calyx?"

"Both." He added, "And to see you."

She didn't ask who or why, having little interest in their neighbors. "Anyone else?" She liked to hear him talk. The rough, river-hatchling's voice ran just beneath ten years of household polish; it surfaced now and then, unexpectedly.

"Merchants," he said. "In and out again. A tinker, in but not out."

"A tinker?"

"He has kin, he said."

"Ah."

"The Holder sent word to the gate that she will see you whenever you arrive."

Meguet glanced at the third tower. Lights swarmed around it; the great hall looked aflame. "She'll be at supper." The Gatekeeper, eyeing something in her hair, seemed to weigh respect against inclination. He said:

"You had raw weather for a ride upriver."

Meguet looked at him. "I suppose you can tell from the mud on my stirrup which bog I stood in to mount."

"No." He reached out, picked a feather from her hair. "I've seen you wear mud from all over Ro Holding. But the small birds this color orange live only in one place."

Gazing at it, she thought of the small silent white birds caged in Nyx's workroom. She took it grimly, let it flutter free. He watched it fall.

"You saw the Lady Nyx," he commented. There was neither question nor curiosity in his voice, but she was irritated, at him for seeing a feather fall and thinking of Nyx, mostly at Nyx, for causing the tales that linked her to such small birds. She asked sharply.

"Is there anything else I've done that you need to tell me?"

He eyed her, his expression, in the torchlight, hard to read. "You sat for some time on the gutting board of a trapper's boat," he said. She stared back at him, impassive. Then she heard something beyond the tower-ring, across the back meadows and pastures: a weave of light and dark beating the air toward the small lake that lay hidden behind the thousand-year-old wood. She knew that sound, had heard that coming every year of her life.

"And you," she said, "forgot an entire company."

The spare, crooked smile flickering over his face again, into his eyes, made her smile. "Who?" he demanded. "Who entered or left missed my eye?"

"The wild swans of winter."

Two

MEGUET stood in the black tower, watching for swans. Her high chambers overlooked the tower ring, household grounds, sea and the city beyond. It was too dark to see anything; there was not a single star in the sky, not even a splash of moonlight on the lake to show her where it lay. But still she stood there, silent, tranquil, feeling them drop toward the water, a great gathering of black and white swans from the far north, who waited, it seemed, for the fiercest winds to ride across Ro Holding. She had never told anyone but the Gatekeeper that she could feel the swans come and go. In that house, with its long, powerful and eccentric history, it seemed an unimportant matter.

She turned away from the window. Her attendants moved quietly through the rooms, clearing away her supper, the bath water, gathering her muddy clothes. No one else lived in the tower, it was used once every three years for the Holding Council. It held Chrysom's haunted library, just above her, and beneath the tower, the maze where, legend said, his bones were buried. They were guarded, legend said also, by terrifying and awesome beings, whom Meguet and Rush and Nyx had once wasted days trying to find. Such tales clustered around the tower like the thousand-year-old rose vines, making it the most peaceful place in the house. The Holder and her children escaped to Chrysom's library for quiet and conference; cottagers' children crept like mice in and out of the exasperating and tantalizing maze. Other than that, no one used it but Meguet and her hardheaded attendants, who feared neither ghosts nor the long spiral climb to the top.

There was a tap at the door; word came that the Holder would see Meguet in Chrysom's library. Meguet pulled on a long black wool dress that hid the greater part of her oldest boots, and set a braid, Wayfolk-style, to one side of her loose hair. Watching her fingers move in the mirror, she thought of mirrors; Corleu's face looked back at her, innocent and dangerous and bewilderingly compelling.

She rose, went up the final spiral of stairs. There was wine in Chrysom's library, and the makings of a fire and a view of the night from every direction through the ring of glass windows that circled the stones. The room still held obscure oddments of Chrysom's sorcery; Nyx had taken some. It also held Rush Yarr, who had built the fire and was standing at a window with a cup in his hand, looking for stars apparently, but thrown back by the utter dark onto his own reflection in the glass.

"Meguet," he said, recognizing her long, quick stride before he turned. He was a sinewy man with a lean, restless face. He had hair the color of a blood-fox pelt and the blood fox's amber eyes without the wash of red in them. His family, who once fought Moro Ro under the sign of the Blood Fox, had perished at sea in one of their own merchant ships. He had been sent to Ro House at an early age, a year after Meguet had come. There, he fell in love with the Holder's third daughter. The old stones still echoed with their quarrels years before, for she had not told him she was leaving, nor, returned for a visit, would she permit him to travel with her. So, ghostlike, he haunted the room where she had spent most of her time, waiting for her final homecoming, trapped, Meguet thought, unable to love a woman never there, unable to stop loving her.

He poured Meguet wine before asking the question she knew was foremost in his mind.

"Did you find Nyx?"

"Of course I found Nyx," she answered. "The Holder told me to find her."

"Well?"

"Well what?"

"Well, is it true she is eating small animals alive and gossiping with the dead?"

"She was doing those very things when I walked into her house." Meguet sipped wine, and leaned her head back to look at Rush, who was pacing the length of the massive hearth. Ravens and gulls perched half out of the stone beneath the mantelpiece; the Cygnet, carved in black marble, flew above the fire. In that room, with its thousand-year-old collection of books and paraphernalia, Nyx had taken up residence as a child, reading constantly, spells seeping into her pale, luminous eyes, while Rush rifled through old jars and boxes, set minor fires and conjured up terrifying images in cloudy mirrors, which Nyx would summarily disperse. Meguet added with more sympathy, "She said she intends to come to the Holding Council."

"How kind of her."

"She's learning things, Rush."

"Learning what?" He was facing her suddenly, backed by fire and flying birds; something of Chrysom's had somehow gotten into his hand. "A mean, petty magic—pirates pay her to foresee storms, merchants pay her to foresee one another's misfortunes. She pays river-scum to bring her half-dead animals. She is Lauro Ro's daughter. Or at least she was. I don't know what she's making herself into now."

"A mage," Meguet said simply.

"I want to talk to her. Where is she?"

Meguet cradled her wine cup in both hands, contemplated the shiver of light across it. Something in her grew alert, as always when Rush was fretting over Nyx. She said calmly, "Nyx is in a house upriver. Any trapper could tell you where. If you really thought she would listen to you now, you would not be standing here talking to me. She is doing what she thinks she must."

"How can she think—"

"Be patient, Rush."

"She's in the Delta backwater, tearing the wings off birds and burning the bones of the dead." His hand clenched tightly around the thing he held. Meguet, very still, watched needles of firelight dart across it. "None of us knows her anymore. None of us. We saw her last nearly three years ago. For all of five days. And not for two years before that. She is tearing at the Holder's heart. And mine. And you say be patient."

Meguet closed her eyes briefly, against the headache that was threatening. "You could simply forget her," she suggested, not for the first time.

"She could be brought home."

"No."

"She belongs here. She could learn her sorcery here like she did when she was young."

"You weren't this bitter when she stayed for two years in Berg Hold. Or for a year in Withy Hold. Or in Hunter Hold among the witches."

"She was learning things of value then, not—"

"How do you know? How do you know what she was learning? Do you think knowledge always lies in safe, clean places where nothing or anyone is disturbed? That you can always learn by daylight and always sleep without dreams afterward?"

"How can you defend her?" It was as much plea as demand; he stood so tensely, waiting for answer, that he might have been something Chrysom carved on the hearth along with the crows. She picked her words with care; if he wanted a quarrel, she thought, he could go find Nyx.

"She has great power, I think, though it's hardly evident from what she does in the swamp. If she makes mistakes now, she may make great mistakes. But she—"

"Then she may harm herself, along with the swamp life. She should be brought home."

"Nonsense, Rush, you can't just walk into her house and—"

"Why not?" Rush demanded. "You did. So can I. So I will."

"No. You won't," she said flatly. "Because you know her too well. You know that she will only love you freely if you let her come back freely. That's why you are still here, shouting at me instead of her."

Rush was silent, his jaw clamped. He whirled abruptly, having no other argument but confusion, and flung the thing in his hand into the fire.

They both jumped, he in surprise at what he had done, and Meguet because he had actually done it. She finished the movement on her feet. The fire made an odd, keening wail. She threw herself at Rush, who seemed too surprised to move, and knocked him away from the fire. Black smoke poured out of the hearth, obscuring the flames. Something snapped, and there was a stench that sent them both running to the windows.

They flung a few open before, weeping and choking, they headed up the stairs to the roof. The stones flashed green a moment; the smell followed them up, disgorged itself into the wind.

Meguet leaned on the parapet, wiping her streaming eyes. "I wish," she said tartly when she could speak again, "you would stop doing that."

"I'm sorry."

"One of these days you'll throw the wrong thing and blow Chrysom's tower back to the quarries in Hunter Hold."

"I'm sorry," he said again. He leaned against the stones beside her, dragging at the north wind. "It—it tears at me that you can see her, talk to her, and I can't."

She put her hand on his shoulder. "I know. But she barely even talked to me. I startled her, I think, coming out of this world into hers. . . . You'll see her in spring. It's not that long to winter's end. Perhaps by then she'll be out of the swamp, learning something less . . . dubious."

"Dubious." She felt him laugh noiselessly at the word. "There's nothing dubious about what she's doing. It's disgusting."

"Then how can you love her so? Can't you love someone else instead?"

"I've tried."

"And?"

"No one else in the world is a lank-haired, cold-eyed, sharp-tongued woman with enough sorcery in her to stand this house on its head."

"Is there anything at all you like about her?"

"No. Just the smallest finger in each hand, the color that comes into her eyes under a full moon, the way her mouth shapes certain words. My name, for instance. The way she laughs, which she did once, three years ago. A soft, summery chuckle like blackbirds among the rose trees. The way she wears the color green. The way she looks sometimes, like a wild thing listening for another wild thing. The way she reads, as if words are air to be breathed. The way she kissed me when we were barely more than children, out of curiosity, behind the closed doors of the hay barn on the warmest day of the year, and the way she looked at me afterwards, as startled as if she had just invented a world. The way the shadows of the doves flying up into the rafters crossed and recrossed her face . . ." His hand was between Meguet's shoulders by then, his fingers working at the knot from the day's riding. She tilted her head back, loosening muscles, and saw, beyond the curl of the great black pennant whipping above their heads, the full moon revealed with a swan flying across it. She caught her breath; in the next moment the swan had dipped down into darkness and the moon had disappeared.

"I suppose there is no hope for you, Rush Yarr."

"None." He paused, added with a shade of reproach in his voice, "I would have ridden with you to see Nyx, but you didn't tell me you were going."

"The Holder tells me when to come and go. She didn't mention you."

"Must you be so blindly obedient?"

"Always."

"Because she gave you a home?"

"Because I choose to."

"She gave me a home, too, and family. I am obedient and respectful, too, but rarely at the same time."

"You are of Delta blood. You have an archaic desire to rebel against the Holder."

"And you, descended from Astor Ro, desire to obey the Holder, speak meekly at all times with downcast eyes, and never look out of high windows."

"Astor Ro may have been afraid of anything not surrounded by high walls, but she fought at Moro Ro's side during the Hold Wars and she was not afraid to tell him when to change his underwear."

"How do you know that?"

"I read it in some old chronicle."

"You never read."

"I tried, when you and Nyx and Calyx all studied together. I never understood how you could. It made me feel strange."

He gazed at her curiously, his hand still. "How?"

"As if I had read everything before, and yet I never had. As if I remembered things I never knew..." She shivered suddenly and he dropped his hand. "Let's go back. The Holder is coming up. I want to see if there's a library left."

"What do you think that was?"

"What was?"

"What I threw?"

"I have no idea. Dead, it smelled like. A thousand years dead."

A silken green pall hung over the library. They opened more windows, let the north wind scour the air, blow the green shade out to sea. Rush, having enchanted away his anger, left Meguet alone to wait for the Holder.

She came finally, near midnight; Meguet heard her footsteps walk into a dream, and she half-woke, trying to rise at the same time. Lauro Ro's hand at her shoulder kept her still. The Holder crossed to the fire, and picked up a poker to stir the lagging flames. Of all her daughters, Nyx most resembled her, in her dark hair and her movements. The Holder's hair, wild, night-black, flecked with white, was coiled, braided, pinned into submission every morning; by midnight the Holder's impatient fingers had freed most of it. She was tall, big-boned, still slender; her eyes were dark as the Cygnet's wings and her voice could—and did once or twice—carry from the top of Chrysom's tower clear to the Gatekeeper in his turret beside the gate. She wore blue velvet that night, and rings on every finger, which sent jewelled lights spinning around the walls as she fanned the air under her nose with one hand. Rush Yarr considered her a throwback, in her darkness and strength and fearlessness, to Moro Ro himself.

"Has Rush been breaking things again?" she asked, opening a few more windows, and the damp sea winds danced into the room, waking Meguet further.

"He was upset about Nyx."

"He is always upset about Nyx. I am upset about Nyx." She gave the fire a final poke and turned, poured wine. "How is Nyx?" She handed Meguet a cup and sat down finally, near the hearth, with the poker and wood close at hand, for, like Nyx, she loved fires. "Will she come home?"

"She remembered her promise. She will come for the Council."

"But not before."

"No."

The Holder's mouth tightened. She pulled a pin of gold and pearl out of her hair, shook the falling strand free. Her feet worked out of her velvet slippers at the same time; she sat with her unshod feet on the stones like a cottager while Meguet stretched a worn boot to the fire and added, "I think she only does these things to see that she is able to do them. That's what matters to her. She's not destined for a life of petty witchery in the swamps. But this may not be the only strange path she takes."

"She's been away most of nine years," the Holder said incredulously. "How much more of sorcery is there to learn?"

"I don't know."

"I wish I did know more." She brooded at the fire a moment, her elbows on her knees. "Her father was ensorcelled," she added, stunning Meguet, for the Holder never answered questions about her daughters' fathers.

"A swan?" Meguet hazarded.

"No. A wolf in Hunter Hold. In the night hours when he was human, he never spoke of any such knowledge. She didn't get it from him. Or from me." She glanced at Meguet, reading her mind. "I broke the spell over him. I don't know how. We were both surprised." She smiled a little, remembering. Then she looked at Meguet again, her eyes dark and fire, a long look that took in more, sometimes, than Meguet knew about herself. "But you have more to tell me."

Meguet, unsurprised, nodded. She took a sip of wine, held the cup in her linked fingers. "There is someone with Nyx."

"Who?"

"A young man. I couldn't tell at first what he was; he was dressed in rich, antique clothes. I learned later he is Wayfolk, with strange pale hair and a dark, harrowed face."

"From watching Nyx work, probably. An apprentice?"

"Maybe."

"A lover?"

"I hope not."

"Why not?"

Meguet hesitated, received the Holder's full attention. "I only looked at him once, and he never spoke. But something in him drew me back into the house after dark. I could not ride away and leave him there with Nyx, without knowing more. And yet there's nothing to know but that he's Wayfolk, with chaff from the fields of Withy Hold under his fingernails and a love named Tiel in his heart. On the surface."

"On the surface," the Holder repeated. Her eyes were still now, expressionless, reminding Meguet of the ancient, equivocal night in a stone-tortoise's eye. "And under the surface? What exactly is my daughter living with?"

"I don't know. Neither does she. A Wayfolk man with a secret . . ."

"What secret?"

"I don't know."

Memory, to her surprise, seemed as accessible as the memory of the house she had wandered in; small details became clear, including the landscape in her mind that the young man's piecemeal rambling had formed. She began with her unremarked entry into Nyx's house, and ended with Corleu taking the light out of the mirror, leaving Meguet in darkness in a room full of dark mirrors.

"I thought you might have sent me back anyway," she finished. "But even returning there, and listening to them, I have no idea what they're doing together."

The Holder, still through the long tale, got to her feet in a whirl and prickle of lights. She poked at a log meditatively; Meguet could not see her face. The fire flared; she kept up a gentle but relentless nudging until sparks flew thick as stars up the chimney and Meguet cast a watchful eye at the ancient, mysterious, gleaming secrets along the mantel. Lauro Ro put the poker down abruptly, turned. The expression in her eyes startled Meguet; it was something like the impersonal, bone-searching gaze she had favored Corleu with.

"You followed the Cygnet into a room full of mirrors?"

Of all details her memory had woven together, it seemed least significant. "I didn't know which way to go," she explained, surprised. "It was like throwing grass into the air and following. I moved in the direction the Cygnet flew in my mind. That's all. It's nothing but a trick I play on myself. Sometimes when I'm lost impulse will find a path where reason can't."

Lauro Ro sat down again. She pulled the last pins from her hair, tossed them into her lap. Her hair, tumbling forward, hid her face again. But her voice sounded more familiar. "They were searching those old books for a web?"

"So it seemed."

"Instead of waking the Dancer."

"It seemed."

"That's a constellation."

"His tale was full of stars."

"Is Nyx in danger?"

The question started Meguet. "From what? A Wayfolk man who grew up jumping stooks?"

"Then why did you go back?"

Meguet was silent, gazing back at the Holder. She pulled herself up restively. "I don't know," she said, scrutinizing memory to find the bone in Corleu's face, the fleeting expression that had turned her in her path. "Impulse."

"Grass in the wind."

"He disturbed me."

"Before he even opened his mouth?"

"Yes."

"So." The Holder watched her pace. "If the man himself is not the danger, who is the danger?"

Meguet halted mid-step, as if the shadow of a raven flying out of the stone had suddenly barred her way. She stared down at the shadow, whispered, "Is that what I saw? Why I went back?"

The Holder shifted; a sapphire light flashed. She raised her head; her eyes had changed: They grew wide, luminous, vulnerable, like the eyes of a deer catching sight of a hunter's arrow. She said nothing, left Meguet staring at her. Meguet took another step into the raven's shadow, and stopped again.

"Do you want me to go back there and talk to Nyx?"

"Was Nyx settled there for the winter? Or will she move again before spring?"

"She said she has work to busy her there until spring."

"I can imagine," the Holder said, darkly. "I could call her home, I suppose. She could glare at me and pick bats apart in the middle of the night."

She stirred the fire with unnecessary force, scattering embers onto the floor. Meguet kicked them back in, leaning wearily against the stones. She felt bone-tired suddenly, ready to sleep where she stood, propped among the stone birds, beneath the Cygnet.

"How did the Wayfolk man get his hair?" she heard, a riddle in the dark, and realized that her eyes were closed. She said:

"Yes."

"What?"

She opened her eyes, saw her own hair milky in the firelight against her black gown. "There," she said, "is the question." She dragged her hand over her eyes, remembering. "I looked at him, he looked at me. He recognized me. That's what I saw in him. Why I turned back. We recognized each other."

"From where?" the Holder asked. "Have you met him before on your travels?"

"No. Never."

"Then how?"

"That," she said, "I will find out."

"Just be careful," the Holder said somberly.

"I am always. And he is only Wayfolk."

"He may be only Wayfolk, but he is with Nyx, and she is wandering in dangerous country. One of these days she may call up something she didn't expect. She may have already, by the sound of it. Take Rush with you. You should not go alone."

"I would rather take the Gatekeeper," she said, surprising both herself and the Holder. "Rush would only fight with Nyx."

The Holder looked at her silently, her expression unfathomable. "My Gatekeeper?"

"He knows the swamps." She kicked a cold ember back into the hearth. "There are fewer travellers in winter, for him to open the gate to."

"He will not leave the gate. They never do."

"If he will?"

The Holder was silent again, her eyes on the fire. "If he will go," she said slowly, "take him." She shivered suddenly, then gathered pins in her lap and stood. She put her hand on Meguet's shoulder, kissed her lightly. "Watch over my spellbound child. But be careful of her."

"I will."

Asleep finally, Meguet dreamed a moon, and a strange pattern of stars beyond her window, in a windy, blue-black sky. A ragged edge of black cloud detached itself from the wind and sank earthward. As it neared her window, the winds stilled. Moonlight drenched the sky. The casement opened: A wild black swan lighted on the ledge, drew in its wings. It filled her window, huge, mysterious, darker than the night behind it. It watched her. Dreaming or awake by then—she hardly knew—she watched it.

THREE

SHE was forced to wait before she went back upriver. Cold rain fell for days; the entire swamp, yellow-grey with mud, seemed to be sliding into the sea. She and Rush, both restive, took to the armory and threatened each other with antique weapons. Sons and daughters of the Delta lords, descendants of swamp dwellers and half-wild under their wealth and manners, joined them, looking for any sport in the drenched world. Meguet gave lessons to young men whose eyes constantly looked past her for a glimpse of Calyx, and then were suddenly on her, unbraiding her neat hair and studying her flowing, muscular movements. She treated them with a grave courtesy that was dampening, left them searching for Calyx, who was always elsewhere.

She forded the rivers and pools in the outer yard one day near dusk, when the hard edge of the rain had dulled. She surprised the Gatekeeper as she came up the steps along the wall to his turret. With thick sheepskin on the stone seats, a three-legged brazier between them, and their own voluminous, bulky cloaks, there was hardly room under the peaked stone roof for both. But he seemed pleased, if mystified, by her company.

"Lady Meguet," he said. "It was brave of you to cross the yard. Some of the cottagers were fishing in it earlier."

"I don't doubt." She held her hands to the brazier, looking curiously around at the scalloped edgings of marble on the open ledges, and along the roof. "This place was enormous, when I came last."

"Before my time, then. Or I would have remembered you coming."

She smiled. "It was another Gatekeeper, yes. An old man with white hair and black brows. I have forgotten his name. Or maybe I never knew he had one beyond 'Gatekeeper.'" She paused, saw the flicker of smile in his eyes, and surprised him. "Hew."

He blinked. "Yes. Most don't know that, beyond the cottages."

"I asked the Holder."

"Oh." He cleared his throat. "She remembered my name, did she? After ten years?"

"She must have considered it important."

"And you," he said mildly, "have found it suddenly important to know."

"I asked her," Meguet said, "ten years ago, the first time you opened the gate for me alone."

He was silent; she watched a wave, storm-ridden, stumble wildly against the sand and fall a long, long way before it stopped. He reached for a little ebony pipe on the seat beside him, and found a taper. He met her eyes. "What can I do for you, Lady Meguet?"

"The Holder said you may not do it."

"Ah." He carried flame to the pipe with the taper; light flooded his hands, the lower part of his face. She realized then that he had been young, too, when she asked the Holder his name: a boy, straight out of the backwater, catching crayfish one day and guarding the Holder's gate the next. "There is only one thing I would not do for you," he said simply, and she sighed.

"You won't leave the gate."

"I can't."

"But why? You leave it nights to sleep, don't you? Do you? You do sleep."

"Sometimes here, other times I have a small cottage . . ." He studied her, his brows crooked. "I can't," he said again. "But tell me what I can do."

"Tell me what binds you here," she demanded, frustrated. The rain pounded down again; he shifted the brazier from the open window, his eyes straying by habit to the massive closed gate. He puffed on his pipe a bit, then said apologetically at the smoke:

"It keeps me warm, and awake when I'm up late, waiting. . . . Nobody ever asked me that before. Not like that, anyway."

"Is it secret?"

"Even so, I'd tell you. Because you know what you're asking. The old man—the other Gatekeeper—came looking for me upriver. He had yellow eyes; with all that white hair he looked like an owl. I heard he was coming; word travelled faster than him, that some bird-haired old man wearing the Cygnet was stopping everyone, man and girl, and saying one thing to them. I was standing in my boat, hauling in a five-foot pike when he found me. He spoke. That's the last I saw of the pike."

"What did he say?"

"He said, 'I have left the gate.' I remember rowing down-river in such a panic I nearly wrecked myself among the ships coming into the harbor. That's the last I saw of swamp and the first I saw of the city and the Holder's house. I didn't stop moving until I had shut the open gate and climbed up here to watch." He smiled a little. "Later that evening the most beautiful woman in the world came up the steps and brought me supper. She asked my name and welcomed me into her house."

Meguet leaned back against the stones. "What a strange tale. So you were born Gatekeeper."

"Seems so. One day, I'll do the same, leave the gate wide and hobble around the Delta until someone drops crayfish net or butter churn or bill of lading and runs to close the gate."

"What happens if you leave?" she persisted. "For only a day or two. Three."

"Makes my heart pound, just the thought. But why? Why me, of all?" Then he answered himself. "The swamp." And then, "The Lady Nyx."

This time his guesswork did not annoy her. She sighed soundlessly, sliding her hood back, for the brazier had heated the old stones well. "Nyx," she said softly. He waited, pipe going out between his fingers, his odd, slanted, swamp-green eyes grave. "I think she may be in trouble. The Holder wants me to go and talk to her, but not to go alone. I thought of you. You know the swamp."

"So do you."

"You know the tales spread about her."

"So does everyone."

"But you would not spread others, if you saw her. You would be discreet, you would not be afraid of the swamp, and—I think—you would not be afraid of Nyx."

"I've seen swamp magic." He relit his pipe, added, glancing across the yard, "It's a bloody, ugly kind of thing, some. But I can't believe you'd be in danger at all from Lady Nyx."

"She has someone with her."

He said, "Ah," softly. Then: "The Lord Rush Yarr knows sorcery. He is not afraid of Lady Nyx."

"I'm afraid of his sorcery. And his temper. Nyx would toss us both out of her house and guard the door." His eyes were on the yard again; she turned, saw some of their neighbors bundled faceless, splashing through puddles toward the gate. "If you can't come, I will ask him, though. He doesn't know enough to fear the swamp; he won't be discreet with Nyx, but at least he cares for her."

"I'm sorry."

"Do you miss the swamp?" she asked suddenly. "Your freedom?"

He smiled. "That's why I like to see you come and go. Hear where you've been, travelling around Ro Holding like a tinker." He flushed a little as she laughed. "Sorry. I had one on my mind."

"I never met a tinker who roamed as far as I do."

"This one might. Hunter Hold Sign on the back door of his house, and Withy Hold on the side. He could put Delta on the other side while he's here."

"It's easy enough to paint a sign."

"Or tell stories to the gullible." He put his pipe down as the riders neared. "At least he did tell them. Mended pots and told tales, cottage imps in and out of his house. It caught their eyes, his little, black, rolling house. It caught mine."

"You said he had kin?" she said absently, pulling her hood forward.

"No. He said."

"He didn't? He lied to get in the gate?"

"He claimed kin, I heard. But by the time he did his business and told his stories, kinship got confusing. Everyone knew he had kin, but no one claimed him. When they got that sorted out, he had disappeared."

"He left the house."

"No. I never opened the gate for him to leave. He's hidden somewhere. Not even the cottage brats can find him."

She waited for him to rise, followed him out into the rain-spangled torchlight. His story irritated her: too silly to heed, too disturbing to ignore. "A tinker," she repeated, "in hiding in Ro House. Tinkers don't do such things. They mend and move on. He must be somewhere among the cottages."

"You must be right." He stepped to the gate as the riders came up, bid them good night courteously, not missing a name or a half-hidden face. "He could put that dark house in the shadow of a wall, and you'd miss it." He swung the gate shut again, faced her, the rain sliding down his bare head, wet hair hugging the lean lines of his face. "Or I would."

She shivered suddenly, gathered her cloak close. "You wouldn't," she said. "You put him into my eye. Now I'll be looking for him. A little black house in the shadow of Ro House."

*　　*　　*

The heavy rain turned to snow the next day, to everyone's astonishment, for it rarely snowed along the coast. The Holder's children gathered one by one in Chrysom's tower to watch it fall. Even Iris, who thought Chrysom's library gloomy and sorcery incomprehensible, joined them and was entranced by the pale sky falling endlessly into Wolfe Sea. Meguet, staring out at the weather, was not entranced. Her eye fell on the Gatekeeper, in his turret across the empty yard. Even in that cold he kept watch.

She heard her name spoken; Rush was describing the swordplay lessons to Calyx.

"They are all in love with Meguet," he said, "at least while they are with her, and she scarcely sees them." He smiled as Meguet turned; he was slightly drunk. "Meguet loves no one."

"So do I," Calyx sighed. "They all have homes, don't they? Why can't they stay there?"

"Really, Calyx," Iris said. "You might like marriage." Iris, the oldest of the Holder's daughters, had deep chestnut hair and violet eyes, and a head for the myriad small details that fretted each Hold or kept them peaceful.

"I will never marry," Calyx said. "I am going to live in this tower and write a history of Ro House." She sat leafing through an ancient, cracked book, looking like a winter rose, with her fine, silk-white hair, her skin flushed like dawn over hoarfrost on the top of the world. She had eyes the blue-grey of the northern sky, and bones so fine only the smallest of rings fit her fingers. Though the Holder had never told her, it seemed obvious where her father had come from. He was, Rush suggested, one of the ice-spirits of Berg Hold, who lured travellers to their deaths with their stunning beauty. Calyx agreed that, if nothing else, he had probably got the Hold right.

"You're already too much in this tower," Iris declared. "It can't be healthy."

"Meguet lives here. So I will."

Iris eyed Meguet a moment, found answer to her own satisfaction. "Meguet is permitted to be eccentric by heritage."

"This entire family is eccentric," Calyx said, delving back into her book. "We have no known fathers, Nyx is a sorceress, Rush is hopelessly in love with a sorceress, and Meguet wanders everywhere and lives among ghosts. Our mother never married. I take after her."

"Our mother never sat in a tower to avoid suitors."

"They bore me. I would rather read history."

Rush slipped the book out of her hands. "What is this?" he asked, leafing through it. "There seems to be a lot of vegetables in it."

"It's Rydel's book on the growing of herbs and roses. I thought I would."

"Would what?"

"I found a tiny, overgrown walled garden behind the back tower; Rydel wrote that Astor Ro had one that was latticed with vines, so she did not have to see the sky. I think this was her garden. Rydel planted roses there; perhaps some are still alive."

"After three hundred years?"

"The rose vines on this tower are a thousand years old."

"But Chrysom planted those. They must be magic."

"Why must they be?" Iris demanded. "I don't see why everything in this tower must be somehow touched by Chrysom. He's been dead for centuries."

"This entire tower is spellbound," Calyx said composedly. "That's why I like it. The roots of the rose vines are fed by Chrysom's bones, buried in the maze."

"Oh, really, Calyx," Iris said in disgust. Rush laughed; Meguet, glancing at him, realized how rarely he did that, these days.

She poured herself wine, sat where she could watch snow and fire at the same time. Rush paced a little, restlessly, behind her. His feet stopped finally; she felt his hands on her shoulders.

"You look beautiful in that green," he said. She dragged her thoughts back from the swamp, watched him thoughtfully as he moved to lounge on skins at her feet. He met her gaze. "Am I right," he asked, "that you love no one?"

She did not answer for a long time. "You," she said, "love everyone and no one. I love no one and everyone. Even you, Rush Yarr. As you sometimes love me. And sometimes Calyx. But always Nyx."

"So," he said, "you are not indifferent to the young blood foxes you teach."

She smiled. "Of course not."

"Don't you want to marry, leave Ro House for a home of your own?"

"No," she said. "Marry, perhaps. But leave this house? Never. It is my heritage, I think. So old, I am tangled in these old stones. I can't separate myself."

"One day you might," he said, his brows knit. "One day."

She shook her head. "I can't explain it," she said, indifferent to explanations. Calyx, listening, said gravely:

"Meguet is born to love a swan."

"What?" Rush said, turning. Meguet looked at her, startled. Calyx gathered strands of imagination, began weaving them.

"A swan. One of the wild swans that come down late from Berg Hold. A great black swan, who comes once every three years to the lake. Once every three years, in the hour just before midnight, he takes on human form, and one year—perhaps this year—Meguet will stray to the lake under moonlight and find him, in the thousand-year-old wood where the trees will shift and hide them from all view. The mage who ensorcelled him is dead, and no one in the world is powerful enough to free him. So he is in despair of ever regaining human form. Meguet, finding him, will be his only solace, his only happiness. But, unbeknownst to him, there is someone even now growing powerful enough to free him, someone no farther from them than the Delta swamp—"

Iris, intrigued by the tale, interrupted harshly. "Oh, Calyx, she'd be more likely to burn his liver for him than turn him human."

"She would not!" Calyx said indignantly. "Iris, I can't believe you believe every stupid drunken trapper's tale you hear about Nyx."

"They're true." Rush said shortly. "Meguet knows. True, Meguet?"

Meguet sighed noiselessly, disinclined for a tempest. "Nyx would recognize an ensorcelled swan if she saw one."

"Yes, but the question is: What will she do with it?"

"Stuff it and roast it for supper, I suppose."

"Poor swan," Calyx said temperately, opening her book again. "An unhappy end to an unhappy tale."

"Anyway, Nyx may be wicked, but she is not disgusting," Iris pronounced, contradicting herself, and Rush, as always, rose to the bait. Meguet moved from between their argument, to sit next to Calyx. Calyx knew odd things and Meguet had odd questions. Calyx smiled at her. The swan had met its destiny and she was already back among the roses.

"You know that garden, Meguet. Don't you? Where the tower rooms had no windows above the garden wall, so that she would not have to look out."

"Yes," Meguet said. "I read about it once, and I searched for it. I wanted to look at the world out of Astor Ro's eyes. She fascinated me: such fear and such courage. I could read Rydel's books; she talked so much about plants instead of history."

"Which book was it?"

"I don't remember. Odd things, she wrote of, everything. I think Nyx took it. She rambled about her gardens and Timor Ro."

"Timor Ro said she had mysterious powers."

"Sorcery?"

"Something like, but even more powerful. Chrysom, Timor Ro said, stood in her shadow."

Meguet raised a brow. "All she ever did was garden."

"Mysterious, secret powers, they were."

"Calyx, you're inventing this."

"I'm not. He said she used them only for Ro Holding."

"Did he say what powers?"

"No. He said such things were not to be known."

"He must have meant her peach brandy. Calyx . . . if someone spoke of waking the Dancer, what would that mean?"

"The Dancer trapped in ice by the Cygnet," Calyx said promptly. "Guarded by the Fire Bear."

"In the sky?"

"On the top of the highest peak of Berg Hold."

"Berg Hold," Meguet repeated, oddly startled. There was a place, not between lines of a tale, but in Ro Holding, that a Wayfolk man might find if he persisted. "How would—how would the Dancer be wakened?"

"Only the Fire Bear can free her, and it has no more of its fire."

"Then how—"

"But, she may be wakened on the last day of winter."

"Why the last—"

"Then, if you bring her a question, she will wake just long enough to answer or predict, without moving from the ice. Which is safest for us all, since, freed, the Dancer dances chaos into the world."

"Why chaos?"

"Because she is no longer trapped in dreams; she can turn all our waking lives into dreams, and nightmares." She read a page or two, while Meguet, frowning, imagined the Dancer dancing free.

"Why the last day of winter?" she asked. Calyx pondered, smoothing a single shining hair back into place.

"Perhaps," she suggested, "because the constellation of the Dancer sinks out of sight during spring, leaving only the Fire Bear visible, watching her over the edge of the world."

"How do you know these things?"

"I watch the stars," Calyx said simply. "Sometimes it seems that all the constellations exist in a strange, ancient tale that we only catch glimpses of, in our short lives, while they move slowly as centuries through it."

"A piecemeal tale," Meguet murmured, and thought of another piecemeal tale she had heard from within a mirror. "But what, I wonder, is the tale?"

She and Rush went to the armory awhile, and then, sweating, tired, still armed, they flung cloaks over their light shirts and went riding to cool themselves. The sky had emptied itself for a time of rain, snow, wind, and there was nothing left in the pale, silken clouds to fall. The air was still; only a thin, dark thread of crow flight seamed it now and then. They rode across field and meadow, an unbroken plane of white, passing birch a shade whiter than the snow. The thousand-year-old wood, a dark, glistening green powdered with snow, seemed the only color left in the world. They rode to the edge of it and paused, questioning one another silently. The tangled, massive, sweeping boughs had caught most of the snow before it touched ground. The snow itself had caught the frail winter light, leaving a dense, sweet-smelling shadowy world among the black trunks that rose toward a green-black mist higher than Chrysom's tower. It looked, Meguet thought, like a giant's garden.

She turned her horse into it; Rush followed.

"We just left the world behind," he said, glancing back: Towers, gardens, pasture, sky had all vanished.

"Speak quietly," Meguet warned him. "The trees are more restless in winter. Cold wakes them."

Rush stared at her. "It is true, then. I never believed it."

"That they shift?" She looked at him, amused. "Why would you believe everything else that Chrysom said, and not this?"

"I don't know. Moving trees? Maybe if they roamed under my window I would consider it."

"You'll consider it if they start," she said softly, and he eyed her again, askance.

"You've been caught in that?"

"Only twice."

"Twice!"

"Sh."

"What's it like?"

"It's like being lost in a forest the size of Berg Hold. . . . The trees shift, and all their memories move with them, century upon century of dreams, until you don't know anymore what's tree and what's only a dream of tree."

"It's only a small wood."

"I know. But Chrysom took them from the northern forests so long ago there must have been a sea of trees bigger than Wolfe Sea. It's that they remember, I think, and that's the memory you get lost in."

Rush shivered lightly. "Cold," he commented. He reached out to touch one swollen black trunk. Knots and burls like small animals ran up it, peered, frozen, at the riders. "Cold," he said again, as if he had felt the heart of the tree, and Meguet had a sudden image of tree roots, chilled in the unexpected weather, stirring just beneath the earth. She picked up her pace a little. The swan lake lay just on the other side of the wood. Like the trees, the swans were born to a land of fierce winter; the snow, it seemed, had followed them south.

"Rush," she said impulsively, keeping her voice low, and hoping he would, "I must ride back upriver as soon as the weather clears. To talk to Nyx. The Holder told me to take someone. Will you come?"

He was watching her as he listened, his face as cold and set as the wrinkled faces of the trees. "Why?"

"Why what?"

"Why do you need company? You never have in your life. Why, to see Nyx? What is she doing?"

She drew breath, her mouth tight. "Rush. Don't shout here."

"I'm not going to."

"You are. Just say yes or no. Shout among the swans."

"I'm not—"

"You are. Please. Say yes. Say no. Then don't say anything more."

"Why—" She stared him into silence, saw his eyes widen in comprehension. He unclamped his jaw, said, "Yes," and watched the trees in an uneasy fascination.

They were nearly through the wood, with a tree or two between them, when Rush vanished. He was there one moment, and then, obscured by two trees aligned by eyesight, if not by distance, he was simply gone. Meguet circled the trees several times, called him softly. He was nowhere, it seemed, or she was. She reined, feeling the blood run quick and cold through her. Trees filled her sight wherever she looked. She moved forward, she thought, toward the lake. Trees shifted in front of her, faded as she circled them, or did not when she rode up to them. She cursed softly, helplessly, feeling the chill damp air clinging to her. "Not now," she pleaded, numbly. "Not now." But trees and the dream of trees rose in her path, huge, tranquil, ancient and endless as the forests of a world a thousand years younger. She called his name desperately, careless now of their peace, and heard a rustle like wind around her. She smelled wood smoke.

She turned toward it with relief, without thinking. Trees opened in front of her to dense shadow. Within shadow was a denser shadow: a small black wagon like a house, its slanted roof painted yellow, Hold Signs on back and side. And in front of it, roasting a swamp lizard: a tinker.

He lifted his black shaggy head, smiled. Gold gleamed in his ear, around his neck, and, she imagined, from his eyes.

"You'll pardon me, Lady," he said. "I'm a solitary man. Crowds like that in the yard when I entered frighten me."

Meguet stared at him. There seemed a patch of sunlight beside his fire, or some odd reflection from the flames. "Why did you come into this house?" she asked, for he was no tinker, nothing she had ever encountered.

"To patch pots."

"We have no need of another tinker."

"You never know," the tinker said. He turned his spit thoughtfully. The lizard's eye, open and emerald green, regarded her.

"You must come with me," she said, dragging her eyes from the lizard. "In the name of Lauro Ro."

"Why?" the tinker asked, wide-eyed. "I have done nothing more than pass through her gate."

"She has a pot to patch."

"She has, in this great house, a tinker for every broken pot."

"She has not yet had you to mend a pot for her." The patch of sunlight appeared to be moving with the tinker. It was his shadow, she realized suddenly, a subversion of light that left her breathless. She kept her body very still, kept her face calm, though it felt cold and white as snow. "You must come with me. The trees are shifting, it is not safe here."

"You are armed," he said surprisedly, and the jewel in the pommel of the sword she wore winked as at a touch of light in that dark place.

"It is my right to bear arms in this house."

"Against a poor tinker?"

"You troubled the Gatekeeper, who has an eye for trouble. You are skulking like a thief in these woods without a broken pot in sight. Since you did not give your true name to the Gatekeeper, you must give it to the Holder, for you are in her house."

He did not answer her. His yellow-gold eyes seemed to reflect fire as he gazed at her. A corner of his mouth had crept upward in a smile. "And you?" he said finally, softly. "You looked straight at me, through those shifting trees; your eyes picked me out of the shadows. Who are you?"

"Meguet!" Rush called, from some place far away, within trees, behind trees, encircled by trees.

"Meguet," the tinker repeated thoughtfully. He turned the spit again; the lizard's eyes were faded now, filmy with smoke. "Meguet," he said again. "Pretty. But who? Who dwells behind your eyes?" He fingered the lizard, picked an eye out of its head, tossed it into the air. Falling, turning, turning in the air, it flashed now emerald, now coin-gold.

Sudden, dark, overwhelming anger drove Meguet forward, past revulsion and fear, to the fire and the charred, one-eyed lizard, and the tinker who dared his ugly sorcery within the Holder's house. She drew the sword at her side, thrust it down through the flames until the tip rested against the tinker's heart.

It was Moro Ro's great sword and it shook slightly in one hand, but the tinker seemed impressed. He looked up at her, still turning the lizard's eye between his fingers. "Meguet," he said curiously, his eyes full of yellow light, and suddenly her mind was full of light, as if the sun had struck her.

"Meguet!" Rush shouted behind her. The fire flared silver, swallowed the lizard, Moro's sword. Half-blind, she swung her horse, confused, trying to see Rush. She saw the tinker's wagon; its back door with the gold sun on it slammed shut. Then the air cracked oddly around her, as if a tree had snapped in two. The dark walls of the tinker's house crawled with flame.

She cried out. Rush tugged at her reins; she jerked free, turning back to stare at the tiny house, with its four black walls and its yellow roof and yellow lintel, until the silver flames engulfed it and Rush wrenched at her reins again.

"Meguet! The trees!"

They were rustling, sighing, drawing back from the fire. "Meguet," Rush pleaded. "He's burning in his house." He looked shaken, white; as usual, Meguet realized, his sorcery must have gone awry. The flames were dying already, without reaching toward the tree boughs; that much he had done right. She let him lead her finally. She glanced back one more time, incredulously, to seek a hint of what she had glimpsed in the fire-chewed bones of the wagon. The lizard in the fire moved its head to look at her. Both eyes were in its head and they were yellow-gold.

FOUR

YOU burned a tinker in the thousand-year-old wood?" the Holder said incredulously. Half the household had stood in windows and doorways, on the parapet wall between the back towers, watching the silver smoke rising out of the trees. Household guard, riding out to investigate, had found Meguet and Rush emerging from the trees, grim, silent, exhausted from the twisting paths of the disturbed and dreaming trees. The Holder, the guard told them, would see them immediately.

"He was not a tinker," Meguet said abruptly, breaking a silence that had lasted from the wood to Chrysom's library, where the Holder and Calyx had been watching the oddly glittering smoke. "And he is not dead."

Rush stared at her. "He's dead. Whatever he is. I burned his house with him in it—"

"Why?" the Holder asked sharply. "What had he done? In Moro's name, why did you set fire to a tinker?"

He closed his eyes. "I did not intend to. I was trying to circle his house with fire. Not burn it down."

"Then why—"

"I missed."

"Oh, Rush," Calyx breathed, hands over her mouth. "You never could do that right."

"He's not dead," Meguet said wearily. She began to tremble suddenly; methodically, she tried to unbuckle the sword belt dragging at her side so she could sit. Her hands shook; the buckle would not loosen. Calyx's hands moved under hers, flicked it open; she sat down finally, the sword across her knees. The Holder touched a pin in her hair, frowning down at Meguet, then swung back at Rush.

"Why?"

"He was threatening Meguet."

"A tinker?"

"She had drawn her sword against him."

"So Meguet was threatening the tinker. And you set him on fire. I gather this was no ordinary tinker. Meguet, why did you take up arms against a tinker?"

"He isn't a tinker."

"Wasn't," Rush murmured.

"He isn't dead." She heard him gather breath; she leaned forward in the chair, gripping its arms, gazing at him. "The yellow star its lintel, the yellow star its roof, the four stars of red and pale marking its black walls, the blue star marking its door latch. That's the house you burned, Rush."

In the silence, the Holder pulled at a pearl hairpin. The pin came out; a strand fell. "That's a Hold Sign," she said harshly. "Meguet."

"Yes." She met the Holder's eyes. She was still trembling; the jewels in Moro's sword and the sword belt shivered with light. "And the dark house that falls from the sky, in the Wayfolk man's tale."

The Holder stared at her, her face waxen against her dark, scattered hair.

"What Wayfolk man?" Rush demanded, and the Holder turned, looking, in the cast of firelight, fierce, dishevelled, oddly like Nyx. Rush swallowed. He said again, more quietly, "What Wayfolk man?"

"A man with Nyx. Meguet saw him."

Rush's face whitened. Meguet found herself on her feet again, speaking as calmly as she could. "A young man wanting a spell from Nyx. He spoke of a little dark house falling out of the sky—"

"That's a song," Calyx said wonderingly. "The house you never leave." She paused, blinking at something in the fire. "And it's a Hold Sign. The Gold King."

"His eyes were gold," Meguet said. Her voice faltered; she finished in a whisper. "The tinker's eyes were gold. He was roasting a lizard. When the house burned, I saw the lizard's eyes. They looked at me and they were gold."

"Sorcery," Rush said flatly. The Holder said nothing. Her eyes searched

Meguet a moment, then hid their thoughts. She pulled at another pin; it glittered to the floor.

"Nyx could fight it," Calyx suggested. "She would come home for this."

"No," the Holder said sharply.

"But, Mother, she has studied sorcery for nine years! If she can protect this house, she will, I know it—"

"I don't want her fighting anyone! I will not bring Nyx into danger."

"But if this house is in danger, we need someone to protect it, and Nyx—"

"No."

"Are you afraid," Rush asked abruptly, "that it's not this house she would fight for?"

The Holder's face flamed. He had struck her wordless; wordless, she struck back. The force of her blow rocked him a step and shook a few pins out of her hair. Rush dropped his face in his hands; she rubbed her wrist. She spoke first, grimly. "This is not the time, Rush Yarr, to show me my worst nightmare."

Rush reappeared; Meguet, shocked motionless, saw the blood between his fingers. Calyx, looking cross, pulled a square of lace from her sleeve and he applied it to his nose. "You hit like a blacksmith," he commented. Meguet, gripping the sheathed sword with both hands, eased her grip and set it down.

"We cannot start fighting each other," she breathed.

"No," Rush said. "I'm sorry." He sat down; so did the Holder.

"So am I," she said after a moment. "It would be easy to blame Nyx for every evil in the Delta now, but for eight years before this, her reputation has been blameless. Don't overlook that, Rush."

Calyx picked pins off the floor, began to tidy her mother's hair. "There's old Diu up in Berg Hold. Chrysom's descendant. We can send for him."

"No."

"Well, Mother, we have a sorcerer living in the thousand-year-old wood who frightened Meguet, who is not afraid of anything. What do you want to do about him?"

"I don't know yet." She looked at Meguet. "Is that why you went into the wood? Did you suspect he was there?"

"No. I didn't know where he was."

The Holder straightened, tugging her hair out of Calyx's hands. "You knew he was in this house? You didn't tell me?"

"I didn't—The Gatekeeper mentioned a tinker in a little black wagon who came into the house and vanished. I wasn't looking for him, no. But I recognized him when I saw him."

"Then why did you go into the wood?"

"The trees were beautiful," she said helplessly, puzzled. "Quiet, mysterious in the snow. They drew me in."

"They weren't quiet for long," Rush said dourly. "They rambled all over, especially after I tried to set them on fire. The tinker must have misjudged my power, or he would not have bothered to hide in his house."

"Or perhaps your ineptness terrified him," the Holder murmured.

"But why," Calyx said, setting a final pin in place, "would a sorcerer disguise himself as a tinker, drive around in a wagon reminiscent of a constellation and hide himself in the thousand-year-old wood?"

"Why," Rush asked, "would a Wayfolk man speak to Nyx of that same house?" The Holder's eye fell on him; he added carefully, "It begs an answer."

"Well," the Holder sighed, "Nyx is the one to ask. But," she added emphatically, "I do not want her back here. I would irritate her and she would upset me."

"Mother, you are being completely unreasonable," Calyx said softly.

"So is Nyx. Meguet will speak to her when the weather clears."

"She asked me to go with her," Rush said. The Holder raised a question with an eyebrow. Meguet shook her head.

"He would not leave the gate."

"Good," the Holder sighed. "It would terrify me if he did. Then go with her, Rush. But," she said severely, "do exactly as Meguet tells you, and do not antagonize Nyx."

"But what about the tinker?" Calyx persisted.

"We'll wait."

"For what?"

"For the pot to break," the Holder said darkly, "and give us something to mend."

"I found your tinker," Meguet said to the Gatekeeper, climbing up the steps to join him later. It was dusk; stone and sea and sky were all of the same raw grey. Children flung snow at each other in the yard; men stood around the forge fires, drinking ale and watching the world go dark. The Gatekeeper, lighting his pipe and trying to rise at the same time, took in smoke; she waited, standing on the top step, until he settled it.

"Sorry—"

She had disturbed him, she realized suddenly; shifting for her to enter, he did not look at her. She saw his jaw tighten in his lowered face. He drew a clean breath finally.

"You startled me. I heard you and Rush Yarr were found among the shifting trees. No one knew there was a tinker involved." He looked at her finally, eyes narrowed against his smoke. "Is that what burned?"

"His house."

"But not the tinker."

"No." He sat very still, pipe still in his hand, waiting. "You must keep watch for the tinker coming or going through the gate. But be careful of him. He is quite dangerous."

He gazed at her, his face dark against the darkening sky. "Lady Meguet," he said finally, "it's not me went in the back wood to roust out that tinker. Is he still there? Or does anyone know?"

"No." She thought of the lizard's gold eyes, and shivered lightly. "He could be anywhere."

He murmured something, shifting; forgetting her, he spat suddenly over the window ledge. "He had trouble painted all over his house, and yet I let him in. He spoke fairly enough, and gave me his reasons. . . . I should have known. A tinker wearing gold, and hardly a pot in sight. What is he, then?" She hesitated, caught his full, angry, insistent gaze. Astonished, she heard herself answer:

"Rush Yarr thinks a sorcerer."

He still watched her. "You don't."

"No. I'm not sure what he is."

"But you guess."

Pressed, she flared at him suddenly. "I'm only seeing shadows. You are overbearing."

"Nyx," he said, and she stared at him, speechless. "You only get like this with me when it's Nyx on your mind. That's a broad leap to make, from this house upriver to the swamps. From tinker to the Holder's daughter."

She stood up so abruptly she hit her head on the low, slanted stone roof. She sat back down, tears of anger, pain, frustration springing into her eyes. "How dare you," she demanded, rubbing her head furiously, "tell me what I am thinking. You have no right to judge Nyx, even if you were born among the small orange birds."

"I'm sorry, I'm sorry—" He had one arm around her shoulder, his head close to hers; it was his hand, then, rubbing her hair. "I'm not judging Nyx, I swear by the next thing comes off the river bottom. I'm Gatekeeper, and it's up to me to put a name to everything on two legs that comes in and out of this house. There's no name for that tinker."

"You assume because the tinker is evil, that Nyx must be—"

"No. You connected them, not me."

"Don't tell me what I'm saying."

"I'm sorry. Nobody ever taught me any manners. I only—I would cut my heart out for this house." He was stroking her hair now, his voice, tense with his own frustration, close to her ear. "And it was me that let the tinker in. I have never made a mistake before."

She lifted her head, sliding her hand under his hand; she sat back against the stones, flushed, her hair dishevelled. He watched her, the small lines gathered at the corners of his eyes. She stood up again, carefully, and saw how his hands lifted as if to guide her, then fell. She said, more calmly, "You were right about Nyx. I am going upriver with Rush to talk to her. Don't tell me to be careful of her."

"No," he said quickly. "I like living."

She opened her mouth, closed it. Her mouth crooked. "I'm sorry," she said. "Nyx worries me so. And this house."

"I know that." He stood up so swiftly she feared for his head, but he was used to dodging the slant. She felt his arm hover protectively around her, above her head as she ducked under the stone lintel. She went down the steps slowly, wanting to look back and not daring. She looked back finally, met his eyes.

She and Rush left two days later. The rains had slowed, but the river was still full, swirling angrily, opaque with silt. Once out of the city, she had to choose her paths carefully; the path along the river bank was under water in some places. In others, the river had spilled far over into other pools and creeks, and they had to backtrack, skirt, go south, Rush pointed out too often, to go north. It was wearisome, with the rain falling intermittently; neither of them spoke much. Rush's face was pale, set; he looked constantly ahead in his mind, seeing a woman he had not seen in nearly three years, instead of what lay under his nose. Meguet had to guide him around soggy bogs, pull him away from the crumbling hillside. It took them an entire day just to reach sight of a tavern she knew that had a couple of rush-filled mattresses, and a meal. She said with relief, "I thought it might have fallen into the water."

"What?" Rush said, roused. "That shack? That's an inn? How much farther is it? Can we get there tonight?"

"We've been slowed by the flooding. Dark falls fast here. I don't know how long it will take us to reach her house, but we can't do it tonight."

"I'd rather sleep in the rain than in that flea-bitten hut."

"Suit yourself," she said tiredly, then saw something within the trees: a black that took her breath away. Rush made a comment she did not hear; her attention was busy, trying to pick the black thing apart from the woods, make a familiar shape out of it. It moved as they moved, toward them; Rush, catching sight of it, fell silent.

It was a woman. Meguet eased in her saddle as she came closer: a woman in black, with her cloak lifted, held against her face, covering nose and mouth. She fluttered oddly, with wind that was not there. She stopped in the middle of the path, waited for them. Meguet saw ash-white threads endlessly circling the dark hem of her cloak; her lips parted.

"It's a witch," she breathed.

"What?"

"From Hunter Hold. Look at the pattern on her skirt and her cloak. Look at her sandals—they make them of bitterthorn. She must have walked all this way. . . . No." A chill ran through her, of wonder and fear. "No. She has sent herself ahead of time."

"She what?" Rush said incredulously.

"She is in Hunter Hold. And she is here. She sent her image along time with a message."

"Are you sure?" Rush asked urgently. "Is it sorcery?"

"No. They only walk the path of time." She quickened her pace then, rode alone to meet the witch.

She was an old woman, grown strong and implacable as thorn and iron in the black desert of Hunter Hold. Her grey eyes were milky, as if she had looked too often at the full moon. She blinked uncertainly at the black-clad rider in front of her, as if desert winds were blowing a fine mist of sand before her eyes. Then she dropped her cloak from her face.

"Meguet Vervaine."

She felt her face blanch. "Yes."

"You must beware."

The witch's voice, for all her stamina, was fragile as a glass bell. Her image flowed in the wind of another Hold. Meguet, aware of the rain touching dead leaf and twig and water with slow, delicate fingers, of Rush's horse stirring wet leaves on the trail behind, answered finally, "Yes."

"You must go back. You must watch."

"What—" She drew breath. "What have you seen?"

"In the last full moon, I looked along the path of time and I saw a lady as beautiful as night walking toward the house of the Holders of Ro Holding. She walks along the line of time, and the great house stands in her path, and as she walks, she grows vast or the house grows small, small enough for her to crush underfoot if she keeps along that path."

"A lady."

Meguet swallowed, her voice shaking. Nyx, she thought, Nyx as dark as night. But the witch had seen a different path.

"She may know the house is there, or she may not. I could not tell, for she is blind. You must watch for her. Will you watch, for the Holders of Ro Holding? You can see. Will you watch?" Meguet was wordless, shivering badly. The woman huddled into her shapeless clothes, took a step back into her own time. "Watch!" she pleaded, in her fine, frail voice. "Watch, for the Cygnet!"

"Meguet," Rush breathed, and she started.

"Watch!" the old woman cried. "You have the eyes."

Somehow her voice came clear, certain. "I will watch."

The sending faded; a darkness crumpled in the air and vanished. Meguet watched the place where she had been, as if she might see the beginning and end of time appearing there. She felt a touch on her arm and whirled, pulling her horse back.

"Meguet." Rush stared at her, startled, disturbed. "What did she say to you?"

She touched her eyes, closed them and saw the dark of night, the dark of time. "We must go back," she whispered.

"Now?" he said sharply.

She opened her eyes. "Rush," she said, "the witch gave warning to the Holder's house. Warning to the Cygnet. Nyx can wait. She is not the danger. Ro House is in danger and it can't wait."

"Warning of what?"

"I don't know. A blind woman." She turned her horse blindly, night falling fast, and the threads of paths through the swamp as tangled as the threads of time. "Some blind woman. She must not enter the House. I must go back and warn."

"Why you?" Rush asked bewilderedly. "Why did she cross your path, and not the Holder's?"

"I don't know."

"Or the Gatekeeper's?"

"Rush, I don't know. She told me to watch. How can I watch anything in the middle of this swamp with night coming on—"

"You can't," Rush said, for once making a decision for her. "Unless you know how to throw your image across the Delta."

"No."

"Then," he said, resigned, for she knew he would not let her ride back alone, with such strange things happening around them, "we will spend the night in the shack and be home tomorrow."

They entered the gate again at nightfall, worn, mud-stained and drenched; the rains had started again. Rush rode ahead to the towers to speak to the Holder. Meguet relinquished her horse at the gate. The Gatekeeper, holding a torch above their heads, took a sharp look at her face and said cautiously,

"Is it Lady Nyx?"

"No."

"Then what?" He drew her to shelter against the wall, beneath the turret, replacing the torch in its sconce.

"You must beware," she said. His eyes widened. "Think," she pleaded. "Think. Has a blind woman entered this house since I've been gone?"

He was staring at her, so still she gripped his cloak, shook him a little, alarmed. "No," he said abruptly. "No." His hands rose, closed over her hands. "No stranger has entered or left, and no one blind."

"She's beautiful, the witch said. A blind woman, beautiful as night." She glanced at the gate; he had closed it securely behind her. "You must watch for her. She must not enter."

"No," he said again. "Who is she?"

"I don't know. The witch didn't say. She walks the path of time toward this house. Blind, she may know or may not know this house is underfoot." She felt him shudder; his hands tightened.

"But who?" he insisted. "She must have a name. Tinker has no name, the blind woman has no name—Meguet, you must find out. How can I guard against something that has no name? How can you?"

"How can I find out? I barely know they exist! I'm not like Nyx to know sorcery, or Calyx who has read everything in Chrysom's library twice—"

"You know they're dangerous. The witch came to you."

She stared at him, wordless, frustrated. "Hew, what do you expect me to do? Stand at the gate and ask her name when she enters? That's for you to do."

"It's for me," he agreed tautly. "And by then it will be too late. You must help me. You grew up in this house. You have ancient memories in your past. The witch came to you."

"She crossed my path. She said my name." She was shivering in the rain; rain rolled down his face like tears. Wind dragged torchlight over them,

pulled apart the cloak of darkness they stood wrapped in. She saw them suddenly as from another angle in the yard, a cottager's window, the alehouse
doorway, a tower casement: she gripping his cloak, he her hands; his face, an
inch or three higher, inclined slightly, the hard spare lines of it dark and fire,
reflections of the pale Delta river in his eyes.

She whispered, "Gatekeeper."

"Lady Meguet."

"I must go."

"Say my name again before you go."

"Hew."

"Meguet."

FIVE

THE Holder sat late with her family that night in Chrysom's library. Meguet, who had shed her drenched, muddy riding clothes for black velvet and pearls, sat on a stone seat against the stone wall. The chill kept her awake, the stones kept her upright; demands beyond that, she felt, were unreasonable. Yet the Holder made them.

"What blind woman?"

"I don't know," Meguet said.

"Tell me again what the witch said. Tell me exactly."

She was pacing back and forth in front of the fire, the swing of her heavy, wine-colored gown mesmerizing. Iris, looking perplexed, was doing some needlepoint. Calyx sat in the shadows listening intently, looking, in white velvet and diamonds, like something carved out of frost. Rush was frowning, his eyes lowered in concentration; he was, Meguet thought, about to snore.

"Beautiful," Meguet said for what seemed the third or eighth time, "as beautiful as night, and blind."

It was then Calyx spoke. "That's simple," she said. "It's the constellation. The Blind Lady who wears the Ring of Time. The Silver Ring of Withy Hold."

The Holder stared at her. She was not prone to throwing things besides her voice, but she did then. The poker struck the hearth with a snarl of stone and iron that brought Rush upright, feeling for a weapon that he had taken off hours ago. He froze under the Holder's glare.

"Another Hold Sign."

"Strictly speaking," Calyx began, "the Blind Lady is not—"

"How could a constellation walk through the gate?" Iris asked.

"The tinker did."

"The tinker is not—"

"If we guard the gate," Rush said. "If the Gatekeeper watches, she can't enter."

"The tinker did," the Holder snapped.

"We weren't warned."

"The Gatekeeper let him in."

"He wasn't warned either," Rush argued reasonably. "This time, Meguet told him."

The Holder paced a step, whirled. "The Gatekeeper is responsible for whoever enters or leaves this house."

"But, Mother—" Calyx began.

"He should have known. As he recognized himself Gatekeeper, he should recognize anything this dangerous to Ro House. The Blind Lady. The Silver Ring. The Dark House. The Gold King. Something is gathering against this house—" She turned again, for Meguet had made a sound. The Holder gazed at her, waiting, her eyes hardened already against what Meguet would say.

"The Wayfolk man," she breathed. "Corleu. He spoke of these things. The Dark House. The Dancer. The Warlock."

"The Dancer is guarded by the Fire Bear," Calyx said wonderingly. "The Warlock is the Blood Fox's shadow. Berg Hold and the Delta."

The Holder's arm swept impulsively toward the mantel, where Chrysom's crystal jars and boxes and cut stones gleamed like jewels in the shadows. Meguet closed her eyes. But Rush spoke a moment later. She had checked her gesture; they were all still alive.

"We'll bring him here. The Wayfolk man."

"No," the Holder said harshly. "Not into this house."

"Under guard, bound, locked away—what more could he do?"

"I will not have him anywhere in this house."

"Then elsewhere," Rush said bewilderedly. "In the city, somewhere—"

The Holder, her mouth tight, picked up the poker, sent a small avalanche of coals rattling through the grate instead of answering.

"Somewhere safe from Nyx?" Iris asked. "Where might that be, Rush? If Nyx wants him with her, she has the power to keep him. Against you, against Meguet, against anyone."

"Thank you," the Holder said icily.

"I'm being sensible, Mother. Someone has to be." She flushed suddenly under the Holder's gaze. She continued with a stubborn, curious dignity. "All I can see is what is obvious, and that is what most of the people of Ro Holding see. You all see through the confusion in flashes of magic and learning. I can't. I just recognize the simple things. If Nyx is doing all this, none of us can stop her. If she is innocent, then she's bound to be in danger."

The Holder set the poker down with a sigh. She said nothing for a moment; her fingers worried at her elegant hair, but for once the pins were too skillfully hidden. She folded her arms instead; her eyes went to Meguet.

"You thought the Wayfolk man was not the danger."

"I think," Meguet said carefully, pulling together the dreamlike scraps of his tale, "he is trying to rescue someone. The dark house fell unexpectedly into his life. The tinker is the danger. Part of it."

"And the tinker is here."

"If we guard against the Blind Lady, keep her from entering—"

"I think we should bring them both here," Rush said implacably. "Nyx and the Wayfolk man."

"Oh, Rush, use your head," Calyx said impatiently. "You weren't listening to Iris. If she is dangerous, do we want her in the house with the tinker? And if she is not, she is much safer being away from here. And what I think—"

"If she—"

"What I think," Calyx said, raising her delicate voice as much as she ever did, "is that if Nyx and the tinker were working together, this is where she would be. Here, in this house, with him. I think we should guard the house against the blind woman. The tinker is doing nothing; maybe he can't, without her."

"What I want to know," Iris asked, "is: Are they sorcerers? Or something to do with the Holds?"

The Holder touched her eyes. "Iris, how can you say such things so calmly?"

"Well, we do have to know."

"I know." She consulted Meguet again, with her eyes. "You've seen more of this than anyone. What do you think? What are they?"

They all turned to her expectantly. She answered after a moment, softly, reluctantly. "The Wayfolk man spoke of waking the Dancer on the last day of winter. That is not sorcery. That is a tale out of Berg Hold, as old as Ro Holding."

She stood in her chambers later, staring out at the night. Rain and wind gusted across the yard. She could not see a single light on the sea. The only light in the world was in the Gatekeeper's turret, and the torches he kept lit beside the gate to guide travellers in the dark. She saw the brazier light obscured a moment, reappear. He was still there, at the cold, late hour, still watching.

She reached for her cloak.

She felt, walking through the storm, as if she walked the surface of Wolfe Sea, with all the spindrift flung about her, and the small, high fire pulling her like the moon pulling tide. He did not hear her mount the stairs; he could only have heard the booming tide, the wild wind. She stood, darkly cloaked, hooded, at the top of the stairs, at the edge of his light, and as he turned his head, she wondered if he could see her face at all, or if he would speak some name other than hers. He looked at her. Wordless, rising, he stepped into the rain. He slid her hood back with both hands, slipped her long, pale hair free until it streamed with the torch fire in the wind. She took his face between her hands, drew it down and down until she tasted the Delta river currents running in his mouth.

The wild rain wore them apart finally. They huddled close to the brazier, dripping, blinking in the light. The Gatekeeper watched Meguet; she watched the shimmering heat, too weary to think. He said finally:

"So green, your eyes. Not a Delta green. Nothing under these mists is that green."

She raised her eyes. There were threads of silt and gold in his hair she hadn't noticed, a line along his mouth, a scar high on one cheekbone, near the eye. He waited calmly, undisturbed by her silence; his eyes, far paler green than her own, had flecks of white in them. She said, "My great-grandfather was of Withy Hold. His eyes got so, looking at the corn, they said. He liked to wander, too. He was a strange man.... Do you mean to stay here all night?"

"Yes."

"The blind woman must not come into this house. Calyx says she is a Hold Sign."

He blinked, as though her words had flicked like rain across his face. "Then I must be careful," he breathed.

"Yes." She leaned back against the wall, all her weariness roiling through her, all her fears. She slid her hands over her face, felt the sting of tears in the back of her eyes. She felt his hands follow her hands, slide down her wet hair, unpin her wet, sodden cloak.

"All in velvet, you came out," he marvelled. "In pearls. You're soaking."

"I wanted to hear your voice." He smiled his tight, slanting smile. She added, "I don't know why."

"The world's a wild place beyond Ro House. You've known a good deal of it. You're not content with what's bred within walls."

"So it seems." She drew breath as he leaned into her cloak, caught her pearls between his teeth. "Hew."

"Meguet."

"Could you be content, in the late hours some night, watching the gate from Chrysom's tower? You must sleep sometime."

He lifted his head; her hands were in his hair. He drew them down, kissed her fingers. "Will you help me watch?"

"I will." She laid her face against his hair. "From my chambers you can see the swans, you can see Wolfe Sea, you can see the barred gate and the turret where the Gatekeeper sat tonight with all the house asleep, but for one woman watching him. Watch until you can no longer watch alone. Then come to the black tower, and I will keep watch with you."

He waited until she thought he would not come. And then he came one night, unexpectedly, in some dark, lost hour adrift between midnight and dawn. She was dreaming of swans, gliding on the lake, white and black, shadows and reflections of one another, elegant, proud, secret. One black swan lifted a wing; she felt the chill of the air it had disturbed, then a play of feathers across her mouth. She lifted her hands, shaped and molded the feathery dark until a man moved under her touch and she finally woke.

He rose after a while, to stir the fire and light candles. He opened a casement to look across the yard at the gate. A mix of rain and snow tumbled past him; he stared down the hard bitter wind without flinching. He shut the casement finally, slid into bed beside Meguet, smelling of winter and cold as iron.

She rolled on top of him; slowly he stopped shivering; the warm firelight lay over both of them. He slid the furs down, fanned her hair across her back.

"Is the gate still closed?"

"Closed and barred." He went on with his task, separating the rippling strands to his liking. "Lady Meguet. Do you remember the first time you left the house on Holder's business, all in black, with the swans flying at your back and side and shoulder?"

"Yes."

"You took my breath away."

"I don't recall you looked overawed."

"I was trying to stay on my feet, not topple over in your wake. You rode through the gate like night itself. I had only just come; I was overawed by anything. You looked at me and thanked me. You wouldn't remember that."

"I do," she said, smiling. "You caught my eye. Brown and hard and half-wild, like you knew all the secret places of the backwaters. I wanted to say more, but you looked so stern and solemn."

"So did you. You scared me silly." He began weaving strands of hair like a net. "Ten years ago, that was. Now you have been all over Ro Holding, and I have seen only as far as I can see from the gate in any direction."

"Don't you miss the river?"

"How can I? My heart is nailed to that gate. I had to come here to find it." She bent her head to kiss him; his net unravelled.

"I could never leave this house either," she said.

"Why so? You'll marry, you'll leave—"

"Do you think so?" she asked, gazing down at him out of her cool, clear eyes. "No matter how far I go, I always come back here. Rush Yarr says that in a place as old as Ro House, and among such old families, more than faces and names are handed down. Memories, he says, echoes of the past. Sometimes I can see it. . . ."

"See what?"

"Back. Far back. As if I'm seeing through a long history." His hands were still now, his breath barely stirring her hair. "When I watched Nyx in secret, inside her house, I felt it then: that others were watching out of my eyes, evaluating what I saw, showing me what to see. . . ."

He made a soft sound, drew her hair back from her face. "Swamp's like that," he said. "Layering year after year, bone on bone; if you dig deep enough, you'd find the beginning of things. And the gate."

"The gate?"

"Watching, I lose time, now and then. A thousand years passed through that gate. A thousand years of names spoken, shadows riding across the threshold. Sometimes I wonder if a few of those whose names I know are ghosts, riding into another century that still exists somewhere inside the house."

She pushed her face against his chest. "Don't talk of shadows." She slid her arms around him, watching her shadow on the wall hold his shadow. "Just once, here, let's leave trouble out in the cold." He turned, easing over her, sliding his hands through her hair as he kissed her, drawing it out along the pillow, like wings.

She was half asleep when she felt him pull back the furs. She reached out, but he was already up.

"Where are you going?"

"Just to the window."

This time she went with him, stood wrapped in furs while the rain blew into her hair. The torches beside the gate still burned; the bar across it had not shifted. Beyond the wind-whipped pools of light, only a tower light or two, a cottage light, broke the wild dark.

"Nothing could be out on a night like this."

"Someone's always up, always thinking, even in a storm like this."

"Not tonight. There's no world left out there. Only Ro House, in an ancient night before there were stars."

"You must be right," he said, his eyes still drawn to the gate. "Before people. Only you and I and the swans on the lake . . ." He turned to her, so quickly his eyes still carried some reflection of the dark. He pulled the fur away from her and lifted her naked in his arms like an offering to the wind and rain and the ancient night. Cold took her breath away, and then he did, head bowed over her body, drinking in the hard rain.

Asleep finally, she felt him loose his hold of her, draw back the furs. She groped for him, murmuring. The winds were singing madly around the tower. "Don't," she pleaded, her eyes closed. "Nothing is out there."

"I must watch." He sounded still asleep.

"Stay with me. Don't leave me yet. Not even dawn is at the gate."

"The gate moved."

"It's only wind at the gate. Only rain."

"I must watch."

"I'll watch," she said, and felt him sink back. She pushed against him; he wound his hand into her hair. "I'll watch," she whispered, and drew his other arm around her.

"You watch, then," he sighed, and she felt his body ease back into sleep. "You watch."

He was gone when she woke again. She rose, went to the casement, and saw familiar movement within the turret. She watched him, wondered if he were watching the black tower. Something strange hit her hand, spilled over the stones, down the wall; blinking, she saw her own shadow. She raised her head, and saw the sudden light fall over the sea.

She dressed quickly, ate something she did not taste. The morning lured her: a taste of spring, though the air was still brittle with cold. She went downstairs, watching for the Gatekeeper's turret in every southern window. Walking outside, between the towers, she saw him again, framed in every archway she passed along the wall. Turning into one, finally, she found her way blocked.

An old woman stood within the archway, half in shadow, half in sunlight fanning over the cobbles. She seemed to be seeking the sun with her face; her heavy eyes could not lift to see. She was dressed oddly, layered with old clothes. A cottager, Meguet thought, someone's ancient kin wandered away from the hearth.

"Are you lost?" she asked. "May I help you?" The face swung toward her, strong and hard, mottled like an apple. For a moment, Meguet felt that she was being scented.

"Ah. Meguet." The old woman lifted her hand to the ragged edge of lace trailing out of a hole in what looked like a skirt made out of sacking, over a longer gown of stained velvet. Her fingers pulled at the threads, twitching. "Lost? No. I found my way here. I came out to smell the spring."

"How did you know my name?" Meguet asked curiously. "You must remember voices. But I don't remember you."

"Your name is here." She held out the threads her restless fingers had woven together. "I have all the names." She pulled up the worn velvet; beneath it was a skirt of tapestry edged raggedly with muddy cloth of gold. Beneath her motley layered skirts, Meguet glimpsed strange boots covered in peacock feathers. "Here they all are. All of Ro House." On the hand that wove she wore a tarnished silver ring.

Meguet was silent. She closed her eyes, feeling the light on her icy face. She could still speak; the horror, a blow falling across a long distance, had not reached her yet. "They said," she whispered, swallowing the burning in her throat, "you were beautiful."

"So I was. So I was."

"How—how did we—" But she knew before she asked. She heard the Gatekeeper's dream-heavy voice: The gate moved. She heard her answer. She opened her eyes, beginning to tremble. The pool of light was empty. A peacock feather watched her from the shadow, then vanished.

She pushed her face against the stones and wept.

SIX

IN the shadows, someone touched her. She whirled, breathing hard, back against the stones. She stared at the Gatekeeper through swollen eyes.

"You left the gate," she said, stunned. "In broad daylight."

"Moro's eyes," he said, staring back at her. "You're weeping in broad daylight." He reached out, pulled her away from the stones, held her tightly. In the yard behind him, stablehands were staring; faces clustered at the thick glass windows of the cider house. "I watched you cross the yard from Chrysom's tower in the sunlight. You disappeared under this arch and you didn't come out."

"Did you see her?"

"Who?"

She pushed against him, hands on his shoulders, to look at him. "Who." She watched the color drain out of his face. He set his hands flat against the wall on either side of her, leaned against them, not looking at her. "It was my fault," she added wearily. "I would not let you watch."

His head lifted; his back straightened, as if her words were something edged, dangerous, that had touched him unexpectedly. "Then, it was?"

"Yes." Her eyes filled again; light blurred into dark around his face. She heard him catch his breath.

"Meguet..." Then he swung his heavy cloak around her, gathered her into it. "Come with me."

She walked with him through the cottages, scarcely seeing the people that gazed, shaken, at the pair of them. He pushed a door open; she sank onto a bench, dropped her face into her hands, trying to think rather than to weep. She heard Hew stirring, hearth-sounds, the snap of fire across kindling.

She dropped her hands finally, said numbly, "I must tell the Holder."

"I'll come."

"There's no need——"

"I let trouble in," he said grimly. "Through my gate, they came. The tinker in his dark house, the Blind Lady——"

"You know her." She stared at him. "You know her."

"I know them both. I have over enough time to think up there, see pictures in my pipe-smoke and put them together. That tinker rolling across the threshold of this house in his black house with the Gold King scowling on the back door, telling his tales, then vanishing——"

"You told me. You tried to warn me."

"And the Blind Lady. 'My lady walks on the moon's road, shod, she is, in peacock feathers, all eyes, she is all eyes, but for her moonstruck eyes.' " He gave a short laugh, not smiling. "A love song, that is."

She was wordless, taking in finally the fragile, faded books that stood on oak shelves against the whitewashed walls, the dark, carved furniture with a flower winding down a chair-arm, a leg ending with a cat's face, both flower and face worn smooth by centuries. Hew poured her wine; she took a swallow; he watched her, the hard lines running along his mouth. He said again, "We'll go together to the Holder."

"Yes." She set her cup down, her eyes going to the fire. "Soon."

"Meguet."

"Soon." She raised her eyes from the fire to his face. "First I have to find them."

"Where?" he demanded. "They move in and out of shadows, they're hardly real——"

"They're in this house. They came in through the gate. They're real enough to have come from somewhere, be somewhere. They know me. I've seen them both; they've said my name. The household guard might raise the dust looking for them and never notice them."

"They're dangerous."

"I only want to find them. I only want to——" Her voice shook suddenly; she folded her hands tightly, steadying herself. "When I tell the Holder that the Blind Lady is in this house, I want to give her something more than just that. Perhaps, if I go quietly, in secret, I might learn what they want here. Why they have come into Ro House. We have to know, Hew. We must know."

He closed his eyes, breathed something. She stood up restively. "Do you have a sword?"

"For what?" he asked. "Skewering the guests?"

"A knife?"

"Bread knife." His eyes opened, withholding expression. "Where will you look? There are people moving constantly up in the towers, down in the cellars, across fields, through cottages, everywhere but Chrysom's tomb. There's no place for secrets in this house."

"Chrysom's tomb." She stopped moving to gaze at him. "The maze beneath the tower."

"That's no secret, either. Every cottage brat old enough to lose front teeth knows how to get into that maze."

"And how far do they get?"

"Never far."

"How far did you get?" she challenged him, and saw the flicker of memory in his face.

"Not past the place where all the rotting strings unwound," he said. "Seemed no one got past there. Unless you."

"No." She touched the window glass lightly with her fingers, her breath misting the blade-sharp edge of shadow the tower wall laid across the light. "Nyx and Rush and I spent days trying to get past the first few turns. We would turn a corner and wind up walking into a closet, or a pantry. Or a cupboard under a stair. Always through some door we could never find again. As if whatever Chrysom built that maze to guard is too precious, or too terrible, for humans."

"Did he build it to guard against a tinker and a beggar woman?"

"Maybe not. Maybe. Maybe they got no farther than the first few turns. But even that's a place to hide. The black tower, where so few come." She turned toward the door. "I'll get—No. If I take a sword out of the armory, they'll wonder. . . . I'll get one off the council chamber wall."

"For what?" he asked her tersely. "Tinker doesn't burn, what makes you think he bleeds?"

"It makes me feel safer."

"Then I'll carry the bread knife. It'll be as much protection."

"No," she said, her eyes widening.

"I'm coming."

"You can't leave the gate."

"Am I at the gate?"

"But, Hew! Who will open and close? What will people think, seeing the turret empty in daylight? They'll think you died. What will the Holder say?"

"What will she say to you, going into that dark and lonely place alone?"

"It's my business," she said obstinately.

"What is? Defending the house? There's a guard for that. What makes it your business to track danger and power into such a place? Are you a sorcerer yourself?"

"No," she snapped. "What business is it of yours to abandon the gate for this?"

"None of mine. None of yours. So." He swung the door open. "My lady Meguet, let us get on with it."

Only one door in or out of the maze never vanished: one set in the stone wall behind the dais in the ancient council chamber where Moro Ro had claimed, in the Sign of the Cygnet, all Ro Holding. As usual, the chamber, which took up the entire ground floor of the black tower, was empty. The banners of Hunter Hold and Withy Hold had been hung; the silver and gold thread winked in the morning light. The vast banner of Ro Holding hung behind the dais, hiding the door, so fragile and old that black swan melted into blue-black night, and only the tarnished threads depicting the stars of the Cygnet in flight seemed to hold the darkness together.

Hew took a torch from the stairway; Meguet chose a sword from the wall of ceremonial swords forged for each Holder, and then held the Cygnet away from the wall until, bending, Hew had carried the fire safely through the small door. She let it fall behind her and entered. Fire ran down the steps ahead of them, nibbled at an ancient dark. She smelled earth, stones, but no wood fires, no lingering odors of cooking. She heard nothing.

Hew, moving down the steps ahead of her, stopped at the foot of the stairs. She whispered,

"What is it?"

"I was only remembering what all the younglings hope to find but are terrified of finding: the fearsome beings, the guardians of Chrysom's tomb. Do you think there's truth to that?"

"Why not? The stars are falling out of the sky and turning into tinkers. If we ever find the center of the maze, I suppose we'll know."

"Maybe it's a Ring of Time, the center. Chrysom walked out of Ro Holding into past or future."

She was silent, hovering at his shoulder, watching gryphons, dragons, hawks, lions, shrug themselves out of the marble walls of the maze. Under torch fire, they raged silently, bidding the trespasser beware. "Why?" she wondered, forgetting to whisper. "All this for his own tomb? What is he still guarding after a thousand years? Are a mage's bones so precious? Do they turn to gold?"

"I've never heard such." He took a step, then stopped, handed the torch to Meguet. "You lead."

"Why? Neither of us is likely to wind up anywhere but in a pantry somewhere, interrupting a cook's apprentice and a scullery boy kissing."

"You're the one bearing arms," he said wryly, and, edgy as she was, she almost laughed. She moved; he followed her. Walls broke between passageways; she slipped at random between them. Passageways split, forked away into the silence, forced her to choose between one shadow and another. She chose thoughtlessly, according to the glint of light in a gryphon's eye, the gesture of a lion's paw. At any moment, she expected, the walls would subtly shift, dissolve and simply vanish into the dark. A door in front of them would open to some tower or another; they would emerge under a stairway, trailing cobwebs and blinking at the light. The small door, closing, would melt into wood or stone around it. But the walls held longer than she would have believed. Hew walked quietly beside her, watching the dark beyond the edge of light around them, sometimes watching her. He said once, softly:

"They'd never have gone this deep, surely?"

"I don't know." She added after a moment, "I've never come this far myself."

"I doubt anyone has."

"Why?"

"No threads left, no candle nubs, no smoke marks on the walls or on the floor . . ."

"It must run underground even past the tower ring. We've been walking forever, it seems."

"Into or out of forever."

She looked at him, surprised. "Do you mean like the thousand-year-old wood? Part real, part dream?"

"No. Well, maybe, or partly a different time. Or a slower time. In our own time, the House time, the maze never goes beyond the tower ring. But in a different time, it is vast and the center can be reached."

"And the House?" she asked, startled and intrigued by the intricate turn of his thoughts.

"Ro House does not exist now."

"Or the gate?"

He smiled a little. "Perhaps the gate. But open or closed? And who watches?"

A tongue of gold fire dropped out of a lion's mouth and fell, burning, at Meguet's feet.

She whirled, the torch outstretched, spinning a circle around her. She saw no one. A coiled snake of fire dropped out of a hawk's talon; a gold eye rolled from a gryphon's face, spilled fire on the floor. She drew her sword, circled again, her eyes wide, both torch and blade probing the empty dark. More fire fell, ringing them both with gold, she saw in horror. "Hew!" she cried, losing him as he circled at her back. He swung his heavy cloak around her suddenly, and gripped her, swept her off her feet. She struggled instinctively, desperately, hating to be bound, needing freedom to move, to fight. The torch slipped dangerously close to his face. He flinched back, gasping. But he kept his grim hold; he lifted her, tossed her away from him over the burning ring of gold. She lost her balance, tangled and weighted in sheepskin; she stumbled to her hands and knees. Turning, she saw only a tower of gold.

She whispered, "Hew." Within the fire something shaped: a woman clothed in stars and night, stars clinging to her black hair, her beautiful face moon-pale, her blind eyes closed. She lifted her hands, pulled a glowing thread taut between them until, under the lick of fire, it began to fray.

Meguet screamed his name. A small dark wagon with a roof of light and a lintel of light rolled through the flames. Its door opened. She saw the Gatekeeper of Ro House rise amid the flames. He walked away from her for a long time, it seemed, or into a different time, while the door in the black house opened slowly, revealing a starlit dark.

Meguet rolled to her feet, flung herself, eyes closed, through the fire. She careened into Hew, knocking him off his relentless path. Groping for balance, he caught at her, dragged her down under him as he fell. She pushed at him desperately, winded; sagging against her, his hand on her shoulder, his arm across her hair, he gave her no help. She edged out from under him finally. When she dragged his arm off her hair, it fell back laxly against the floor. He did not move.

Pulling herself to her knees beside him, reaching out to him in bewilderment, she saw the blood on the knife in his hand.

A sound came out of her, echoed off the corners of the maze in a harsh, terrible tangle. Laughter wove into her cry. Lifting her head, she finally saw the Gold King.

He stood within the fire. He wore armor hammered of gold; his hair and eyes and the seven-starred crown on his head were gold. Only his laughing mouth was dark, a hollow that might open into another world, another time, and she knew he laughed at her because she did not know, seeing him, if she knelt beside death or dream. In sudden fury, she pulled the knife from Hew's hand, flung it with deadly accuracy into the Gold King's open mouth.

A darkness burst out of the tinker-king, flooded the walls, buried flame and torch fire until she could see only the barest, silvery outline of stone animals in the wall. She got to her feet and ran.

The stones began to come alive under the strange glow. A hawk cried; a gryphon shifted a wing; a dragon pointed her path with an upraised claw. She ran without hesitating, not even considering choice, and as she wound deeper into the maze she realized, chilled, that she recognized the path she took.

I have walked this before, she thought, prickling with terror, knowing it was not true. But, as memory guided her, she made choices: right at the gryphon's snarl, left at the lion's roar, between walls at the graceful shift of a unicorn's horn. *Who sees out of my eyes? Who walked this before me? Whose memories have I inherited?* And then, rounding a corner beneath a dragon's outspread wing, she knew that she had shifted into a different time.

That was why the stones moved, she realized; in her own life they might have spent a century lowering an eyelid. She swallowed drily, trembling, sensing movement around her from those that dwelled in the dark of this time. Walking into a small, circular chamber, she caught glimpses of colored horn, of fur, of rich cloth, of sword blades so massive she could not have lifted them. Here were the huge and terrible creatures of legend white-toothed, masked, prowling at the edge of an eerie, silver-green glow that came from a globe hanging over a black effigy and tomb. Chrysom's tomb, she thought in horror, but its guardians recognized something in her and let her pass among them. As she stepped beyond time, she stepped beyond wonder, beyond terror, beyond any thought of her own. She gazed at the effigy; then the globe above it dragged at her eyes. Staring into it, she saw back along her own history: a past full of names of those born to see, to watch, hers among them, though at that moment she could not remember which was hers.

The tomb faded into its own moment; the globe changed shape.

A huge, faceted crystal, suspended from nothing upon nothing, glowed like a moon at the center of the maze. Its facets blazed with a white light that slowly faded, until, blinking away splinters of light, she could see the black swan flying in every plane. The swans faded; faces began to appear within the globe, of men and women she should not have recognized but did: Rydel the gardener; the mage Ais; Tries, physician to Jain Ro; the Lady Scirie, historian and poet; Paro Ro's horse trainer Jhen; Eleria Ro's cousin Shadox; all of them descendants of Astor Ro, all secret guardians of the Cygnet. She saw her own face last, broad-boned, green-eyed, and then realized, from the pearls braided into the long hair, and the darker, straighter brows, that she looked at Astor Ro.

Motionless, submerged in her heritage, she felt no surprise. The face within the crystal spoke:

"Who are you?"

She answered, her voice expressionless, a dreamer's voice. "I am Meguet Vervaine."

"Why were you born?"

The answer, like her movement to the heart of the maze, came without hesitation. "I was born to serve the Cygnet."

"To what are you sworn?"

"To guard the Cygnet. With my life. For all of my days. Beyond my days and my life."

"You will walk in the Cygnet's eye. You will guard. You will defend."

"Yes."

"Our memories are yours, our eyes are yours. Your heart is ours and your body and the strength of your hand."

"Yes."

"Our gifts are yours. Our experience is yours. We will guide you, watch with you."

"Yes."

"You will obey us."

"Yes."

"Why have you come here?"

"The Cygnet is in danger."

"What must you do?"

She felt an ancient rage within her, honed thin and sharp as the mage-forged blades she sometimes practiced with. She said, "I will seek the danger to the Cygnet. I will hunt it down. I will destroy it. For this we were born."

"Meguet Vervaine, Guardian. Put your hands to the Cygnet's eye."

She reached out, placed her hands on the cold planes of the prism. Astor Ro's face faded. Through the white fire that flooded the crystal, the black

Cygnet flew, imprinting itself in her eye, in her mind. A whispering began, within the prism or her mind. The fierce light died. She held the night sky and the constellations between her hands. As the stars slowly revolved, she drank in knowledge with the night.

The crystal vanished when she finally dropped her hands. The moment of time that had opened for her closed again, hid its treasure. In another moment, she saw Chrysom's effigy on a tomb of black marble, the globe above it, the huge, strange guardians moving restlessly around it. And then that layer of time also hid itself. She stood in the dark at the center of the maze, and watched torchlight mold the stone animals out of the darkness at the top of the wall, before the torchbearer turned the final corner and illumined the moment around her.

She stood in a small circular chamber. The guardians of Chrysom's tomb no longer moved; they surrounded her, half-sculpted out of the marble wall and painted. There was no sign of globe or tomb or effigy. There was only a shadow slanting across the ceiling, which the busy torchlight searched and shaped into the Cygnet in flight.

The Holder carried the torch.

SEVEN

SHE said softly, "I thought so."

Meguet felt the last, familiar layer of time slide into place; she stood again in her own present. "You know what I am."

"I know," the Holder said. "The powers that protect the Cygnet do not keep the Holders ignorant of its guardian. For some time now I have wondered about you." She paused. There was not a pin left in her hair; it flowed wildly down her back. Her eyes looked weary, bruised by conjecture. She added. "You would not have come down here, the Gatekeeper would not have left the gate, unless there was dire need."

Meguet put the back of her hand to her mouth. "The Blind Lady has entered." Her voice trembled. "We looked for her. They were both here, in the maze. Blind Lady and tinker."

The Holder stepped closer; firelight ran over Meguet's dishevelled hair, her singed skirt. "You found them," she said harshly.

"The Gate—Hew—I left him. He was hurt. Dead, maybe." She swallowed, calmed her voice from habit, though she had begun to shake. "I must find him. I had to run—"

"Yes."

"I ran—beyond time, I think. Into the heart of the maze."

"Here."

"Yes, only—within. Within this place. I must go back and find Hew. He fell on his knife."

The Holder closed her eyes. "Moro's name. You cannot go back there."

"I must find him."

"No. I'll send the guard."

"They won't get far enough. They won't get past the periphery. No one does. Except you."

"I came another way," the Holder said obscurely. "Gatekeepers don't kill themselves without regard for the gate."

"He didn't—I knocked him down."

"Oh."

"He was walking into the tinker's house. I—he might have been dead then, I don't know. I tried to kill the tinker."

"It does seem futile." She touched her eyes delicately with her fingers. "The powers you have inherited are formidable, but I don't think you are able to use them to rescue a Gatekeeper. They rouse to protect the Cygnet."

"I know, but—"

"Those two may be waiting for you."

Meguet felt a familiar stillness settle through her, as when she had chosen a path or an action and choice lay in the past, in another time. "Then," she said, "I will meet them."

"Meguet Vervaine, I forbid you to do this!"

"Will you let me take the torch, anyway?" She added, under the Holder's outraged stare, "I am overly fond of your Gatekeeper."

"So you would leave me in the dark."

"I'll light your way back first. It's not far, is it? The way you came in?" She looked around, at the strange menacing figures surrounding them, wearing their bright masks of paint. She had seen them many times, she knew, through many centuries. "It's quite close...." she said surprisedly. The Holder watched her, face impassive. Her fingers lifted, worried her hair for a phantom pin. She gave up, tossing her hand in the air.

"I dislike changing Gatekeepers." She gave Meguet the torch. "Lead."

Meguet bowed her head; the torch shook in her hand, then finally steadied. She turned, and, stepping forward, flung a circle of light around the Gatekeeper.

She stopped, catching breath. He kept moving, slowly, with a weary, dragging persistence, until he was close enough to reach out, gather her against him with one arm. She whispered, "Hew." She put her free arm around him tightly and felt him wince.

She drew back, still holding him lightly. He carried his singed cloak under one arm; there was blood in his hair, a streak of blood along one torn side of his tunic. He smiled a little, then started as the Holder stepped into the light.

They looked at each other for a long time. Then the Gatekeeper let go of Meguet, bent his head respectfully, and the Holder said, "Hew, what are you doing here? This place is for mages and Holders, not Gatekeepers."

"I heard Meguet's voice, my lady. I followed it. Hours, it seems I followed."

"Are you badly hurt?"

"I've been worse, my lady."

"I thought you were dead," Meguet said numbly. "I saw you walking into the tinker's house."

He looked at her wearily. "It's not a tinker you were fighting, my lady Meguet. It's not a tinker lives in that dark house. Down here, there's no one to keep secrets from, unless this cheerful crowd around us."

"That may well be," the Holder said grimly, "but until I know better what danger we're in, I prefer to have only a tinker under my house."

"And a blind weaver, my lady. She got past my sleeping eye."

"I'm not surprised."

"How did you escape from them?" Meguet asked. He shook his head.

"I didn't. I woke up and it was dark and they were gone. So were you. I thought they had you. Then I began to hear your voice. Here, around this corner, there around that, words I couldn't quite hear . . . I was circling you, I think, forever it felt. You never sounded frightened. Never troubled. You were safe, I thought, but I could never find you. It helped me, hearing you, kept me from sitting down and falling asleep." He was holding his arm tightly against his side. Meguet saw him blink away sweat. The Holder said abruptly:

"The house must be in a turmoil by now. Meguet, lead us back up."

Meguet raised the torch above her head, illumined the tall, still, half-human figures ringing them. A horned face, its human part blue, its horns gold, gazed back at her out of blue and gold eyes. She reached out impulsively, touched its clawed, jewelled hand.

It swung gently aside, revealing steps. The Gatekeeper made a sudden noise, of recognition and wonder. "We came down those," he breathed. "My lady Meguet, is there a maze or is there not? Or is this all in the mage's mind?"

"You should know; you walked as much of it as any of us."

"While you spoke, who were you speaking to all that time?"

The lie came easily to her, she found, as they must come, she realized, for the rest of her life. "Only myself," she said, "guiding myself, feeling my way . . ." She opened the small door at the top of the stairs, pushed the heavy, dark banner aside. Through the open doors of the tower, the Gatekeeper's empty turret hung like a delicate carving against a blue-grey dusk.

With the Holder's permission, Meguet helped him back to his cottage. He sat stiffly on the hearth bench, the jagged tear in his side cleaned and dressed, watching her gaze dubiously at his pots.

"I can cook what I have hunted," she confessed finally. "But I'm no good in a kitchen."

"Never mind," he said. He stretched out his good arm. "Sit with me a little, Meguet." She dropped beside him on the bench. Her skirt was torn at the knee where she had fallen; her braid was coming apart; there were, she was certain, smudges of sweat and dust on her face. He kissed her for a long time. Night laid dark wings against the windows; the world was oddly silent.

"No wind," she said at last, surprised. "No rain."

"Stars, maybe. Entire constellations . . ." But neither of them moved to look. "Spring, soon."

She leaned against him, watching the fire, thinking of the tinker's fire. "What happened to you," she asked, "in that gold ring of fire? I saw you walking toward the Gold King's house. Do you remember the open door of his house? It was full of night and stars."

"All I remember is falling."

"That was after, when I pushed you away from the house."

"No, before. When I threw you away from the fire. You hit me with something."

"I didn't."

"You did. That sword you carried. I saw its pommel coming at me. That was that for me until I woke alone in the dark."

"Then you walked in your sleep. Or maybe it was an illusion of you, walking. Or a sending through time, like the Hunter Hold witches. The Blind Lady pulled a thread between her hands while you walked. . . ."

"They didn't harm me." He looked down at her wryly. "You did most of it."

"I did," she said, startled.

"They didn't hurt you?"

"No. I threw your knife at the Gold King. He was armed in gold, then, and crowned, and laughing at me. I hit him."

"Did he drop dead?"

"Not noticeably."

"Then what?"

"Then I ran."

"Did they follow you?"

"I don't—I don't think so."

He grunted. "They were in hiding. Waiting, it seems like. We disturbed them, they showed us a trick or two and then hid themselves again."

"Waiting."

"So it seems."

She was silent. A finger of fire caught color from sap and turned gold. She started. She turned abruptly, caught his arms so tightly he winced. "Hew. When is spring? When is the last day of winter?"

"I don't know. Soon."

"How soon?" She shook him a little, when he didn't answer. "That's what they're waiting for! The Dancer, the Blood Fox's human shadow, the Warlock—"

"The Warlock?"

"The other Hold Signs!" She loosed him, sprang up to pace, thinking furiously. "How many weeks of winter left?"

"Days, more like." He watched her, nursing his side, his face hard, expressionless as always when he was disturbed. "I must watch for a Warlock now, at the gate. And all the Hold Councils themselves beginning to come soon. What do you see in all this, Meguet?"

She whirled, her face white. "I have to stop him."

"Who?"

"The Wayfolk man with Nyx. He's going to Berg Hold, to wake the Dancer. On the last day of winter."

"He'd be gone by now," Hew said, and brought her to a halt in front of him. "Unless he can fly across Ro Holding. Wayfolk don't fly. But they're not afraid to travel."

She swung to the hearth, brought her fist down on the stones. Then she dropped her face against her arm. "I'll leave now. Tonight."

"You'll never make it. Never to Berg Hold by winter's end. You might make it past the Delta."

"Then what?" she said bitterly. "Will we stop the Dancer coming in the way we stopped the Blind Lady? I can't do anything right. I try and try and only make things worse."

"Why is it you who should be trying? You, more than the Holder or Nyx or Rush Yarr? Why, Meguet? Why is it you must stop the Wayfolk man in Berg Hold?"

Because I can! she said fiercely, but only to herself, her eyes still hidden in the crook of her arm. She felt him pull at her gently.

"Don't. Not twice in one day. I'll watch, this time. I swear. Day and night."

She turned her head, gazed down at him, dry-eyed. "I must get to Berg Hold."

"But how?"

"Rush. Maybe he learned something useful from Nyx. Or the witches of Hunter Hold. Maybe they know a way I could walk through time. I could get to Hunter Hold before winter's end."

"Rush Yarr's sorcery might land you in the middle of Wolfe Sea."

"I have to risk something! It's because of the Wayfolk man these things are happening. I don't know how or why, but he is dangerous, and I must stop him."

"With what?" he demanded. "With what power? Moro Ro's sword that you have to hold steady with both hands? Why you? Why you that must fling yourself across Ro Holding into the endless snows of Berg Hold to keep the Dancer from dancing?"

"For the same reason that you watch the gate, night and day, summer and winter. Because you must. I have old eyes in me, Hew. Old voices. They make me see, they make me do what I can. I was born rooted to the past in this house." She added, "The Wayfolk man needs no power to be stopped. I could threaten him with Moro Ro's sword and he would take it seriously. All I need to do is get there. . . ."

"Take the house," he suggested. "It used to fly for Moro Ro." She stared at him. "That way I wouldn't have to fret about you."

"Chrysom moved it."

"Did he?"

"During the Hold Wars."

"Well," he said, "from the sound of it, that's what we may be heading toward. Did he take that power with him when he died? Or did he leave something to the next Holder, in case of trouble in the Delta?"

"I don't—I don't know."

"Who would know?"

"I don't know." She pushed her hands against her eyes.

"Rush Yarr?"

Her hands dropped. She gazed down at him, then she bent swiftly and kissed him. "Calyx."

"You want to move my house where?" the Holder said incredulously.

"The highest peak in Berg Hold," Calyx said. She was at a table in Chrysom's library, walling herself up with books.

"It would fall off," Iris said practically.

"Well, then as close as possible to the top. Meguet could climb the rest of the way. If people are meant to consult the Dancer, there must be a way for them to get up."

"I'm coming with Meguet," Rush said. "To protect her from the Fire Bear."

"This house hasn't moved in centuries!"

"Does everything go?" Iris wondered. "Barns, hen coops, the thousand-year-old wood?"

"Tinker and Blind Lady?" Rush asked. The Holder, gazing at Meguet, toying with the amber around her neck, shook her head.

"It's no longer possible. Is it?"

"The house was made to move."

"Across Ro Holding?"

"Legend," Calyx murmured with satisfaction, "says so. Legend says that during a siege by the Delta armies, the house moved to the northern fields of Withy Hold."

"Legend," Iris said sharply and poked her needle through cloth. "It's a thousand-year-old tale."

"So," Rush said grimly, "is what we've got living beneath this tower."

"Either this house goes to Berg Hold," Meguet said, "or Rush must find a way to send me there."

"If you want to get there, you'd better take the house," Calyx said.

"I think it's safer to guard the gate against the Dancer," Iris said. "What will people think if Ro House vanishes?"

"We'll bring it back," Calyx said, flipping pages. "The question is: Who actually moved it, during Moro Ro's time?"

"Chrysom must have," the Holder said.

"Maybe he left a spell," Rush suggested.

"I'm looking," Calyx said. She added, "You could help, instead of pacing around and shaking Chrysom's things up." Rush, tossing something iridescent in his hand, moved to her side. Meguet watched them turning pages in rhythm, their heads bowed over books, absorbed. She saw Iris watching also, a curious smile in her eyes. She threaded her needle through cloth and put it down.

"If the witches warned of the Blind Lady, why didn't they warn of the Dancer?"

"The Blind Lady weaves time," Meguet said. "The witches explore it. They consider the Blind Lady nothing more than a childish tale of life and death. Until she walked down one of their paths, and they saw the Lady's face."

"I don't understand any of this," Iris sighed. "I don't see how you could make any sense at all of a tinker in Chrysom's maze."

"The house," Calyx said suddenly, "was moved two hundred years after the Hold Wars." Her face was suffused with a delicate rose; finding a foot-print on the trail of some historical mystery gave her pleasure.

"By Chrysom?" the Holder asked.

"No. He had been dead for fifty years. By Brigen Ro's oldest son. He moved it from the Delta to the black desert of Hunter Hold."

"Why?"

"It's not clear. . . . Brigen Ro was upset and made him bring it back im-mediately. There is a reference by Brigen's son to one of Chrysom's books."

"Nyx probably has it," Iris said, picking up her needlework again.

"No, it's here. Brigen's son, apparently, just moved the house to see if he could. He sounds like you, Rush."

"Thank you."

"But what," Meguet asked, "made him think he could?"

"Let's find out," Calyx said, picking up a small, frail book with letters on the cover in faded silver, "what Crysom has to say."

They watched her, while she turned pages silently. Meguet too restless to sit, moved next to the Holder beside the fire, and wished that, when she had changed out of her torn skirt, she had put on a string of beads to worry. But she stood with her usual calm, back against the hearth, hiding a terrible impatience.

Calyx made a satisfied noise. "Here we are. According to Chrysom, the power to move Ro House is passed from generation to generation of Holders' children, who are born with an innate ability, for the Holders instinctively seek out as mates those who may inspire the power within the child conceived."

The Holder looked startled. Iris murmured, "Really, Calyx."

"So Chrysom says."

The Holder cleared her throat. "All children? Or one, specifically?"

"Nyx," Rush said shortly.

"No." Calyx looked solemnly at her mother. "Always and inevitably the first."

They all gazed at Iris. She put down her needlework uncertainly, flushing. The Holder's brows had risen. She pulled pin out of her hair absently, her mind running down the past; a smile, reminiscent, wondering, touched her eyes.

"Mother," Iris said accusingly.

"Well, I didn't know," the Holder said. "He seemed a very practical man."

"I can't move this house."

"Chrysom says you can."

"He's been dead for nine hundred years!"

"Eight hundred and fifty," Rush corrected.

"I don't have any gifts for magic! I never had any."

"You have one," Calyx said. She sat back in her chair, smoothing a strand of hair back into place. She narrowed her eyes at her sister. "Iris Ro, you are not going to sit there and tell us you won't even try! You must. For the sake of this House. It is your duty."

Iris stared back at her, mouth pinched. Then she looked at Meguet, standing motionless at the fire, her eyes enormous, dark with urgency in her pale face. She flung her needlework down and got to her feet.

"It won't work."

Calyx smiled.

Iris was still protesting on the night before the last day of winter, but with less conviction. Midnight was the preferred time, Chrysom suggested, if possible, since people and animals would be less disturbed than by leaping in broad daylight from one Hold to another. Meguet and Rush spent the day finding merchants, guests and other assorted visitors, and persuading them to shelter somewhere in the city. At dusk, when the household was sorted out, and the last visitor had departed, she had climbed wearily to the Gatekeeper's turret, sat with him silently, watching the sun go down over the grey, crumpled sea. She could smell spring now, from the swamps: a hint of perfume over the layered scents of still water and mold, all overlaid with the wash of brine from the outgoing tide. A single swan rose high above the lake; the Gatekeeper said drily, watching it. "This'll save them a flight north."

Near midnight she stood on top of Chrysom's tower, with Rush and the Holder and her children. The wind-whipped Cygnet flew above them on its black pennant. Above it the constellation itself flew in and out of thin, bright clouds. The full moon that had blinded the Lady of Withy Hold hung white as bone in the sky.

Iris stood silently, apart from them. She must, Calyx instructed her endlessly, root herself as fast as Chrysom's rose vines to every stone, mouse, dirty pot, child and chick, sleeping peacock, weed, swan and thousand-year-old tree within the rambling walls of Ro House. Iris had explained as endlessly that she couldn't, no one could, it was not possible. . . . But she said nothing now; her profile, under flickering light, looked unfamiliar in its calm. She was gazing down at the yard, one hand on the stones, as if she were watching a horse race, or children playing. She had stood like that for an hour.

Clouds swarmed over the moon, swallowed it. Meguet, watching a fleet of night fishers on the sea, saw them vanish suddenly, as if they had all slid down into the black water. Her lips parted; she held the parapet stones, waiting for the wind to hit. She heard Rush's sudden breath. But no wind came: There was only a dark like the darkness in dreams through which they floated, a quick scratch of light across the ground below now and then, and all the constellations shifting in a stately dance above. She smelled a hint of green from Withy Hold, no more than a thought of leaves in the quickening trees. In the charmed silence no one spoke. Meguet sensed stirrings behind her, a gathering that she dared not turn to see, as if the ghosts that frequented Chrysom's tower—mages, guardians, the odd son or daughter drawn to sorcery—had come up to watch the stars. If she turned, she knew, she would see nothing: They might have been there, in the endlessly folded tissue of time, or they had never been there.

She smelled snow. In a moment or two the wind struck: a blast as bare and merciless as frozen stone. A white peak loomed over Ro House like a jagged tooth. The stars had disappeared. Snow, torn like spindrift off the crest of the mountain, scattered over them. Calyx reached out to Iris, gripped her hand, and she lifted her head, startled. They all ran for the stairs.

They huddled next to the fire, shivering, drinking wine. The shadowed, vulnerable expression in Iris's eyes caused the Holder to say fretfully, "You will only have to do this once more. Then never again, I hope."

Iris, crouched close to the flames, looked at her. She said softly, "I carried everyone's dreams . . . it was like moving the world in a bubble. I even saw my child's dream. I know where that ring you lost is, Calyx. I know where all the mice live, in every crevice. I know what the peacocks see in the dark. I sensed those in the house that do not belong here. Only they were hidden. Only they . . . And the Gatekeeper. I had trouble keeping track of the Gatekeeper. I kept mistaking him for other things."

"The gate, most likely," Meguet suggested. "Sometimes I think he himself gets lost in it."

"And you, Meguet. I kept mistaking you for ghosts."

"Ghosts," Rush repeated. The wild winds fluting through the tower seemed to echo the word. Iris smiled at him tranquilly.

"Oh, yes. They all came, too."

Meguet woke before dawn. She could scarcely see the Gatekeeper at the wall, though by the faint red glow of his brazier she knew that Iris had not forgotten him. She dressed swiftly, went down to the armory where she found Rush choosing a sword. Horses were already saddled, waiting for them. The household, considerably startled at finding itself snowbound, had not ceased its smooth operation. The early winds eased as the sun rose. A wave of fire washed down the mountain, splashed around them: the warning of the Fire Bear.

The Gatekeeper opened the gate, his face impassive as Meguet rode through. She looked at him briefly, her own face settled into a stiff, deceptive calm. Neither spoke.

The path up the mountain was narrow, rubble-filled, steep. The edge of the world fell away from them, it seemed, on one side; on the other, bare slabs of rock, the bones of the mountain, pushed upward toward the top of the sky. They rode until the path grew too rough for the horses. A gold, raging face sprang at them as they rounded a turn on foot, breathed fire over the white world below. Meguet, shielding her face from the sun, said breathlessly, "I can smell it. I can almost taste it."

"What?"

"The end of winter." A sudden panic seized her; she pulled herself over crumbled boulder, past the solitary, twisted, stunted trees. "Hurry, Rush."

"We'll break our necks."

"Hurry."

Shadows were peeling off the mountain as the sun climbed higher. Meguet, sun in her face constantly, wondered if the Fire Bear had roared this golden light at the Cygnet. She increased her pace, breath tearing at her, and saw, from the very top of the mountain, a blinding flash of silver.

She cried, "Rush!" He was beside her, then not, as she pulled herself up, clinging to anything solid: rock, icicle, even, she thought, the blinding surface of the snow, light, and shadow.

Something bulky blocked the sun, hissed at her. She nearly slid down the mountain. The Fire Bear was white as snow, with red eyes and red claws; it paced just above her on a flat, bald slab of granite, shaking its shaggy head, trying to hiss fire. Then, fretfully, it turned away, its attention caught, and she pulled herself onto the stones, the breath running in and out of her like fire. She heard Rush call her name, but she could neither move nor speak.

The Fire Bear was busy eating fire. It was a blue-black flame the Wayfolk man had laid on the snow, and it seemed to take its fuel from the snow. Corleu's back was to her; the Fire Bear was between them. He stood looking down at a smooth ice sculpture that lay like a statue on the top of the peak. He spoke.

Meguet moved forward. The Fire Bear saw her move, but busily ate its fire. Corleu's eyes were on the beautiful face trapped within the ice at his feet; he said, as Meguet stepped beside him, "Is that all you can tell me?"

He was shivering, lightly clad; his face looked raw in the cold. Meguet wondered suddenly how he had climbed the mountain in those clothes, and what he had done with his footprints.

"Ask the Blood Fox," the Dancer murmured, her eyes open, but unseeing. "Take him a gift."

"What gift?" There was no answer; he raised his voice desperately. "What gift?" Then he saw Meguet, a tall, black-clad figure holding with both her hands a sword that hovered near his heart.

He stepped back, his breath scraping in horror. He recognized her; she saw that in his eyes, as well as a reckless despair that made him tense to run, to attack. But there was nowhere to run, and Moro Ro's sword was dogging his every move.

"In the name of the Holder and the Cygnet, you must come with me."

The Fire Bear roared.

Black flame washed over them. Blind, Meguet leaped, felt cloth, bone in her grasp. Then she stumbled; they both fell against the ice-statue, who turned under them, murmuring, then turned again. Corleu pulled free; Meguet, finding him again in the dispersing mist, saw him stop mid-pace, stare at the Dancer.

She rose in a fluid, graceful movement. Smiling, she stepped out of the pool of melting ice. Her hair fell to her feet, one side white, the other black. She shook it back, laughing, and raised her hands to the sun.

Corleu shouted, "No!" He backed a step, another. And then a silver circle floated around him, and he vanished into it. The Dancer turned a circle, faster and faster, until her hair whipped around her, black and white. The black and white blurred into snow and shadow.

The Fire Bear blew a final breath of night and shambled over the edge of the world.

Meguet stood alone, on the top of a mountain on the top of the world, listening to the spring wind.

PART THREE

HEART
OF THE
CYGNET

ONE

WHO is she?" Corleu demanded. "She stood in front of me with her eyes the only color in the world. She came out of nowhere to the top of that mountain like she knew I would be there, on that one day of all days in the year, she knew I would step across time from Delta to Berg Hold, and she came to meet me. I turned and there she was, holding that blade at my heart and all I could see was green, like the green of the cornfields of Withy Hold in late summer." He was pacing; Nyx, curled in a chair, listened without moving, except her eyes, following him as he wove a convoluted path between chairs and book piles and the tiny round jar holding time. "Her eyes and her hair like when you tear the green leaves off corn and the pale silk holds to your fingers."

"Why," Nyx asked curiously, "are you comparing my cousin Meguet to a corncob?"

"Because that's what I think of when I see her. My greatgran's tale of Rider in the Corn. Green, she said, his eyes corn leaves and his hair corn silk. That's all she ever said of him. He lay with her among the corn and then rode on."

Nyx gazed at him expressionlessly out of her colorless eyes. Her fingers found a loose button on her sleeve, toyed with it. "That's a preposterous idea."

"I know."

"You and Meguet related."

"Moonbrained."

"She is a descendant of Moro Ro's wife."

"And I'm nothing but Wayfolk. Almost nothing."

A thin line ran across her brow. "What I want to know is what she was doing on that mountain. Did she hear you speak to the Dancer?"

He closed his eyes, sank into one of the chairs that for some reason were cluttering the workroom that morning. "I don't know." He dropped his hand over his eyes. "Dancer is freed."

"What did you expect when you gave that fire to the Fire Bear?" she asked. He stared at her, felt the blood leap furiously into his face.

"You did—You knew—" He was on his feet suddenly, his fists clenched. Her cold eyes did not flicker. He whirled, found a door and let his fists slam into it. From within he heard the fluttering of startled birds. He dropped his face against the door, felt the sting of tears in the back of his eyes.

"Corleu," she said softly, "to get what you want, you must give what they want. What did the Dancer say?"

"She said," he whispered into the wood, " 'ask the Blood Fox.' " She was silent. He turned finally, found her gazing in conjecture at a twisted candle.

"Blood Fox . . . Last of the Hold Signs." She drew breath. "So. That is why Meguet went to meet you in Berg Hold. Those powers you are waking must be finding their way into Ro House." She rose abruptly, turned to him; he saw a shadow of color the candlelight dragged into her eyes. "You ask the Blood Fox."

"That'll be Warlock." He swallowed drily. "I saw his shadow once."

"Did the Dancer say anything else?"

"She said, 'The thing sought lies always in the same place, but always in a different place, and that place is never far from the Cygnet.' It's no help."

"Of course it is. Something near the Cygnet . . . a web. The Cygnet flies above it day and night. . . . What gift did she say to give the Blood Fox?"

"She didn't. But I figured out that one. Any smallfolk knows. 'Shadow fox, fox shadow, hide your face, hide your shadow—' It's a hiding a game."

"Go on."

" 'Red star, blood star, find your eyes and see, find your—' "

"The Blood Star."

"Cygnet broke the Warlock into pieces and trapped him in the Blood Star. What—what will happen—"

"I don't know." Her face seemed colorless in the shadows. "But it's too late to undo."

"How do I get the Blood Star to give it?" he asked her. "Hang on the horns of the moon and pick it out of the sky?"

"You make it." She began pacing then, her feet following an independent path of thought. "And you make it fast. I don't know how Meguet got to Berg Hold, but I doubt that she took the long way. Rush helped her, maybe. When she returns to the Delta, she'll come to this house. She knows where to find you. And she wants you."

"Why her? Why did she come for me?"

"I don't know. She's a mystery to me. She never was before this. She was only Meguet."

"There's nothing 'only' about her," he said. "She nearly sent me diving off the mountain, with her eyes and her sword. How do I make a Blood Star? With a wish and an adage?"

"Almost. It's a very old, very primitive sorcery. The Blood Star does not threaten, foretell, defend. It is all but useless except as a kind of lantern or guide between separated lovers. The effort far exceeds the results, which is why the making is rarely heard of, now. There are much simpler ways of keeping track of people than fusing your heart's blood into a glass ball."

"Mine."

"A drop or three."

"I can spare that, likely. Where do I take it, though? Where would Blood Fox be, in the Delta?"

"There's a place upriver, a strange place that resonates with ancient power. Long ago someone sensed the power, and carved statues among the trees there. One statue was of the Blood Fox as human. Or as warlock."

He nodded. "Trappers passed that place when they brought me here. I remember the Blood Fox."

"You'll make the Blood Star there. The Blood Fox will find you."

He was silent, remembering the shift of tree into blood fox into man, all one, all rooted in the still water. "She'll know this is the last of them."

"Meguet?"

"Will she know this place?"

"She has roamed in and out of the swamps since we were children. She'd know it, I think, but perhaps only as a garden of statues, not as a place of power."

"Because she has no power," he said evenly.

She eyed him. "Maybe it's not such a moonbrained idea after all. She does have some kin in Withy Hold. Do you want to see her again?"

"No."

"Then I suggest we assume she will be at your heels like your shadow. Get something to eat. Then I will teach you how to make the Blood Star."

Later, he borrowed the boat from the silent ghost, who bestirred herself in her pearls and laces to fade into the afternoon. He placed a lit, shuttered lantern at the bow and rowed through slow, tangled paths where the hanging vines were just beginning to flush with green. On a sandy bank beside the statue grove, he pulled the boat ashore. In the dying light he gathered wood. The night fell quickly, a dense darkness unrelieved by stars or moon. The bitter cold that he felt did not disperse when he lit the fire with the boat lantern. The fire itself—made from odd things—was yellow as a hunter's moon.

He carried pale, damp, rough sand from the bank and added river water to it. He worked it into a ball the size of his fist. As he molded and smoothed it, he murmured under his breath, over and over, the old rhyme he had known since he could find his feet and walk. Sweating, fire-scorched, mesmerized by his own monotonous voice, he laid the ball of sand in the fire. He watched it thoughtlessly, still murmuring, as the gold fire licked it. When it had turned black, he lifted it out again and broke it in half.

He slid a tough razor-edged piece of marsh grass over the forefinger of his left hand. Then he teased a bit of flame out of the fire onto the grass, laid the flame carefully in the center of one of the broken halves. He fed the flame three drops of his blood. The flame ran from gold to blood red. He closed the halves, laid the ball into the fire again. After a time, during which swamp animals came rustling to the edge of his light to watch, he pulled the ball out again. This time, with the heated blade of the silver knife he had taken from the house, he began to sculpt the sides of the ball. Molten silver from the blade, blood from his hand, streaked the dark sand as he worked. Sweat rolled into it from his face; words seeped into it, mingling with the river water. He layered the sphere with flat planes angling against one another. When he finished that, he was ringed with watching eyes.

He put the faceted ball into the fire. His voice stilled finally. Around him the night was soundless, in the slow, lightless empty hours between midnight and dawn. The fire flared, flared again, washing silver, crimson, black. The small dark ball in the heart of it began to glow.

The eyes around him blinked suddenly out, like vanishing stars. He heard the sighing passage through the underbrush of many small, invisible animals. Then he heard something else: a blood fox's sharp bark in the distance. Another answered, just behind his back.

He heard that as from a distance, too. Everything seemed detached from him: the heat of the fire, the burns on his hands, his dry aching throat, the appalling, lonely silence of the night. More eyes ringed the fire, some high as his knee and higher, others close to the ground. All were a smoky, red-tinged amber.

The ball in the fire had turned clear as glass, red as blood.

He did not touch it. The fire sank around it, yellow again. He stood up. A great blood fox walked into the light. The fur on its massive shoulders was bristling. Its eyes were cloudy, yellow with the fire. It was dancing a little, singing its high, eerie whine before it barked and attacked. The shadow stretching from its hind paws beyond the fire's circle was not an animal's.

"Shadow Fox, fox shadow," Corleu said to it. His voice was so hoarse it might have been the blood fox's growl.

"Hide your face, hide your shadow.
Red star, blood star,
Find your face, find your shadow,
Find your heart and follow."

He reached into the fire, drew out the star that hid a pearl of blood in its heart and caught fire in all its glittering facets.

The blood fox stood silent as the trees around it. Its eyes burned into Corleu's; they seemed suddenly faceted, like the Blood Star. For a moment, his detachment vanished under that inhuman gaze; he wanted to wrap the dark around him like a cloak and slip away before he became a human swarm of blood foxes, furious with him for disturbing the Delta night.

The Blood Fox faded away. A darkness formed where it had been, shaped a man in the firelight, a patch of night with a face that shifted, blurred, re-formed. Corleu stared at it, his thoughts reeling between terror and wonder; he felt as if he were falling again through that long, black, starry night in the Gold King's house.

"You have something I want," the shadow said. Its face stilled enough to form: long, sharp-jawed, red-browed; then the lines of it fractured again. Its voice was deep, husky, a blood fox voice. Corleu swallowed.

"I made it for you."

A shadowy hand reached toward it, passed through it, darkening it briefly. At the cold touch Corleu, trapped between shadow and fire, would have backed into the fire if he could have made himself move. He glimpsed eyes, amber flames swarming across them.

"What do you want for that?" the shadow asked with a snap of teeth.

"Just—just a small thing."

"That's a small thing. That's my heart you hold in your hand. Be careful what you ask for, or I'll set a blood fox shadowing you to nuzzle out your heart."

"I'm not—It's not for me I'm asking."

"Who then? Who sent you?"

"The King in the dark."

The shadow made a complex sound, part human, part blood fox's curious whine. "So the King goes hunting. . . . You put your heart's blood into that. Into my heart. You want something worth that much to you. Corleu. That's your name. You've said my name now and then in your life."

"I'm sorry I ever learned to talk," he said starkly, and the shadowy face gave a lean, sharp-toothed grin.

"There is no idle chatter in the world. So here you stand with my heart in your hand, asking nothing for yourself?"

"I'm to be paid later."

"To be paid. Or to pay?"

His voice shook. "Both."

"I know that King, with his heart of fire. He stalks everyone's days. What does he want? What small thing?"

"Something hidden away in secret for safekeeping. The Gold King told me to go to Withy Hold, offer the Lady there a peacock feather and ask. She told me to take fire and ask the Dreamer on the top of the world. Dreamer told me to ask you. All of them gave me pieces of a puzzle, none of them a whole answer. So I made this for you." It burned in his hand with cold fire. He wiped at sweat and smoke on his face. "I need you to finish the puzzle."

"How small is this thing that sent you wandering the world?"

"Small as the heart of something wild that flies by night over Ro Holding."

The shadow was still; even the lines hinting of bone-structure stilled briefly, and gave Corleu a clear glimpse of its honed, red-furred, feral face. It made a soft whistling noise, like a branch keening on the fire, and blurred again. "He's been thinking, that King. . . . And you are feet and hands and eyes to find it. What of yours does he hold hostage?"

"My heart," he whispered.

"Give me mine. I will tell you what I know."

"How?" he asked, his heart pounding in sudden hope. "How do I give it?"

"Lay the Blood Star in the fire."

Corleu knelt close to the flames, let the prism slide among them. Just before the flames closed over it, he saw the jumbled patchwork of a man in all its facets.

The shadow stepped into the fire. Flames flared high above his head, closed like the petals of a burning flower. Corleu flung himself back, watched, breathless, as the flames swirled and parted, died down again and the Warlock stepped out of them.

He stood over Corleu, grinning his fox's grin, lean-flanked, his shoulders bunched with muscle, the hair on his head and body the red of the blood fox's pelt. He tossed black, broken pieces of the prism in his hands, juggled them a moment into a whirling black circle.

"The thing you seek is well hidden, even from that King's gold fingers, which go everywhere. But I have heard, in all my eons of wandering, dragged after a Blood Fox with its nose to the wind and its ear pricked to every whisper: The thing you seek will be reflected in the eye of the Cygnet."

"Reflected in—But what does that mean?" he cried. "It's only another riddle!"

"That's all I know."

He let the pieces of the prism fall into one broad palm. Then he covered them with the other. When he opened his hands again, the black glass had fused into a swan in flight.

He dropped it into the fire. It exploded, flinging glass, burning wood, shards of flame, into the night. Corleu, still crouched, ducked behind his arms. All around him he heard the whisper and crackle of leaves as the animals scuttled away.

"Thanks," the Warlock said. "I'll remember you."

"The web. The eye. The Cygnet."

Nyx was pacing. Corleu, slumped in a chair, watched her. It had taken him the rest of the night to return, and for what, he wondered bitterly, as he climbed the shivering stairway near dawn. What he sought was only tale. Just a story, a lie, to set him moving, rousing all the sleeping powers in the Holds. The thing was a dream, a lure to catch a Wayfolk fool, to trap his thoughts, keep his eyes from seeing what his hands were waking.

He said as much to Nyx. She stopped mid-step, looked at him with her cold, searching, inscrutable eyes.

"If you think that, you are a fool. The thing itself is of more power than what you are waking. Why else would it be so carefully hidden?"

"What's to be done, then?"

"Be quiet and let me think. . . ." She paced barefoot, a heavy gown of grey velvet swinging as she turned. She had been awake all night, he judged; her eyes looked luminous, and her temper was short. "If these powers disturbed Ro House enough to catch Meguet's eye, then that's where they all will gather. The place where the Cygnet flies, day and night. That's the place of power that draws them: Ro House. Tell me again."

He told her wearily, for the hundredth time. "A secret at the center of the web, over which Cygnet flies, day and night. That was Blind Lady."

"The Dancer."

"The thing sought lies always in the same place, but always in a different place, and that place is never far from the Cygnet."

"The Warlock."

"The thing you seek will be reflected in the eye of the Cygnet."

"Cygnet. Cygnet. Cygnet." She whirled, to contemplate him again, her arms folded, her mouth taut. "The thing you seek, Corleu, belongs to the Cygnet, I would guess. An ancient power that's waking other ancient powers. Not even Chrysom hinted of anything like this. I want it, as badly as I do not want the Gold King to keep it."

"You're still not forcing me to tell you."

"That wouldn't be finding it, would it. You'd never see Tiel again, and you would hate me, and refuse to find this thing at all. Then we'd have chaos on our hands at Ro House. If not already. Ro House . . . A web. The Cygnet flying . . ." She stood still then, still as one of the carved, dead trees in the statue grove, her hands open at her sides, her head bowed, contemplating her reflection in the water. He couldn't hear her breathe. Finally he heard the statue speak. "The maze."

"What?"

She lifted her head, her face white, still. He had never seen such color in her eyes. "Chrysom's maze. The black tower. The Cygnet pennant that flies on the tower roof, summer, winter, day and night. The secret of where to find this thing is at the center of Chrysom's maze."

"Where is that?" he asked wearily. "Where do I go this time?"

"To the house of the Holders of Ro Holding."

Two

MEGUET stood at the edge of the lake beyond the thousand-year-old wood, watching the swans. Iris had brought the house back to the Delta; the swans, casting black and white shadows on the surface of the water, wove a tranquil dance among themselves. Used to flight, they seemed unsettled by the flight of Ro House. Meguet, drawn out of sleep by a dream of them, had slipped out at dawn. Every image in the dream, every word, had transformed itself into swan, until their elegant, masked, enigmatic faces had crowded into her mind. She had carried all their faces across the misty pastures, past the dark, dreaming wood. Finally, at the lake, the swans had shifted from her mind into her eyes: The great company clustered in the lake as usual, busily feeding. She felt her mind empty of them, grow still, peaceful.

A swan detached itself from the group in the middle of the lake. It glided toward the shore where Meguet stood. She watched it thoughtlessly. It was huge, as black as if it had flown straight out of midnight. Its smooth, steady drift toward her was soothing, almost a dream itself. It drew quite close, so close she could see the dark, steady gaze of its reflection. She blinked, surprised, for the swans kept to the far shore. It breasted the shallows, came on, its graceful head lifted as if to meet her eyes. Fully awake now, she watched it, not moving, not breathing. It stirred the muddy bottom, so close she might have touched it, or it her, extending its strong, quick, danger-ous neck.

It roused so suddenly that she started. For a moment the air was black with feathers. Its wings beat; rising, it drew a wet wing tip across her lips. Darkness thundered around her, tangled in her hair. She caught her breath; lifting her face, she saw the sky again. Sunlight shot across the lake. She tasted lake water on her lips, felt it on her face. The great swan had vanished, like the night, into light.

She turned finally, startled, wondering. Sunlight raced across meadow, pasture, illumined the back towers, but could not reach across them to Chrysom's tower, still shrouded in its darkness. As she looked at it, wings filled her mind again: dark crow wings rustling with uneasiness.

In the west tower, all the kitchen chimneys were smoking. The first of the Hold Councils was due soon. A messenger, arriving to request a guide through the swamps for a Council, assorted family, curious kin, retinue, bag and baggage, had spent a night wondering where Ro House had gone. The house was back the next morning. Meguet, greeting the messenger, had seen him torn between asking and appearing lunatic. "Hunter Hold Council," he said, and the household bustled with preparations.

Meguet, walking into that tower in search of breakfast, found the Holder, surrounded by half the tower staff. She caught Meguet's eye, sent them all flying, and gestured Meguet into an antechamber.

It was a tiny room off the main tower door, close as a bear cave and chilly even in midsummer, with a double thickness of stone. Even the chairs were stone: ledges beside the fire, in the windowless walls. There Moro Ro had taken council with Chrysom, where not even a mouse could overhear without being seen.

The Holder swung the door to with a thud that cut short all sound. It was, Meguet thought, like being entombed.

"Tell me what you dreamed," the Holder said abruptly. She looked pale, edgy; Meguet tensed at the question.

"I dreamed of swans."

"Living or dead?"

She felt the blood leave her face. "Living."

"I dreamed all my children were dead." She turned, grabbed the poker, toppled the neatly burning pile of logs on the grate so that they nearly slid onto the floor. "Rush dreamed that Nyx had become something so terrible that he did not recognize her. He shouted at me this morning because I refused to let him ride upriver with you. If this is something—" She stopped, began again. "If this is something of Nyx's doing, I can't let him go there."

"No," Meguet said flatly, and the Holder looked at her, hope waging against suspicion in her eyes. "I would sooner suspect the Gatekeeper of intending harm to this house."

"Then what is troubling this house?" the Holder demanded, her voice rising in relief. "Even Iris was in tears this morning. Iris hasn't cried since she was two. I haven't even seen Calyx. She shut herself up in Chrysom's library."

"The Dancer is troubling this house. The Dreamer of Berg Hold. We brought her with us."

"But how? How did she get in? The Gatekeeper never left the gate, he never opened the gate—that was my command."

"I don't know." She rubbed her eyes wearily. "I don't know how she got in. Maybe she followed me off the mountain top. I couldn't even stop an unarmed Wayfolk man from getting away from me. How could I stop the Dancer?"

"You're supposed to know such things! It's your heritage, your duty to protect the Cygnet."

"I know," she whispered.

"Then, where were those in you who should advise you? Weren't you listening to them?"

"I thought—I thought so. Maybe I haven't learned how yet."

"You'd better learn fast. We have the Hunter Hold Council on our doorstep and a mad dreamer under our beds. What's next?"

"Worse," Meguet said tightly. The Holder's eyes widened.

"What worse?"

"The Warlock."

The Holder pulled a pearl out of her hair and flung it across the room. "Send the Gatekeeper to me."

Meguet gave him the message, then sat in the turret, watching the gate and waiting for him. A company of hunters rode out; no one requested entry. The Gatekeeper returned soon, his face impassive. Meguet asked him, as he joined her:

"What did you dream?"

"Of you." He reached across, took her hands, warmed his own. "No good watching for the Warlock."

"Why not?"

"He'll get in. Like the Dancer, he'll come when he comes."

Meguet slumped back against the stones. "Did you tell the Holder that?"
"Yes."

"Did she believe you?"

"No. I told her Dancer must have danced herself over the wall, because I kept a lizard's eye on that gate night and day in Berg Hold. What did you dream?"

"Just swans."

He smiled his quick, tight smile. He leaned forward, kissed her gently. "Don't blame yourself so."

"If we hadn't gone to Berg Hold—"

"The Dancer would have come to us here." He watched her. "And if, and when the Warlock comes?"

She shuddered. "Don't say it. Words come to life, these days."

"What then? What are they gathering for, like crows on a carcass? What's in that maze but a wizard's time-picked bones?"

"It's a place to hide."

"For what? Until when?"

"I don't know!" she flared. "Don't push at me with questions, I am so tired of hearing that answer from myself. I don't know, I don't know, I don't know." He was silent; she raised her eyes finally, found a curious, dispassionate expression in his light eyes.

"You beg such questions," he said abruptly. "If only because you're the one in this house thinking for the house. And you get angry with me because I see that."

"I told you," she said helplessly, "I am part of this house. A lintel, a casement, a stone seat in a stone wall, some old walled-up grate that hasn't been on fire since Chrysom's time."

"A lintel." He pulled her hands to his mouth. "An old grate. A tower, more like. Chrysom's tower, strong, mysterious and covered with roses." He opened her hand against his mouth, said, breathlessly, head bowed, "Will I come to you, or will you come to me?"

"Come to me." She opened her other hand, laid it against her eyes. "At least in the tower you can see the gate."

"For whatever use."

"The Holder should send for Nyx."

He removed her ring finger from his mouth. "Nyx."

"She could fight a Warlock. She's a sorceress."

"And bog witch, which is of more use. They don't fight clean." He kissed the center of her palm, then relinquished her hand. "She's coming home for the Council. So I heard. Gossip about Nyx doesn't stand around idle."

"I think," Meguet said, "that won't be soon enough." She rose, edged past him. "We've given the yard enough to talk about this morning. I'm leaving tomorrow to ride upriver."

"With Rush Yarrow?"

"No. With an armed guard. I want that Wayfolk man. He's the one who can answer questions."

"When will you leave?"

"At dawn."

"So," he said, meeting her eyes. "Meguet."

A swan wing, glistening, crossed her mind. She said, "Midnight."

She rode across the yard the next morning with twenty of the household guard behind her, all in black, with a black, silken pennant flying overhead. The Gatekeeper, crossing in front of her to open the gate, looked up at her briefly. She saw night in his eyes, swamp leaves, secret, wind-stirred pools. His thoughts dragged at her; she closed her eyes, set her face resolutely toward the gate. Behind her eyes were moving, fire-edged shadows. A silver goblet spilled wine over white fur. She heard the gate open. She rode forward mechanically, her eyes on the road between the gateposts, where the Gatekeeper, moving, laid his shadow across her path.

Slowed as they were by spring-swollen ground, by water flooded with storm-pushed tides and snow melting in the upper lands, they reached Nyx's house at mid-morning two days later. It looked more shrunken than mysterious in the spring light. Vines tugged at it here and there, threatening to encroach beneath a window sash, to pull off a corner beam. A motley gathering of old boats set the company on the dock. Meguet took two guards with her; they climbed the stairs cautiously.

Nyx came out to meet them on the porch. She looked dishevelled, dressed in threadbare velvet; her long dark hair fell untidily past her waist. Her face was pale, lean, smudged with tiredness and what looked like old ashes. She said, frowning:

"Meguet." She cast a glance at the group on the dock, and her frown grew pinched. "If you've come for me, that's far too many for courtesy, and far too few to do any good. I told you I would return home in spring."

"If I had come for you," Meguet said evenly, "I would have come alone. And unarmed. I have come for the Wayfolk man."

"Why?"

"The Holder wishes to see him."

"The Wayfolk man is gone."

"Gone where?"

"He stepped through his circle of time. He might have gone anywhere."

"He might have." Nyx's colorless eyes met hers, expressionless. "He might have gone upriver. He might have gone into a room in this rambling, changing, shifting house. He might have—"

Nyx's eyes narrowed. "How do you know this house shifts itself?"

"I came back to spy on you."

"Really." She drew breath. "Really, Meguet. You do take chances. Did it ever occur to you that wandering around in a bog witch's house might be dangerous?"

"Has it occurred to you yet that the Wayfolk man is dangerous? I came back that night when I saw you last, for only one reason: I looked at him and was warned."

Nyx was silent. She pushed her hair back from her face absently, studying Meguet. "You never even spoke to him."

"I know."

"You saw him last in Berg Hold. He told me."

"Yes. I came for him then. He disappeared into silver."

"That was the Ring of Time. He stepped through it again two days ago. I cannot tell you where he went."

"And why did he leave you so precipitously?"

"He is only Wayfolk," Nyx said. "My work must have troubled him."

"He stayed with you a long time before it troubled him."

"Did my mother instruct you to question me?"

"She instructed me to find Corleu. I will find him."

Nyx's eyes flickered, a touch of color in them. "You even know his name."

"Yes."

"He is Wayfolk. Powerless."

"He made a Ring of Time. He wakes power wherever he goes. And those powers are disturbing Ro House. I want him. Let me search the house."

Nyx did not move. She said softly, "Meguet. You must not stand between the Wayfolk man and those powers."

"Someone must," Meguet said tautly. "Will you? Where do you stand? With the Wayfolk man, with those powers, or with Ro House?"

"I stand for myself," Nyx said sharply and stood aside.

Meguet beckoned the guard up from the dock. She went first into the house. When she passed through the hallway, she heard Nyx's cold voice behind her: "Stop."

She held one arm across the door. Meguet waited, poised for anything from Nyx: charm, nightmare, a moment's private conversation. Nyx spoke privately to the air. "These belong to the woman who entered. You will not harm them."

She dropped her arm, turned away, letting the guards enter. Meguet's skin prickled. "Who were you talking to?"

"My doorkeepers. They guard me, day and night. They never sleep. No one passes them without my permission." She put her hands on Meguet's shoulders, held her lightly. Her eyes seemed enormous, mist-cold. "Except you, my cousin Meguet. Except you. I have often wondered why." She loosed her, as the guard, taking the stairs cautiously, began to file in. "Search."

"The rooms in the house shift constantly," Meguet said to the guard. "Don't let it alarm you. If you get lost, you will be found."

"By what?" someone wondered dourly.

"I will find you." Nyx glanced at her sharply. She said no more, led the way through the single door opening out of the workroom. The hearth had been cold, she noticed, empty even of ashes. The air smelled only of a slight cellar damp. *Nyx*, she thought, *is leaving*. The guard separated, opened other doors, scattered themselves through rambling corridors, where the threads of time frayed and broke and knit again. Meguet wandered with them until she was alone, in a room empty but for a great loom, the thread in the shuttle a color not used before.

She opened the only door in that room, wanting one room, expecting one room, and found it: the room full of mirrors. She felt a sudden chill down the corridor, like a wind from a broken window, or the swift turn of a sorceress's attention. She closed the door abruptly. All the mirrors were black.

"Meguet!" The door latch rattled, the door shook. "Meguet!"

She did not answer. Standing in the middle of the room, she watched the mirrors. All her thoughts were focused on one thing. The house heard her, showed it to her: the Cygnet in flight in all of its eyes.

They darkened again. *Corleu*, she thought, holding his face in her mind. *You saw where he went from this house. You heard. Show me.*

Others watched in her; she sensed their sudden waking interest, alert to her focused attention. They had watched him from the first, she realized then, before she even knew them. They had pulled her back into Nyx's house, to hear his voice, listen for his name. The Wayfolk man was the danger to the Cygnet.

Fire flared in the heart of each dark mirror. A hand held the fire. The flame moved slowly, revealed a slab of marble, a lion's paw, a gryphon's eye. The flame shifted across the mirrors, across the dark between walls. Travelling, it illumined, briefly, a Wayfolk face.

"Meguet!" There was a shock of noise that should have broken the door. But Meguet, intent on the mirrors, held the door firm with nothing more, it seemed, than blind desire, and the old house strained to do her bidding. The blood had washed from her face: she could not move, she could scarcely breathe. The Wayfolk man had stepped through time into Chrysom's maze.

The mirrors shook around her. The walls of the room shuddered, undulated. She whispered drily, "Not yet. Not yet," and they held, as if the hands of all the ghosts of her ancestors stood with the ghosts of the house to buttress them.

Faces formed under the flickering light: brightly masked, half-human, half-animal. The flame moved from one carved, motionless face to the next. Meguet put her hands to her mouth, made a sound, another. He had found his way to the center of the maze.

"How?" she shouted furiously, and found no answer within herself, only a strange, watchful silence. "How?"

"Meguet!"

She turned, flung herself against the trembling door, felt the power threatening it, pushing inward against it, beating through her, like a heart, like wings. "Who is he? Nyx, who is he?"

He stood in the dark, surrounded by statues, in the small, empty chamber that all passages but one led away from. He had found the one passage. But he could not breach time itself. He turned in the dark, she saw from the changing light, like one uncertain. "He cannot," she whispered through dry lips. "He cannot go within time." The door bucked, throwing her. "Nyx!" she cried, still watching, as she picked herself up. "Nyx!"

"Meguet!"

She clung to the door again, felt a thousand years of power within her shielding the door to watch Corleu. "Who is he? Nyx, who is the Wayfolk man?"

"He said he is kin!"

"Kin to what?"

"To you! Meguet, what are you?"

Meguet closed her eyes. The door exploded inward with a sound like all the sorrows of the house. It flung her against a mirror, and then into the mirror. For an instant she saw room after room in the overburdened house torn by the conflict of powers in it. Walls and corners drew together, flattening; walls shrank. Ghosts thinned like spun thread. Guards tumbled, crying out soundlessly, terrified. Then they merged into wood, into warped glass. Meguet screamed, "No!" She felt glass against her mouth, glass tears falling from her eyes. Then the glass itself spun and spun toward nothing. Dimly, she heard it shatter.

She sat up slowly, amid an odd debris: a few rotten boards, a pink shoe, a pair of spectacles, a broken cauldron. She was sitting on bare, muddy ground where the house had stood. As if they felt the weight of her gaze, the ancient stairs gave up their hold on the leafless shrubs, slid with a dry clatter, like a pile of old bones, onto the dock. The drowned ghost stood up in her boat, staring upward under her hand. She vanished quite suddenly. So, inexplicably, did her boat. Guards in torn, mud-streaked uniforms pulled themselves up-right, looking sour. Nyx, surrounded by a pile of old books and some bro-ken jars, stirred near Meguet. She turned on her side, wincing. A book slid down the hillside, hit the river and floated.

She followed it a moment with her eyes. "Chrysom's," she said wearily. "They are indestructible." She sat up, brushed old leaves out of her hair, then surveyed the destruction she and Meguet had wrought between them. She turned her head finally to stare at her cousin. "What exactly are you?"

Meguet slid her hands over her face, as much to evade that sudden, in-tense scrutiny, as to try to contain the headache that was rioting behind her eyes. "Desperate." Her voice shook badly. "Nyx, what is the Wayfolk man doing in Chrysom's maze?"

"Looking for something."

Meguet dropped her hands, feeling the thousand-year-old fear like some icy wind, blowing off a place the sun never touched. Nyx's eyes, catching at hers, seemed the color of that wind. "Looking for what?" she asked sharply.

The force of Nyx's attention lessened finally. "He never told me. He is under duress not to tell. Something of Chrysom's, I would guess, of great, secret power he may have hidden in the maze. Except that . . ."

"Except?"

"Not even Chrysom had power like yours," Nyx said simply. Meguet, staring back at her, felt the chill again: this time, oddly, not an ancient fear for the Cygnet, but one a small night-hunter might feel for its bones, at owl wings darkening the moon. She got up too abruptly, had to quell the brawl-ing in her head.

"It was only your power," she said recklessly, "seeped into that crazed old house. I could not cast a spell of my own to save my life." She counted heads swiftly, saw with relief that no one had been rendered into glass and framed. She held out a hand to Nyx. "We're getting no farther than nowhere, sitting in the mud."

For a moment it seemed the hand grasping hers was of stone, and the weight she pulled at was the stone-tortoise's ponderous, time-burdened shell. "There are two things of great power in Ro House that I never knew existed," Nyx said softly. "One is hidden in that maze. The other is you. If you will not tell me, Meguet, I will find out what you know, how you know it. One way or another, I will find out."

White, mute, she set her teeth, pulled against Nyx's grasp. Nyx, rising suddenly, nearly sent them both tumbling down the hillside. "Please." She freed herself from Nyx's hold. Her fists were clenched; the river blurred. "Please," she whispered. "Just come home. Help us."

The Gatekeeper found them a day or two later, trailing the twilight into the gate, a bedraggled company that caused him to lose his habitual impassivity.

"Lady Nyx," he said, helping her dismount from behind Meguet. "Welcome." Nyx, barefoot as the house had left her, grunted sourly as her foot hit a stone.

"Hew," she said. She gestured a stableboy toward the great sack of books another rider carried. Then she folded her arms over her worn, archaic, velvet gown and surveyed the towers. "At least the house is still standing."

The Gatekeeper held Meguet's stirrup. She dismounted wearily, her face stiff. She could not smile at him; she could not even speak, until he touched her gently, as to help balance her, and then she could look at him, let him calculate the impossible distance the hand's-breadth between them was. His hand rose toward her cheek, cupped air, dropped.

"You had a rough journey," he breathed. She nodded, looking away from him until she could answer steadily.

"It isn't over yet. Did the Hunter Hold Council arrive?"

"Not a sign of them. They'll be a few days crossing the swamp. Lady Nyx, do you want a mount to ride to the towers?"

She shook her head. "I'd rather crawl, after that ride. I'm used to walking barefoot." She took a step and stumbled, grasping at Meguet to keep her balance. Brows pinched in pain, she turned up a dirty foot. Blood welled across it.

She eased down, still clinging to Meguet, and picked up the glass she had stepped on. "What is this?" she asked, and Meguet tensed at the sharpness in her voice.

She took it from Nyx; red, it was, with curved, jagged edges. "It looks like part of a glass cup," she said, puzzled. "A hollow ball of some kind. Why—"

"One of the juggler's," the Gatekeeper said shortly. "I missed it, lying there. I beg your pardon, my—"

"What juggler?" Nyx interrupted. Meguet stared at him.

"You let a stranger in the gate?"

"Not that I know," he said, and she saw how his eyes had darkened with weariness, and the skin hugged the sharp bones of his face. "Unless he slid like a shadow under the gate. I took him for a cottager, juggling for the children. Smith, by the look of his shoulders."

"You don't know him," she whispered, cold. "You don't know his name."

He hesitated. He put his hand to his eyes and said tiredly, "I never saw his face. Only his back and his juggling. Always those red glass balls. If he is a stranger, I don't know how he got in."

"You said it: a shadow under the gate." Nyx took the glass from Meguet, dropped it. It shattered into fine sand, lay sparkling in the torchlight. "He is no stranger," she said grimly. "He's the Warlock with a heart of glass, and he has just laid blood across this threshold."

THREE

CORLEU sat in the center of the maze. The mage-fire he had made and carried through time into the maze burnt on bare stone in front of him. Other fires he had not made lit the strange statues circling him. Their eyes, slitted like goat or cat, painted unexpected colors, seemed to watch him.

The Dancer leaned among them, sometimes putting on one of their nightmare faces. The tinker sat next to Corleu, sharing bread and cheese, or providing it from somewhere, since he ate little but a bread crumb now and then. The Blind Lady sat mumbling names to herself, weaving from an underskirt of muddy linen. The juggler paced. Sometimes his shadow, pacing over Corleu, was the Blood Fox's.

"It's here," the tinker said patiently. He broke more bread off a loaf, passed it to Corleu. "I can feel it."

"Thread ends here," the Blind Lady said. She cocked her head at some mysterious trembling in time, and found a dangling thread in her sleeve. She snapped it abruptly; Corleu jerked. "Time, for that one."

"I can smell it," the Warlock said, standing over Corleu. He dropped his hands on Corleu's shoulders, and sniffed at the air above the fire. "Mage-fire," he said.

"I made it."

"I know. But who taught you?"

"My great-gran," he said recklessly, and the Warlock grinned his fox's grin.

"Great-gran taught you to make the Ring of Time," the Dancer said. She turned a scarlet face to him among the shadows, with gold-rimmed eyes and delicate gold cat's ears. She settled her long, lissome body along a statue. "I heard Great-gran's dreams. I danced in them. White-haired man among the corn she dreamed, now and then, all her life. Her last dream was of green corn. I was kind to Great-gran. She never dreamed the Ring of Time."

"She was Wayfolk," the Blind Lady said, chuckling. "They see into time in little toad hops. A morsel of future here, there. Never great daylong strides of it."

"Did Great-gran teach you to make my heart?" the Warlock marvelled. His fingers dug painfully into Corleu's shoulders, then let go suddenly. He paced again. Corleu chewed stolidly, his mouth dry.

"Great-gran," he said, swallowing with an effort, "had odd talents."

"You take after her, then," the tinker said, passing him a water skin. "Thirsty? What other talents did Great-gran have?"

"She could read. She gave my granda books. Odd books, with odd things in them."

"Many odd things," the Warlock agreed, turning noiselessly on bare feet. "A wizard's blood in amber, for instance," Corleu, tilting the water skin, lowered it without drinking. He met the Warlock's eyes a moment; they were smoky amber red. He lifted the skin again, drank.

"You owe me," he said shortly. "You all do. I promised to find what I would find, not loose you into the world."

"You haven't found it," the tinker commented, carving a sliver of cheese with his knife.

"I'm near enough. I found the place."

"We found it before you."

He was silent, swallowing bitterness with his bread. "So," he said to the tinker, "you knew this place all along. You only needed me to wake your friends. If you know so much, you don't need me now. You can find the Cygnet's heart by yourself."

Hissing, the Warlock was behind him again, one hand over his mouth, the other tightening over his throat. The tinker put a finger to his lips.

"Things listen, in here."

Corleu heard only the blood drumming in his ears. The Warlock loosed him finally; he sagged forward, blinking, until the darkening fire burned bright again.

"I made your heart," he said hoarsely. "You said you would be grateful."

"I smell a trap," the Warlock growled. "I smell sorcery."

"What sorcery could stand up to you when I find this thing for you?"

"What sorcery?" the tinker said genially. "You can answer that one." Corleu picked up bread silently. "You won't answer." He cocked a brow at the Dancer. "What sorcerers have been dreaming of this thing we want?"

She discarded her mask, let her face flow into various faces. Nyx's face came and went quickly; Corleu froze mid-bite, then chewed again, expressionless. "None dreaming," the Dancer said, "not of this."

"Of him?"

"Only one," she said smiling, "still dreaming. Like me, before you woke me." She wore Tiel's face. Corleu caught his breath on a bread crumb.

"Easy," the tinker said, pounding on his back, handing him the water.

"I told—I told no one."

"Not even Great-gran? Not even whispered to her grave? Not even to a green stalk of corn?"

"No one."

"Then who taught you?" the Warlock demanded. "Whose sorcery brought us awake?"

"You wanted that," Corleu said tersely. "You wanted freedom. I couldn't do it without learning somewhere, from someone. You said find it. I chose how."

"Silver Ring of Time is a powerful magic."

"So are you. I couldn't free things of power without power."

"What did you pay this teacher?"

"Nothing."

"What did you promise?"

"What does it matter?" he said. "It's my promise, my payment. Nothing to do with you."

They were silent, looking at one another, even the Blind Lady, casting about with her fallen eyes.

"He paid for sorcery," the tinker said, "with nothing we need worry about." He cocked a brow around the chamber, then regarded Corleu, hand rasping at the dark stubble on his cheeks.

"What would Wayfolk pay with?" the Dancer asked. "All they own is time."

"A man searching for treasure could promise that in payment," the Warlock said, prowling the edge of the light. His eyes flared at Corleu. "Did you?" Corleu stared back at him. He turned to the tinker.

"You didn't pay me for this," he said. The Warlock snarled beyond the fire, then barked the Blood Fox's attack, and he felt the cold sweat break on his face. But he kept his eyes steady on the tinker, who smiled a faint, thin smile.

"Wayfolk. Always one for a bargain." He waved a remonstrating hand at the Warlock. "You should be a little grateful."

"I'll be grateful," the Warlock said with a snap of teeth, "when he finds this."

"You owe me," Corleu said baldly, "not just tinker, you all do." He reached for the knife, his hand trembling in the shadows. "You told me ask for myself."

The Warlock, snarling, leaped over the fire. Corleu jumped to his feet, the knife in his hand. A blood fox's weight crashed against him, bore him back against one of the statues. Its orange lizard's face smiled over his shoulder, its cloven hand pushed into his backbone. The knife burned like a coal in his hand; he dropped it, crying out, and heard it shatter like glass on the stones. A blood fox's eyes looked into his, feral, furious.

"You alone in this. Not with some faceless mage behind you. Who is it?"

The tinker chuckled. "Don't eat him. We need him yet. Who, Corleu?"

"You may not need to know." He stopped, catching his breath; the Blood Fox eyes still glared into his, all he could see. "Ever. How could—how could anyone threaten you, once you have it?"

The Dancer pirouetted along the statues, turning herself gracefully from embrace to embrace until she brought herself against Corleu. She put her hand on his hair, murmured against his mouth, "But how will we know who to protect, if we are threatened?" Her face became green suddenly, with fierce blue oval eyes and a sharp raven's beak. He jerked his head back, banged it against the stones. She laughed.

"Pass the knife," the tinker asked politely, "if you're done with it."

The Warlock loosed Corleu slowly. He bent, growling, picked up shards of glass and flung them to the tinker. They reshaped in the air; the tinker picked the knife out of it, cut more cheese.

The Dancer turned across Corleu, continued her dance. Corleu slid down to the feet of the statue, closed his eyes.

"Now," he heard the tinker say, "let's begin again. You want something more for your pains. For the worry and trouble. That seems fair. We told you you might want more. But here is the point we stick at, Corleu. There's the small matter of the thing itself." He cocked an eye up at the painted Cygnet flying across the small round ceiling, then down at the floor. "Even Wayfolk know not to barter with air. You find this small thing. Then ask."

Corleu looked at him, wondering if any Wayfolk in all history had ever strayed down such a mysterious path to end sitting in the dark beneath the Holder's house, surrounded by tales come alive and speaking. He said slowly, "You knew this place before I did. Why do you need me now? You gave me pieces of the puzzle. Is that all the pieces you have? If it's not here, I don't know where to look. I don't have your magic. You could find it easily as me, now."

"It's here," the Blind Lady murmured, and snapped another thread absently. The tinker's yellow eyes smiled their faint, glinting smile.

"Another fine point. But so easily answered, you answer."

"You can't find it without me." He shook his head, bewildered, as the tinker's smile broadened. "I'm Wayfolk," he protested. "That means back roads, herb magic, no corners. Ignorance, field dirt, living and dying in a wagon. I'm nothing. If you want me for more than my feet and hands, there's little to find. Why me? Why me to find it?" They were silent. The tinker gazed into the fire; the Dancer beside a statue imitated its distant stare. The Blind Lady picked at thread; the Warlock picked a red glass ball out of a gryphon's mouth, set it flaming in a niche in the wall. Corleu's hands closed tightly. "You do need me," he breathed. "So I have more than air to barter with." The Warlock's face flashed toward him, snarling, but noiselessly, and he did not move. The tinker picked his teeth thoughtfully with the knife.

"It's an unusual position to bargain from. You alone can find this thing. But you don't know how to get at it."

"Hear him," the Dancer murmured. "It costs nothing. And it may amuse." She strayed to Corleu, traced his ear with her thumb. "What more does the Wayfolk man want? A house? A palace?"

"I don't like walls."

"Wealth?"

"Wayfolk can't count. They use coins for buttons."

"A sorcerer's power?"

"I've had a bellyful of sorcery."

"Knowledge?"

"I'm getting that, just breathing."

"Then what, Corleu?" the tinker asked. His smile was gone; his voice had thinned. He tossed the knife in the air, caught it. For a moment, wheeling in the firelight, it turned gold. Corleu's hands clenched; he looked at them blindly, testing the demand silently, against the straight doorposts and towers, the safety of the ancient house above his head.

"I want," he said, "a promise. That no harm will come to the one who helped me, or to her house, or to any who know her name."

There was dead silence from the gathering he had wakened; they gazed at him, remote and eerie as the statues around him.

Behind him, the statue he leaned against seemed to shift.

Meguet and Nyx entered Chrysom's tower. Nyx had paused to heal her foot, standing in the middle of the yard, with one hand on Meguet's arm. No one greeted her; no one stared; no one, Meguet found bemusedly, noticed either of them. Then she saw the yard as from another angle, a world without them, and she said, feeling an odd mingling of uneasiness and freedom:

"Have you made us invisible?"

"For a moment," Nyx answered absently. "Just until we reach Chrysom's tower. I have things to do; I don't want to be distracted."

"You will see the Holder first."

"No."

Meguet caught her breath. "Nyx, she has waited years!" Nyx's grip on her tightened slightly; she stared down at the dark head, hair swept impatiently behind one ear, what she could see of the pale, lean face quiet, absorbed in work. Nyx answered finally:

"She will be here when I have finished. If I don't begin, neither she nor I may be here in the end."

"And if you don't return from the maze? You will not go to her first, even to let her see your face? Nyx Ro, that is cruel."

Nyx straightened, tested her foot on the bare ground. "I haven't your warmth," she said, "which you extend so unexpectedly. Even to Gatekeepers, apparently. Even to me." She added, at Meguet's silence, the ghost of a smile touching her mouth, "Hew, I can understand. But you use so carelessly, at times, something that to me is simply another source of power."

"Love?" She felt the blood in her face, a confusion of anger and helplessness, as if she were without arms or armor in some vital battle. But the word touched Nyx; her eyes flickered, following a thought.

"Not even Chrysom suggested that as a source of power," she commented. "It's an interesting thought. I only meant that you allow yourself to be distracted by so many small things. To focus power you must first focus your attention."

"I am," Meguet said shortly. "It's all in that maze. If you are finished."

"First I must go to Chrysom's library."

"Moro's eyes! We have no time! If you haven't learned it by now, you don't need it."

"But I do." She looked at Meguet, her eyes distant, unreadable. "There is something vital in that library. I will need it in the maze. It may save our lives."

Meguet hesitated. Her attention drained inward, to the still, secret place where a great prism hung in darkness. She sensed disturbance in a layer of time around it, but, so far, it was itself undisturbed.

"All right," she said tensely. "But hurry."

In the library, she paced, picking bog leaf out of her hair and rebraiding it. Nyx searched through books, letting pages dance through her fingers, a mysterious task which spun Meguet's calm to a fine, frayed thread.

"Nyx," she breathed. "We must go." Nyx did not answer. She closed a book, opened another. Meguet closed her eyes, turned on her heel. Her hands fell to her sides, clenched. She forced them open. Nothing had happened, yet. Nothing, yet ... "Nyx."

"Be patient," Nyx murmured. "In matters of sorcery there's nothing more dangerous than haste."

"What are you looking for?"

"A puzzle piece."

Meguet drew breath, held it. She listened to the silence a few more minutes. Then she wheeled, went to the door, opened it. She got Nyx's attention then.

"Where are you going?"

"Down. Catch up with me."

"Wait, Meguet. Please wait. We may lose each other in the maze."

"Will you at least let me send word to the Holder?"

"The guards must have told her by now." She waited, her eyes on Meguet, looking faintly troubled, until Meguet's hold on the latch loosened. She resumed reading. Meguet stood gazing at the half-open door. She closed it finally, leaned against it, head and shoulder against the wood as if she might hear voices from far below carried upward through the ancient stones.

"Rydel." Nyx's flat voice nearly made her start. She closed a book sharply. "Secret powers. Powers not to be known. To be used only for Ro Holding." Meguet turned incredulously to face her. "Rydel," Nyx reminded her, "was your ancestor. Chrysom himself, Timor Ro said, stood in her shadow." She took a step toward Meguet, her eyes wide, speculative. "The enormous powers of the mage Chrysom were overshadowed by the powers of Timor Ro's eccentric gardener. That's how you could walk past my doorkeepers."

"Your doorkeepers," Meguet whispered. Then she heard herself shout, an unfamiliar sound. "Nyx, what are you doing wasting time reading about gardening? This house is in danger!"

"Gardening is not at issue, and the acquisition of knowledge is never a waste of time. You stood against me in my house. You. My cousin Meguet, who could never find your way through a book, let alone a spell. I want to know how. I want to know before we go into the maze. I want to take this thing Corleu is searching for, and I need power. Power like Rydel's. Like yours."

Meguet stared at her, stunned. She whirled abruptly. "You stay and look for it, then. I'm going down." She wrenched the door so hard it should have swung back to boom against the stones. Instead it pulled her off balance, brought her up hard against it.

She leaned into the wood after a moment, her heart pounding. "Nyx."

"Open it."

"I can't!"

"You could fight me in my house."

"I wasn't fighting you! I was watching! I can't—"

"Open the door."

"I can't use those powers at will!" She stopped, appalled at what she had relinquished: an ancient privacy, a secret between Holder and Guardian. But it had already been relinquished, by consent, in Nyx's house. She stood quietly then, her face against the wood, calming herself out of long habit, as for a bout. She turned finally, trembling slightly, her face white, feeling unskilled and clumsy at battles of will instead of movement. She said softly, waiting for an inner uproar of voices that did not come, "The powers are ancient. I may use them for one purpose. Only one purpose. I can't use them at my own need. They are kept always secret, and through some generations they are never used."

"Power is power," Nyx said. She stood as calm as the stone Cygnet carved above her head, unfamiliar, suddenly, as if her own past in that room, in that house, could no longer lay claim to her. "It can be worked with, changed, manipulated, shaped in whatever ways you choose. I only need to know its source."

The black prism, the Cygnet's eye, formed in Meguet's mind. She said, trying to find Nyx in the dangerous stranger in front of her, "The source itself is ancient. I obtained power by being born, only that. It is my heritage.

And but what for you and the Wayfolk man have wakened, I might have lived and died without using it."

"Use it now. You can. Open the door."

"I can't. The power is not mine to summon."

"It could be. Only learn how. If the need is there, the power will come. You know that yourself. Desperation spawns power. Open the door."

The Cygnet's eye was still dark, untroubled, in its secret rings of time. . . . She shook her head, not trusting herself to speak further, for desperation would spawn nothing more magical than anger and anger was a beggar's blade. Without moving, it seemed, Nyx stood in front of her. She laid her hands against the door, on either side of Meguet's face. Her eyes, misty, unblinking, drew at Meguet.

"There must have been a place where you first knew your powers. A moment in time when you first recognized them for what they are. When was the time? Where is the place?" Meguet turned her face away; Nyx lifted one hand from the door, turned it back gently to meet her gaze. "Tell me."

"I cannot," she whispered.

"Why? Who stops you? What?"

Meguet closed her eyes, shaking with anger. In one of her lithe, skilled movements, she had ducked away from Nyx, put distance, mentally and physically between them in this peculiar battle, before Nyx realized she had moved.

But she had not: She had only thought the movement. She was still backed against the door, pinned under Nyx's gaze, with the anger in her turning into a nightmarish panic. She tried again to move. Her voice broke away from her in terror.

"Nyx, I can't—"

"You can move. If you choose. Find the way."

"How can you do this to me, how can you—"

"Don't panic. Find the power. Use the source."

"It is not—I cannot—it is not mine to use!"

"It is yours. Take it. Have the courage to take. To use."

"You don't understand—You think you know so much, you understand nothing."

"What? What don't I understand?"

"How to know without using."

"Power is to be known, is to be used, is even to be shared. You must share this knowledge with me, Meguet. It might save my life. If that, at this particular moment, does not move you, then think of the safety of this house. I can help, but you must help me."

"Nyx—" She could not even blink; she felt as immobile as one of the strange statues in the maze. She could only speak, and her voice shook badly. "You have brought your swamp ways into this house. The power does not belong to me. If even the thought of using it so crossed my heart, I would lose it. Do you think I would risk my own heritage only because I can't move a finger or open a door? Ask me what my heart is worth to me, or my life. Then make me an offer. Ask me." Nyx, a hair-fine line between her brows, said nothing, waited. Meguet's breath caught suddenly, painfully; she was going to cry, in sheer frustration, she realized furiously, and she could not even wipe away her own tears, or turn her face to hide them. "I never judged you before," she whispered. "I never knew the things you know. It seemed that what you sought might be worth a long journey, a stay in the desert, a lonely life, even the life of an animal or two. But now I judge you. I know you as the small birds know you. You cut out their tongues so they cannot speak, you cut off their wings so they cannot fly. They look at you and know you. You make what you are. When you burn their hearts, it is your own heart burning in the fire."

Color flared into Nyx's face. Her eyes seemed enormous, luminous. The door latch rattled suddenly and she started. She pushed herself away from the door.

"Nyx!" It was the Holder. "Open the door!"

She pounded on it impatiently. Meguet, freed suddenly, turned her whole body, hid her face against the wood. She reached out, at the insistent pounding, pulled the door open with shaking hands. The Holder stood on the threshold, looking at the lank-haired, barefoot woman whose back was turned to her. "Nyx?" she said tentatively. "The Gatekeeper told me you had come."

Nyx turned slowly, met her mother's eyes. They were both silent then, their faces reflecting the same faint surprise at the still unbroken bond between them. The Holder spoke first, her voice soft, shaken:

"Nyx." She looked at Meguet then, her eyes suddenly vulnerable, haunted. "You went upriver for the Wayfolk man. Not Nyx. Not now."

"The Wayfolk man is here," Nyx said.

"Here! Where?"

"In Chrysom's maze. He came to look for something."

The Holder's face whitened. "What is he looking for in my house?"

"I don't know. He never told me. He is coerced. I promised him help. That's why I came back with Meguet. We are going together into the maze—"

"No," the Holder said sharply. "Meguet will go. I don't want you in danger."

Nyx paused, looked at her oddly, a touch of color in her eyes. Then she linked her hands tightly together; her brows pinched. She answered carefully, "Meguet will need help."

"Meguet may need help, but—"

"Mother, I did not spend nine years wandering Ro Holding for no reason. Almost nothing can stand against me. Almost nothing. And I promised—"

"I don't care what you promised the Wayfolk man and I don't care if you can harry Chrysom himself out of his tomb, I want you here with me. Or better yet, out of this house. Go back to the swamp."

Nyx's eyes narrowed. "I thought you wanted me out of the swamp. Your fey third daughter eating toads under a full moon, causing gossip across four Holds—"

"Then, take that as a reason to be sent back to the swamp," the Holder said sharply. "Better there than here. This house is not safe."

"That is why I came back. To deal with the danger. When I have done that, I will be gone. If that is what you want."

The Holder closed her eyes. "Moro's name. I have wanted you home for nine years. Now I want you home tomorrow. Not now."

"Why?" Nyx asked, and answered herself, coldly, evenly. "You don't trust me. You don't know me anymore. You don't know anymore which daughter is yours: the one who lived so innocently among the witches, or the one who dwelled among bones in the swamp. Which one will go into the maze? Which will fight in this house?"

The Holder was silent; Meguet saw the confusion of anguish and guilt in her eyes. So did Nyx; her head bowed slightly, away from her mother's expression. She added softly, "There is only one way for you to find out. You must let me go into that maze."

The Holder's face looked pale, brittle as the pearls she twisted between her fingers. "No," she said. "For many reasons." Nyx did not move, or change expression, but Meguet, watching her, felt something twist in her own heart.

She said abruptly, "Nyx is right. I will need her with me."

The Holder turned to her, startled. "Meguet, no. You cannot take her. She has only a mage's powers."

"And at this moment, I have none at all." She paused. She had fought back tears, but her face was colorless, and her voice unsteady with anger and shock. The Holder said sharply:

"What's wrong?"

Meguet's shoulders straightened, lined to the stones at her back. Nyx gazed at her expressionlessly, asking nothing, forcing nothing. Meguet said evenly, "Everything is wrong. I keep blundering a step behind the Wayfolk man. I could not stop him in Berg Hold, I missed him in the swamp, and I may well miss him again unless I get into that maze. If it is only sorcery to be dealt with in the maze, I will have only a sword to fight it. I will be helpless without Nyx."

The Holder drew breath, her eyes flicking between them. The strand in her fingers broke suddenly; pearls ran like mice at her feet. She threw the last of them down.

"Then go," she said huskily to Nyx. She did not look at her daughter. "If you do not return, you will break my heart."

They were nearly at the foot of the tower stairs before Nyx spoke. "You could have told her. I thought you would. It would have been just. And," she added dispassionately, "she has already judged me."

"I fight my own battles," Meguet said shortly. "And I may well need you. I have no idea what is down there in the dark by now."

"I do not mean to harass you." She touched Meguet's arm lightly and for a breath, once again, Meguet froze, so precariously balanced between steps that if Nyx had shifted a finger she would have tumbled headlong to the floor. She felt the dark anger beat like insect wings in the back of her throat, in her wrists. "I only want to understand you, and the great secret power that uses you. I want to see its face."

In the heart of the tower, Corleu saw the small chamber he sat in waver around him. The fires went out, hiding the still faces of both stone and the living. Time closed over him like water. A globe lit the room now, silver-green, hanging from the center of the ceiling above a marble effigy and tomb.

The stone statues began to move.

FOUR

THE tomb guardians, colorful and fierce, prowling silently around the tomb on their half-human legs, the black stone effigy itself, of a tall old man frowning faintly, it looked, at the doings in the tower, impressed Corleu fully but briefly. His eyes kept returning to the globe.

Just a light, his brain told him. But his hands wanted to hold it; he wanted to see into it. Nothing in it but a green-white mage-flame, his eyes told him, but his attention fluttered around it like some frantic moth. *There,* he wanted to say, *there.* But it wasn't there.

"Nothing there but fire," the tinker said. Corleu dragged his eyes from it finally, turning. He opened his mouth to answer, then could not, stunned finally in that chamber full of wonders.

The Gold King stood in his gold spiked armor, masked in gold, crowned with the seven gold stars of his house. The edges of his scabbard rippled like flame. The chain he dragged went just so far across the marble floor, then simply stopped in the middle of a link, as if it continued elsewhere, in another chamber, perhaps, or somewhere among the stars.

Behind him the Warlock, dressed in the black of his night-shadow, juggled the stars that limned the shadow, and the one red star that was his heart.

"We're close," he said. His red-furred, feral face looked intent, watchful, the blood fox scenting the hunters, perhaps, or the prey. It was an ancient expression, Corleu thought suddenly, seeing the first blood fox in the Delta waiting, wide-eyed, still, for what it smelled flying low over the swamps on the wind.

His heart pounded. There was too much power. Tinker, he had told Nyx; old blind beggar woman. The Blind Lady wore peacock feathers from throat to foot. Her long black hair tumbled away from a delicate oval face. Her eyes were closed, a faint frown between her brows. Her ringed hand wove threads of palest silver; like the Gold King's chain, they stopped short in the air, continued elsewhere. Her face was so calm she seemed elsewhere as well, but she spoke. "A little farther, Wayfolk man. Take us farther."

He stared at her, not knowing how he had gotten even that far. "You must promise," he said desperately. "You haven't promised what I asked."

The Dancer chuckled. One side of her hair was black as night, the other white as snow. She wore a Fire Bear pelt; her fingers were its curved ice-white claws. She looked old as night one moment, then, at a shift of light or expression, as young as morning. "We gained ground without a promise."

"Then I won't move. I'll go no farther." He sat down at the foot of the effigy, his arms folded. "I'll stay here with the dead until you promise." His face was blanched; his old man's hair, he thought, would have turned white anyway at this point. The Gold King turned his imperious mask of gold at Corleu, and he had to drag at air, just at the movement.

"Tell us who might be waiting for us," the Gold King said. "Tell us who might have taken an interest in whatever you searched for, who might have turned a thought toward taking this thing I want. How can we promise without a name?"

"I won't name until you promise." He had reached out, clung to something solid on the tomb, in the face of the Gold King's wrath. The guardians swung their horned, beaked, goat-eyed heads at him as they roamed around the tomb. But no fire came out of their mouths, no roars of warning. "And she doesn't know what or where. She can't be there waiting."

The Warlock paced, juggling, with one hand, small worlds of fire.

"Then why are you afraid for her? This ignorant, innocent sorceress who has no interest in why we wake? If she's nowhere, how could we harm her? I know mages, witches, sorcerers. Their minds are always turning, always busy, nosing out this, that. She pointed your way here. You'd have spent years searching on your own for this maze. But she would not come with you if only to see for herself what you might find? She was not curious? She had better things to do? And why," he added, tossing a star and catching it, "would we harm her for helping us?" Corleu, gripping stone, stared at him, dry-mouthed. "No answer from the Wayfolk? Then I'll answer. Because she intends us harm."

He threw a glass ball in his hand hard across the chamber, straight at the globe. Corleu, on his feet before he realized it, saw the ball pass through the globe as if it were air, and rebound against the wall. The Warlock caught it. Corleu molded stone in his hand, still searching the globe, for a crack, injury, a wavering of its light. He moved finally, took a step toward it, touched it with one hand.

He flinched away from hot glass; it was only mage-light, burning for centuries, likely old as the maze. He turned, found an audience out of nightmare watching him.

"What do you see," the Dancer asked softly, "in there, Wayfolk? It's only a round globe of light."

"Nothing." He sat down again, cooling his hand against the cold marble: It was the effigy's left foot, he realized, he had hold of like a spar off a swamped ship. He moved his hand quickly before the effigy stirred in annoyance.

"I looked into a round globe of light once," the Blind Lady said in her low, grave voice. "I saw what I saw and never saw again. Be careful, Wayfolk, what you look too closely into."

"It's too late for care." His eyes wandered back to the globe, then dragged away from it, to meet the Gold King's expressionless, armored face.

"There," the Gold King said softly. "In there, Corleu?"

"No."

"Maybe in its shadow?"

He did not answer; his face turned resolutely from it. But it burned in his thoughts. "You must promise," he said doggedly, "or none of us will ever know. She could never harm the likes of you. She could never take from you."

"Could she not?" They consulted one another silently; so did the fey-eyed tomb guardians.

"Never harm," the Warlock said thinly, tossing balls again. "Never take."

"But would she try?" the Dancer asked, revealing her ancient furrowed face. "There's the question. If we promise, and she tries to harm, then what, Wayfolk man? Will you come to our rescue?"

"She can't harm you," he said again, wearily. "No one could. You're old as story. You never die. Nothing's got more power than a dream. Or time. Or sun. You'll take what you want and walk through her like glass through that globe. She'd maybe throw a spell or two, but what's that to do with you? You'll go on forever. Promise."

"Name her."

"Promise. Her, and her house, and all who know her name."

"Name her."

"Nyx."

Rush's voice, pleading, breathless, caught them across the black tower. Meguet, pushing the Cygnet banner away from the door, saw Nyx's eyes widen, expression cross her face, before she finally turned.

"Rush." It sounded like a sigh. He was armed, but for his heart, which had no defense against Nyx anywhere, it seemed.

"I heard you had come home to fight for this house."

"Rush, we cannot wait—"

"I'll come with you."

Meguet closed her eyes. An impatience like some deadly acrid desert wind shook her. The Wayfolk man had breached time. She saw his face, turned upward, gazing, pale, entranced, puzzled, at the silver-green globe over Chrysom's effigy. "Nyx," she whispered. "We have no time left—"

Rush swept a torch out of its sconce, crossed the floor toward them. "You'll need help. I have some power, Nyx—"

"No."

"I won't let you go there alone."

"Rush," Nyx said, her voice cold as the gate hinges in midwinter, "you have been saying that for nine years. And for nine years I have gone my way and I have gone alone. You don't have the power to follow us. I will not be distracted trying to guard you."

"You won't." He had reached her. His eyes narrowed slightly, as if he were trying to fit a face of memory over the sharp-boned, expressionless, intent face in front of him. "I'll take care of myself. I'll guard Meguet—she has only her sword against those sorcerers."

"I need only Meguet," Nyx said flatly. His temper flared a little, sending blood to his face.

"I'll come with what I have: The house is in danger. You can't return after three years, give me a glimpse of your back and your shadow and then disappear into that convoluted puzzle out of a dead mage's brain, and expect me to wait—"

"I never expected you to wait!" Nyx's cold, calm voice, raised in sudden, genuine despair, startled Meguet. "I never wanted you to wait! You kept thinking I would return to love you—if it was love I wanted, I would never have left! You can't understand, you never could, that I could want knowledge more than you, experience and power more than you. You love a shadow that left this house nine years ago. I have nothing in me of that woman. I have travelled a strange country, and I have changed myself to live in that magic country. Love is not what I have learned in nine years, Rush. It's what I left behind."

"I don't believe that," Rush said. He was shaken, white, but grim, clinging with a blood fox's death grip to something that, to Meguet's eye, had given up life years ago without a protest. Nyx's mouth thinned; her eyes looked silvery in the torchlight. "For nine years, yours was the first face I saw waking, the last I saw sleeping, no matter who lay beside me. How could I be that mistaken? You must have given me something, each time you returned—the way you spoke my name, the way you turned your head to catch my voice— You can't have turned so far from love—"

"You did," she said flatly. "It was you who turned away from love, these nine years, turned away from those who might have truly loved you, to wring love out of a memory, a ghost, air. You loved nothing, Rush. You loved no one. Not even me. At least in nine years I learned something."

She turned abruptly, pulled aside the banner. Rush stood blinking, his face patchy, as if she had thrown more than words at him. For a moment he almost heard her: Meguet saw the hesitation in his movement. Then, obdurately, he stepped forward. Nyx spun so fast she blurred; there was a sound like air ripping. A line smoldered across the stone in front of Rush.

"You will wait," she said, her voice shaking with anger, "and you will wait, and you will wait in this dark tower—"

"Nyx," Meguet breathed.

"Until the woman you will love freely frees you from your waiting."

"Nyx, what have you done?" He stood very still, looking half perplexed, half frightened, as if he had come to that moment, to that place, by choice, and then could not remember why. Nyx turned again.

"Nothing more," she said with grim weariness, "than what he has laid on himself for nine years. You said to hurry." Meguet, with a final, stunned glance back at Rush, followed her down the steps. "We'll have to elude Chrysom's tricks," Nyx added, "to reach the center. We might have used Corleu's Ring of Time, but it frayed when the house and all its odd time-paths broke apart." She paused at the bottom of the steps; a mage-fire in her palm illumined a lion's face at the first wall, turned to gaze back at her. "However, there are other ways of passing through time—"

Meguet, impelled by a thousand years of voices incoherent in their urgency, did not bother to speak. She gripped Nyx's arm, pulled her forward through the wall into the center of the maze. For a moment, the strange stat-ues appeared around them, then Meguet, all her attention focused on the prism, changed that moment. The statues disappeared; black walls rose around them, enclosing the black eye of the Cygnet. It slowly paled, turned its fire-white gaze on them.

Meguet let go of Nyx then, her eyes flickering at the shadows. She drew Moro Ro's sword, out of habit. Nyx, standing stone-still, her back to the prism, blinked at the sound.

"He's close, the Wayfolk man," Meguet said, prowling, tense. "He changed time at the center. I don't know how." Nyx moved, turned her head slightly to follow Meguet's movements. "Only a Guardian can do that."

"Meguet." The word was almost inaudible, but in that chamber any word ran clear as crystal to the ear. "What is this place?"

"The heart of the maze."

"How did you find it?" Still she had not moved; expression had not yet come back into her face. "Who showed you the way?"

"You did," Meguet said a little bitterly. "Those that you and Corleu woke hid themselves here. I came here to search for them. They attacked, I had to run. Time opened. I ran here." She stopped pacing finally, leaned against the wall, watching Nyx. "You should not know about this place. I could have left you behind easily. But you said you wanted to see the face of power. I don't know its face. But there is its eye."

Nyx turned. She moved then, swiftly, to stand beside Meguet, staring at the great prism that, moonlike, was affixed to nothing but time. "What is it?"

"The eye of the Cygnet."

Nyx was silent, testing it, Meguet knew, recognizing the intent, detached expression, as if she were trying to breathe it like air, swallow it with her mind. "It yields nothing," she whispered. "Who made it?"

"Astor Ro. Chrysom made the maze to protect it. She was the first of us."

"The first——"

"Of the Guardians."

"What is it——exactly that you guard?"

"The Cygnet."

Nyx stared at her. "You never even wanted power. You never cared. You couldn't get through the maze when we were young. Is this what gave you power?"

"Yes. It needs hands, eyes, a mind living in the world. Other minds, older Guardians, woke in me to give me advice."

"What advice are they giving now?"

"They are silent. Listening."

"Listening?"

"To you. For any sign of danger from you."

"Toward you?" Nyx asked with a certain wariness. "Or toward the Cygnet?"

"Toward both."

"They did not help you before."

"The danger was only to me, not the Cygnet. Now, it would be to both, but"—she shrugged slightly, a small gesture she regretted—"now you could not touch me."

Nyx's gaze flicked away, back to the eye. "Why you?" she asked. "Why were you chosen?"

"We are all related, in some way, to Astor Ro. Beyond that, I don't know why."

"And you never knew. As we grew up together, you never sensed this power."

"I never needed it. The Cygnet was never in danger."

Nyx was silent, searching her face. The fire-white prism drew any hint of color from her eyes. "The thing he seeks belongs to the Cygnet," she said slowly. "Or is it a danger to the Cygnet? Does the Cygnet give holding power to the Holders of Ro Holding? The power of the Holders turns on a tale? A constellation? But where is the Cygnet? Four Hold Signs and their faces of power are gathered in this maze. But where is the Cygnet's face? You, Meguet?"

She shook her head, wondering, herself, what mask the Cygnet might choose. "No. I'm simply a Guardian."

"My mother?"

"Perhaps. But these powers only wear their faces to give them a human aspect. Tear the mask away, and you would have other words for them. Take those words away and—what?"

"The power itself," Nyx said softly. She looked at the prism, her arms folded, her face intent in a way that made Meguet alert, uneasy. She was no longer overawed; her busy mind had begun to weave again. "The eye of the Cygnet . . . What is in there?" Meguet did not answer. Nyx threw her a curious glance. "May I look into it?"

"Be careful."

"Is it dangerous?"

"No. But that's what the Wayfolk man is reaching toward, through time."

"Where is he?"

"Here."

"Here?" Nyx said, startled.

"In this chamber. In the same moment, but in a different circle of it. The wall is a Ring of Time. Not like you make them, from one place to another. But in one place, one moment, and deeper into the same moment. It is part of the knowledge within that eye." She paused, wishing she had bitten the word in two and swallowed it before she flung it to Nyx like bait. She added carefully, "As I said, all the power it gives is transitory; it can be used only for one purpose."

"Perhaps. I think power is malleable; it can be used to suit purpose. How much knowledge must have collected there, in a thousand years . . . And you might never have such power again in your life. This place could close like an eye closing, never to be seen again while we live. How much of it do you know, Meguet?"

"I have no idea," Meguet said shortly. "But it will be enough to stop the Wayfolk man."

Nyx was silent. All her attention had withdrawn from the prism to focus, suddenly, on Meguet. She put her hand on Meguet's arm, gently, as if to coax her to turn, to look at something. "Meguet"—she picked words slowly—"whatever Corleu is searching for, he has been compelled to find. He is not acting by choice."

"Compelled," Meguet said flatly, "he may have been, but he has found his way step by step to this time, to this place, and he has always known exactly what he wanted. And I am born to defend it."

"He is Wayfolk, powerless. I had to teach him spells a cottage brat could work, to get him this far."

"He should never have taken the first step." Nyx's fingers tightened on her arm; she moved slightly, left them closing on air. She eased into shadows again, her face shadowed. "He threatens the Cygnet. That is what the powers within me will see."

"Meguet." Nyx's face, with the color washing into her eyes, seemed candle-pale. "He is an innocent——"

"How would you recognize innocence anymore? You have no mercy for any who love you, why would you defend someone you yourself coerced, except to get what you want?"

"I did not coerce him. He needed me so he could rescue some Wayfolk girl——"

"And that moved you, I suppose."

"It did, oddly," Nyx admitted. Her brows were pinched; expression had broken through the cool detachment in her eyes. "I know he looks for something of great, dangerous power. But he wants nothing from it. All he wants is to rescue his Wayfolk love. It is a kind of innocence. A kind I never knew. I thought I could take what he found, and then use the power in it to protect him, send him unharmed back to his life. Back into that innocence. It seemed—even to me, living that way in the swamp—something worth protecting."

Meguet closed her eyes. "Then why," she breathed, "did you send him here? He could never have known about the maze without you. What kind of innocent dream does this look like to you? You knew I wanted him. What did you think I would do when I found him in this house? Why should I believe what you tell me, rather than what I see with all the power within me? He is here. He is searching not for the face of power, but for its heart. You have sent him here to die."

Nyx caught her breath, a small, unguarded sound, a half-formed word. She vanished abruptly. Meguet, startled, had time only to tense, and then she found herself adjusting her vision like a telescope, pulling Nyx out of the air, focusing clearer and clearer, until she could see even the changing expression in Nyx's eyes.

The great swan-etched broadsword wrenched itself out of her hands. It stroked the air with silver, a line drawn straight toward the shining prism. Fast as it moved, Meguet was faster, folding the moment in her mind, stepping across time to seize the sword with both hands, stop it an instant before its tip broke the facets of the prism. It resisted her, in midair, dragging against her on its determined path. Then the desire that had held a door against Nyx's power filled her; the need to see, to protect, became stronger than the threat, and she pulled the blade down and whirled.

"Nyx!" She caught her breath, furious and terrified. Nyx had disappeared again; Meguet's eyes picked her out from behind an illusion of black stone wall. She looked unfamiliar in concentration, detached, unreachable.

"You can move like thought," Nyx said softly. "You can see through illusion, your strength is formidable. You can walk through stone, you can walk through time. What else can you do? What else did that eye teach you that not even I know how to test? You guard a living power. I want it."

"Nyx, be careful," Meguet begged, white, trembling. "Please stop—"

"What mind is in that eye?"

"You will go too far—too far even for me to protect you. Nyx, please—"

The dark walls blinked, hid Nyx. Meguet turned, drawn as always toward the Cygnet's eye, and found her there, reaching out to it with both hands.

Finally the voices within her spoke. They checked her, stilled a thought that would have transfixed Nyx within that moment, left her always reaching, never grasping. *Wait,* the Guardians said. She waited; their voices stilled, left a silence in her like the silence in the face of the moon. Nyx's hands touched the prism, held it.

In the misty light between her hands, the Cygnet flew.

Corleu saw it within the globe. It left him no time to think, no time to move; he stood at the globe, reaching for it, his hands settling on it before he had even gotten off the tomb. He never felt the hot glass. Here, it was, he knew: The thing that trapped him and would set him free, the Cygnet, flying through that mist between time, to the place where it had hidden its heart.

A face formed out of the mist; mist lingered in the eyes. "Nyx," he said, a small word startled out of him that seemed to echo in whispers behind him. She also looked surprised, at something he could not see.

And then he saw.

FIVE

HE dropped his hands, spun in horror and nearly impaled himself on the blade burrowing against his throat. Down the length of it, he saw Meguet's eyes.

They stared at one another: he seeing green, hearing the green rustling corn leaves and knowing what they whispered of in their dry, ancient voices. *Nothing*, he heard, *nothing, nothing, nothing*, because that is what he glimpsed between him and the blade poised so surely in her hands that the light on it did not even tremble. She saw him dead. He had crept into the heart of time and held the Cygnet's secret between his hands, revealing it to the wild, dangerous powers he had brought with him. She saw, held him transfixed with what was in her eyes. But her hands did not move to complete the image.

Kill, she heard within her, and felt the ancient, killing anger sweep through her. Light shook down the sword. He saw Tiel's face, smelled the lavender in her hair, and then sorrow thrust a sharp, heavy blade into his throat. He opened his mouth, breath grating through him, and realized that he was still alive.

He was powerless against her, she sensed. Powerless to lift a finger to help himself: He did not even carry a knife. Still stunned by what he had seen, he could not even speak, beg, bargain for his life. Only his eyes spoke: of a terrible despair. Powerless as a swamp bird in Nyx's house, and yet he had made his way to a place not even Nyx herself had found. He had known where to look. He had recognized what he had seen. . . .

She heard her own voice finally, among the clamoring winds of centuries. The voices cried at her; she beat them back with her own: *I am your eyes and feet, I am your killing hand. I live in this world, I look into the eyes of those you tell me to kill. I have the right to be heard. How could he have reached this place without a Guardian's powers? He has looked into the Cygnet's eye. He is born to guard.*

She could barely speak, among the wild voices. Neither had moved, except him to take a breath. Together they had formed a private moment within a slow, slow drawing out of time around them. Nyx still held the prism, walls were still changing, Chrysom's effigy shadowed the air, faces were still coming visible around her. "Wayfolk." Her voice shook. "What are you?"

"I—" He stuck, mute, forgetting how to talk as his eyes ran again over her face, her hair. "I never knew," he said helplessly.

"What did you see in the eye?"

"The heart of the Cygnet."

"What you have searched for."

"Yes," he whispered. Light flashed from her blade again; it bit at him and he jerked, feeling the sweat run down his face.

"I should kill you."

"Likely."

"Why do I recognize you?"

So he told story, his life hanging on his great-gran's tale. Her green eyes narrowed at him through the tale; her face was hard and pale as marble. But it reached her. He felt the blade shift slightly against him. Something flicked into her eyes, memory, expression, something that was not death.

"My great-grandfather," she said tautly. "He was a restless man, with odd, stray power. He lived in Withy Hold until heritage drew him here. He would have taken a Wayfolk girl in a cornfield."

"How she remembered," he said, "was she saw and took as well. It was what she came back to all her life. The place where time stops. Where green never fades. Where story begins. When I saw you in that house, I saw what she told: corn-leaf eyes and corn-silk hair. But that wasn't all. It wasn't even close to all, what I saw in you."

"No." The voices within her were all silent now, waiting, it seemed, for judgment from her of this dangerous, bastard power. She lifted the blade finally, held it an inch or two away from him, still tense, still watchful. "You found what you need here. What will you—"

"How can you ask?" he cried, seeing it again: the black swan flying into the mist of Nyx's eyes. "I couldn't lift a finger against her. When I told the tinker yes, it was stories I was thinking of: the heart kept inside a nut inside a tree, or locked in a box on one side of the world with the key in the other. I didn't know it would be in someone living! And she——she wanted this thing I looked for. She said she wanted its power."

Meguet was silent. She lowered the blade, let the tip fall to the floor, her eyes wide, troubled. "Nyx," she said softly.

"You'd think a bird would have chosen better."

"She wasn't always so . . ." Her eyes searched around them: Nyx's hands had fallen, the effigy had seeped back into its own time. The forces gathered against the Cygnet had pulled themselves clear into the moment. She said quickly, "Hide. Go back through time."

He shook his head. "I can't. You know I can't. Cygnet is in danger."

"Do you have a Guardian's full power?"

"I'll find out, likely. If not," he added bleakly, "maybe I'll stand a better chance at finding Tiel as a ghost. But who is it the Cygnet is in most danger from? Gold King's heart or Nyx's?"

He was unprepared for time roiling back over them like a fierce, moon-tossed tide. Nyx's hands finished falling away from the prism. She turned, her face still wearing a private, startled expression at what she had seen within it. Then the Warlock stepped out of the shadows.

Her hands were moving before she even changed expression. A huge red ball formed around him; he snarled soundlessly, testing it with his hands. The Gold King drew a sword that was a blinding stroke of light, and dragged his chain toward the Cygnet's eye. Meguet, stunned by his flat, metallic sun-face, the lines wrought into it of fury and cruelty, recognized the tinker only by the gold he wore, and the tricks he played with light. She moved into his path, her back to the prism, holding the broadsword between them with both hands. She heard him laugh. The Warlock exploded out of his glass prison, throwing splinters of fire everywhere. The Blind Lady, gathering them out of the air, began to weave a net of flame.

The Gold King's sword wheeled, moving so fast it left its reflection across an arc of air. It caught one of the Cygnet wings along the grip of Meguet's sword and wrenched it from her hands. It flew across the room to-ward the Dancer. As she looked at it, the swans on the hilt and pommel, etched along the blade, startled away from it, flocked together as they flew, tiny birds turning desperately along the curved walls.

Meguet pulled the Gold King's relentless path along a fine, slow, narrow line of time; he walked his halting pace toward the prism, but the distance he crossed was minute. The Blind Lady lifted a hand toward them, reshaped the Gold King's path, and he pulled himself close to Meguet. He was molten, she saw; blisters of gold appeared and disappeared along his armor. Nyx swung toward them. Her face seemed as detached as ever, concentrating, as she juggled spells, but her eyes were wide, and there was a desperate edginess to her movements. She flung out a hand, frowning. The Gold King's chain lifted ponderously, began to wrap itself around him.

He only laughed again, the dark, jangled, echoing laughter that Meguet had heard before. He was so close to her, she could feel the heat within him. She would not back; Corleu, behind her, gripped her finally, pulled her a step or two closer to the Cygnet's eye. The Warlock sent the small birds scattering out of the air, dead at Nyx's feet.

She stared down at them, a moment that cost her. The Blind Lady flung her web. It fell over Nyx, a weave of fire and light that tangled around her. She cried out suddenly. Meguet, her heart pounding at the sound, left the Cygnet's eye to Corleu and moved to her, so quickly that the Gold King, swinging his chain at her, tripped only empty air.

"Wayfolk," the Gold King said, facing him. He put out a burning hand; Corleu flinched back from it. His shadow, flung forward by the light within the prism, fell over the Gold King. For an instant he was tinker again, with shaggy night-black hair and smiling golden eyes. "You found what I wanted. Why fight me? I'll return what's yours."

"I didn't promise you someone living!"

The tinker shrugged. "Who will miss her? She's swamp-mired. Her heart is full of little bones. Who would want her ruling Ro Holding?"

"The Cygnet—"

"A bird, like the ones she pulled apart?"

"It's more than bird," he said desperately, but the tinker smiled his mocking smile and shifted out of Corleu's shadow. Armed again, masked in light, he swung his hand at Corleu, his upturned face glowing pale in the light from the prism. The spiked armor hit Corleu like stone. Thrown out of the Gold King's path, he hit the wall and clung, blinking, trying to stay on his feet while the wall moved against him. The floor bucked suddenly; he fell to his knees.

Wayfolk, he heard suddenly, deep in him: the frail, whispering winds of voices. *Watch his shadow.*

It lay under his hands, the Gold King's shadow, stretching away from him. Its hands reached toward the prism's reflection, a complex dance of light thrown along the wall. The shadow of a swan flew into the fractured light.

Shadow-hands closed around it. The bird eluded, flew again into the light. Again the hands grasped. The bird flew.

The rhythm of it transfixed Corleu; the action seemed of a world apart, a different time—small, silent movements he could draw out, he felt, if he wanted. In his mind, he changed one color trembling on the wall. The Cygnet flew, the hands grasped. He changed another color, made it a different reflection, in a different time. The hands grasped, closed, empty; the bird flew. He changed a color. A different shadow, a different time, a different world. The hands closed. The bird flew.

How many worlds? he wondered, fascinated. How many times?

Then a blood fox's shadow leaped across the wall. Corleu heard its bark. His mind, a sparkling prism, moved too slowly to shift into the Warlock's time. Something struck him. He slid helplessly on a tide of splintered light. The wave broke, slammed him against the wall, then let him fall onto his back, half-stunned, blind, heaving for breath. He smelled blood fox, felt a warm, snarling weight on his chest. And then he felt its sharp claw over his heart.

Meguet saw him fall. The Warlock was invisible, but its blood-fox shadow hunched over Corleu, clear on the wall. Her mind was tangled in the Blind Lady's net, tracing its threads of fire and time one by one, breaking them. As fast as she broke, the Blind Lady wove. Nyx and the Dancer were fighting over Moro Ro's sword. Birds flew, fell dead; the blade formed, turned to peacock feather; the blade formed again, made of fire, streaked the air toward Meguet. Flame crumpled against something invisible, blew out, re-formed. It was an idle but desperate game, to keep Nyx from freeing herself from the net. The time in its threads was slowing her movements, measuring them to its flow. Soon, Meguet knew, the sword would form, slip beyond her, strike.

She glimpsed the Dancer's chaos then: panic, nightmare. *I cannot hold them,* she thought, almost in wonder, for failure was unthinkable. She saw Corleu move under the blood fox, like a drowned man touched curiously by fingers of tide. Then he lay still again. The blood fox lifted its muzzle, barked.

I need help! she cried down the centuries, then saw the Gold King's hands close within the prism.

No bird flew.

Her desperate unweaving faltered; unravelled lines of time snarled in her mind. She heard Nyx cry. "Meguet!" The great, flaming blade flew at her again. Nyx's hand, rising to stop it, was a scant moment late. It bore onward. Meguet, her attention snared between Nyx trapped in time, and the small bird trapped in the Gold King's hands, hesitated, torn. Nyx turned to follow the sword's path, tightening the net around her. She swayed, her face glistening, white with exhaustion, as if time were wearing at her. "Meguet!" Her voice was husky with weariness and horror. "Use your power! Save yourself!"

But she had been given no time for herself: Time was divided between the Cygnet and its heart. She could only pick apart one final thread in the web of time around Nyx, and then the great sword severed the future in front of her eyes. She did not see it swerve; it impaled her breath as it flew past her, or through her, left a deadly edge of silver in her vision. She closed her eyes, shaken by her own heartbeat, and felt time knit itself again as she found her breath. Opening her eyes, she saw Corleu lift his head finally, groggy, bewildered. Silver caught his eye. He turned his head, saw it come.

"No!" Nyx snapped. A thread in the fiery net snapped in response. She dredged a word from somewhere deep in her; Meguet did not recognize her voice. Another thread snapped. She threw both hands upward, shaped the word out of shadows, it seemed, and white fire torn across the air out of the shining prism. The starry fire fell over Nyx, dissolving the net of time. She reached up again, drew at air with her entire body. Air sculpted her, lifted her. Meguet saw her eyes as she flew past, pale lavender, strange in a swan's face.

Then the white wings shifted time as they fell; in a fractured movement, the swan was across the room, ahead of the flaming sword, swerving in the air to push it out of its deadly path. But the sword, searing the air in front of Corleu's eyes, was faster. He caught a confused image of silver fire, white feathers; he heard Meguet's voice, crying out with his own.

The sword formed its own wings. A swan's neck extended along the blade. It came so close that for an instant Corleu saw a night-black eye, with a pearl of light in it from the prism's light. Then it pulled itself up, climbed the air, its black wings thundering past his face. He gasped. The swans wheeled together in the small chamber, one black, one white, turning and turning endless circles that gradually lost their frantic speed, slowed to an endless, timeless spiral, as if they had all the night and all the stars to fly through.

Then there was only one swan, and its black shadow; one angled down to meet the other. The white swan touched its shadow; Nyx reappeared, standing beside Corleu.

There was not a sound in the chamber; Gold King and Blind Lady might have been among the statues Chrysom had made. Meguet stood as still, feeling something build in the silence, like another wild, powerful, mysterious word. Nyx felt it, too. She looked around her, hands poised to work, her shadow falling protectively over Corleu. But no one moved; faces only stared back at her, wordless, motionless, masked.

She began to tremble suddenly, gazing back, incredulously, at what she had been fighting. "What are you?" she breathed. "What is it you are looking for?" She looked at Corleu when they did not answer. The Blood Fox, its human shadow lying beneath Nyx's feet, moved its paw from his chest. It sat back on its haunches, grinning its fox grin as Corleu pulled himself up. Even he could not stop staring at her.

"You saved my life," he said in wonder. "You did all that, became swan, just to save a muckerheaded Wayfolk man who brought all this on you—"

"But what—" Her voice broke away from her, echoed off the high stones. "Corleu, what have you been searching for?"

"The heart of the—" He paused. His eyes widened on her face, as all the threads of the tale they had made among them wove into place. She wavered under his sudden, burning tears. He whispered, "Your heart."

It was such a rare and startling sight, Nyx weeping, that Meguet felt her own throat tighten. Wordless, spellbound, she watched the Gold King loose what he held in his hands: A shaft of sunlight struck the prism. Color danced along the walls. Her eyes widened; she put her hands suddenly to her mouth.

"Just story, you see," he said to her, and was tinker again. "Just a piece of sky." He reached up, snapped the gold chain around his neck. The sound it made as it hit the floor boomed ponderously against the walls, then faded into the rustling wings of small birds. The Blind Lady was busy reweaving her net, gathering its fiery, broken threads into a patch over a hole in one of her skirts. She whispered as she worked, whispered story, Corleu knew, all the story in the world.

"But you always fight the Cygnet," he said dazedly, as the tinker reached down, helped him to his feet. "In all the tales."

"Look again," the tinker said, "and it's Cygnet fighting us: whatever sun touches, whatever dreams, whatever works magic, whatever flies. . . . When the heart casts a shadow instead of dancing light, there story begins."

The Blind Lady finished her weaving. She took the ring off her finger, tossed it in the air. The Ring of Time opened in the heart of the maze, a blinding silver that enclosed the night. She stepped back. The Fire Bear lumbered through it, sending a soundless roar of its black fire across the stars. The Blood Fox leaped through, dragging its tantalizing shadow. The shadow flung something behind it before night swallowed it. A small red prism cracked in two on the stone floor, a drop of darker red glistening within it.

The Blind Lady's sightless face turned toward Meguet before she left. "You have some talent," she commented, "with my threads." A white peacock feather drifted to the floor as she vanished.

The tinker stepped toward the Ring. "Wait!" Corleu cried, and he turned, his eyes luminous, smiling his thin, equivocal smile.

"Don't fret, Wayfolk. I always pay my debts." He put his hand over his heart, bowed his head to them both. "Thanks," he said, and added to Meguet, "I'll do a bit of tinkering for you, when I go."

He walked through the Ring, into a darkness squared by stars, one gold star rising above it. The Ring dwindled; stone walls patched the night. The Ring fell to the floor, a tiny circle, then a stroke of silver, then wings and circling swans on a flawless, sun-forged blade.

Corleu picked it up, held it out to Meguet. She met his stunned and weary gaze; she took the sword in one hand, and slipped her other arm around his shoulders. Their pale heads touched. Together they watched Nyx wipe her face on a threadbare velvet sleeve. She turned away from them without speaking, moved into some private vision under the Cygnet's eye.

The Holder and her children stood waiting beside Rush in the black tower. It was morning, Meguet saw, startled, as she pushed aside the Cygnet banner. The rich spring light tumbled down from the high, narrow windows, lay in slabs across the stones. They all looked worn, fretted, sleepless. Even Calyx's hair had tumbled down.

Nyx went to the Holder. She said huskily, her head bowed, "In my house in the swamp, there was a room full of mirrors. I looked into them. I never saw what they reflected. Their reflections seemed to have brought me here, forced me to look again."

The Holder touched her hair, drew it back from her face. "I don't understand," she said wearily. "But you are safe and Meguet is safe, and that is all I need to know now."

"The House is safe." She added, "The Wayfolk man fought for the Cygnet."

The Holder looked at Corleu. His face burned; he felt Wayfolk to his bones under that dark, powerful gaze. Then she moved it to Meguet and he could breathe again.

"How?" she demanded.

"It seems," Meguet said, "my great-grandfather met his great-gran. In a cornfield."

The Holder made a blackbird's noise. "It's unprecedented."

"His hair is like yours, Meguet," Calyx exclaimed. "Are we all related, then?"

Corleu stared at her delicate face, which surely must bruise under a whisper. Iris said tiredly, "Work it out later, Calyx. What I want to know is how, when Meguet and Nyx went into the maze, Meguet and Nyx and a Wayfolk man came out of it."

"What I want to know," Calyx said, "is will you take the spell off Rush, now?" She patted his arm soothingly as he stood there, silent and pale, looking, to Corleu's startled eye, remarkably like the Warlock's distant descendant. "I can understand why you didn't want him wandering around in the maze, setting things on fire at random, but he's harmless now."

A touch of color rose in Nyx's face. "I forgot about Rush." Her eyes flicked, troubled, to the Holder; the Holder's eyes narrowed.

"Now what have you done?"

"I'm not sure. . . ." She looked at Calyx, standing close to Rush, then hid her eyes behind her hand. "I'm very tired," she sighed. "Calyx, just talk to him. I'm afraid he'll shout at me."

"Rush," Calyx said. She stood in front of him, her hands on his arms, her pale, weary, smiling face coaxing his bemused, distant gaze. "Rush, wake up. It's morning and the house is still standing. Nyx is here."

He was looking at her suddenly, blinking, as if she had just wakened him out of a dream of nine years. "Calyx?" he said, and touched her face. Meguet heard Nyx's faint sigh of relief, met her eyes a moment.

"Nyx is here," Calyx said again, her smile deepening; he lifted his face, jerking himself farther out of dreams.

"Nyx," he said. A long look passed between them. He drew breath. "You never wanted me to follow you," he said ruefully. "But last night you went too far. Farther then I could ever go."

"I know," she said softly. "I hope you will forgive me. What happened—whatever happened down in the maze was my doing also. My fault. You were right: I wandered too far. Corleu and Meguet brought me back. That is how I would tell the story," she said to Corleu, "if I were telling."

"If I were telling," he said, "I would say you brought yourself back."

"What I would say," Iris said, "is that someone should tell us what happened all night down there. Meguet?"

She shook her head quickly. "No, not me," she said, remembering the Gold King's molten face swinging toward her, masked and furious, and the tinker in the woods, smiling as he picked out the lizard's eye, and the sword flying at her, and then the swan. . . . "I only saw pieces of it."

"Corleu, then."

"No," he said with sudden intensity. "I'll never tell. It's not mine, not for me. I only want to find what I lost, which is," he added, "near enough like what was almost lost in the maze."

They were silent; the blood fox eyes moved to Nyx. "Then you," Rush said, "must tell."

She met his eyes. "It's a very long story, Rush. And not yet over. I still have things to learn."

"Nyx," the Holder breathed, "not again!"

Nyx put a hand on her arm. "I have things to learn in this house," she said gently. "You must teach me."

Horns sounded outside the gate, a startling fanfare that made the pigeons whirr outside the windows. The Holder closed her eyes, touched her wild hair.

"Not Hunter Hold. Not now."

"Now," Calyx sighed.

"Meguet—" The Holder paused, eyeing Meguet's stained uniform, her fraying braid, and flung up her hands. "At least you're dressed and armed. Go to the gate and wait for us. Corleu, don't leave this house. I want to talk to you. Nyx, did you come all the way from the swamp without shoes?"

A stable girl led her horse out as Meguet ran across the yard. It was saddled and caparisoned; the Gatekeeper had seen the Council coming. She pulled herself up wearily, rode to the gate. The impatient, golden flurry sounded again. The Gatekeeper did not come down yet. But he looked down, and his impassive expression strained badly at the sight of her.

The Holder joined Meguet finally, after the horns had sounded a third time. Her children and Rush Yarr sat mounted behind her, in such astonishingly tidy attire that Meguet suspected a sorceress's hand in it. She looked for Corleu, saw him standing with some cottagers near the smithy. Too far, she judged, to slip through the gate unnoticed, in the tangle of entry.

The Holder nodded. Meguet rode to one side of the gate, stood guard, according to ancient ritual, Moro Ro's sword outstretched before the gate. The Gatekeeper opened the gate.

The Gold King stood outside: the Hold Sign of Hunter Hold, the crowned King in his dark house on a field of dark blue, newly sewn, for the silver thread depicting the stars glittered like water in the sun. Cedar Kell's two young children held it, one on each side, their faces immobile with terror at the sight of the Holder before them. The Holder began the ritual that in Moro Ro's time had cost blood for every word.

"Who speaks for Hunter Hold?"

Cedar Kell stepped in front of the banner, looking tired, dusty from travelling, but cheerful.

"Kell speaks for Hunter Hold," she said in her booming voice, that must have laid threats on her children, for not a smile or a tear touched their faces.

"Under what sign?"

"The sign of the Gold King."

"Under what stars?"

"The yellow star its lintel, the yellow star its roof, the four stars of red and pale its walls, the blue star marking its door latch. Under this sign the Gold King holds Hunter Hold."

"Does the Gold King recognize the Cygnet?"

"The Gold King recognizes the Cygnet."

"Under the sign of the Cygnet, the Gold King holds Hunter Hold. For the end of time, the Cygnet holds the Gold King under its eye, beneath its wing, within its heart. None shall break this bond."

"The Gold King holds Hunter Hold, the Cygnet holds the Gold King. Under its eye, beneath its wing, within its heart. So bound are they, so bound are we. Truth in my words, peace in my heart, Lauro Ro."

"And peace in mine," the Holder said, and smiled. "Welcome to my house, Cedar Kell."

Meguet lifted the broadsword, turned her horse away to let what amounted to a small travelling village through the gate. She remained mounted, sword sheathed, until the Council members, families, kin, retinue had entered. When the baggage and supply carts started rumbling in, she dismounted, gave her horse to the stablers. She found Corleu again, looking tense and frayed in the crush.

He seemed relieved when he saw her. "I must go," he said. "Can you tell the Holder that? I'll come back, but there's only one thing in the world I want to do now—"

She put her hand on his shoulder. "I know. But you can't leave. Not yet. You are half-Guardian—"

"And all Wayfolk at this moment," he said, his face turned to the open gate. "I've been in walls too long."

"Don't be afraid. You have kin within these walls."

He looked at her, silent. Then he sighed, his body loosening finally under her touch. "Seems strange. Last night you nearly killed me. Now, you're the only reason I might stay."

"You must do better than might. Be patient. You have a formidable inheritance. You'll never be able to stray far from this house. The heart that

brought you here will bind you here. Wait for the Holder." His eyes moved to
the black tower. She saw him draw breath and hold it. "Wait," she said again.
"The Holder will send for you soon."

"How much," he asked abruptly, "do I tell her?"

"You tell her everything. But only her. No one else in this world."

He nodded, his eyes still on the tower, with the Cygnet flying over it, by
day and night. He sighed again, sagged against the smithy wall.

She left him there, to watch him from the Gatekeeper's turret. She felt,
climbing the stairs, that there was no end to them. Then she was at the top,
sitting thoughtlessly, watching the sea, and the Gatekeeper help ease a wagon
through the gate. The sunlight touched her eyes gently, closed them.

She was asleep when the Gatekeeper came up finally. He smoothed her
hair from her face, in small, gentle touches; she woke dreaming of wings.
Then she saw the burning sword fly at her again and she started. Sword
turned to swan, swan to Gatekeeper's taut, tired face.

She caught her breath at the vision. Then she leaned forward, quickly,
into the warm, familiar dark of his embrace. She slid one hand around his
neck, where she could feel the blood beat. "It's over," she said finally. "The
House is safe. They've all gone."

"Have they? Through which gate?"

"The gate they came through."

"There is only one gate to this house."

She nodded against him, her eyes closed. "And you are the only Gatekeeper."

He was silent; she felt him begin to speak, hesitate. She lifted her head; he
held her face between his hands, looked into her eyes. He said at last, very
softly, "Why is there a swan in your eyes?"

"There always is," she answered. "Have you never noticed? A great wild
black swan, who sometimes watches me sleep . . . The only swan that never
leaves this house, summer or winter." She smiled a little, at his stillness. "It's
only story."

His head dropped; his lips touched hers, feather-light. She closed her
eyes and heard, from some distant corner of the yard, children's voices,
chanting to some game:

In a wooden ring,
Find a stone circle,
In the stone ring
Find a silver circle . . .

She felt Hew move; sun spilled over her face. She saw the back of his head as he leaned out of the turret, looking over the wall.

"What is it?"

"We have a guest, it seems."

"Who now? The whole world just came in."

"Wayfolk by the look of her."

She caught breath, leaned across him to look down as he spoke to the visitor, as courteously as he would have spoken to a lord's daughter. The girl was slight, with long, straight, heavy black hair, and wide-set dark eyes. Wayfolk to the bone, yet standing alone, and prepared to cross a threshold.

"How can I help you?"

"I'm looking for someone," she said, her voice, gentle and timid, barely carrying above the tide's voice. "We came down from Withy Hold. A Wayfolk man named Corleu. We passed a tinker said he might be here."

The Gatekeeper got up to open the gate. Meguet, trembling, closed her eyes again, felt the sun lay its hand across her face, catch her sudden tears.

Corleu, slumped against the wall, his eyes on the dark tower, turned his head at the sound of the opening gate. His heart saw before the light relinquished the dark, slender figure to his eyes: He felt the green timeless secret place bloom in him again, with all its scents and still pools and sweet, rustling shadows.

Tiel crossed the threshold as he began to run. They met within walls, in a place with no walls.

The Cygnet
and the Firebird

For Howard Morhaim,
the Dark Knight of the Soul,
with love (and no cholesterol)

ONE

MEGUET Vervaine stood at the threshold of Chrysom's black tower, swans flying at her back and shoulder and wrists, swans soaring out of her hands. She had stood so for hours. Dressed in black silk with the Cygnet of Ro Holding spanning silver moons on mantle and tunic, she held the ancient broadsword of Moro Ro, unsheathed, tip to the floor, guarding against stray goose and cottage child's ball and wandering butterfly, for within the broad, circular hall the councils from the four Holds had gathered to discuss their differences under the sign of the Cygnet and the formidable eye of Lauro Ro. In Moro Ro's day, the threshold guards would have faced both chamber and yard, prepared for violence from any direction, not least from the volatile councils. Meguet, armed by tradition rather than necessity, faced the hall to keep the sun out of her eyes. She had gathered her long corn-silk hair into a severe braid; her eyes, green a shade lighter than the rose leaves that climbed the walls of the thousand-year-old tower, kept a calm and careful watch over the sometimes testy gathering. Members of the oldest families in Ro Holding had made long, uncomfortable journeys to meet for the Holding Council in a place where, not many weeks before, Meguet had found herself raising the sword in her hands to battle for her life. She did not expect trouble; it had come and gone, but some part of her still tensed at shadows, at unexpected voices.

But only the councilors themselves had provided any excitement, and that was contingent upon such complexities as border taxes. There had been sharp debate earlier in the day between Hunter Hold and the Delta over mines in the border mountains, which had kept everyone awake on the ninth day of the long council. Now, the heavy late-afternoon light, the pigeons murmuring in the high windows, and Haf Berg's young, pompous, querulous voice maundering endlessly about sheep, threw a stupor over the hall. Meguet heard a snore from one of the back tables. She stifled a yawn. A sudden wind tugged at her light mantle. The air was a heady mix of brine and sun-steeped roses on the tower vines: it seemed to blow from everywhere at once: from past and future, from unexplored countries where wooden flowers opened on tree boughs to reveal strange, rich spices, and sheep the colors of autumn leaves wandered through the hills. . . .

She felt herself drifting on the alien wind; a sound brought her back. The hall was silent; she wondered if she herself had made some noise. But it was only Haf Berg, sitting down at last, working his chair fussily across the flagstones. Lauro Ro watched him impassively. She sat at the crescent dais table, the Cygnet flying like a shadow through tarnished midnight stars on the vast, timeworn banner behind her. Her elegant face was unreadable, her wild dark hair so unnaturally tidy that Meguet suspected Nyx had bewitched it into submission. The Holder's heir sat at her right, wearing her enigmatic reputation with composure. Lauro Ro asked, "Will anyone challenge Haf Berg's painstaking examination of the problems of sheep pasturage on the south border of Berg Hold?" There was a daunting note in her voice. Only a pigeon challenged. Iris, on the Holder's left, consulted a paper and whispered to her mother.

Rush Yarr sat beside Iris, and Calyx beside Nyx. The two younger sisters, one fair and reclusive, the other dark and distinguished most of the time by extraordinary rumors, bore the intense scrutiny of the council members calmly. When Calyx spoke, pearls and doves did not fall from her lips. When Nyx spoke, toads did not fall, nor did lightning flash. But it had taken days for the anticipation to fade.

The Holder spoke again. Linden Dacey of Withy Hold wished to bring up the matter of . . . Meguet tightened her shoulders, loosened them. A knot burned at the nape of her neck. She shifted slightly, easing some of her weight onto the blade she held. Across the room, the sorceress lifted her eyes at the flash of light.

They looked at one another a moment: cousins bound by blood and by secret, ancient ways. Memories gathered between them in the sunlit air. The

swans on the hilt and etched blade in Meguet's hands had taken wing, Nyx
had transformed herself from bog-witch into Cygnet's heir so recently that
the sorcery in that hidden time and place beneath their feet must still be re-
bounding against the labyrinth stones. The sorceress's eyes, mist-pale in the
light, seemed mildly speculative, as if, Meguet thought, she contemplated
turning her cousin into a bat to liven up the tedium. Meguet, returning her
attention to the proceedings, half-wished she would.

Linden Dacey had brought up the matter of a border feud between
Withy Hold and the Delta. A river had shifted, or been shifted; the south
border, defined for centuries, was suddenly uncertain... The great Hold
banners swayed and glittered above her head as she spoke; eyes caught at
Meguet. The Blood Fox of the Delta prowled on starry pads; one eye glinted
as if thought had flashed through its bright threads. The Gold King of
Hunter Hold, the crowned and furious sun, glared out of his prison of
night. Meguet, gazing back, felt a sudden chill, as if the face of spun gold
thread were alive again and watching.

Someone from the Delta interrupted Linden Dacey. There was an interesting squabble on the council floor. Old Maharis Kell jerked mid-snore out
of his nap. The Holder let it rage a moment, probably to wake everyone up.
Then she cut through it in a voice that must have brought a few cottagers in
the outer yard to a dead stop. Rush Yarr slid a hand over his mouth. Calyx,
catching a tremor in the air, glanced at him. Rush, Meguet noted, had recov-
ered his sense of humor—or discovered it, she wasn't sure which, for he had
loved a sorceress who was never home for so long that likely even he didn't remember if he had one. Calyx had entered the doorless walls of the tower he
had built around himself, and he found her inside his heart.

Linden Dacey, finished finally, yielded debate to the chastened Delta
councilor. Gold streaked suddenly through a west window. Meguet eyed her
shadow, guessed at the time. Another hour, if that... The Delta councilor
bit a word in half and was still. Meguet raised her eyes. On the dais, no one
breathed. Behind her the yard was soundless. Not a child's shout, a groaning
wagon wheel, an iron blow from the smithy, disturbed the sudden, bewitched
silence. Meguet stared at Nyx, wondering if, bored or day-dreaming, she had
thrown some spell over the council. But Nyx was entranced by the table, it
seemed; she gazed at it, wide-eyed, motionless.

Someone had slowed time.

In the weird stillness, Meguet heard a footfall in the grass behind her. She
whirled, her heart hammering, and brought the broadsword up in both
hands. A man stood within the tower ring, staring up at the solitary black

tower. The flaring arc of silver from the door as the broadsword cut through light startled him; Meguet felt his attention riveted suddenly on her. In the brilliant, late light, the stranger cast no shadow.

She drew a slow, noiseless breath, tightening her hold on the blade, trapped in a world out of time by his sorcery and by her peculiar heritage: the sleepless compulsion to guard what lay hidden within the tower's heart. The man's face, blurred by the dazzling light or perhaps by shifting time, was difficult to see. He seemed a profusion of colors: scarlet, gold, white, dust, blue, silver, that sorted itself out as he moved, crossing the yard with a strong, energetic stride.

Tall as she was, Meguet was forced to look up at him. His hair and skin were the same color as the dust on the hem of his red robe and his scuffed yellow boots, as if the parched gold-brown earth of some vast desert blown constantly through sun-drenched air had seeped into him. A strange winged animal embroidered in white wound itself in and out of the folds of cloth at his chest. The robe was belted with a curious, intricate weave of silver; silver glinted also at his wrists beneath his sleeves. A pouch of dark blue leather was slung over his shoulder; another, of dusty yellow silk, hung beside that. He stopped in front of Meguet's blade. She saw his face clearly then, as surprised by her as she was by him.

His eyes flicked over her shoulder at the motionless hall, then back to her. His broad, spare face was young yet under its weathering; his eyes, a light, glinting blue, were flecked with gold.

He said, amazed, "Who are you?"

Meguet, abandoned, with only a broadsword to protect the house against sorcery, found her voice finally. "You are in the house of the Holders of Ro Holding. If you have business with the Holder, present yourself to the Gatekeeper."

He glanced behind him at the little turret above the gate, where the Gatekeeper leaned idly against the stones, a motionless figure in household black watching something in the yard. "Him." He turned back. "He looks busy." He touched the blade at his chest with one finger, but did not turn it. He grunted softly, his eyes going back to Meguet. "This is real."

"Yes."

"Well, what do you expect to do with it? You can't keep me out of this tower with a sword. How can you have the power to see me through shifted time and still wave that under my nose? What are you? Are you a mage?"

"You have no business in this tower, you have no business in this house, and you have no business questioning me."

"I'm curious," he said. "You eluded my sorcery, and I had only thought to come and go so secretly no one would ever know."

"Why?" she asked sharply. "Why have you come here?"

"I want something from this tower."

She felt herself grow so still that no light trembled on the blade. "You may not enter."

"There are a thousand ways to enter a tower. Every block of solid stone is an open doorway. You can't guard every threshold."

All fear had left her voice; it was thin and absolute. "If I must, I can."

He was silent, puzzled again, at the certainty in her words. "It can't be the sword," he said at last. "The magic is in you, not that. True?" He caught the blade in one hand, so quickly that not the flick of an eyelash forewarned her. She wrenched at it; it might as well have been sunk in stone. "Not," he mused, "the sword, then." He loosed it as abruptly. She steadied herself, breathing audibly, while he studied her, his eyes quizzical, secret. "Perhaps," he said finally, "it's what you guard in this tower that gives you such power. Is that it?"

She raised the blade again, swallowing drily. "No one may enter the tower at this time without permission from the Holder. Those are my instructions. You may not enter."

"But the Holder will never know," he said softly. "What I want has been hidden for centuries. No one knows it is here, and no one will miss it when it is gone. I will never return to Ro Holding. Let me pass. If all you're brandishing against me is a point of honor, you won't be dishonored. No one will ever know."

"I will," Meguet said succinctly. "And so will you. Honor is a word you would not bother to toss at me, if it meant nothing to you. You may not enter."

He was silent again, so still he might have put himself under his own mysterious spell. His eyes had narrowed; light or memory flashed through them. "What made you time or honor's guardian?" he breathed. "You have seen a few of its back roads, its crooked lanes and alleyways. Haven't you? But you are not a mage. Or are you?" She did not answer. He stepped closer; she did not move. He stepped so close that the blade snagged the golden eye of the winged beast across his chest. He said, "If you do not let me enter, I will turn every rose on this tower into flame."

"Then you will burn what you have come for."

He moved closer. The blade turned a little in her hands as if the animal had shifted under it, and she felt the sweat break out on her face.

"I will seal every door and window in this tower, and turn it into a tomb for those you guard."

"It is already a tomb." Her voice shook. He stepped so close the blade slid ghostlike into him. Her shoulders burned at the sudden weight, but she held the blade steady under his expressionless gaze.

"If you do not let me enter, I will kill you."

"Then," she said, as sweat and light burned into her eyes, and the clawed, airy animal whipped beneath the blade like a desperate thing, "one of us will die."

He stepped back then, as easily as if the great sword were made of smoke. The animal turned a smoldering eye at her and subsided into the cloth. The blade trembled in her hands; still she did not lower it. The mage's face changed; the expression on it startled her.

"You deserve better than a doorway," he said abruptly. "What kind of upside-down house is this where no power but honor is pitted against the likes of me? You can't stop me. You can barely hold that sword. It is shaking in your hands. It is so heavy it weighs like stone, it drags you down. It is heavier than old age, heavier than grief. It falls like the setting sun, slowly, slowly. Watch it fall. Watch the tiny flame of light on its tip shift, move down the blade toward your hands. Watch it. The light trembles among the silver swan wings. What is your name?"

"Meguet Vervaine."

"Is it night or day?"

"I do not know."

"Are you awake or dreaming?"

"I do not know."

"Are you a mage?"

"No."

"Have you a mage's powers?"

"No."

"How do you have the power to see and move through shifted time?"

"I have no power."

"Then who gives you power?"

"No one."

"You have power. You are standing here talking to me when no one else in this house can move."

"I have no power."

"What gives you power?"

"Nothing."

"You are guarding something from me as steadfastly as you guard this door. I will enter this tower. Do you have the power to stop me?"

"You may not enter."

"Do you have the power to stop me?"

Meguet was silent. Wind brushed her face, a cool breeze smelling of twilight. For a moment she stared senselessly at what she saw: the inner yard, the towers, the outer yard through the arches, where cottagers' children flung a ball back and forth, and the Gatekeeper on the ground, his back to her, opened the gate to a couple of riders. Then she looked down at her hands. They were locked so fiercely, so protectively around the hilt of Moro Ro's sword that her fingers ached, loosening. The smell of roses teased her memory. *I fell asleep,* she thought surprisedly. *I had a dream....*

Then the Holder's voice snapped across the chamber. "Meguet!"

She turned, startled. The sword slipped out of her hold, rang against the stones like a challenge, and she saw beside it the rose that had flung itself off the outer wall into the room to lie burning in her shadow. She dragged her eyes away from it to the dais.

Nyx had vanished.

Dream shifted into time, became memory; she felt the blood leap out of her face. She reached down, snatched up the rose and began to run.

On the dais, the sorceress had felt the sudden shift of time.

Intrigued, she simply sat still, not a difficult thing to do for one who had spent nights in the black deserts of Hunter Hold watching the constellations turn and the orange bitterthorn blossom open its fullest to the full moon. She saw Meguet bring up the sword in her hands, turn. The fair-haired stranger stopped at the threshold. Nyx's attention focused, precise and fine-honed, on her cousin, who was waving a blade of sheep grass against the wind. Their voices carried easily across the eerie silence.

She watched, unblinking, while the stranger came so close to Meguet only the swans on the sword hilt protected her. Light sparking off a jewel in Nyx's hair would have alerted the mage; when he forced her to move, he would not see her. But he backed away from Meguet, passed around her, left her defending a breached threshold in a dream. He had paused, for some reason, to pick a rose off the tower vines. He dropped it in Meguet's shadow. He passed among the councilors with no more interest in them than if they had been hedgerows. At the stairs, beneath the Blood Fox prowling between green swamp and starry night on the Delta banner, he hesitated. The power within the tower was complex, layered as it was with Chrysom's ancient wizardry, household ghosts, the impress upon the centuries of every mage or Cygnet's guardian who had left a trace of power lingering in time. Beneath that lay the entombed mage and the vast and intricate power within the Cygnet's heart. He would not recognize that power, but he would be aware, like a man stepping to the edge of a chasm at midnight, that something undefined was catching at his attention. To separate what sorcery the stranger had come to find from the emanations of power and memory within the ancient stones would require at least a walk up the spiral stairs. When the stranger had felt his way through the lingering magic beyond the first curve, Nyx rose. She formed an image of Chrysom's library in her mind, book and stone and rose-patterned windows, and stepped into it.

She waited.

The sight of Nyx reading at one of the tables made the stranger pause a heartbeat, as if his glance into the council chamber had snared her in his memories. But she gazed down at the page—a list of cows who had calved four hundred and ninety years before—with rapt attention. In that magic-steeped chamber he would not notice her mind working. He had reached his goal; his attention flicked like a needle in a compass toward what he had come to steal.

The stone mantel above the fireplace was littered with thousand-year-old oddments of Chrysom's that had somehow survived accidents, misplacements, pilfering and spring cleaning. Nyx had no idea what they were, besides volatile and unpredictable. The stranger glanced briefly at them. He stood in the center of the room, sending out filaments of thought like a spider spinning a web, into tables, hearth, book shelves, ancient weapons, cracked, bubbled mirrors, tapestries on the wall. He ignored Nyx, who, surrounded by mysteries, was reading about cows. He moved finally, abruptly, across the room to kneel at the hearth. His hands closed around one of the massive cornerstones that was crusted with centuries of ash. He tried to shift it. Now that he had shown her where it was, Nyx asked before he found it,

"What in Moro's name are you looking for in there?"

He was so startled that he nearly leaped back into his own time. Parts of him faded and reappeared; a wing on his robe unfolded in the air and folded itself back into thread. He did not so much turn as rearrange himself through shifting moments of time to face her. She recognized the white animal then, from some of Chrysom's ancient drawings: She thought he had imagined it, from some tale so old there was scarcely a word for it in Ro Holding. The mage, his face a few shades paler than dust, studied her while he caught his breath.

He said abruptly, "You were in the hall, down there. I remember you now. Your eyes."

She lifted a brow. "You saw me watching you?"

"No. I remember their color, when I passed the dais. Like a winter sky. You are a mage. It's hard to tell, in this house."

"People who belong in this house recognize me easily." She rested her chin on her palm, contemplating him. "You are a thief. You are not from Ro Holding, or I would know you by now; your remarkable power would have caught my interest."

"You have some remarkable powers yourself," he said with feeling. "You nearly turned me inside-out, scaring me like that."

"I know a few things," she said.

"You don't know what's in this stone. You never knew anything at all was in there. I can name it. That makes it mine."

"Fine," she said drily. "I will let you keep the name. You may take that and yourself out of this tower. How dare you bewitch this entire house and wander through it, pilfering things? What kind of barbaric country taught you that?"

"Only one thing," he pointed out. "One pilfering. That's all I need. Something you have never needed. Let me take it and go. I'll never return to Ro Holding again."

"You have more than theft to answer for. You disturbed my cousin Meguet. You threatened her and tried to coerce her." He opened his mouth to answer, did not. Nyx continued grimly, running one of Calyx's pens absently in and out of her hair, "You used sorcery against her."

"I'm sorry," he said. "I was curious."

"You were cruel."

He drew breath, his eyes flicking away from her; she saw the blood gather under his tan. "I was never taught," he said finally, "to make such fine distinctions. In my country, ignorance is dangerous; curiosity can be ruthless. But I would never have harmed your cousin. I only wanted to know—"

"I know what you only wanted to know." She paused, her own eyes falling briefly. She took the pen out of her hair and laid it down. She folded her hands in front of her mouth and looked at the stranger again. "But it's none of your business. Now leave this house in peace."

He paused, his eyes narrowed faintly, light-filled, hidden. "You're curious, too," he said slowly. "You want this thing only because you don't know what it is." She nodded, unperturbed. For a moment their eyes held, calculating, and then, abruptly, he yielded, tossing up a hand. "I never expected to find this tower so well-guarded. And now I have run out of time. . . ."

And he was gone, to her surprise, as easily and noiselessly as light fading on stones. Distant sounds wove into the air again: children shouting, cows lowing as they came in from the back pastures. The Holder, she remembered suddenly, would be discovering the empty chair beside her. But Meguet would reassure her. Nyx knelt at the hearth, touched the stone with her hands, and then with her mind. Neither moved it. She wrapped her thoughts around the stone, feeling its weight and texture, its size: a single block of charred marble in a hearth so old the stones were all sagging into one another. As she studied it, she felt something watching her. She lifted her head. A crow winging out of the mantel gazed at her out of its black marble eye.

She reached up, touched the eye. Nothing moved. Above it, in relief, the Cygnet flew the length of the mantel through a black marble sky, its eye aligned with the crow's eye. She had to stand on air to reach it. The Cygnet's eye moved nothing. She stood thinking, her own eyes flicking across the scattered convocation of crows, until in all their black stone eyes the pattern formed.

It was a constellation: All the eyes were stars, depicting the Cygnet flying across the night. A riddle, she thought, no one outside of Ro Holding would have guessed. She felt a rare impulse for caution, but dismissed it immediately, too close to the mystery, too curious. One after another she touched the dark stars. The stone, its mortar sifting drily into the firebed, swung free.

She barely had time to look into it, when something struck her—a wind, a thunderbolt—and flung her at the mantel and then into it among the crows. She cried out, startled; her mouth was stopped with stone. She concentrated, found the face of one of the crows and gathered herself like a thought in its stony mind and then into a point of light within its eye. Beneath her, she saw the mage looking into the hollow stone.

Meguet, slamming the library door wide, knocked a shield off the wall. The mage, barely glancing up, flung a hand out impatiently, murmuring. The animal leaped from his breast, a sinuous blur of white that poured to the floor, bounded upward again, catching air with its wings, claws out, aimed at its prey. Meguet threw up her arm, wielding a rose against it. Something— the streak of red in the air, a sound she made—caught the mage's attention. His head snapped around. For an instant the rose stunned him. Then he spoke sharply. The animal halted in mid-flight; white embroidery thread snarled in the air. Nyx dropped like a tear out of the crow's eye, reappeared

in front of Meguet. The air seemed to snarl in her wake as she dragged rem-
nants of the mage's spell from the air and threw them back at him. The mage
began to fray in different directions at once, as if he were spun of fine
threads of time, all unravelling. He cried something before he vanished. The
cry skipped like a rock across water, snatched the gently falling thread. Cry
and thread whirled away into nothing.

Meguet sagged against the open doorway, felt air and brought herself
upright. "Moro's name," she whispered. "What did you do to him?"

Nyx, her eyes flooded with color, untangling herself from her sorcery,
looked bewitched herself, something only half human. "I'm not sure," she
said. "I've never done that before."

"Is he still alive?"

"I have no idea." She drew a deep breath then; her eyes relinquished color,
became familiar. She glanced toward the noise that had followed Meguet up
the stairs. She touched her cousin, who, having fought some ancient and very
peculiar sorcery not many weeks before, seemed oddly shaken by a tidy piece
of work. "Stay here. Keep them out. If he comes back, this time not even
that rose will stop him."

She crossed the room quickly, knelt at the hearth. Meguet, watching the
air for a warning of color, was jostled by the first of the guard who, weapons
drawn, flung themselves precipitously toward the threat to the house. Several
of the more agile councilors were among them. Meguet heard the Holder's
voice farther down the stairwell.

She turned briefly, stilled the guard with a gesture. They quieted, peering
over Meguet's shoulders at Nyx, who was gazing meditatively into a cracked,
charred stone adrift from the hearth. The silence spread; subdued whisper-
ings passed it back to the crowd at the top of the stairs, until it reached even
the Holder. Meguet felt her coming in eddies of movement as the guard
pushed a path clear for her. She joined Meguet, who was guarding yet another
threshold, eyed her daughter, and went no farther.

"What is it?" she asked. She had evidently flung a trail of pins down the
stairs; most of her hair had fallen loose. She was frowning deeply; her black
eyes were expressionless, wintry, but she kept her voice low. "Was she harmed?"

"No. There was a strange mage, a thief, trying to steal something—she
may still be in danger."

"Moro's eyes, she knows enough sorcery to make Chrysom sit up in his
tomb—why didn't she just let him have what he wanted?"

"Because she doesn't know what it is."

"I thought she knew everything by now."

"She's trying to be careful."

The Holder stared at her. "Really. And how did this thief get past the Gatekeeper?"

"He slowed time."

The Holder's response caused even Nyx, feeling through the stone for mage-traps, to raise her eyes. The Holder, still furious, lowered her voice mid-sentence, "—in the middle of the Holding Council, wandering among us at will, it's unthinkable, intolerable. You couldn't stop him?"

Meguet sighed noiselessly. "I tried. All he wanted was something of Chrysom's, nothing more serious. I had no power against sorcery. Nothing but a sword."

The Holder was silent, gazing at her quizzically. Her eyes dropped to the rose in Meguet's hand. Meguet, staring at it, felt the color blaze into her face. She lifted her other hand, pushed it against her eyes, and saw the rose again, lying beside the sword in her shadow.

She let it fall, as if a thorn had pricked her. "I was bewitched."

"Apparently," the Holder said curiously. "But, I wonder, by what?"

A murmuring rippled through the crowd at Meguet's back; she looked up to see what the mage wanted so badly out of the stone that he had stopped the world.

Nyx held it in her hand: a golden key.

TWO

NYX was crouched under a table in the mage's library a day later, picking at a crack in the stone floor with her fingernail, when the firebird flew over the gate. Engrossed, she did not immediately hear the effect of its arrival. The Hold Councils and most of the household were at supper; strings and flutes from the third tower played a distant, ancient music in the peaceful twilight that wove among the reeds and drums from the cider house. Nyx, dressed for supper, had forgotten it. Cobwebs snagged in her dark hair; absently, she had rearranged the elaborate, jewelled structure until pins and strands of tiny pearls dangled around her face. Her black velvet dress was filigreed with dust; she had walked out of her shoes some time ago. Her eyes, usually the color of bog mist, were washed with lavender. Her face had taken on a feral cast; she seemed to be scenting even threads of smoke ingrained in the ancient stone.

The disorderly clamor of people and animals finally intruded into her concentration. She straightened abruptly against the table top. Someone pounded on the door, then opened it.

"Nyx!"

It was Calyx, who, looking high and low in the shadows, finally looked low enough. Nyx, rubbing her head crossly, said, "I thought I locked that door. What in Moro's name is that racket in the yard?"

"It's a bird," Calyx said dazedly. "What are you doing under the table? And what have you——" Her voice caught; color washed over her delicate face. She found her voice again, raised it with unusual force. "Nyx Ro, what have you done with all the ancient household records I was studying?"

"Over there," Nyx said, waving at a cairn of books as she crawled out. "A bird. What bird?"

"They're all jumbled up! I had them all in order, a thousand years of household history—And look what you've done to this room!"

A pile of chairs balanced on a tiny wine table; shields and furs and tapestries hung in midair above their heads; bookshelves climbed up the stairs to the roof. Spell books, histories, accounts, diaries, rose like monoliths from the floor. Nyx, her arms folded, stood as still among them, eyes narrowed at her sister.

"Calyx," she said softly. "What bird?"

"Look at this mess! And look at your face! There are black smudges all over it."

"That would be from the chimney. Calyx——"

"You put your face up the chimney?"

"Evidently."

"Why," Calyx asked more precisely, "did you put your face up the chimney?"

"Because I'm looking for something," Nyx said impatiently. "Why else would I crawl up a chimney?"

"I have no idea. I thought, after studying sorcery for nine years, you'd pull an imp out of the air to do it for you. Maybe I can help you. What is it we're looking for?"

"Most likely a book."

Calyx stared at her. "Did you," she asked ominously, "look on the bookshelves?"

"Oh, really, Calyx." She wiped at ash with her sleeve, her breath snagging on a sudden laugh. "You do keep dwelling on nonessentials. After studying sorcery for nine years, I have learned how to clean up a room." She picked her way through the chairs to the windows. From that high place, she could see the parapet wall linking the seven white towers, most of the cottages clustered beyond the wall, and the vast yard with its barns and forges and craft houses that dealt with the upkeep of the household and the lands that rambled endlessly within the outer wall. One thing caught her eye instantly at that busy hour.

"The Gatekeeper is not at the gate."

And then she saw the flash of fire that scratched the air with gold and turned a rearing cart horse into a tree with diamond leaves.

Meguet had been sitting with the Gatekeeper in his turret when the bird flew over the gate. Dressed in corn-leaf silk the color of her eyes, strands of tiny jewels braided into her rippling hair, she had abandoned guests and musicians in the supper hall, pulled on her oldest boots and wandered into the summer twilight to talk to the Gatekeeper. She had seen nothing of him the day before; at the Holder's request she had stood watch in Chrysom's library most of the evening, while Nyx puzzled over the key she had found. Some of the gossip had evidently found its way to the gate; as she entered the turret, the Gatekeeper handed her a rose.

She eyed him; his lean, sun-browned face, with its silvery-green swamp-leaf eyes, was expressionless. She said, "It was red, not white."

"I hoped you'd like this better." Then she saw the beginnings of his tight, slanted smile, and she sighed and slid onto the stone bench next to him.

"I was hoping no one had noticed. Does gossip blow on the wind across this yard? Or do you hear through stone?"

"People like tales." He put his arm around her shoulders. "For nine days you've stood at that tower door with a sword in your hands. When you suddenly toss it aside for a rose, it causes comment. What was he like, this mage who gave you the rose?"

"You should know," she said grimly. "You let him in."

He stirred; his eyes flickered away from her, across the wall, where the lazy tide sighed and broke. "He did get past me. Odd things have, in this house. Tell me what happened. No one saw him but you and Nyx, and the tales being spun around this mysterious mage make me afraid to open the gate."

She smiled at the thought. "You'd open the gate to winter itself. Or time, or the end of it." She brought the white rose to her face, breathed in its scent. He opened her other hand, dropped his lips on her palm where thorns had left an imprint.

"You fought a battle with the red rose."

"I nearly lost it," she said, and heard his breath.

"Tell me," he said, and listened with the hard, expressionless cast that his face took on when something disturbed him. He applied a taper to his ebony pipe before the end of it, blowing smoke seaward, his eyes hidden. She told much of the tale to the rose, turning it in her fingers, finding memories in its whorl of petals.

"Is he expected back?" he asked. "Or did she kill him?"

"She doesn't know. She told the Holder that if he is alive he might return, since he seemed that desperate."

"For a key? To what?"

"Nyx thinks a book. Some secret magic book of Chrysom's."

"I thought she had all his books."

"So did she."

He turned his head, tossed smoke downwind. "What kinds of things would a mage keep hidden?"

"That," she sighed, "is why Nyx refuses to let the stranger have what he wants, which is the advice that, at some length, the Holder gave her. If she knew, she might let him take it and stop threatening the house. But she is spellbound by this book that she can't even find."

"So is the stranger, it sounds, stopping time and threatening to burn the house down for it."

"What was that like? Did you feel time stop?"

He shook his head. "Your corn-silk hair caught my eye; I turned to look at you. I was hoping you would turn. Then I blinked, and there was your face. Then you vanished into the tower, and what caught my eye was the blade of silver light on the stones just inside the door. A moment later one of the tower guards ran for help. And I guessed what the light must be. I nearly left the gate. But I didn't want to risk trouble letting itself out while I was gone, though it had wandered in without my help. So I waited. And the tales started flying like birds out of the tower, each one more colorful than the last." He touched the rose in her hand. "They all said you were safe." He paused, his eyes going seaward again, where white birds flashed over the water and dived. "I caught the gist of it: a mage, a key—"

"Don't say it."

"And a blood-red rose."

She looked at him, said recklessly, "You were watching; you must have seen him pick it."

He blinked, wordless, then pulled her close suddenly; she heard his heartbeat. "What do you think? That I would have stood here sunning myself like a tortoise while you defended a sleeping Holding Council alone against a mage who could have left you lying on your shadow as easily as the rose? Is that what you think?"

"Yes," she said, for there were gates within gates into the house, and she suspected he watched them all. "No. Yes. What I think is that you know exactly what comes and goes through that gate."

He was silent. His hold eased; he dropped a kiss on her hair, and said finally, "So I do. And in case the mage considers knocking at the gate next time, tell me what I should look for."

"A man," she said, "taller than me, by a few inches. With hair a dusty golden-brown and light eyes like water. The animal is embroidered on his robe." She paused, thinking back. "He wears silver at his wrists—"

"Old?"

"No older than you. Taller than me—"

"You said that."

"And he moves like a man accustomed to space."

"You noticed a lot in an eye-blink," he commented drily. She looked at him, her eyes still and clear as the sky where the sun had set and the memory of light lingered. He swallowed a word. His face dropped toward hers. Their lips touched. And then he turned abruptly, snatching her breath along with his, and she saw the firebird over his shoulder.

It seemed to blow out of the sea like spume, so white it was, and so fast it flew; then, as it passed the turret, she saw the fiery wingtips and the long, graceful plumes that trailed behind it like flame. Its talons were silver. It gave a cry of such fierce fury and despair that it drove the blood from her face and brought the Gatekeeper to his feet. The busy yard stopped as if it were spellbound again. With the cry came fire: a forge-fire, and a hammer, and the hand holding the hammer froze into silver.

Meguet hit the ground running before she realized she had moved. There were cottagers' children transfixed by the swooping bird; there were animals everywhere, it seemed—horses, cows still coming in to be milked, chickens, hounds. The bird, crying again, turned a corner of a barn into bronze, and nicked a hound's ear. The hound bellowed, blundered into the cows; there was a small stampede toward the bewitched forge. Stable girls hurried to take in the horses, ducking their heads under their arms as at pelting hail. The bird wheeled above a group of barefoot children who had twisted themselves into a knot with a piece of harness. Meguet and several of the cottagers ran toward them as they struggled frantically. The bird's fire missed the children, hit a cat slinking away into the shadows and turned it into a jewelled sword. Meguet snatched it up. Wielding it above the children, she startled them into tears. She cut them free of each other; they scattered, wailing, then turned again, too fascinated to find shelter.

She saw Rush Yarr and a few of the younger councilors on the tower wall with bows; household guards were racing to position themselves along the crenelation. She saw Rush fix an arrow, draw back and aim. She slowed, feeling a sudden, unreasonable dismay form like a shout in her throat. The bird, a swirl of white and red, cried its enraged sorrow; fire swept the wall, and all the archers ducked. The stones themselves turned gold.

"Nyx," she breathed. The Gatekeeper, struggling with a panicked cart horse, shouted at her.

"Meguet!"

"I'm going to get Nyx! Tell them not to shoot!"

"It's not the bird in danger," he retorted, holding the horse as stablers un-hitched the lurching cart. "It's you standing there waiting to be turned into a silver rose."

"It cries so," she said, puzzled, hearing it again, a sound that made her throat constrict. The horse reared, throwing the Gatekeeper; it elongated it-self as the fire hit it: Its dark hide turned to wood; harness rustled through its still, shimmering leaves to the ground. Meguet, hand to her mouth, sti-fling a cry, stared at the Gatekeeper. He glittered no more than usual, and, rolling promptly under the cart, seemed unharmed.

He shouted at her, "Go!"

She went, still carrying the transformed cat, out of habit, and dragging her skirt high above her boots as she ran. Nyx, who seemed to have fallen like a rose off the vines, appeared abruptly in front of her outside the dark tower.

"I'm here," she said, putting a hand on Meguet's shoulder to keep from being run over. The bird cried above them; transfixed, they followed it with their eyes. Calyx, hanging precipitously out a window, ducked suddenly in-side. A shower of bronze apples scattered on the grass.

"Roses," Nyx said tersely, eyeing them. "Not Calyx."

"Moro's name," Meguet said, dragging at air. "What is it?"

"A firebird."

"It cries like wood might cry in the fire. Why does it cry like that?"

"They do, according to sources. The cry of the firebird is fierce, desper-ate, terrible. So Chrysom wrote of, he thought, a fabled bird."

"It sounds human," Meguet said simply, and Nyx looked at her, a color-less, dispassionate gaze. A line ran between her dark brows; she opened her mouth to answer, then turned her head as the guard, followed by curious guests, fanned across the tower yard. The bird cried again, wheeled at them, and they retreated beneath the archways of the tower wall. Fire washed through the archway at their heels, glazed the cobbles with opal. "Nyx, can you do something?" Meguet pleaded. "Before it gets hurt?"

Nyx glanced at her again. "You have a peculiar fondness for birds," she said drily. She lifted her hand as to a falcon; the bird circled the dark tower, circled again. Meguet, watching, thought she saw a thread form between Nyx's uplifted hand and the bird, a gossamer strand of air that shimmered faintly with light against the evening sky. The bird cried once again, spiralling down toward them. Onyx roses swayed on the vine, broke free. Something else flashed in the corner of Meguet's eye: Rush Yarr's blood-fox hair. She turned, running again across the yard as he crouched in an archway, following the bird with his arrow.

"Rush!"

She knew his aim; it was far better than the sorcery he was evidently breathing into his bow. Concentrating, he did not hear her. He shot. Behind Meguet, Nyx flung out another thread. It caught the arching arrow mid-flight; the bird, riding air to meet it, picked it up like prey and cried its fiery rage. The fall of red and gold streaked the dusk. Meguet, running headlong into it, felt a moment of complete astonishment before her eyes filled with gold and then with night.

The evening was suddenly very quiet. The bird flew up the black tower and disappeared. Rush's bow, dropping on the bespelled cobbles, seemed to echo within the tower ring. Nyx, motionless at the foot of the tower, met his stunned eyes. After a blank moment of shock, during which her brain seemed capable only of grappling with analogies, she regathered her attention and picked at the weavings of the force that had transformed Meguet. The spell, at first touch, seemed oddly seamless. Calyx, emerging breathlessly from the tower, bumped into Nyx; she stirred, blinking, overwhelmed again. As if the still emerald leaves had beckoned, they drew the three, along with guards and fascinated guests, to stand staring, speechless, trying to see Meguet among the leaves and roses.

"Oh, Rush," Calyx whispered reproachfully.

"I didn't—I swear I didn't even see her!" He touched a glassy leaf tentatively; his eyes sought Nyx's. "Can't you do something?"

"I was trying!" she flared, exasperated, and Rush flushed a dull red.

"I'm sorry. I am so clumsy with sorcery. It makes me blind and deaf and extremely stupid."

Nyx did not bother to answer. She touched the rose-tree here, there, with her mind. It was a great jewel of malachite and emerald, with ruby, garnet, amber and moonstone blossoming among closed buds of paler jade. Within the jewel was Meguet; seeking her, Nyx found veil after veil of fire, and, at last, the face of the bird.

It was masked, like a swan, with red plumage; its eyes were golden. Sens-

ing her, it cried. The Cygnet in front of it, flying on a long triangle of night
sky, melted into a strange vine with swan-shaped leaves.

The bird was on the tower roof. Nyx spun her thread again, flung it like
a message: *I am the one you seek.* The bird landed a moment later, noiseless,
glowing faintly, its white and fiery red bruising the dusk, clinging, with silver
talons, to the malachite leaves.

The faces around Nyx resolved themselves again. The Gatekeeper's was
among them, pale, expressionless, hard as the jewel he stared at.

"Apt," he commented. His hand slid among the leaves and silver thorns,
closed gently around the stem. Nyx saw him swallow. "It was me put the idea
into its head," he added, ten years of courtly smoothness swamped suddenly
by his river-brat's accent. "Me shouting at her like that." Like Rush, he sought
Nyx's eyes. She said slowly, her arms folded tightly,

"It's an intriguing spell. I can't seem to find her, only the bird. It should
be simple, but it's not."

"I'll wait," the Gatekeeper said.

"The bird is waiting, too," Calyx said wonderingly. "It's not screaming
now. Is it real? Or sorcery?"

"I can't tell yet," Nyx said. She held its eyes, looking, with her smudged,
jewel-framed face, as fey as the firebird. Voices disturbed her; they all turned,
saw the Holder and her oldest daughter, surrounded by household guard, half
the Hold councilors and their assorted families.

"There it is!" someone cried, as they crossed the yard. They gathered in
sudden, perplexed silence around what it clung to. The Holder, her hair
nearly as dishevelled as her daughter's, studied the firebird grimly. The guard
ringed it, arrows poised; Calyx cried in horror,

"Don't shoot it! You'll hit Meguet!"

"Meguet," the Holder exclaimed, then took in the truant Gatekeeper, his
hand, and what he held. Her dark eyes widened; her voice, raised, caused even
the firebird to shift. "Moro's eyeteeth! I'll wring its neck!"

"Mother," Nyx breathed.

"That's Meguet? Are you sure?"

"Magic seems to follow her in that shape," the Gatekeeper said.

"Why," Lauro Ro demanded of Nyx, "are you just standing there? Are
you waiting for the roses to bloom?"

"I'm waiting," Nyx said tartly, "for some peace and quiet."

"After all that time in the bog, what you don't know about birds, inside
and out, you could thread a bead with. How could you let this happen? Can
she breathe in there? Is she even alive?"

Iris, her stately and practical eldest, glanced at Nyx's frozen face, and then at the guests fascinated by the sorcery and by the threat of explosion between the Holder and her unpredictable heir. Troubled, she touched her mother's arm. "Mother, Nyx knows what she needs to work with, and if it's peace and quiet, you could at least stop shouting. How could anything possibly be Nyx's fault? Do you think there is anything she wouldn't do for Meguet?"

The Holder looked at her dusty, barefoot heir, standing dark and still, with the first wash of light from the rising moon spilling over her shoulder. She gestured at the guard; they lowered their bows, but kept their tight, watchful circle. Nyx, her voice low, taut, said,

"There is no reason to think she isn't alive. But the bird's magic is random, uncalculated, and very strong. What I need to know is if the bird is the sorcerer or the sorcery. The maker of the magic, or simply its bewitched object. For some reason, it's difficult to tell. It shouldn't be this difficult, but it is. I can't find Meguet at all. You'll have to be patient. Please. If you startle the bird, it may scream again, and I'll have twice the mystery to undo."

The Holder sighed. Arms folded, pins dangling in her wild hair, she looked much like her magical daughter. "I'm sorry," she said. "All this sorcery makes me edgy. It's quiet, now. And not afraid of any of us. It didn't, most likely, fly into my house to turn Meguet into a rose-tree. Was it looking for you?"

"I think so."

"The guard say it snatches arrows out of midair."

"It caught mine," Rush said. "Meguet was running to stop me; she got tangled in its cry."

"There's a blacksmith in the yard with a silver hand," the Holder said grimly. "If this bird is the sorcerer, it has much to account for. May we watch? If it turns you into a black rose-tree, may I wring its neck then?"

Nyx smiled a little. "Please." The smile faded; her brows twitched together again. "What intrigues me most is something Meguet said. She has no power of sorcery, but sometimes she can make very complicated things very simple, by looking at them from an angle I miss. She said about the bird: It has a human cry. That, I think, must be what makes its cry so terrible."

The bird had not stirred since the Holder startled it; it clung like something carved of marble to its spell. A curve of moon rising behind the east tower caught in its silver talons; they flashed like blades. Its eyes, flooding with moonlight, turned milky. Nyx looked at it, leaving her mind open, still, tranquil, an invitation for whatever violence or enchantments or speech it might be moved to. It gazed back at her, as still as she. She tried again to find some thought of Meguet within its spell: Leaves moved through her eyes, endless leaves and petals of carnelian and beaten gold, as if she wandered through an enchanted garden.

Moonlight touched the jewelled leaves, spilled its cold fire over the bird. It roused abruptly, crying its fierce and terrible cry, but its fire only fell pale and spent, harmless as the risen moon's light. As it moved, leaves trembled. The Gatekeeper, still holding a stem, found his hand at Meguet's neck, her hair falling over his arm. For a moment her eyes were malachite, and then they were her own, blinking, surprised, at the Holder's face. The bird landed at her feet in a flood of light. The cry it gave, as it transformed itself, was fully human.

THREE

HE looked without expression at the arrows aimed at him, as if he did not recognize them, or as if such things, in his peculiar life, were commonplace. Meguet, stooping instinctively for the sword she had dropped, started as it slunk away under her hand. No one else moved; his cry held them spellbound. But nothing of its raw fury and despair lingered in his face; he did not seem to realize he had made a sound.

He was oddly dressed, in a tattered dirty tunic of blue silk, and an embroidered belt of raw red silk. Beneath that he wore a close-fitting garment of gold thread or mail. His soft leather boots were torn and scuffed. He wore strange metal bands at his wrists, intricately fashioned, as if strands of molten metal had been poured over each other in a wide filigree. They looked fire-scorched, so blackened they might have been made of iron. His hair, thick, black, fell past his shoulders. The moon, striking his face at an angle, illumined half: a dark brow, long bones at cheek and jaw, skin drawn tightly across them. The other side of his face was dark.

He did not speak; he seemed resigned to whatever impulses his actions might have inspired. Nyx, connecting moonlight with the pale fire that had come out of the bird before it changed, asked abruptly,

"How long are you human?"

He seemed surprised that she had thought to ask. "Until midnight." His voice was nearly inaudible. "Then the bird hunts."

"What," the Holder asked sharply, "does it hunt?"

"I think mice."

"Who are you? What kind of outlandish place are you from, flying into my house, frightening my household, turning my niece into a rose-tree?"

Meguet, glancing around for the niece in question, took a step backward suddenly, found her own shape against the Gatekeeper.

"The bird cries. It changes things." His voice held a hollow, haunted weariness. "I cannot stop it. Are you the mage?"

"No. I am the Holder of Ro Holding."

"Ro Holding." The blankness in his voice was stunning. Then he added, "The realm of the Cygnet. I have seen the black swan flying on warships' sails. Or the bird has. One of us. Or perhaps it was only a picture. I don't remember."

"Do you remember your name?" Nyx asked. He looked at her for a long time before he answered.

"You are the mage."

"I am Nyx Ro. And mage, sorceress, bog-witch, something of everything." She was holding his eyes, speaking slowly, calmly, using words like tiny grappling hooks to draw and fix his attention. "You are ensorcelled. You came for help."

"Yes," he breathed. "The bird cries for help—it transforms its cries to jewels, gold, anything precious to catch the eye."

"How did you know to find help here?"

"The bird knew."

"You are the bird."

He opened his mouth, closed it. His face changed suddenly, like shifting flame: For a moment he was going to scream. And then it changed again, forgetting. "No. The bird is the sorcery."

"How long have you been ensorcelled?"

"I do not know. A week. A month. A century. I do not know."

"Where are you from?"

"I have forgotten."

"What is your name?"

"I have forgotten," he whispered. Nyx was silent; her own eyes, catching the moon's pale fire, turned misty, inhuman. Meguet, resigned to the expression in them, knew she had ensorcelled herself by her own curiosity. After a moment, Nyx loosed the man, turned her gaze to the Holder. Her brows crooked questioningly. The Holder, equally resigned, flung up a hand.

"All right. I am curious, too. But I will have no more sorcery from that bird. Keep it out of sight, and in Moro's name give the man something to eat besides mice."

The man slid to his knees. His head bowed; he held his arms together as if they were bound, elbow to upturned wrists that the strange, latticed metal protected. His fingers spread wide and flat, a gesture that riveted Nyx's attention. "This to the Cygnet," he said. "All the time I hold."

The Holder sent him, under guard, to be fed, washed, clothed and presented to Nyx's scrutiny in the mage's tower before the bell in the north tower changed night into morning. Nyx returned to what a hasty eye might have deemed the disaster in the library. So orderly was her chaos that she saw at a glance Calyx's futile attempts to straighten things. Musing, the stranger's gesture repeating itself in her mind, she stared into the eye of the Cygnet flying through black marble above the mantel. Beneath the Cygnet, things glinted in candle and torchlight: tiny opaque bottles, dark glass boxes that refused to open, mysterious things carved in amber, wood, gold, that had no openings yet when shaken moved from the liquid rolling within them. She fingered a seamless cobalt box; something buzzed in it like a furious insect. She still did not know, after years of wandering, study, work, what magic lay within that tiny box. What she had finally learned was why she was still ignorant.

The door opened; Meguet, about to enter, stopped in the doorway with an amazed face peering over her shoulder. She turned with barely a flicker of expression, and took the tray that had followed her up. The door closed; she stood, with more expression, looking for a place to set Nyx's supper.

"Just let it go," Nyx said. Meguet, who had been transformed into a rose-tree with less notice, yielded calmly to the whims of sorcery and left the tray hanging in midair. "Thank you."

"Your mother asked me to bring it. She said you hadn't eaten all day."

"How could she remember that? I didn't." She waved the tray across the room. Meguet, glancing around, caught sight of ancient weapons hanging like icicles above her head. She moved promptly, joined Nyx at the hearth, where nothing hung overhead but a faded tapestry. Nyx, bread in one hand, cold chicken in the other, asked,

"Where is he?"

"In a bath, I think. What is it in you that causes furniture to behave in such a peculiar fashion?"

"I prefer a world in a constant state of transmutation," Nyx said with her mouth full.

"Is that what you will tell the Holder?"

"Is she coming up?"

"She's hardly in the mood to leave you alone up here with a man who turns cart horses into trees by breathing."

"Oh."

"So she said."

Nyx shrugged. "The bird's spells wear away by moonlight. Luckily. You made a beautiful rose-tree."

"A rose-tree," Meguet said with feeling. "In front of half the household. Why did you wait for the moon to rescue me? You could have spared me some dignity."

"I couldn't."

"Why not?"

"I don't know."

Meguet gazed at her. She folded her arms, leaned against the mantel. She rarely made unnecessary movements; the heel of her boot ticked uneasy questions against the hearthstones. "You mean you couldn't."

"I couldn't." She put down a chicken bone, eyed it with a bogwitch's speculation, then licked a finger. "That's what fascinates me so. To break a spell, you simply unweave it, strand by strand, until the spell does not exist. Of course, doing this, you are liable to catch the attention of the sorcerer who cast the spell, who may look askance at your meddling. I couldn't undo the spell over you because I couldn't find a single strand. It was of a piece, that magic, like a single jewel. Very beautiful."

"You mean if the moon hadn't risen—"

"Eventually I would have worked it through. There is always a way. Always. But the moon worked faster."

Meguet was silent. A night breeze drifted through the windows, scented with roses; she saw in memory the rose on her shadow. She asked slowly, her fingers gripping hard on her arms, "Is there a connection between the mage and the firebird?"

"I don't know." Nyx poured wine, stared into it without drinking, her dark brows knit. "Is there a connection between a mage looking for a key and a firebird flying over a wall? If the mage had come a month ago and the firebird tomorrow, I would say no. But they came one after another, and both from lands beyond Ro Holding."

"He spoke of warships."

"Then the spell may be very old and the mage dead. Which may make it easier for me. Or more difficult, if the spell is archaic. How long has it been since warships sailed under the Cygnet on Wolfe Sea?"

"Centuries." Meguet shivered suddenly, envisioning time. "Ensorcelled so long, no wonder he cries like that. But will the mage or sorcerer be dead? Didn't Chrysom live for centuries before he even built this house for Moro Ro?"

"Legend says."

"What did he say?"

"Chrysom said very little about himself; he hid his life behind his spells. And apparently he hid a few spells as well, locked away in a secret place. . . . Meguet, if you had something to hide in this room, where would you hide it?"

"Up the chimney. Under a hearthstone. In a table leg. Unless I were a mage. Then——" She shook her head helplessly, blind to sorcery. "I don't know how mages think."

"I do. I want to know what you think."

"What am I hiding?"

"A spellbook. It may not look like a book; it may look like a doorknob. It might even be a book within a book, lines hidden between lines, words within words, but I've searched every book in here that was made before Chrysom died."

"Someone took it."

"No."

"How do you know?"

"Because the spells would have become common knowledge by now. I've suspected for some time that a book had been lost or hidden. What gave the visiting mage a clue to look for the key, I have no idea. Perhaps he will come back and I can ask him. Perhaps he realized what I did: that Chrysom hints now and then at spells which are unknown, even to the mage Diu, for he never told me."

Meguet nodded blankly. The ancient mage Diu, a descendant of Chrysom's, was such a legendary figure it was difficult to conceive of him still alive and swapping spells. "Why? What made you suspect?"

"These," Nyx said, touching the mysteries on the mantel. "He never makes use of them in any book I've ever seen, and I thought I had all his books. And because I came across an odd mark now and then at random, in the margins of his spellbook: a C or a crescent moon holding an M in its arms. The key has the same design on its handle. I've always thought the spells he marked with that sign were incomplete, or so old they are little more than curiosities. But now I know he completed them in another place. A secret place, locked by the key he hid."

"But why would he hide them?"

"That," Nyx said softly, "intrigues me most of all. What kinds of spells did he feel compelled to hide?"

Meguet recognized the gleam of compulsion in her eye: the sorceress in pursuit of the unknown. It had led her most recently into a morass, and the house into turmoil. Meguet said resignedly, "So you tore the room apart searching for this secret book that may or may not exist."

Nyx nodded, unperturbed, chewing again. "Every crack, every glass rose, every stone and every stone bird in this hearth. I've searched as a mage searches, and I've searched with nothing more than my eyes and my bare hands."

"Then it's not here."

"I think it is here. . . . Chrysom kept everything he used in this room. He lived here; his bones are still here, buried beneath this tower. Even after a thousand years, these old stones are saturated with his magic. They send a signal like a beacon, a ghostly signal, but visible to those who can see the imprint of power. . . ."

"Like the bird? Is that what drew it?"

Nyx was silent, her eyes on Meguet while she mused, using the calm in her cousin's face to focus her thoughts. "I still don't know," she said at last, "where that bird's sorcery comes from. Perhaps it was simply made to find this place. Or any place of power."

"For yet another mage?" Meguet looked shaken. "Nyx, how many mages will we have to contend with?"

Nyx shrugged. "It's only speculation. I'll worry when I find something to worry about." She paused, listening, the wine halfway to her lips. She put it down abruptly. "Like now. My mother is coming."

The room composed itself in an eye-blink, as if, Meguet thought, its tidy self had been simply waiting in abeyance around the moment of time Nyx searched through. Carpets and skins lay underfoot, weapons and tapestries hung on the walls, books surrounded them on shelves and pedestals. The account books Calyx had been studying lay open on a table, her pen angled on a page to mark a place. The mound of chairs that had been balanced in an impossible pyramid on the wine table fanned around the hearth; not a shadow or a flame had been misplaced. Nyx picked her supper out of the air and set it on a table. The door opened.

The Holder entered, followed by her two older daughters, and Rush Yarr; a pair of armed guards flanked the stranger. Even dressed in more civilized fashion, he looked formidable, tall and muscular, something of the

bird's wildness about him. Meguet, remembering the rage and desolation in
his cry, wished she had thought to arm herself, for he was a man unaware of
his own anger. The bird's fury shaped itself into jewelled leaves; what form
the man's might take was as yet unknown, perhaps even to himself.

But, entering, he seemed quiet enough. He barely glanced around himself; his eyes found Nyx and clung. Nyx gestured at a chair; he sat hesitantly,
as if he had forgotten how. Meguet moved unobtrusively to a table near him,
leaned against it. Rush joined her. The guards stood behind the Holder and
her daughters, silent, watchful. Nyx, at the hearth, studied him, fingering a
strand of tiny pearls sliding down over one ear.

"Is there a name I can call you?" she asked. "One you might remember to
answer to?"

He was silent, dredging unknown fathoms of memory. He said finally,
"Every name I reach for eludes me. It might be anything. Or nothing."

His face formed suddenly, clearly, under Nyx's absent gaze, as if, until
then, she had only seen the firebird. His eyes reminded her of something. She
slid the strand of pearls behind her ear and remembered what: the little
cobalt box on the mantel behind her. She blinked; the entire room was still,
everyone fascinated, it seemed, by her silence. She gathered her thoughts,
which had been fragmented by a color. "Two things I must do first. I want
the bird's fire and I want its cry."

His lips parted; he whispered, "How?"

"I'll tell you how after I have done it. I don't want to be turned into a
gaudy pile of leaves every time it looks at me. And the cry that bird makes is
like the crying of every bird I have ever tormented in my sorcery. It would
wear me to the heart."

He was staring at her, transfixed, as if she had just changed shape, or
taken shape, in his eyes. He made a sudden movement, muscles gathering, his
hands closing on the chair arms. The cry came and went like lightning in his
face. Silver flashed from behind the Holder as one of the guards moved.
Meguet caught his eyes, held him still. Nyx continued, her voice grim but de-
liberate, "Mages find themselves sometimes on strange roads, in strange
places. You can trust me, but you don't know that. My past casts a shadow. If
you want a mage without a shadow, you must fly farther north, to a mage
called Diu, who is very old and tired, but would do a favor for me if I asked.
You must—"

"The bird found you," the man said. He was still gripping his chair, but
he had made no other movement. Nyx waited; he added, some feeling breaking into his low voice, "I don't know how long the bird flew to find you. But,

entering this house, it cried its magic until you listened. You must do what you can. What you want. The bird will choose to stay or go. It's no question of trust. Or of choice, for me. I have no choice."

The Holder opened her mouth, closed it as the sorceress's eyes flicked at her. Nyx said, answering her unspoken question, "I cannot know how the bird found me, or why, or if it was sent until I begin to work. I suspect that the spell was cast very long ago, and that the bird came here simply because it sensed a thousand years of magic in this tower. So I will assume that, for now, all I have to do is remove a spell."

"And if the bird was sent?" the Holder asked. "Perhaps by the mage who appeared yesterday? You may put the entire house in danger."

"Well," Nyx said softly, "it won't be the first time."

"But—"

"You have heard that bird cry. Is there anything you would not do to stop it, if you could?" The Holder was silent; jewels sparked on her hands as they clasped, containing a mute argument. Nyx added, "I can stop it. I can help. If I bring down sorcery on this house, then we will find a way to deal with that. But now, the bird is here and the sorcerer is only a possibility. I must begin with the magic I see, not with the ghosts and shadows conjured up by fear." She looked at the man again. He had not moved a muscle or an eyelash while she spoke; still she was not certain how much he understood besides hope. "So," she said, toying with an earring, a circle of amber ringed with pearls, "we will wait for the bird to return. Tell me what you remember of your wanderings."

"I remember sea. I remember the bird flying through a storm of burning arrows. I remember the face of a small boy just before he was caught in the bird's fire. I remember waking in snow, in mud, sometimes in trees, sometimes falling out of the air and running from hunters."

"And before you were spellbound?" The earring fell off; she caught it in her palm. She dropped her other hand toward the metal on his wrist, but did not touch it. "What are these?"

He gazed at them without a flicker of recognition. "Armor, of some kind, I think."

"May I see?"

"They don't come off."

"Do you remember any place? A city? A house?"

He paused, made an effort. "I remember a doorway."

"A doorway?"

He shrugged slightly. "Nothing more. A marble doorway, with a marble pot of flowers beside it."

"What was inside the door?"

"A noonday shadow. That's all I remember, except that I saw it, not the bird, because I remember the scent of the flowers and the soft air. It could be any door, anywhere. It means nothing."

"What did you mean when you said to the Holder, 'All the time I hold'?"

He was on his feet, then, with no warning. Meguet, pushing away from the table, saw the cry beginning in his face. Then she heard the midnight bells, and saw the fiery plumage streak his back. She checked her instinctive movement to Nyx's side, having no desire to be caught in the enchanted fire. The bird finished the cry in midair. Fire swarmed at Nyx; Meguet heard Calyx cry out behind the silken, red-gold wall. Nyx opened her hand, held up her defense: an amber earring.

Fire kindled in the amber, a reflection of the onslaught of flame. It kindled in Nyx's misty eyes, washed them with color. For a time her mind was an amber, fire-filled jewel guiding the magic, inviting more, expanding endlessly as it flooded into her, while, to watching eyes, the small jewel in her hand focused and ate the fire. The gorgeous and magical imagery of the bird's enchantments changed and changed again in her mind as it tried to change her: black roses, emerald leaves, snowflakes of silver latticed like the odd armor, birds with sapphire wings and eyes, golden lilies, bird-eggs of topaz and diamond. The threads of the spell were a tapestry of tiny detail worked by a skilled hand. Dimly, as she dragged the fire and rich images endlessly out of it, she heard the bird's ceaseless cry.

Then there was only pale moonlight in her mind, a final rose the color of mist. She could see again; she dropped her hand, blinking. The bird, perched on the chair, was silent. The air darkened slowly, candlelight and shadow. The faces gazing at her looked haunted, exhausted by the cry. She lifted the amber, red-gold now and cracked like glass, and put it back in her ear; her hand trembled slightly.

"So the bird knows where it is," she said.

"Nyx," the Holder breathed, and nothing more. Beside her, Calyx lifted her face from her hands; tears slid between her fingers. Rush, stunned by the sorcery, moved behind her, put his hands on her shoulders. The guards' faces looked pinched, as if they had been standing in a freezing wind. Iris had gone. Nyx's eyes moved to Meguet. Her face was composed, watchful, as always, but so white it might have been carved of snow.

"That must have wakened the house," Meguet commented. Her voice shook suddenly; she put her hand to her mouth, hearing an echo of the fury and the sorrow. "Can you find a jewel hard enough to hold its cry?"

"Maybe," Nyx said softly. Her eyes were wide, luminous; they seemed to look through Meguet. "Maybe one." Meguet, recognizing that expression, felt herself grow very still; she seemed to pick out of Nyx's mind the jewel that hung there. "You do it so easily, Meguet, when you need to, but I have never tried. Yet I saw it all within the Cygnet's eye. . . ."

"What?" Calyx and the Holder asked together.

"All the fractured moments within the whole, like light fractured within the prism . . . a moment shifting into all its layers. If I could throw the bird's cries into another layer of time, we would not hear them and it would still have its voice. I have taken its fire. That cry is its heart and the only word it knows. I will not take its heart." She paused, her eyes clinging to Meguet in lieu of the great dark prism beneath the tower that was the Cygnet's eye. "I looked into the Cygnet's eye, and saw its power. But did it only show me things I could never know? Or did I take that power?" Meguet, transfixed, birdlike, could not look away. The room was soundless. "You wander through the walls of time at need; so did I, that one time, flying faster than thought. But can I wander at will? I am the Cygnet's heir: Did it give me only what I needed, or what I wanted? I wanted everything I saw. . . . For that one moment, I flew within time, but did I fly? Or did the Cygnet?" The black tower walls wrapped around her like the small, circular chamber at the heart of Chrysom's maze. Concentrating, her gaze still on Meguet, she saw the black prism, the faceted eye of power, hanging in the still darkness within a triple ring of time. "You could cry into that silence," she told the bird. "I did."

The bird cried. She heard it standing once again beneath the great prism, which was no longer dark, but fire-white, sculpted with planes of light. The cry filled the chamber, buried deep where only the Cygnet would hear it. It cried, and cried again; the stone walls echoed with its tale, as if it had found the safe and secret place to tell it. Nyx, gazing into the prism, listening for one familiar word, saw Meguet's face reflected in every plane. Then she saw Meguet, in the shadows on the other side of the prism, caught in the tangle of cries, as if Nyx, using her face to open memory, had pulled her into the fractured time.

She blinked; the prism faded, and she saw Meguet's face again, a stillness in it like the stillness of stone. The mage's tower circled them again, with its triple ring of stone and night and time. Color flooded suddenly into Meguet's face; she stared, incredulously, at Nyx. The bird cried, but its cries were soundless now, its story hidden.

The Holder and Calyx were both on their feet.

"Where did you go?" Calyx demanded, astonished. "You both vanished."

"I sent the bird cry into the heart of the maze," Nyx said. She ran her hands through her hair wearily, scattering jewels, her eyes on Meguet. "I seem to have pulled us both along with it."

"That's not possible," the Holder said. She appealed to Meguet. "Is it?"

"No." She drew breath, shivering slightly. "There was no need for me there."

"I needed you," Nyx said. "You took me there in memory. Who knows which of us guided whom? The bird is crying to the Cygnet instead of to us, which means we can all sleep soundly." She dropped her hand on Meguet's shoulder, and smiled a little, tightly. "Maybe that's all we did: walk back into memory, and leave, appropriately, a bird cry there."

Meguet, still standing tensely, shook her head. "You shifted time," she said simply, "not memory." She paused, listening to her words, or to other words echoing under the moonlight. The Holder said softly, her dark, troubled eyes on the sorceress's face,

" 'All the time I hold.' "

FOUR

MEGUET watched the dawn unfurl like a wing of fire across the Delta. She had wakened early, anticipating a summons, and had seen the Gatekeeper, anticipating dawn, extinguish the torches beside the gate. Beyond the wall, the waves picked up light, rolled it into scrolls and unrolled it again, like a spell in some forgotten language across the sand. She dressed quickly, without waking her attendants, pulling swans down her wrists and across her shoulders, for despite the mysteries and magic, there was yet another prosaic day of council ahead of them, if they could dodge the sorcery falling headlong out of the air. She braided her hair as she went down. Crossing the yard, she caught a breath of the moist, dank sweetness of the inner swamps, lily and mud and still, secret waters. The Gatekeeper's face turned toward it; she wondered if he had smelled it, too, if he were breathing in memories. And then he saw her.

His breakfast followed close behind her. He shared it with her, the tray balanced between them in the tiny turret. He buttered hot bread for her, offered pale, spiced wine from his cup, peeled quail's eggs. She nibbled, weary and absent-minded, listening, in some deep part of her, for the Holder's voice.

He said, "I saw light all night from the mage's tower."

Her eyes, following the white thread of a gull's flight, flicked to his face. "Then you were awake all night."

"I thought it best," he said wryly, "the way things have been getting past me." He cut wafer-thin strips of melon and passed her one. "I don't know what to expect next."

She saw then the familiar shadows under his eyes, that came when he saw too little or too much in the small lonely hours of the night. She set the tray aside abruptly, shifted to sit beside him.

"Nobody knows," she said, and told him what the firebird had said, what Nyx had done. When she finished, her head in the hollow of his shoulder to dodge the flood of morning light, he commented,

"She has a way with birds."

Meguet lifted her head, eyed him narrowly. He let her see the faintest line of a smile beside his mouth. "You had better be smiling," she said dourly.

He smoothed her hair. "It's not so long ago that she had us all dancing at shadows because of birds. Now here's another over the gate so fast it left the Gatekeeper of Ro House standing with his mouth open in a wake of pin-feathers. I might as well row myself back to the swamp."

"Take me with you," she sighed. "I'm housebound with this council. I want to pick lilies in a bog and have you braid them in my hair."

"They must be getting edgy, the Hold Councils."

"They're curious. I'm edgy. The Holder looks as if she swallowed a thunderbolt. Her house was spellbound by a mage with no good intentions who may or may not return, and her heir is up in Chrysom's tower with a bird who may be trouble or may not, but most likely has trouble on its tail. In the middle of this, she has to sit through speeches about sheep."

"What kind of trouble does she look for from the firebird?"

"The mage who cast the spell."

He made a soft sound, stirring. "Another one? How many mages are we looking at?"

"Maybe this one will knock on the gate."

"They don't seem in the habit of knocking. Why would a mage twist a man out of his shape for all but a few moonlit hours? Only to make him remember that he's human?"

"That's all he does remember."

"Not what he did to get himself turned into a bird?"

Meguet was silent, thinking of the cries that came and went across the man's face like lightning across a barren landscape. She said, "The bird remembers."

"But not the man." His eyes strayed seaward. "So I must watch for a dangerous and cold-blooded mage."

"If he's still alive. And if—" She paused again, her brows crooked uncertainly, her eyes on another bird: the Cygnet, flying across the mantle of the bell ringer entering the north tower to summon the councilors together.

"And if what? What do you see, Meguet?"

She blinked, her thoughts clearing. "I see that I must leave you."

"If what?" he asked insistently, holding her with nothing more than the tone of his voice, his eyes. She gazed back at him, perplexed, hearing again the terrible, desperate cry of the firebird.

"If," she said, "the bird is innocent."

Nyx, present to the outward eye during the council that day, was so preoccupied that Calyx touched her once or twice, wondering obviously if she were still breathing. All her attention was focused in the high tower room, where the mage might return. He would want the key. He would guess that she had hidden it in a different place. She had spent some time before dawn trying to turn it invisible, or change its shape into one of Calyx's hoary household records, or a rose among the hundreds on the tower vines. It resisted all enchantment. She gave up finally and put it in her pocket, a solution which would have horrified the Holder. Nyx did not approve of it herself, but she had run out of ideas by morning. The mage might disrupt the council, demanding the key, but the worst he would most likely do would be to give everyone something to talk about besides border tolls. The bird, she suspected with no particular evidence, might fare differently. So she had separated them, the key and the bird, in hope that the strange, ruthless mage, seeking one mystery, would ignore the other.

She carried the key with her to the great hall in the third tower, where the councilors ate savory delicacies with their fingers, drank wine, and continued their endless debates while families and guests slowly gathered from woods and gardens, city shops and neighbors' houses, for supper. She had promised the Holder that for one evening at least, she would not shut herself up behind another locked door with yet another bird. But birds and rumors shadowed her, it seemed. As she bit into melted cheese wrapped in butter pastry, young Darl Kell of Hunter Hold, who had eyes like some of the frogs she had used in her fires, asked with a bluntness he meant to be charming,

"Is it one of yours?"

She raised a brow mutely, her tongue busy dodging hot cheese.

"The great bird in the tower. A bit of your leftover magic from the swamp?"

She coughed on a pastry crumb. "No," she said when she could speak. "If nothing else, I'm tidy. If I transform something, it stays transformed, and I don't leave it a voice to complain with."

Darl Kell flushed to his broad ears. "You're not like your sisters," he said, and stalked off to gaze at Calyx. Nyx brushed crumbs off her silk and wished she could be as tidy in life as she was in art. Someone pushed wine into her hand and said, his voice too close to her ear,

"He could stand some room for improvement, if you're in the mood to transform."

She looked up, into the smiling eyes of Urbin Dacey, whose father led the Withy Hold Council. He was tall and black-haired and amber-eyed. She had noticed those eyes several times during the council, and had wondered what perversity they watched for. She took a sip of wine, and answered equably,

"I don't transform by whim. And I don't practice such sorcery on humans."

"Pity. His ears could stand some." He turned deftly, lifted a plate of stuffed mushrooms as she opened her mouth. "What sorcery do you allow yourself to practice on humans?"

"As little as poss—"

"You have been practicing some on me."

"What?"

"I've felt it in the council chamber. You meet my eyes with your pale moon eyes. You draw at me. Calyx is very beautiful, but she is day, and you are night, secret, beautiful, mysterious, perhaps dangerous. Are you dangerous at night?"

Nyx gazed at him, a mushroom halted midway to her mouth. "What in Moro's name are you talking about?"

His smile never faltered. "I believe I make myself clear. I am falling a little in love with you."

"Oh, don't be ridiculous." She bit into the mushroom, added, chewing, "Love is the last thing on your mind."

He was silent, looking down at her so long that she wondered if she had left mushroom in some unsightly place. "It's a game," he said lightly. "You should learn to play it. It gives the world grace."

He slid the glass from her hand, took a sip of wine, and slipped it back between her fingers. She said softly, "And how well you play it. You must practice often."

"I'll teach you."

"Unfortunately, I lack grace." She set the glass on the table and stood quietly, not moving or speaking, simply looking at him until his smile finally faltered and he turned away.

She picked up the glass again, took a hefty swallow. Someone else stepped to her side and marvelled, "You made Urbin Dacey blush."

She lowered the glass with some relief. "Rush."

He brushed a crumb off her sleeve. "It takes a complex sorcery to discomfit Urbin. He won't give up easily, though. I've seen him watching you. He plays a game he hates to lose."

"I have no time for games," she said, feeling the weight of the key in her pocket. Rush looked at her silently a moment; she glimpsed a familiar curiosity in his eyes and wondered what realm she had neglected to explore. He asked the question in his eyes.

"Does sorcery preclude love?"

"I wouldn't know. It's not in Chrysom's books."

"Is that all you——" he began, then saw he was being teased. He smiled a little, still curious, while she helped herself to a plate of tiny biscuits rolled in poppy seeds and spices. She said, because he wanted to know,

"I take after my mother, who roamed Ro Holding when she was young and found three fathers for three daughters. Sorcery does not preclude curiosity, and I have satisfied my curiosity at times. But——"

"With whom?"

Like her mother, she ignored the question. "But you have to stand still for love. I could never stand still."

"Like Urbin," he said, then flushed a little. But she mulled that over calmly.

"Maybe. But at least I'm honest."

"Yes," he said, not looking at her, but she saw the memories in his eyes. "Urbin has a thousand ways of saying one thing. You don't hide behind language, which is why he can't find, among his thousand ways, the one way to make you listen. Neither could I," he added, but lightly, and she smiled, seeing no bitterness in his eyes.

"Now," she said, "we listen to one another." She touched his arm and turned, to find Arlen Hunter in her path, who had come to tell her what he believed about her, and what he didn't, feeling it was important for her to know. She extracted herself abruptly from his muddle of awe and prurience, deciding that no effort to please her mother was worth becoming civilized for this. She slipped away to wait for moonrise.

Across the hall, Meguet, disarmed, dressed in red silk and gold, found siege laid against her own patience. Tur Hunter, blue-eyed, golden-haired, heir to Hunter Hold, had lost, he said, his heart to her green eyes. He was smiling, but relentless, burning hot and cold, and willing to fight a slight to his pride. She said carefully, "My own heart is bound to this house; my eyes are not free to stray."

"Not from the gate?" he said, his smile thinning, and she felt the blood rise in her face. "Your whims are your business, but you should have some respect for your own heritage. What in Moro's name can you do with a Gatekeeper?"

"Love him," she said simply, with no tact whatsoever. Tur Hunter snorted, flushing.

"What will you do? Marry him and live among the cottagers?"

She shrugged slightly. "I hadn't thought. If past is status, some among the cottagers can trace their families back a thousand years, when Moro Ro's status in Ro Holding was that he had a bigger cottage than anyone else and a bloodier sword."

"And what does your Gatekeeper have?" he retorted. "Born among tortoises and river rats, he still has the swamp in his voice. You'll tire of that soon enough."

"Then," she said, keeping her voice steady with an effort, "it is not worth your breath to interfere, since I will cast him aside eventually over the cadence of lilies and slow dark water and small birds in his voice."

Tur was silent a breath, then changed weapons. "Now," he said solicitously, and took her hand in his, "I have put you in the position of having to defend him. I have made you angry. That was hardly my intention. If the Holder hasn't interfered in your infatuation with the murkier side of the Delta, it must be because she is wiser than I am, and knows it is like the elusive, colorful swamp lights, of little substance and will burn itself out. Tell me what I can do to persuade you to forgive me."

She almost suggested something. But the Holder was beside her suddenly, as if summoned by the swamp lights smoldering in the air between them.

"Tur," she said, fixing a dark eye upon him, "stop trying to lure my niece to Hunter Hold; I need her here. She is one of the foundation stones of this house, like my Gatekeeper, and I won't free her for all the gold in Hunter Hold. Go and get me wine and take it outside and drink it." She took Meguet's arm, forcing Tur to loose her hand, and led her to the hearth. It was cold, unoccupied, and offered a moment of privacy within the crowded hall.

Meguet said softly, "I can fight my own battles. Though I didn't think I would have to."

The Holder, who loved fires, eyed the empty grate wistfully. She said, "Neither did I, but then I never admitted to anything I had to defend. Anyway, I wanted to talk to you. When you are not guarding the Holding Council, I want you with Nyx."

Meguet, startled, said, "There's not much I can do for her."

"I know that and I don't care. I don't want her alone with that stranger, and you're the only one in the house she would put up with." She kicked the grate moodily, and turned, gazing at the placid, murmuring hall as if mages were concealed in the hangings or underfoot beneath the carpets. "I want you with her in those night hours when the bird becomes human."

Meguet was silent, seeing again the rich and stunning shapes the bird's cry had taken in the yard. "I wonder where he came from . . . I wonder if anyone is alive to miss him or search for him."

"I'm wondering who cast that spell and when Nyx's meddling will bring yet another mage to my door."

"If that mage is still alive."

"There are too many mages." Her fingers lifted to her hair, searching for pins to pull, but they were too well hidden. She folded her arms instead, frowning at her shadow in the torchlight. "Nyx assumes the mage is dead. I assume otherwise, for the sake of my house. That is why I want you with her. She trusts you, and you have more common sense than she does."

"Only for an ordinary world."

"That's the one I want to keep her alive in," the Holder said grimly. "She has so much power, and she has hardly scrubbed the mud off her feet from that morass she trapped herself in."

"The power was given to her freely."

"It's not her heart that worries me now, it's her magpie curiosity that picks at anything glittering of magic. She's facing a twisted sorcery unfamiliar even to her. She may have terrorized the population of birds in the swamp, but she never made anything human cry so desperately. And all she can see of the sorcery is something she can't do herself——she's blind to danger. Even the young man seems dangerous to me."

"Yes."

"I don't think he's just an innocent under a spell. He looks powerful and unpredictable."

"Like Nyx, not long ago."

The Holder's brooding attached itself to her. "Meguet Vervaine, are you counseling compassion over common sense?"

"Never," Meguet said flatly, "where Nyx is concerned. But given the murkier sorcery she has dabbled in, she may have more success with a bird with a questionable past than a mage with a tidier history would."

The Holder made an undignified sound. "Let's hope his past is tidier than hers. Wherever his past is. Or was."

"Perhaps he is from Ro Holding and he simply can't remember. He does remember the Cygnet flying on warships."

"He'd have to be a very old bird."

"Or a young man trapped outside of his time."

The Holder touched her eyes. "That is something Nyx would find irresistible. But how much does she know about time? Is that common knowledge among mages?"

"She pulled me within time to stand beneath the Cygnet's eye. For all I know she may have all the Cygnet's power."

The Holder drew breath. "Moro's bones. It's unprecedented." Her eyes moved over the hall, searching. "Where is she? I asked her to stay through supper."

"I saw her talking to Rush. And then to Arlen Hunter."

"I don't see her."

"She must be here," Meguet said, failing to find her. "She doesn't forget things."

"She forgets unimportant things," the Holder said darkly. "Supper, her shoes, sleep, time. Maybe that mage returned without our knowing, ensorcelled us all again between a bite and a swallow. Maybe," she added, with some hope, "he has found the book himself and vanished back into his own secret country."

"It can't be all that secret," Meguet pointed out, "if he has heard of Chrysom."

The Holder closed her eyes. "Don't raise side issues," she said tersely. "Find Nyx before the moon rises and I lose her again to that demented bird."

The bird's eye reflected a sorceress within its golden iris. It perched on a window ledge; its shadow, cast long and black by the torch beside the window, cut across the sorceress's path to take shape against the hearth: a faceless dark beneath the stone Cygnet. Nyx was aware of the bird's scrutiny and its shadow. She moved imperturbably through both, continuing her search for the missing book and waiting for moonrise. She had explored everything but the oddments on the mantel. There, she reasoned, it must be: the mage's voice buzzing inside the cobalt box, the barely perceptible shift of weighty thought within the emerald bottle.

The bird opened its beak. No cry came out of it, no fire, but the sorceress turned to face it.

"Be patient," she said. "I haven't forgotten you."

She folded her arms, leaned against the mantel, frowning slightly, studying the bird. The red on its folded wingtips made an elaborate chessboard pattern against the white. Its longer plumes trailed down the stone, delicate puffs of white that stirred at a breath. Its sharp talons caught light like metal; the mask of fiery feathers around its eyes gave it a fierce and secretive expression. Nyx, slowly dissolving within an amber eye, saw only herself in its thoughts. Whatever language it spoke—bird or human—was hidden.

"You are well guarded," she commented, returned to herself on the hearth. The bird did not shift a feather, as motionless as if it had become one of its own enchantments. The fire still hung in Nyx's ear. She toyed with it absently. The bird opened its beak soundlessly, in recognition.

Red the color of the bird's mask snagged her eye. She turned her head, studied a tiny red clay jar on the mantel. It was shaped like a hazelnut with a flat bottom and a cap of gold. The clay was seamed with minute cracks, as if whatever it held had seeped out centuries before. Nyx picked it up, weighed it in her hand. Chrysom, who had, centuries after his death, gotten suddenly more complex, might have left an empty bottle on his mantel, or a mage's trap. A day or two ago she had known how he thought. Now, she was not so sure.

"Well," she said, and met the bird's intent golden stare. "Better sorry than safe."

She gazed down at the jar, letting her thoughts flow like air or water into the spider web of cracks. The rough, dry edges permitted her only so far, no farther, into their tiny crevices. What stopped her, she couldn't tell; it had no substance. The gold cap, molded into the clay by the slow shift of particles of metal, seemed solid; touching it, her thoughts turned into gold.

It was of a piece, like the bird, like the bird's enchantments: a weave of magic so fine she could not isolate a single thread. Baffled, she withdrew from it, fascinated by her ignorance.

She put it back on the mantel, picked up a round bottle of opaque, swamp-green glass, no bigger than her palm. Its neck was short, slender, and had no opening. But it was not empty. Something within it shifted against the glass sides; the bottle tilted sluggishly in her hand, then rolled upright. Her thoughts grew crystal, rounded, green, then eased inward, dropped away from the glass into the tiny pool of magic it enclosed.

She fell into a great pool of nothing. The world lost hold of her, sent her tumbling headlong into an endless mist. Startled, she nearly withdrew; then, curious, she continued falling, seeing nothing, hearing nothing, moving toward nothing until she realized she could fall forever in that tiny bottle and never reach the bottom.

She withdrew slowly, finding stone walls beyond the mist, books, the bird's unblinking eyes. It took some effort; she rested a moment, wary now, but still intrigued, before she explored farther. She chose something black: glass or stone carved into a little block of shadow. It was wrapped in a web of silver filaments that wound around one another and parted and crossed again in an endless, intricate pattern. Concentrating on a single filament, she found herself on a silver road.

She did not need to move; it moved beneath her, swift as wind. Darkness dropped away from the road on both sides, as if the small block enmeshed in the silver had no reality itself. The silver turned and coiled, looked back, crossed itself, moving so fast she felt she had left her thoughts at some forgotten crossroad. The road went everywhere and nowhere, it seemed. On impulse, she dropped off the rushing silver into the darkness within it.

She found herself in a cube of night, with the silver running in front of her, behind her, underfoot and overhead, like a net. She tried to withdraw, but she could not reach past the silver. It was too intricate, it moved too quickly; catching hold of it was like trying to hold water pouring down a cliff.

So I am caught, she thought, *like a fish in Chrysom's net. But what is the net made of?* The way out of the trap was to become the trap. . . .

She could not hold a single, wild thread; she might, leaping out of the dark, out of herself, hold the entire moving, glowing web. Unthinking, forgetting even her own name, she expanded into the darkness, and then, at all points and loops and crossroads, into the rushing current of silver.

The flowing pattern froze. Suspended, her mind the intricate net of filament, she saw what the dark had hidden: cubes within cubes of patterned silver, each a completely different weave, growing smaller and smaller but never vanishing. If she could move between them from one cube to the next, if she could walk each pattern . . . But what were they?

And then she remembered the filaments, blackened with age and fire, on the wrists of the stranger. His hands opened wide, as if to loose some lost power within the patterns. He spoke . . .

She whispered, "Time."

She was suspended within tantalizing spells for time. But what spell opened the paths to use? How could she get here, there, or anywhere on those fantastic silver roads that led nowhere outside the box? How, she wondered more practically, could she get herself outside the box?

I got in, she reminded herself. *I can get out.*

But if she had flung herself down a deep, dry well, that would be easy to say and not so easy to do. She swallowed, for the second time in her life, the little, cold, pebble-hard fact that all her will and all the knowledge she possessed might not be enough to find her way back to the world.

I am looking into Chrysom's eye, she thought. *Into his mind, which until now I thought I knew. This is one of the puzzles in the missing book, which is why I cannot solve it. Yet.*

Later, after she had contemplated the frozen, glowing paths without inspiration, she felt again the feathery touch of fear.

They will find me, she thought, *in the library, silent, blind, motionless, holding the box in my hand. Will they have the sense to leave me with it? Rush wouldn't. He would smash it, to set me free. I could be trapped in its broken shards forever . . . I should have taught Rush more sorcery. But I never had the patience. And he would never stop to think.*

She quieted her unruly thoughts, focused them again. Nothing to do, it seemed, but pick a path again, see if her thoughts might lead somewhere, if the path wouldn't. She narrowed her vision, dropped onto the nearest pattern. Instantly she felt it move, dividing, looping, flowing everywhere and nowhere, as it had before, and she was powerless to control it.

Time, she thought. *What is it? A word. To endow a word with power, you must understand it.*

Settling into that one place to begin to understand Chrysom's spell, she saw a man in the distance ahead of her.

His head was bent slightly; he did not turn or speak. He simply walked, his eyes on the flow and weave of silver as if, out of the endless twists and turns, he fashioned a solid path and followed it.

She found the path he left, a stillness in the wild flow, a single strand of silver frozen among the rushing patterns. Amazed, she followed it, wondering if Chrysom had set a shadow of himself within the paths to guide the unwary mage. The road beyond the guide began to blur into darkness. Nyx quickened her pace; as if he felt her sudden fear, he slowed. Closing the distance between them, she recognized him.

She caught her breath, stunned at the sight of the long black hair, the warrior's straight line of shoulder. Turning, he met her eyes, held them. She blinked, and the tower stones formed around them, the moon hanging in the black sky beyond a window. Gazing at her, still caught, perhaps, in some twist of past, for an instant he recognized himself.

"My name is Brand."

FIVE

WITH the name came memory. He flinched away from it as from
fire; for an instant his human face became the firebird's cry. Then his
eyes emptied of expression: the dreamer waking, the dream forgotten. She
whispered,

"You were with me in Chrysom's box. You led me out."

He only gazed at her blankly. "I don't remember."

"Brand." She added, at his silence, "That is your name. You just told me."

"I don't remember."

The door opened. Preoccupied, she did not loose his eyes, just held up a
hand for silence. She received it, so completely she wondered if she had
thrown a spell across the room. "You remember," she said. "Your eyes remember. The bird remembers."

"The bird—" He paused, bewildered. "The bird is sorcery."

"It cries your sorrow."

"It cries jewels as well as sorrow. Are those mine also?"

"Perhaps. If you are a mage."

He was silent again, throwing a net into the still black waters of memory.
The net came up empty. "Why would I be that?"

"Only another mage could have rescued me from Chrysom's spell." She
heard something from the door then, not sound so much as a rearrangement

of disturbed air. She asked, because it had to be asked, not because she had much hope of answer, "Do you know the mage who wears a white dragon on his breast?"

His head lifted slightly; he gazed beyond her, as if dragons were gathering soundlessly in the shadows just beyond the candlelight. For an instant he seemed to see what lay beyond the light: the country where he had been named. The memory faded; he shook his head. "I cannot see that dragon."

"The mage?"

"What?"

"Do you know the mage?"

He started to speak, stopped. All color left his face then; his hands clenched. Nyx saw the firebird cry in his eyes, of grief and rage and danger.

Red shimmered in the corner of her eye. She turned her head, saw Meguet, dressed for supper, slide a blade noiselessly off the wall. Whether she wanted it to fight mages or dragons, Nyx wasn't sure; either, it seemed suddenly, might blow in unexpectedly on the night wind. She turned back to Brand, touched the metal patterns on his wrists lightly. When he made no protest, she lifted his hands in hers.

"Is this the path of time you followed here?" He looked at them, mute. "All Chrysom's paths are silver. How did these get so black?"

He shook his head, seeing nothing of mage or time or color in the blackened metal. "I don't understand. The bird brought me here. Not these."

"You are the bird," she reminded him patiently, and as patiently he replied,

"The bird is sorcery."

Meguet tugged at Nyx's attention. She still stood silently at the door, but her face was pale and her eyes flicked at every breeze-strewn shadow. She met Nyx's glance, asked softly, "Is the mage looking for him?"

"Probably."

"Nyx—"

"It's an interesting problem," Nyx admitted. "It's hard enough to hide the key, let alone the bird."

"Where did you put the key?"

"In my pocket." She added, at Meguet's expression, "It refused to change its shape, and I couldn't think what else to do with it."

"So you took it to the council hall?"

"Well, I could hardly slide it under a carpet. If the mage returned, I wanted to be there."

"I didn't," Meguet said succinctly. She made a move toward a chair, then drew back to the door, looking, Nyx thought, with the gold threading through her loose hair, and the ancient sword, almost as tarnished as the metal on Brand's wrists, half-hidden in the silken folds of her skirt, unlikely enough to startle even the mage again. Nyx said,

"You might as well sit. I doubt that either dragon or mage will use the door."

Meguet did so, but reluctantly, still holding the sword. "Dragon," she said, "being the little winged animal made of thread."

"According to Chrysom, who must have roamed farther than I ever realized, dragons are made of flesh and blood and fire, and most are not small."

"How big," Meguet asked after a moment, "is not small?"

"Huge. So Chrysom said."

Meguet shifted uneasily, hearing dragon wings in the rustling wind. "Well," she sighed, "at least they can't come through the windows. Did Chrysom happen to say where there might be dragons?"

Nyx shook her head. "Like the firebird, he considered them fable. Or he wrote as if he did. Now, after coming out of that black box, I'm not sure what he knew, where he travelled, or when. He—"

"What black box?" Meguet's eyes fell to what Nyx still held in her hand, and widened. "That? You were in there?"

"My mind was."

"Moro's name. Why?"

"It seemed a good idea at the time. Not," she admitted, "one of my better ones. I wanted to see if any of those odd things were the missing book. This is full of paths, twisting, turning, looping strands of silver. I think they lead to different times, moments within moments, perhaps the sorcery the mage used to slow time. But I don't know how to use them, and I think the knowledge is in the missing book, as well as in the firebird's memory."

"That was the spell he rescued you from?"

"Brand. Coming out, he remembered his name. But nothing more, not even that he had walked a path of time with me in that box, and led me out."

Meguet closed her eyes, dropped a cold hand over them. "I don't know why your mother bothered to send me up here."

"I don't know, either. Why did she?"

"I'm supposed to guard you. At best a futile notion, at worst laughable."

Nyx turned, set the box carefully back on the mantel. "My mother worries too much."

"How can you say that? The mage is not only looking for the key you are carrying around in your pocket, but for the firebird, both of which are in the place he will obviously return to, unless you spun him into thread so thoroughly he is still trying to untangle himself." There was a tap at the door; she nearly jumped, then rose with more dignity. "That will be Brand's supper. The Holder requested your presence in the hall."

"I can't go now," Nyx said absently. "I'm thinking." She sat down, slipped her shoes off and propped her feet up. Arms folded, she frowned at midair. A wide-eyed page set the supper tray on a table, seemed inclined to linger to watch the firebird eat, and encountered Nyx's eye. Meguet, left between the pensive sorceress and the ravenous man, sat tensely, watching for a thread of white dragon-wing, a dust-gold face in the shadows, and wondering what raw deed the firebird's jewelled enchantments hid. She murmured,

"There are too many mages."

Nyx's eyes rose, fixed on Brand. She nodded, still frowning. "He could have ensorcelled himself."

"And the other mage is following to free him?"

"It's possible. There is a way to find out."

"How?" Then she leaned forward, gripping the sword hilt. "No."

Nyx shrugged. "I don't see how we are to get closer to the truth this way. The man retreats constantly into the firebird. If we let the mage find him, Brand might remember himself along with the mage."

"Not here. Not in this tower, in the middle of the Holding Council. They may be bitter enemies. The entire house would be in danger. I think you should hide the firebird—"

"Where?" Nyx asked. "In the maze beneath the tower?"

"Of course not."

"Then where?"

"In the thousand-year-old wood. Not even the mage would find him among the shifting trees."

"I could find him easily there. What I can do, I must assume the mage can do."

"Then somewhere in the city, or in the swamp—"

Nyx's mouth crooked. "I can't disappear into the swamp with a bird. My mother would spit lightning. I would prefer to face the mage."

"I'll leave," Brand said abruptly. They both looked at him, startled, as if they had forgotten he could speak. Disturbed, he pushed away his food. He came to stand before Nyx. "I didn't know the bird would endanger you."

Nyx checked her immediate response, said patiently, "You might walk out of here, but the bird would return. It's you who must learn to cry jewels. To cry sorrow. Or the bird will never set you free."

He shook his head at her obtuseness. "All I know," he said, "is that the bird came to you, sorcery to sorceress. First you must deal with the sorcery. Then I will be able to remember."

She drew breath. His eyes held some of the bird's fierceness, but it was the fierceness of desire, of determination. "All right," she said at last, wondering that he had guided her so skillfully out of one maze, only to be so blind in another. "I will work with the spell awhile, instead of your human memory. One can't be more difficult than the other. But I have already tried to find my way into the spell, and gotten nowhere."

"Try again," he pleaded and sat down on the window ledge where the bird had waited for the rising moon.

She found the bird's face within his thoughts; its spellbound mind yielded nothing to her of memory or enchantment. When the bird itself reappeared, Nyx slipped within its mind, as easily as she had dropped into Chrysom's tiny box. For a time, she wandered among the bird's enchantments that bloomed ceaselessly behind its eyes, and faded again without the fire that fashioned them. They formed like dreams around her, thoughtless, intangible, with nothing of either mage or Brand in them. She found her way out again, and said, studying the bird with some perplexity,

"This is exasperating. The bird won't give me a path into the man; the man won't give me a path into the bird. It's as if they exist in separate worlds. I might as well be back in Chrysom's black box for all the sense I can make of this."

"There is always a way," Meguet said sleepily. "You told me that." She received no answer; Nyx had disappeared again. To Meguet's eye, she looked pensive, very still, as if she were chasing the tag-end of some sudden, imperative notion in her head. She did not move; she scarcely seemed to breathe. Meguet sighed noiselessly, and settled back in her chair. Just before her eyes closed, she saw the white dragon's golden eye in the shadows beside the hearth.

She was on her feet almost before she had opened her eyes. The dragon was gone; Nyx had not moved.

"Nyx," she whispered, shifting toward her, the blade poised in her hands. "Nyx."

Nyx did not answer. Meguet, glancing at her, saw her frowning at the bird, her arms folded. She did not move, she did not blink. Meguet raised her voice. "Nyx!"

"She won't hear you," the mage said. He was still invisible, though she caught the flick of a dragon's wing, the shift of a claw here and there, as he moved noiselessly, restively, in front of the mantel. Listening, she heard faint music, soft laughter on the parapet wall. He read her mind. "I didn't meddle with your time. I didn't come for trouble. I came only for the key."

Meguet screamed Nyx's name. Nyx remained oblivious, but through a south window Meguet saw one of the turret-torches raised aloft, as if the Gatekeeper had felt her desperate need. She heard voices within the tower, guards and pages tossing alarms down the stairwell, a flurry of running in the outer yard.

"I sealed the door," the mage said. "They won't get through. Where is the key? Just tell me that. I'll find it and go." He spoke softly, as if not to disturb Nyx, but Meguet heard the strain in his voice. She wondered if he hid himself from Nyx or from the firebird.

"She put it somewhere."

"Where?"

"I think in a book. One of the household records over there, I don't remember which—"

"You're lying." He sounded amazed. "I didn't think you could lie. Where is it really?"

"Among the roses on the vines."

The dragon eye came closer; she shifted a step or two toward Nyx. "A good place to hide it. One rose among a thousand roses. But even if I picked them all, I'd never find it there. Where is it really hidden?"

"The firebird changed it with its cry," she said desperately, and he was silent, as if at last he believed her. Fists battered at the door; voices, impatient and furious, made improbable suggestions about makeshift battering rams, and Rush's makeshift sorcery.

"Meguet," said the air, startling her with her name. "I can't wait for tomorrow's moonrise. Where is the key? If you don't tell me, I will turn this household, one by one, into screaming firebirds. Beginning with the Gatekeeper."

"So," she whispered, her mouth dry, "this is your spell."

"So it seems."

Nyx turned abruptly, pulling amber from her ear lobe. She held it up. The bird, freed from her mind, cried soundlessly. Its enchanted fire leaped from the amber, illumined the mage for a breath. He vanished before the fire struck him, but not before the firebird had seen his face.

The bird cried. Its noiseless cry became the man's cry, of such fury and agony that it froze both Nyx and Meguet and silenced the crowd outside the door. Brand moved under their amazed eyes, tore swords off the wall. The white dragon leaped to fly. The blades in Brand's hands spun and flashed in a whirling, singing dance of death too quick to follow. Meguet, mesmerized by its glittering intricacy, moved a fraction too late to intercept the dragon in its deadly flight. The blades soared upward, turned again, came down so fast at the dragon that when the mage halted them in midair, Brand lost his balance, stumbled against them. He was instantly surrounded by a ring of swords, shear-edged, gleaming like ice. The white dragon slipped under his blades and flew headlong into the amber fire. A swirl of leaves the color of bone and pearl scattered to the floor.

Brand, his face white, set with fury, was thwarted only for a moment by the blades. He changed himself; the firebird cried within the ring. It caught air, flew above them. Nyx's searching amber found the mage again: a flickering just visible beside the windows. He shifted. The fire continued out a window; Meguet heard an outraged shout from the yard. The firebird circled, its wings brushing wall and torch fire, silver talons outstretched to tear the mage out of the air and hold his shape. The fire swept over him again. He moved, fading, but not quickly enough; the bird's claws raked his outstretched arm before he vanished. Nyx, sweeping the amber fire across the dark, following his movements with a mage's eye, nearly transformed Meguet as he reappeared beside her.

"Give me the key," he said to Nyx. "Or I'll take her with me." His voice shook; Meguet saw the blood under his tattered sleeve.

"Take the spell off Brand," Nyx said with disconcerting control, "and we'll discuss the key."

"He is fighting his own way out of it," the mage answered. "If I take your cousin, you'll never find her."

"Brand is fighting you," Nyx said evenly. "He is still spellbound. Remove the spell."

Meguet, disinclined to being haggled over, slid smoothly out of the mage's grip, whirled away from him. He vanished again; this time he threw up a mist to scatter Nyx's fire. Meguet, swinging her blade, attacked a sudden shower of rose petals as the fire hit the mist. The bird snatched at them as futilely; she ducked as one of its claws tangled in her hair.

"Moro's eyes," she breathed. The bird became man, desperate, furious, bewildered, and then bird again, taking wing. Gold fire flared, limned the mage, and encased half the household records in amber. The bird swooped at random, swooped again, then cried noiselessly as its talons snagged the mage and dragged most of him into light. The mage spun away; the bird's claws scored his shoulders just before he vanished.

Someone cried: Brand or the mage. Brand appeared again, blurred, half-bird, half-man; blood dripped from his fingers. The bird wrenched him out of shape, took wing, and Meguet saw its broken, bloody talon. She cried, a sudden, helpless pity snagging at her voice,

"Nyx, stop this! Can you stop this?"

Nyx cast her a glance, frowning slightly. The color had come into her eyes. "This makes no sense," she murmured, and the amber flared again. Something flew through the window, shadow-dark, as graceful as the dragon. Meguet, expecting dragons, saw it in the corner of her eye and turned her head. The fire transformed it instantly: A black swan circled in golden flame became a white rose falling through the fire into shadow.

Tears pricked her eyes, for no reason, she insisted to herself: Everything was enchanted, even the air. The mage was at her side again, and then the firebird overhead, swooping, talons open, descending toward him.

He seemed to slow the bird; Meguet saw its movements overlapping, image fanning out from image in the air. But he could not stop it entirely. In that charmed moment gold turned and turned through the air, clinked finally at the mage's feet. Bending, he eluded the bird's grasp; its talons flashed, scarred empty air just above him. He could not seem to balance himself; he gripped Meguet, dragged at her until she stumbled. The stones rose like water around her; a key floated on them into her hand. Then whispering air and fire slashed down again at the mage. He gasped, reaching for the key as for a spar in the shifting world. His hand locked around Meguet's wrist. She gave one terrified cry and then he pulled her into stone.

Nyx, staring at the stones where Meguet had vanished, found her nowhere. The firebird, searching as futilely for its prey, gave a soundless cry and glided to the window, with Brand as lost inside it as Meguet was inside the mage's time. She whispered, "Meguet."

A deep, rhythmic thumping began at the door; they had brought up something for a battering ram. Nyx lifted her head, her face mist-white in the candlelight. The floor was littered with the fire's enchantments. She checked her first, absent impulse to open the door to the battering ram, which would have proceeded across the room and out a window, taking the bird with it. She raised her voice instead.

"Stop—" Her voice caught; she cleared her throat. "Stop pounding! I'll open the door."

"Quiet!" the Holder said sharply, and the din outside the door ceased. Nyx broke the mage's spell; the door opened, spilling guards into the room. They stared at the glittering debris from the fire: pearl leaves, rose petals, books sealed in amber. Then they saw the blood on the firebird, and a whispering began.

The Holder tugged at the pearls at her breast, her eyes, wide and dark, reflecting something of Nyx's expression. "What happened?"

"The mage came back," Nyx said. "The firebird attacked him. They seem to know one another." She stopped, pulling at a strand of sapphires in her hair. She frowned, searching for words, her eyes going back to the stones. The Holder read her mind.

"Where is Meguet?"

"The mage took her."

"Took her! Moro's bones, took her where?"

"Somewhere. Some time. Some place."

"Why?"

"She was attached to the key I threw him." The strand of sapphires came loose, dropped to the floor. She touched her eyes and added, "He'll be back. Probably to exchange Meguet for the key."

"Moro's bones," the Holder breathed again. "How many keys does he want?"

"Just one. I gave him a false key to make him leave." She paused, feeling the weight of the Holder's still, black gaze. "There are things that are not making sense—"

"You," the Holder said succinctly.

"I mean, other than that."

"What in Moro's name possessed you to put either of your lives in danger for the sake of some moldy sorcery no one has paid attention to in a thousand years?"

"It's not—"

"Why didn't you give the mage the key the moment he came back for it?"

"Because—"

"Instead of jeopardizing the house and losing Meguet in some time beyond memory and some place without a name? And why is that bird still a bird? You've been immersed in sorcery since you learned to read—what's so difficult about turning a bird back into a man? Surely you've done more complex things with birds. How do I know this one won't attack you next?"

"Because, I don't think—"

"And where in Moro's name is my Gatekeeper?"

Nyx glanced around the room. "I saw him come in. I think it was him."

"If that mage stole him as well as Meguet—"

"No, it was my fault. I was fighting with the bird's fire. I must have changed him into something."

The Holder closed her eyes, pushed her hands through her hair. Pins flew. "You're a sorceress. Do some sorcery. Disenchant that bird. And my Gatekeeper. Find Meguet. And if that mage returns, give him whatever he wants, including the bird, if he wants that. I want no more bloodshed, mage's battles, stopped time or misplaced people. I want to end this council in even less excitement than it began. I want it to be a dull reference in the history of Ro Holding, not an entire flamboyant chapter."

"Yes." Nyx's voice came with effort. "I am sorry."

"And do it by dawn."

She did not quite slam the door. Nyx sat down, blinking, her face stiff. She stirred a couple of garnet rose petals with her foot, trying to think; her mind only filled, like the tower room, with enchantments. The door opened softly. She lifted her head. Calyx entered, side-stepping spells.

"I'm sorry about the books," Nyx said wearily. "They'll change back at moonrise tomorrow."

"Never mind the books." She touched Nyx's hair gently, removed a dangling pin. "I only wanted to tell you that the Gatekeeper is at the gate."

She straightened a little, blinking. "Is he?"

"He could never have gotten through the door. You only thought you saw him."

"Most likely."

"Should someone tell him about Meguet?"

"He knows." She added, at Calyx's puzzled expression, "Rumor is faster than thought in this house."

"Besides," Calyx said comfortingly, "you'll find her by dawn."

"Only if the mage brings her back from wherever he went. I don't even know the names of places beyond Ro Holding. Do you?"

"Just what Cado the Peculiar mentions."

"Who?"

"He was the fourth son of Irial Ro. He was called Cado the Restless when he was young. He signed on a merchant ship, disappeared for eleven years and then came back to astonish his family with tales of one-legged giants, women made of gold, flowers with eyes, sorcerers with tails. According to the historian Blaconnes, it is most likely that Cado went ashore at Hunter Hold, lived an obscure and happy life digging for gold in the Junil Mountains, until the woman he lived with ran away with a rich miner. Then he shipped himself back home, whereupon, meeting his wife again, he thought it prudent to invent a few marvellous lands."

"Oh." Nyx's eyes strayed to the firebird, its eyes hooded in the torchlight. "The firebird would know where the mage went."

"The bird can't speak."

"And the man can't remember." Nyx sat silently, contemplating the pair, then touched Calyx, who was working the pins back into her hair. "You'd better go. If I lose you as well as Meguet to the mage, I'd be better off living an obscure and happy life as a swamp toad."

"Our mother ordered supper sent up to you."

"She's still feeding me. That's a good sign."

"You're too much alike, that's all." Calyx bent, kissed Nyx's cheek. "Be careful."

Alone, Nyx studied the sleeping firebird. Her supper came; she ate a few bites, pacing, her eyes, colorless and heavy, focused on the bird, while her mind drew constant, fraying patterns between the firebird, the man, the mage, the blackened weavings of metal on Brand's wrists, the silver paths within Chrysom's box.

"You know," she whispered to the bird, who had tucked its head under its wing. "You know where they have gone."

But all its memories were enchanted.

She sat down finally in a chair beside the firebird, waiting for the mage to return. He would know the difference between a key made by Chrysom's hand, and one by hers; he might have felt it, her mind instead of Chrysom's as he fell back through time, if Meguet hadn't been holding the key. He hadn't been too hurt to work a spell; most likely he could heal a scratch or two. And his white dragon lay in a pile of pearl leaves; if it were more than thread, he might return for that. And where was the book he so desperately wanted? He must have it already, she reasoned, since he wasn't contorting time to look for that, too. A book without a key was far more valuable than a key without a book. . . .

Her eyes closed. The key floated behind her eyes: gold, with an ivory-and-gold haft, a C or a crescent moon holding an M in its arms. Mage Chrysom. Chrysom's Magic . . . the key . . .

She woke at the sound of the council bells. The sun was up; it flung the bird's shadow over her and glittered in amber, garnet, as if its own fire might wake the things frozen in time, waiting for the moon. She felt the key in her pocket, heard the bird pecking water from a bowl. There was no sign of the mage or Meguet.

She slumped in the chair, feeling the tear in the tidy fabric of household life where Meguet should have been. The mage must return for the key. If he did not bring Meguet with him, there would be a mages' war in the dark tower, despite the Holder's wishes. It was inconceivable that he would not bring Meguet. But why had he not returned? Was he afraid of the firebird?

Would he return at moonrise, when the bird changed? Would Brand remember him? Would the Holder wait patiently through another moonrise?

"She has no choice," Nyx murmured. "All she has is me."

She pulled the key out of her pocket, baiting the air with it, in case the mage lurked in some moment where a flash of magic from Chrysom's tower would snag his attention. She turned it over in her palm; the gold caught a fiery tear of light. The crescent moon arched over the upside-down Mage.

Her lips parted. She felt a stirring deep in her, as if small birds had suddenly scattered through her into light.

Chrysom's Work.

She whispered, "The key is the book."

SIX

MEGUET watched the sun rise over a nameless land.

She had been sitting for hours on bare ground, thoughtless and stunned, under a sky full of unfamiliar constellations. There was some protection in the night. Unless she looked up, her eye did not have to acknowledge that she had travelled beyond Ro Holding: the dark might have belonged anywhere. She sat quite still where she had fallen, waiting for Nyx to rescue her, while the night stirred constantly around her, winds roaring and subsiding, hissing sometimes, the warm, malodorous breath of something she refused to imagine. Now and then the mage murmured, moving restlessly, but he never woke. She did not try to rouse him. Nyx would find her, take the key, and they would vanish before she caught a glimpse of this strange place somewhere beyond the Cygnet's wing.

But the morning light seared the land's image into her mind. It unfolded desert, vast, barren, gold as a hawk's eyes, with juttings of bare stone like fantastic towers and crazed palaces. It was noisy; the winds blew unexpected notes through those stones. It smelled of sulphur and something charred; it hissed and steamed, in the distance, from boiling underground waters.

She drew against herself, feeling dangerously exposed, as if the stones had eyes. They might, in that weird place: the ground itself had mouths. Mages might be riding the air above her head. And there she sat, dressed for

last night's supper in a gown as red as fire that flowed like fire on every passing breeze. Her thin velvet slippers would have sailed away in the wind; her
sword had vanished somewhere between here and there. And even shod and
armed and fitted for a journey, she could not have chosen here instead of
there: Ro Holding might lie beyond the distant, shimmering peaks or, as easily, within the winds.

Light sparked everywhere in this hard, bright place, finding flecks of
gold in the sandstone, turning silvery in the steam. It snagged under the
mage's shoulder, and from there, leaped painfully into Meguet's eyes. She
blinked, saw the gold key half-hidden under him. He had that, she told herself; he had no use for her. But would he bother to send her back? She could
take the key, hide it from him, bargain with him . . . But he had seen the key
across time itself; it seemed unlikely that his mage's eye would miss it under
a rock. Both eyes were still closed; not even the sun had wakened him. She
reached for the key quickly, slid it into her pocket. He did not move. She
shifted closer after a moment, touched him.

She heard his breathing then, shallow and erratic, saw the chalky white-
ness beneath the sweat and dust on his face. Pain clawed furrows between his
brows. He stirred a little, as if he felt her gaze; he murmured something,
wincing, and lay still again, while the dust drifted over him.

Horror, fine and dry as the dust, prickled over Meguet: that he might die
and leave her alone in a strange land which might as well have been on some
distant star. She stood up, panicked, searching the plain for a blue thread of
water, a dark thread of wood smoke, symmetrical shapes of houses or a village among the broken tumbled towers of stone. They might have been the
only living things in the world, she and the mage, and he was only half-alive.
What water there was bubbled and stank; shadows on bare ground provided
the only shelter she could see. She knelt again, trying to calm herself. The
mage might have broken a bone, falling. But, running her hands over him, she
felt nothing out of place. He didn't seem to notice her, not even when, with
some effort, she rolled him on his side to study the marks the firebird had
scored across his shoulders.

The weals were long but shallow; they looked irritating but hardly
deadly, unless the bird carried some unexpected venom in its talons. The
thought panicked her again; she closed her eyes, felt the desert sand in her
throat, the hot sun melting into her skin. She must find shelter, water to clean
his wounds. The nearest shadow, flung by a jagged and oddly folded stone,
she could reach in a dozen steps. But the distance between shadow and mage
seemed insurmountable. She rolled him gently on his back again, and slid her

hands under his arms. It was only when she tried to lift him that he came alive, jerking out of her hold, crying odd words, names out of dreams or nightmares.

She let him lie and knelt beside him, wondering what he might have inadvertently summoned. She stroked his hair, murmuring. She had missed something; the bird had hurt him in some deep, subtle way. She contemplated the problem, her eyes wide, gritty, her thoughts stark as light, while she drew her fingers across his cheek, his hair, until he quieted again. Then, slowly, carefully, she coaxed his boots off.

They were fine leather, scuffed and scratched, big enough to fit over her feet and her shoes. He lay still, in the safe, private place where he sheltered against his pain. He did not stir even when she checked his robe for pockets. She found one in a side seam, and rifled it. She drew out a worn, jagged triangle of crystal or glass larger than her palm, the broken leaves of some dried herb, a tiny cube of gold etched on all sides with a delicate pattern not even the heavy crystal battering it had scarred. She sniffed the leaves: something pungent, unfamiliar. She could start a fire with the crystal and the dried leaves, though there was nothing to feed it. The sun had already burned everything. As she returned his odd possessions, the mage murmured again, frowning at the light; already it had become fierce, heavy, burning brass. She had to move him, find water, or she would die there beside a stranger under a strange sky. She stood up, blocked the sun on his face with her own shadow, scanning the land for one place more likely than another.

Above her, a shadow blocked the sun.

She looked up. The sun had vanished; an odd mass of air had swallowed a piece of sky overhead. She could not see what hovered; it was nothing, of no substance, but it cast a shadow all around her. She forced her eyes down finally, not wanting to look, but seeing it, black and clean-lined in the light: the shape of the little white-winged dragon of thread, but huge enough to swallow the sun.

Winds flew across the plain; blowing between cracks and towers of stone, they sounded deep, wild notes. Other voices bellowed among them from beyond the edge of the world. Meguet heard her own voice making an unfamiliar sound. She dropped, huddled against the mage, hiding her face from all the hidden eyes around her.

"Don't die," she pleaded numbly, scarcely hearing herself. "Don't die. I can spin hope for us out of a stone's shadow, but I cannot deal with dragons. Please wake. Please."

The mage did not answer. Shadow peeled away from the ground, left her to the sun. The winds blew dust and great stone flutes, but the otherworldly voices had sunk to a distant murmur. Steam shot a feathery plume out of the ground. The earth shook a little, as if something enormous, invisible, had walked across it. The steam dwindled; earth settled itself. Meguet straightened cautiously, wondering what other sorcery to expect from that exuberant, deadly place.

It seemed for the moment quiet. She rose, went in search of water.

She found, not far from the boiling pools, great thin crescents of something as darkly iridescent as beetles' wings. Upright, they were nearly as tall as she, but they were light enough to drag. She took four of them, made her way slowly, doggedly, through the heat back to the mage. She looked back once; the crescents trailing from under her arms grooved the earth behind her like some great claw. She closed her eyes against the sight, trudged on, awkwardly, her footsteps echoing hollowly in the mage's boots.

She dug shallow holes with the sharp end of one claw, balanced the claws on either side of the mage's body like four bedposts. Then she tore her skirt loose from the bodice, and picked apart a side seam. She dragged the length of silk across the claws, forced it down the sharp ends so that it stretched like a rippling canopy above the mage. He stirred, his face easing. She tore the sleeves from her bodice and wiped the sweat from his face. She rose again, as oddly dressed as she had ever been in her life, in tattered red silk bodice, long white linen shift and oversized boots, to look for water.

There was water everywhere, it seemed, but it boiled and stank and grew crusts of oddly colored crystals where it splashed. She wandered in a wasteland of heat and steam and bubbling mud-holes, her hair plastered down her back, her mouth so dry she would have drunk what steamed in the rifts and crevices of rock if it had not been too hot to touch. She sat wearily on a sandstone ledge, searching for green in a parched land, while her eyes teared at the smell, and behind her, she heard the sudden hiss of jetting water and steam. She leaned back, resting in the shadow, and felt a drift of cold on one cheek.

She found a cave of ice.

It was small, dark, and it steamed like the water holes. Its mouth was rimmed with icy teeth; the threshold was solid ice. Beyond the threshold lay shadow so black she guessed the earth had fallen away there into some deep chasm of time. From the chasm, icy air blew constantly. There were noises, too, shifts like stone against stone, a kind of subdued, rhythmic bellowing, as if a mountain were snoring. She broke off a piece of ice, sucked it. It tasted of earth rather than rotten eggs. She stepped out of one boot and used it to knock down a fat icicle. Limping, the ground burning through her slipper, she made her way back to the mage, carrying a boot full of ice.

She bathed his face with ice, forced it between his lips. Then she turned him over, washed the dirt and dried blood and torn cloth out of his wounds. He scarcely stirred until she touched a corner of one ragged cut above his shoulder blade. Then he stiffened, crying sorcery and dreams carelessly into the wind. She looked more closely, saw something the color of silver trapped there.

She drew it out: a broken piece of the firebird's talon.

She was trembling and nearly in tears when she finished; the mage, having wakened every snoring dragon in the world, finally subsided when she put ice against his back. On impulse, she felt in his pocket again, drew out the broken leaves. She lay one on the ground, caught the sun in the crystal, and focused it until the dry leaf smoldered. She held it under the mage's nose.

His eyes opened. He stared at her expressionlessly, then at the silken canopy, the dark curved spikes that held it up, the icicle melting in his boot. He tested his back, wincing a little. He gazed at her again, this time with amazement.

"Did you do all this?"

She sat back on her heels, answered wearily, "No, of course not. I summoned my attendants."

"You did this without sorcery?"

She closed her eyes briefly, looked at him again. His face was pale as old ivory; he carried his voice from word to word with an effort. She asked, "What else was I to do? You dragged me into this wasteland dressed for supper. You refused to help me. I could have sat here and wept, I suppose. But you only would have died, and I need you to take me home. Why in Moro's name did you pick the middle of a desert to fall into?"

"It's my home," he said simply. He drifted a moment, asked, when she thought he had fallen asleep again, "Where is the key?"

"I have it."

He held up a hand, his eyes still closed, and murmured, "Let me see it."

She did not move. "Swear to take me back to Ro Holding. What I've done for you, I can undo. This time I have a weapon." His eyes opened; she held up the little shard of silver. "I will use it."

She heard his breath stop. Then he drew air deeply, blinking. "Of course I will take you home."

"How can I trust you?"

"I don't know. Maybe you can't. But it's hard for me to believe you would put that sorcery back where you found it. It would be a bloody and noisy piece of work. And you would still be forced to keep me alive. Unless you want to wait here alone, hoping that someone will rescue you. If you choose to do that, remember that the only thing you'll want to eat are the rock lizards. The smaller black ones, not the yellow. You can boil them in the steam pools. They're less tough that way, than if you roast them. There's not much to burn, anyway. But if you do want a fire—" He stopped, shifting ground a little. Meguet, still clinging to the shard, her only argument, said tautly,

"What do I burn?"

"I'll make you something, before you kill me."

"I don't want—"

"You will, with that. It is a dark magic that goes straight to the marrow." He added, at her silence, "I'm trying to persuade you to trust me."

She ran one hand over her face, felt the fine dust clinging to her everywhere, even beneath her eyelids. "How can I?" she demanded. "You attacked my cousin and stole from her. You cast a spell over the Holder's house. You did such terrible things to Brand that he can't speak of them, he can't even remember them. He can only cry the firebird's rage. I don't trust you. The only reason I did all this for you is so that you will stay alive to take me back to Ro Holding."

He stirred again, wincing, his eyes straying to the bare, distant crags. He said tiredly, "I doubt that your cousin tossed the real key to me. She just wanted me out of the tower. So, you see, I may be forced to return to Ro Holding for the true key."

"You dragged me into this crazed, dragon-haunted place because of a fake key?"

He lifted one hand, touched her arm, speechless a moment. "You've seen dragons?" he asked huskily.

"I saw a shadow. You cried out such strange things when I tried to move you. I thought you summoned it. It hovered above us, hiding the sun. It was invisible and yet it cast a shadow."

"A shadow."

"It looked like a shadow your white dragon might have cast. Only a hundred times bigger. I was afraid—I was afraid it might attack."

"Oh, no. They never do."

"Your white dragon did."

"That's sorcery. I made it from a petrified dragon's heart. I'm not sure how real it is. But I've grown fond of it. I left it there, didn't I," he added, remembering. "In the tower, with the firebird."

"It is, I think, a pile of white leaves."

"Until moonrise. And then it will change and Brand will see it."

"Who is he?"

"Brand Saphier. His father, Draken, rules Saphier. This is the Luxour Desert in south Saphier. The edge of the world, some call it. I was born here."

That explained his coloring, she thought. "And why," she asked steadily, "did you turn Brand Saphier into a firebird?"

He moved abruptly, as if the tiny blade of talon in her hand had touched his back again. He answered, his eyes shadowed, heavy, "If I had made the firebird, the magic would be part of me. It could do no more harm to me than my reflection could. The spell that enchanted the firebird is deadly to me."

She was silent, weighing his words against every inflection in his voice, every change of expression in his face. "Assuming it's not yours," she said tautly, "then who cast the spell?"

His brows drew together hard; his eyes shifted away from her, toward some memory. "It's not a thing," he whispered, "I want even the wind to know."

"Then why did the firebird attack you?"

"I think it was made to kill me."

Meguet stood up. Standing brought her into the stifling light, but movement helped her think. In this case, thinking proved futile. She dropped her face in her hands, saw the fierce light behind her eyes. "I don't know how to believe you." She lifted her head, blinking the mage's face clear again. "I don't know what's truth and what's lie, between you and the firebird."

"You don't have to trust me," he said simply. "You're entirely at my mercy. No one knows where you are. Brand would guess his father's court. If he remembers Saphier at all. You can threaten me with that sorcery, but if you hurt me you will only be forced to care for me so that I won't die, so that I can take you home...."

"And if the key is the real one?" she demanded, torn. "You'll vanish with it, leave me stranded here among the dragons. Why should you take the trouble to return me, and face my cousin and the firebird again?"

"It can't be the true key." He turned his face restlessly away from her. "Your cousin is too shrewd."

She knelt, chipped a piece of ice with the crystal, and put it to his lips. There was color in his face now, a feverish glitter in his eyes. "Why," she asked abruptly, frowning down at him, "did you pick that rose for me?"

"Because," he said softly, "you made me remember what words like honor and courage mean. Why did you pick up the rose instead of the sword?"

She sighed, defeated. "I wish I knew." She turned, lifted the dripping icicle out of his boot. She held the boot upside-down; the key dropped out onto the ground.

He picked it up, studied it curiously. He traced the crescent moon of ivory with his forefinger, and then the letter that clung in gold to the dark of the moon. She watched his face.

"Which is it?"

He shook his head. "Every spell carries somewhere in it the mage's signature. It may be the order in which things are done. Or the favorite spellbook used. Or some familiar element. Chrysom liked riddles. Unexpected images. Your cousin had no time for that. This has no centuries clinging to it. No riddles except for its shape. Nothing of Chrysom's; something of a mage I wouldn't have recognized."

"How do you know so much about Chrysom? Is Saphier in another time? Or are you a thousand years old?"

"I like to wander . . . sometimes I wander in and out of time. I learned things, watching Chrysom. I would go and build his fires, fetch things—"

"You spoke to him?"

"He never asked where I was from. But we spoke of time, how it turns and loops. . . . He knew I didn't belong there. He spoke of a spellbook of time he had written. He had hidden it, but he gave me hints, from time to time, when I came. From time to time." He smiled a little, holding the key one way, and then another. His smile faded; he saw the shadow behind the key. "So you see I must return to Ro Holding."

"Why?" she asked wearily. "What more do you need to know of time? You and Nyx will only fight each other."

"I must have the key. I need it. Your cousin only wants it out of curiosity. I need it for my life."

"Tell her that," she said, startled. "She'll help you."

"Mages don't help one another."

"In Ro Holding—"

"Not in Saphier. And I can't tell her why. I can't even whisper it to air. Not in Saphier. And most certainly not in that tower in front of the firebird."

"Why? What are you to the firebird?"

He kindled a tiny flame out of nothing, set the crescent moon on fire. "Once," he said, "we were friends." He let the flame devour moon and letter and shaft, like a candle, until the flame danced on a tear of gold on his palm. He blew it out, let the tear melt into the ground, and buried it. "Now," he explained, "there is only that much of your cousin to be found in Saphier. What is her name?"

"Nyx Ro."

His brows went up. "She is—"

"The Holder's heir."

"And you, Meguet Vervaine?"

"Her cousin."

"And?" He smiled a little at her silence. "The woman who sees into time. You saw the dragon's shadow. It takes a great, complex power to find the dragon." His eyes wandered to the jagged, barren thrusts of rock, the varying hues of gold and dust, the plumes of steam. "That's why I love these deserts. From the time I was young, I could catch glimpses of the dragons. A shadow. A wing folded into a rock. A roar that is not wind. Light that is not sun. If you saw an entire shadow, it is more than most see in a lifetime. I dream of seeing them emerge from stone and air and light. . . ."

"Are they ghosts?" she asked, entranced.

"No. I think they shift in and out of time. Which is why," he added obscurely, "I need that key."

"Can't you open the book without it? If you know Chrysom's ways?"

"I do know Chrysom's ways," he said, but no more. He slid his hand into his pocket, brought out the little cube of gold. "You used a dragon's tooth to start that fire," he commented. Her eyes widened, going to the crystal. "And claws for the canopy. They leave pieces of themselves around."

"I heard one snoring, I think, in the ice cave."

"I tried to see that one. No light will shine in that dark, not even fire. It lives in some black plane so cold its breath freezes even in this heat. It must look like its own shadow, to the human eye." He set the cube down on the ground.

"What is that?"

"Supplies. For when I travel." He murmured something. One side of the cube opened; he shook a water skin out of it. "Size," he said, as Meguet's eye tried to fit the full skin back into the tiny cube, "is illusion. I didn't want to frighten you before, with my sorcery." He shifted to hand her the skin, then sagged back wearily, settling himself into the ground as if he drew some deep, healing comfort from it. "I have a house in a village on the edge of the desert. I can take us both that far. I need to rest before I return to Ro Holding. You saved my life, but there wasn't much of it left. If I hadn't taken you with me, I would be lying here dreaming while the sun and the sand and the carrion snakes worked their magic on me."

She brought the skin down incredulously, splashing herself. "You deliberately brought me with you? To help you?"

"I hoped you would. I was desperate. But I didn't expect—" He shifted again, his eyes on the dark spikes holding up her billowing skirt above his head. "I didn't expect you to find ice in the desert. I didn't expect you to see the dragon's shadow."

She looked at him, frowning again, but feeling the strange desert working its magic of light and illusion into her bones. She said abruptly, "Do you have a name?"

"Yes," he sighed. "I thought you'd never ask. My name in Draken Saphier's court is something he gave me, and that only mages use. In this place I love, where I was born, my name is Rad Ilex."

SEVEN

IN the black tower, Nyx waited for the mage and the moon.

The Gatekeeper came before either one of them, at evening when the household had gathered for supper and the yard was calm. Nyx, deep in contemplation of Chrysom's key, which opened nothing in itself that she could find, scarcely heard him knock. She lifted her eyes to find him in front of her, an occurrence so rare that for a moment she wondered if the tower were the gate and the Gatekeeper watched them both. Then she remembered why he had come.

"Hew." She pulled her bare feet off the nearest chair. "Sit down."

He shook his head. "I came to ask you—"

"About Meguet." She was silent a moment, studying him, her eyes luminous with sleeplessness. Gatekeepers of Ro House were rooted like stone and vine to the house. When they grew old, they wandered away looking for an heir to some peculiar power which Nyx had never explored. The Gatekeeper, his own face set and shadowed with weariness, did not look accessible to exploration. But a part of him had gotten tangled in the fire's enchantments, the night before; she was aware he had been there, though in what form she was not quite certain. Instead of waiting, like the mage's dragon, for moonlight to free him, he was on his feet in front of her, looking perplexed. If, as she suspected, he saw everything that came and went in and out of Ro House, including ghosts and portents and the Cygnet itself, he would have known Meguet had gone. But not where.

"I thought," he said, "the bird might have told you something by now about where it came from."

"It's a good guess that's where the mage took Meguet," Nyx said. "But where is still a mystery. He left something here; he may still return."

"With Meguet?"

"If not," she said grimly, "I'll search for her."

He sat down then, his head bowed, his eyes on the floor where it had opened like a mist to Meguet's falling. Would it, Nyx wondered suddenly, open also to the Gatekeeper who opened and closed every door? But he did not seem inclined to dive headlong into solid stone. He asked, "Where would you look? Or would you just fling yourself blind into time beyond Ro Holding? Did the bird or mage give you a word to guide you?"

"Not yet. Why? Do you know of places beyond Ro Holding?"

"Me? No. I know the gate and the house and the back swamps of the Delta. The winds don't blow me names of other places. And even so, what name would mean more than another? Unless you could tell me."

"And what would it be worth then? Would you leave the gate for Meguet?"

He lifted his head, met her eyes, his own colored like the silvery bog-mosses and about as transparent. "You would leave the house for her."

"My mother told me to find Meguet. I have no intention of finding out what life is like with my mother and without Meguet." He said nothing, still waiting for an answer; she added, "I'll find her. If the mage brings her back, I'll do what I must. If I have to search for her, I do have the means and I'll discover how and where any way I can. It's only a question of time."

"I have more than enough of that, during the night at the gate."

She was silent again. Something vital hovered beyond her memory: He had been in the tower, seen the mage and Meguet, but in what shape? Had she seen his face? Or only something she recognized as Gatekeeper that had entered a mage-locked room, and had been transformed by the bird's fire just long enough to have known what became of Meguet? She eased back in her chair. Meguet would remember. She said softly, "What time you have is counted by the movement of the Cygnet's stars. I'll find Meguet. If you leave the gate, my mother will only have me searching for you as well."

He stirred a little. "And if you leave? Who will search for you? How far beyond the Cygnet's eye can you go, before you come to a gate without a Gatekeeper to open it?" She stared at him; he met her eyes again and said more plainly, "There is only one gate in this house and everything enters and leaves by it. Including the odd mage. It's bad enough losing Meguet to a place with no name. But you are more than mage, and if you vanish from this house without the Holder's knowledge, if you leave the named world, then you must either find yourself another Gatekeeper, or pay the one you've got with a time and a place to find you in. Gatekeepers grow old at the gate; they don't get thrown out of it before their time. Which is what will likely happen to me if I let you out under strange stars."

"You let Meguet go. And the mage." He said nothing; she straightened, frowning. "Hew, what are you seeing that I missed?"

"I only want to know where you go when you go. That's all I'm asking."

"You're not asking. You're making demands. You're only asking what little you're asking so that you can search for Meguet if I fail."

"Both," he said softly. "Both of you."

"How? If you cannot leave the gate?"

"It's not a question anyone will bother asking if the Holder loses you. Least of all me." His face eased a little, at her expression. "It's only what you didn't notice, following Chrysom's path into sorcery. A little household magic. It's an ancient house, and it has its ways and means. I'm one of them. That's all."

"Is it?" she breathed. "Is that all you are? A little household magic?"

"You know that. It's why you've been talking to me, instead of telling me politely to mind my business and let you mind yours."

"You could stop me from using all the power of Chrysom's sorcery to go where I want?"

He shook his head. "It's a power with a singular purpose. To protect the Cygnet. Only that. Tell me where you are going, beyond the Cygnet's eye, and you are free to go."

"But why you?" she asked, fascinated. "Why must it be you who will come searching for us? You are bound by household magic to the gate."

"And by other magics to Meguet," he said softly. "That's why it must be me. How is what I'll figure out later." He rose; she watched him, wordless. His eyes flicked at the firebird, then back to her. "You must make him remember. Or time, for you, will begin and end at the gate to Ro House. It's the way of the house, to protect."

"Will I know these things when I am Holder? All the household magics? Or should I begin to ferret them out now?"

He smiled his tight, wry smile. "I don't know. It's my guess that whatever you want the house will give you. There's never been a mage-Holder of Ro

Holding. Once you start looking, who knows what you'll find?" He bent his head and left her staring at the door he closed behind him.

After a time, she transferred her gaze to the firebird. It was nearing moonrise; the sky at the bird's back had grown milky. "You," she said, "must find a way to remember."

The bird cried its silent cry, then was still again, waiting for the moon. Moonlight touched it. The bird spread its white wings, dropped down from the ledge. As it reached stone, it changed: Brand stood in a mingling of moonlight and candlelight. Other enchantments changed: The amber-sealed books were free; garnet and opal petals swirled together to form a glittering mist that slowly dispersed. Beside the hearth, leaves of pearl and bone drew together, formed the mage's dragon. Hovering in the shadow of the wrong world, it seemed both real and unreal. Fire picked out a scallop of thread along one unfurled wing, turned it into a delicate layering of flesh and bone.

Nyx, marvelling at it, froze it with a word before it could fly. She heard Brand move and turned quickly, but he had only stepped closer to see the dragon. Memories struggled into his face. He whispered,

"Where is he?"

"Who?"

"Rad Ilex. The mage I fought last night."

"He hasn't come back yet. Why do you want to kill him?"

"Because——" He stopped, linked his fingers over his eyes. His voice came harsh with pain. "He betrayed my father. He betrayed me. He trapped me in the firebird's shape. His face is the last thing I remember, the first thing the firebird saw."

"Why?" She stood as motionless as the dragon, scarcely daring to ask questions, lest the sound of her voice disturb the fragile cob-weave of his remembering. "Why did he put you under that spell?"

He was silent a long time; his shoulders dragged. "I don't remember," he said bitterly.

"Do you remember who you are?"

"I am Brand Saphier." His hands slid away from his eyes; he turned. His face looked ashen, haunted, but his past had etched expression back into it. "My father is Draken, Lord of Saphier."

Nyx's eyes flicked, at the name, to the dragon at his feet. "Draken?"

"His father was a dragon."

Wordless, Nyx found herself staring at him, searching for the dragon. She found the firebird instead, its beautiful, proud, ruthless face within Brand's face, as if some boundary between enchantment and truth had grown strangely fluid. She said finally, softly, "Sit down." She sat at the table, still studying him, wondering if the spellbound man would prove even more exotic than the spell.

She said, "In Ro Holding, there are no tales of dragons. You could walk the four Holds and find maybe four people who even know the word. Setting aside physical complications, is that customary behavior in Saphier, humans mating with dragons?"

He shook his head. "Some say there are no dragons in Saphier, only the memories of dragons. But my father's mother went to the desert in south Saphier and came back with child. She ruled Saphier, and if she said her child was dragon-seed, no one would argue. The dragon was a great mage, she said, capable of changing shape. My father——" His voice caught. He gripped the arms of his chair, his eyes widening, as other memories shifted into place. "My father." He rose, paced, the tower room no longer a haven but a cage. "I wonder how long I have been gone. If he knows what happened to me."

"He must be searching for you."

"He may be mourning me, for all I know." He added savagely, "With Rad Ilex beside him."

"Is Rad Ilex your father's mage?"

He looked perplexed by the question. "My father's court is full of mages. My father is very powerful; he trains mages, those with special gifts, like Rad. It's not like this house. You seem to be the only mage. And you have little sense of order." She drew a breath, but found no argument. "Or manners."

"What?"

"No mage would speak to my father the way you speak to the Holder."

"She's my mother," Nyx protested.

"Perhaps it is because you have all the power in this house." He turned, pacing again; she stared at his back. "The mage would be stripped of power."

Nyx's brows lifted. She picked up a wine cup, blew the dust out of it and filled it. She took a sip, watched him turn, pace back. "Is that where Rad Ilex took Meguet? To your father's court?"

"I don't know. Perhaps, if my father still trusts him."

She took another swallow, set the cup down. "Fortunately, Meguet's manners are better than mine. Who is this Rad Ilex? Do you remember?"

"Yes." He stopped, turned his face away. Nyx saw him tremble, in rage or grief, she couldn't tell. "He was born in the Luxour Desert, and he came to my father when he was a boy and said there were dragons everywhere in south Saphier. There have always been rumors of dragons. Crystals that look like dragon's teeth. Spiky plants that die and turn black and look like claws. My father always wanted to see dragons. He wanted to become one, like his father. He wanted to find his father, be taught by him. He says that a mage-fire like no other power runs through the blood of dragons and he wants that power. So when Rad said he saw dragons, my father took him into the house to train."

The door opened. Servants summoned by moonlight entered, bearing supper. Brand roamed again; Nyx watched him, wondering if he had come to the end of his memories, or the heart of them. He came back to the table, stood gazing down at the trays. "That's what I can't remember," he said at last, tightly. "That's where the wall is. I can remember loving Rad. And now I hate him. I would kill him as quickly as I tried to destroy his dragon. But I don't remember why."

"The firebird remembers."

He looked at her, his eyes dark, bruised, but he did not answer. Nyx pushed a tray toward him. "Eat something. If Rad Ilex wants the key and his dragon, he'll return here. But I want no blood shed in this tower. My mother forbade it."

He made no response to that, either. Nyx broke into an elaborate crust, found duckling flavored with orange and rosemary. She ate hungrily a few minutes, then asked, "Did your father find his father among the dragons?"

"No. He went with Rad to south Saphier. Rad was able to show him something—I don't know what. Enough to give my father some hope, whether it was truth or lie. In the Luxour, some villagers collect big, iridescent lumps of stone they say are dragon's hearts, and sell them. Those who buy them call them one thing, those who don't, another. Rad said he knew a way to draw the dragons into time, but that he had to find something. A key."

Nyx made a sound. "Not a book."

"He said key."

"How could he have known to find it in Ro Holding?" she breathed. "He knows too much, this Rad Ilex."

Brand stirred edgily. "And where is he, if he wants this key so badly?"

"Being cautious, I suppose. Coming here, he must face you or the firebird. Perhaps—"

"I have remembered," he interrupted. "He will face me, not the bird."

"You have not remembered everything. We'll know at midnight."

His knife hit the edge of his plate; he pushed away from the table and rose, his shoulders bowed as if the firebird clung to his back. "What kind of a mage are you that you can't break a simple spell?"

She picked a bone out of a bite, watching him. "I suppose, by the standards of Saphier, not very apt. But I am considered adequate in Ro Holding."

He came back to her, head bowed. "Forgive me. You took me in, tried to help. It's not your fault you are pitted against the most devious mage in my father's court."

She frowned, thinking again of Meguet. "Where is Saphier? Do you cross a sea to get to it? Mountains? Maybe, if you could get home, your father could help you."

"Saphier is the world," he said absently. "I never looked beyond it." Then his eyes widened, and she saw the sudden flare of hope in them. She pushed back her chair, rose.

"What do you remember?"

"These." He turned his wrists up, spread his fingers, as if the tarnished metal wove through blood and bone into his fingertips. "They are all the paths to Saphier."

"Paths of time." She drew her finger down a weave lightly. "I thought so. But are they always so tarnished?"

"No," he said, puzzled. "They should be silver, like the paths inside your tiny box. You need to know the path before you travel it: that's why you couldn't find your own way out."

"You led me out," she said abruptly. "You are also a mage."

He shook his head. "I am a warrior. I don't have mage's gifts."

"But you wear these. You can use them."

"Yes." He hesitated, still perplexed by them. "It is something my father taught me."

"Do you always wear them?"

"I don't think so."

"Then why are you wearing them now? As if you know you might need them? Or you were working a time-spell, or travelling a path when you were transformed?" She saw his face change, as he veered dangerously close to memory. He said quickly,

"I don't remember."

"Do you remember," she asked after a moment, "how to use these?"

"Yes." He rubbed at one, trying to polish it with his thumb. "They are so dark. As if some enormous power ran through them." He looked at her; she saw Saphier in his eyes, future instead of past. "I can go home."

"Yes."

"Tonight. Now. Before I change."

"Yes," she said, breathless at the thought. "But if you leave, and Rad Ilex does not return with Meguet, how will I ever know where to look for her? Can you wait a little longer for them?"

He gave her a distant, masked glance: the firebird's eyes. "I forgot he must come here."

"I will give him the key and his dragon for Meguet," she said. "I will not give you to him, or him to you. If you fight him, it must be in Saphier, or my mother will never forgive me for that as well as for a few other things she won't forgive me for by now. Please," she added, at his weary, desolate expression. "Only a little longer."

"And then what? If he does not come?"

"Then," she said steadily, "you will teach me the path to Saphier and I will look for her myself."

He was silent, studying her, as if she had flung some peculiar spell over herself. "You would walk into a strange land to search for her?"

"She searched for me once in a strange place. She is part of Ro Holding, part of this house. It's inconceivable that she is wandering around lost in some other country."

"You are eccentric."

"Even," she said drily, "in Ro Holding."

"My father's court is structured according to precise law. Within that law, nothing disorderly exists for long. Either it shapes itself to law or it is destroyed."

Her brows rose. "Does that include guests?"

"It is my father's working philosophy," he answered simply. "Out of order comes art. The art of government, the mage's art, the art of poetry, the art of war. We do not give ourselves the luxury of eccentricity."

"Perhaps freedom is a luxury," she said. "But that aside, there must be someone you would wander through a stranger's land to find."

She saw it again in his face: the sudden, desperate aching shadow of memory, the firebird's cry. He whispered, "No one has come searching for me."

She blinked, shaken by a glimpse into something more complex than she could unweave, or even imagine. She touched him; he looked at her, mute again, unable to give her either dragon heart or stone.

"We'll go to Saphier now," she said abruptly, and felt her own heartbeat. "It's cruel to keep you." And safer, she thought, remembering the spinning swords, than another battle in the tower. "Take me to your father's house. If Meguet is not there, then teach me the paths so that I can return to look for her if I have to. Will you do that?"

"My father can, easily. And he will, in gratitude. The Holder will not

even know you have been gone. Thank you." He took her hands, dropped his
face against them. "You took me in when no one in the world recognized me
as human. Whatever else the bird knows, it knew enough to come to you."

And not, she observed with a certain grimness, to Saphier.

The word, spoken aloud in the tower, would find its way to the Gatekeeper, following its own peculiar path within the house's time. Brand held
out his hands, spread his fingers as if to channel the flow of light from the
silver. The bands remained black. He closed his eyes, walking the path in his
mind. After a while, he put the bands against his eyes. Nyx felt pity well up
from some deep place within her, as if hidden water had broken through layers of earth and hoary stone and old leaves. She put her hand gently on his
shoulder.

He whispered, "I am half man, half bird, and I am lost, with no way
home."

"There is always a way," she said. "Always."

He looked at her, read the promise in her eyes. After a while he moved to
his place at the window, and waited silently for oblivion and the firebird.

EIGHT

MEGUET sat rapt beneath the risen moon.

In its light silver feathers of steam or dragon-fire glittered and faded. The high, jagged towers of stone transformed themselves. Here a great wing unfolded against the stars almost as slowly as the stars behind it moved. There an eye shone, moon-white or darker than the night. A craggy head lifted, or had just lifted before she saw it. A moon shadow, massive and curved, lay across the ground, cast by nothing visible. Crystal flashed. Vague, dark, iridescent colors swam against the stars and vanished.

Beside her, the mage lay watching with her. Sometimes he watched her; she felt his eyes. "You see," he murmured now and then. "Did you see that?" His voice, worn, fading, sounded tranquil; he was lost in some fever-dream of dragons that he had pulled her into. She saw through his eyes, she thought, most likely. But still she watched, as he dreamed dragons and set them free into the night.

"We should go," she said now and then, for he shivered, though warm wind or dragon-breath sighed over them. She had taken down her canopy to see the sky. Things that had come out of his cube—wine, salted fish, bread, dried apples and figs—littered her skirt.

"Yes," he said, but made no effort to move. "I wanted you to see this, if you could."

"I see," she said softly. "But I don't know what I see."

"Time shifting. Dragon-paths. Chrysom saw this. He made the key to unlock their paths into time."

"Can they see us?"

"Oh, yes. Oh, yes. Far better than we see them. We glimpse them indirectly, and with the heart more than the eye."

She looked at him. An odd, heavy, nameless feeling pushed through her; she scarcely knew what to call it. Hunger? Sorrow? Desire? "I wish," she whispered. "I wish."

"What?"

"I don't know . . . I wish I could watch you free them with that key."

"You can. Stay here until you have seen the dragons fly. Until I draw them out of stars and stone, until bone and blood cast shadows instead of dreams. Stay until you have seen the dragons' fire."

She dragged her eyes from the stars, still heavy with the strange, impossible yearning. "I cannot. The white dragon waiting for you in Chrysom's tower must be enough for me. I was not born to see dragons."

"They get into your blood. They call you in some secret language spoken by stones. They show you a shadow, they leave a bone behind. And so you spend your life searching for them . . . Stay until I free them."

"I don't dare," she whispered. "You were born under the dragon's eye. I was born under the Cygnet. I have never in my life come so close to forgetting that."

"The Luxour will make you forget."

She was silent, remembering the desert by day, hot and golden as some vast wing stretched taut to catch the light, the massive framework of its bones visible just beneath the surface of the stones.

"We must go," she said, but did not move, still riding the dragon that was the Luxour through the stars. Finally she felt his hand, and saw her skirt attach itself to her again. Everything had vanished back into the little cube. Only the dragon claws, scattered in the sand, told where they had been.

"We must go," he said, and the stars blurred together to form their path.

Night, where the path ended, was unexpectedly still. Here and there a light that was not a star burned, illuminating a circular window or a door. Even the winds were silent. Pebbles shifting under Meguet's feet as she turned sounded loud enough to wake the sleepers within the small stone houses. The handful of them, huddled together in the vast dark, seemed an unlikely place for a mage to dwell.

The mage, rising, lost his balance; Meguet caught him. He dropped an arm over her shoulders, and was still a moment while the earth settled. She whispered, "Where are we?"

"On the south edge of the Luxour." He added obscurely, "Safe. Even mages have trouble crossing the Luxour. This is my house."

She helped him toward one of the simple wooden doors. It had no latch. He placed his hand flat against it and it opened. Sudden light spilled over them. Within, the little house was bare and tidy as the desert. The sandstone walls were unpainted; a single rough-woven rug lay on the stone floor. His table held none of the disorder of magic and mundane—books, apple cores, crystals, bones, assorted nameless things—that Meguet had come to expect of mages. Except for a layer of dust, it held nothing at all. Another door opened to a tiny chamber that held a wooden chest and a pile of skins and neatly folded blankets. Only the collection of colored desert rocks on the stone ledge above the hearth was unnecessary. Other things, a couple of copper pots, a clay water jar, oil lamps, sat neatly in their niches and, like the table, gathered dust.

She said, helping him sit on one of the unpainted benches beside the table, "You don't come here often."

"Not as often as I want." He smiled at her as she moved through the lamplight. "There are some clothes in that chest. People will think I conjured you out of gold and fire and ivory, the way you are now."

She eyed him. He did not seem in much pain, but his eyes were bright with fever and he moved and spoke slowly, as if air were too heavy to shift aside, too heavy to breathe. Worried, she asked, "What will heal you? Are there desert plants I can find?"

"No. I need to rest."

"How long?"

"I don't know. I've never been attacked by an enchantment before. I'm sorry," he added, at her expression. "You'll have to wait. I'll take care of myself if you don't want to look at me."

She sat down on the opposite bench, dropped her face in her hands, felt the desert grit behind her eyes. "Nyx will be waiting for you to bring me back. In exchange for the true key. She'll wonder when you don't come."

"Most likely, she'll assume I died."

"And left me stranded. Moro's eyes. What does that key open?"

"Stone. Sky." She looked up at the longing in his voice. "It opens time itself to reveal the dragon's face."

She felt again a touch of his desire to wake dreams, to step into them. But she said only, "There are no dragons in Ro Holding. Nyx only wants the key because she does not know what it is. When she finds out, perhaps she won't want it anymore."

"Some say there are no dragons in Saphier, either."

"There are no tales of dragons in Ro Holding. Why would she want a key to unbind dragons in Saphier?"

"Because it exists?" he guessed. She was silent at that, knowing Nyx.

"But if you told her what danger you are in—"

"I can't speak of it," he said. He didn't; she was left listening to the silence. It took on an eerie quality then, as if the sandstone walls were paper-thin and something crouched beyond them, listening to her listen. She stirred finally.

"Tell me what to do for you."

"Mages," he said, with a faint grimace as a memory clawed his back, "are easy to care for." He glanced into the other room: Skins and blankets had sorted themselves into a bed on the floor. Another formed beside the hearth. A thought struck her; he looked at her, reading her expression, or her thoughts. "Water. There is a river behind the house. It's slow and warm even at night. If you want to bathe in that, I'll set something on the bank to guard you."

"I'll guard myself," she said, uneasy at what guardian he might conjure up. But he sent one anyway, she noticed later, as she stood in dark water that mirrored a silvery stream of stars. An upright bar of light, elusive as color in moonlight, stood near her clothes. Exactly what it might do, she never knew; nothing disturbed the night. She emerged finally, dried herself with a blanket, and dressed in long, thin, flowing garments the colors of the desert. She sat on the blanket, combing her hair with her fingers and letting it dry, thinking helplessly of Nyx and the Holder, and the Gatekeeper, who had opened the gate for her into a stranger's country. She lay back on the blanket, wanting the river to speak with his voice, the night to curve itself in his shape against her. *Hew*, she said without sound, wanting to protect even his name from the vast, dangerous, magic-riddled land.

After a while, she went in, found Rad Ilex asleep at the table. She touched him; he vanished so abruptly that horror flashed through her: He had not been real at all, only some sending of himself. Then he reappeared, looking dazed.

"Meguet. I forgot you. You frightened me. I was dreaming of the firebird. Only it had a human face."

"Whose face?" she asked, wondering what faceless mage he feared. But he said nothing more. She helped him rise; the bed, it seemed, was too far for his strength. He walked two steps and sagged into the pile beside the hearth, so deeply asleep he did not feel her undress him and wash his wounds with something besides the ice of dragon's breath.

At dawn she stood at the open door, watching the village wake. A patch of stone houses beside a river's bend, it seemed little more than a scattering of pebbles between two planes of earth and sky. The south Luxour was flat as water, but she could see far in the distance the tiny, fantastic shapes of stonework among which dragons, or tales of dragons, dwelled. Along the river, in patches of green, sheep and goats grazed. People bringing buckets to the village fountain looked at her curiously. They did not speak, but their eyes said: *The mage is back.* Their faces looked brown and tranquil, like the desert stones. One old woman driving a cart stopped in front of Meguet, handed her a stone that had been rolling among some sacks in the cart.

"For Rad," she said. She had a broken tooth, and a face as wrinkled as a root. "For healing my donkey, last year."

"But what is it?"

The woman's sparse brows and the reins flicked up at the same time. "A dragon's heart." The reins came down, the cart lurched forward. "I'm going out again for stones. Tell him to stay home, this time. There's nothing good beyond the Luxour."

"How do you know?" Meguet asked curiously. "How does news find its way here?"

"People come and go. And they come back again, for they leave their hearts in the Luxour and they wander back all hollow looking for them. Sometimes," she added with a half-smile, "I find them first. I keep them safe on my shelves until they're claimed." She ticked to the donkey; Meguet stared after her. The dragon's heart, big as a cabbage, crystal under a thin, worn layer of stone, weighed heavily in her hands. She wondered if the ghosts of dragons came back through time, searching for the hearts that the strange old woman harvested in her cart. Most likely, she thought, taking another look, it was just a rock.

She turned to go in, and coax breakfast out of the sleeping mage. Something blocked her way.

It was as if the shadow in the doorway had become a sheet of night with a constellation flying across it, and once she stepped into that night there was no way out of it, no book of time, no gate, just the icy outline of a great dragon with eyes and teeth and talons of stars, breathing a pale, glittering cloud of stars into the dark. She stood transfixed, staring into the dragon's fierce and empty eye, until, with terror and astonishment, she recognized the challenge.

She made some noise. She was aware that, beyond the dark, something fought towards her. A hand reached through the stars where the dragon's heart blazed, a furious, white-hot jewel pulsing with the fires it breathed. The hand caught her, pulled her into the dragon, and then into light.

"Meguet?"

She dropped the dragon's heart. It shattered on the stone floor, shards of crystal flying everywhere. She stared down at it, sorrow for the old woman's simple gift knotting the back of her throat.

"I'm sorry," she whispered. "She left it for you."

"Meguet."

She looked up finally, to meet the mage's eyes. They were lucent as the morning sky, vast as the desert. She blinked, and was suddenly no longer in his hold, but on the other side of the room, watching expression break into his face. He seemed to hold himself upright with an effort, as if, caught in the wake of her movement, he had lost his balance. He looked less feverish, but the weariness dragged at his shoulders. He said finally, "You are a mage."

"No."

"There's a power stirring in you. I can feel it. You hid your thoughts from me. You folded time as you moved." He waited, then pleaded tiredly, "Trust me. Please."

She was silent, feeling the warnings of her heritage wash over her like a slow, endless tide. *The Dragon hunts,* the tide said. *The Dragon hunts the Cygnet.* Then the warnings passed and she could speak again. She said with rare bitterness, "All you care about is power. All of you."

He made a soft sound, shaking his head, the shadows deepening on his face as if she had somehow hurt him. "That's not true. But I can sense it in you— something unusual, unnamed. The power that permitted you to see me when I cast the spell over Ro House. The power that forced you to guard the tower, to see through sorcery. But you aren't a mage. What is the power?" She was silent, backed against the wall, splinters of the dragon's heart glistening, sunlit, at her feet. He sat down finally, listening to her silence. He said to the table top, "It's my fault. I have a mage's habits. I wander where I have no business going. I won't trouble you with my curiosity. You don't have to be afraid of me. But you're afraid of something, in a land that never even existed for you before yesterday."

It was a long time before she answered, and then because she had no other hope of understanding what she feared except for the mage she was afraid to trust. She whispered, "A dragon made of stars, hunting through the stars. A threat to Ro Holding. To the Cygnet."

His head went back; his face, stone-still, was white as bone. "How could you—" he breathed. "How could you know that?"

She moved then in sudden fury, leaning over the table, her hands coming down flat, hard on the wood. "You knew."

"Listen to me." He gripped her wrist. "Listen."

"You talk too much, Rad Ilex. You make me see dragons among the stars, but you don't show me what they hunt. You say you want a key, only a key, just a small key to unlock the gate to an unarmed land that doesn't even know the word dragon. You drag me here and I can't even warn—" She lifted her hands again, let them fall helplessly, beating at her own futility. "I can't even warn. But I can fight. This is where the danger begins. Where there are dragons."

"Meguet—the dragon—"

"How far is Draken Saphier's court? Is it close? If you won't tell me, the villagers will. I'll walk across the Luxour if I must. I'll ride in that old woman's cart."

"Gara. Her name is Gara." He stopped to catch his breath. "Walk out of the door. I won't stop you. The Luxour may stop you, or it may not; I won't. But when you get to Draken Saphier's court, the dragon there will stop you. He will sense the power in you, and he will test you and test you until you can't call your own bones private. The Dragon of Saphier is dragon-born, a mage who trains mages. He trained me. What he wants more than anything is to find the path to the power within the dragon's heart. His father's power. For that he needs a certain key."

Meguet gazed at him. She began to tremble suddenly. She sat, her face hidden behind her unbound hair, behind her hands. "Nyx," she whispered, so softly that not even the dragon's heart broken at her feet could hear. The mage heard; his own voice was feather-soft.

"Yes."

"You must get the key from Nyx. Then, with the key in Saphier, the danger to Ro Holding will no longer exist."

"The danger will still exist. And it may well be insurmountable."

She lifted her head, stared at him again, her own face pale, stunned with shock. "Then I will go to Draken Saphier's court. If the danger must be fought there."

"You cannot fight Draken Saphier," he said flatly. "Your power comes and goes apparently, and from what I've seen, when it goes you can't even fight a dragon made of thread."

"If I must go there, I will be there."

"How——"

"I will be there." She linked her hands tightly, dropped her face against them, avoiding his curious, questioning eyes. "You must go back to Ro Holding and get that key."

"She won't give it to me without you."

"And the Holder will never let me return if I go back now. The danger showed its face to me here, not there. If I leave Saphier, how will I recognize danger when it reaches Ro Holding?" She paused, trying to think. "I'll give you a message for Nyx."

"You'll trust me with a message?"

She shook her head a little, wearily. "I trust you to get that key you want. Little more. Tell Nyx——"

"She'll never believe you chose to stay. She'll think I coerced you. I did once before."

She frowned at the dust on the table, brushing at it, as if to find some message hidden in the wood. She felt drained, hollow, as if she had left her heart somewhere in Saphier and could not return home until she found it. Her finger shaped a swan's wing in the dust; she saw the black swan flying through the tower window, just before she vanished into Saphier. She said abruptly, "Tell her to tell the Gatekeeper of Ro House that he is about to find a dragon at his gate and only the key she has will lock the gate."

He looked dubious. "You want me to give her a message for the Gatekeeper?"

"He is no ordinary Gatekeeper."

"Is that so." He leaned forward a little, caught her eyes, curious again. "A Gatekeeper," he mused, and she felt her face warm. "And this will persuade Nyx not to fight me."

"I don't know. I do know you'll get the key any way you can. Tell her I had a vision of what the dragon is hunting."

"Come with me," he said insistently. "Home to Ro Holding. It's Saphier's dragon. I'll fight it."

"If that were true," she said sharply, "I would not be seeing visions in your doorway. You love Saphier's dragons too much to fight them."

He swallowed, said heavily, "Then promise me you will wait here for me. You will not cross the Luxour without me."

"I will go where I must," she said. "I cannot promise anything."

He opened his mouth, closed it. He stood up, holding her eyes, as if the path to Ro Holding lay there, not within his memories. He closed his eyes at last, his face white as tallow, his shoulders straining against some enormous burden. She saw him vanish finally. And then he was back, no longer standing but fallen among the glittering fragments of the dragon's heart.

She made a sound, staring at him, for he seemed, amid the light and stone and scattered crystals, another vision, a foretelling. But, touching him, she felt his weight, and heard his ragged breathing. He lifted one hand weakly, dropped it over his eyes.

"I'm sorry, Meguet. It was too far . . ." He fell asleep there within the broken heart. She closed her eyes, felt the long, dark tide of dread and warning well through her. Its ancient voices finally ebbed and she could move again. She picked shards of crystal from beneath the mage, and saw the Cygnet's eye in every shattered piece.

NINE

IN Chrysom's tower, Nyx stood spellbound, exploring the gold key she held. The sunlight had faded some time ago; the long summer dusk had filled the tower room and darkened. She scarcely noticed light or lack of it; her mind had become the size and shape of the key. The key was the book; the book, she suspected, was the key to the paths of time in the little black-and-silver box. It would teach her how to pick one path, control its speed, follow its turns, focus its end. She could find a path to match the twists of time on Brand's wrists, if she could find a spell, if she could open the book . . . The book remained stubbornly a key.

Her thoughts turned around themselves, like the graceful lines of gold. *The key is the book, the book is the key. The key is the key to itself, it unlocks itself.*

It might unlock a path to Saphier, she knew, for Chrysom had seen dragons. Had they been the elusive dreams of Saphier, becoming real as he looked at them?

The key is the key. The key opens itself. Her mind roamed within its gold and ivory. *Chrysom,* it said at every touch. Power was implicit in it, like the power in a tuned, silent string. There was a way to touch it, make it sound. . . .

Chrysom, she said within it, but the name did not change it. She tried other words from his ancient spells; none revealed the book. She tried her own name, and then Moro Ro's name; the key ignored both of them. *Time,* she guessed. *Book. Open. Mage. Unlock.* Finally, she told it what it was, and what it must become. *Key*, she said within it, and the key blossomed like a flower in her mind.

It remained a key in her hand; she was aware, in some distant place, of its shape and weight. But the spells, written in Chrysom's clear, precise writing, turned slowly, page after page, in her mind. Some were labelled incomprehensibly; others dealt directly with the oddments that still survived after a thousand years to be recognized. The pages slowed under her scrutiny, stopped when she studied them, turned easily when she wished to go on. She found the box finally: the drawing of a dark cube scrolled on all sides with silver ink.

Time-Paths, the spell said. Pages of miniscule explanation followed. Nyx, engrossed, wandered down path after path of spells, and found at last the one she wanted.

Saphier, it said. *Here Be Dragons.* She followed it, memorizing its patterns. Other spells and paths, labelled strangely, wandered through Saphier; Chrysom, evidently, had found something there to fascinate him. But she concentrated on the path that ended at the ruler's court, hoping that, after so long, it was still there, or that Chrysom's journeys had led him into a time more recent in Saphier's history than his own.

She became aware, dimly, that stars had been burning in the dark around her for some time, a curiosity which coaxed her out of the key finally to investigate. She found candles lit throughout the room. Brand, his supper finished, sat in a window waiting for her.

A moon-paring hung over his shoulder, high above the swamp. She slipped the key back into her pocket, rubbed her eyes tiredly. Movement felt strange; she tried to remember how long she had been standing there, bewitched with Chrysom's knowledge. His taut, uneasy face told her: long enough.

"What were you doing?" he asked. "You didn't move, you wouldn't speak. I thought some spell had been cast over you by that key."

"No." She drifted to the table, her thoughts inlaid with winding paths of silver. She ate bits of cold peppered meat, and bread and a stew of mushrooms and leeks, until she felt she had climbed out of the little black cube into her own time again. She poured wine, drank a mouthful, then turned. In the candlelight her eyes held a trace of lavender. "I found Chrysom's path to Saphier."

She heard his breath catch. He moved away from the window, relinquishing the bird's familiar place. "I can go home?"

"I'll take you."

"How?" His fingers twisted the blackened path on one wrist. "How?"

"The black cube. You came into it once, to rescue me. Do you remember?"

"No." Then he shook his head a little. "Perhaps. It's like a dream—"

"It was real," she said soberly. "I was lost and you led me out. That's when you remembered your name."

"I don't remember," he said, but for once with regret. He added, "I would like to remember that I did something for you."

"You will." She nibbled pieces of slivered carrots and almonds with her fingers, thinking. "Where would Rad Ilex most likely have taken Meguet?"

His face tightened at the name, but he did not retreat from it. "My father's court," he said after a moment. "It's where he lives."

"He'd go there even after casting a spell over you?"

"He wouldn't expect to see me. He is still free to come and go from Saphier; my father must not suspect him."

"Well," she said, "it's a place to start."

"My father will help you. He can send his mages searching across Saphier, even across the Luxour if need be. Not every mage can cross the Luxour. So I've heard. They say ancient magics, old as the beginning of the world, blow across it like wind. But some mages learn to anticipate the winds."

"Rad Ilex?"

He was silent, struggled again; he nodded briefly. "Yes. And my father. And some others."

"It sounds fascinating."

"Perhaps. I never understood his love of the Luxour."

"Your father's?"

"Rad." Blood streaked his face suddenly; he turned away from her, but she saw him tremble. She wondered uneasily what jagged edge of truth waited for him in Saphier. She dipped her fingers in orange-scented water, wiped them on a napkin, then pinned up a stray coil of hair. She said slowly,

"I should tell my mother that I'm going."

"Will she let you go to a strange land?"

"Most likely she'll be so amazed I told her that she won't ask where. But I don't know how long it will take me to find Meguet, and I don't want her thinking I'm in danger."

"My father will protect you," he said swiftly. "Nothing will harm you in Saphier."

Absently she looked for her shoes, found them on her feet. She brushed a crumb off her skirt. "I'd better change. I can't wear silk shoes across a desert, if it forces me to walk."

"There will be no need for you to go. The mages will search the Luxour."

She stared at him. "A desert full of magic, and you expect me to sit in your father's house trying to watch my manners?"

He blinked. "I forget," he said, "how much freedom you have. You choose to come and go; my father's mages do his bidding. You also do things for love." His face closed abruptly, before she could question him. She said to his set profile,

"I'll be back as soon as I speak to my mother."

His brow crooked anxiously. "It's late," he reminded her.

"I'll hurry. If Rad Ilex comes——"

"Do you expect——"

"No," she said quickly. "Though it would be worth this key and more to find Meguet here instead of there. If he comes, tell him to wait for me. Don't touch him. Don't let the firebird break out of you."

"How can I stop the bird?" he demanded.

"Find a way. Do anything to keep Rad Ilex here. The heart of sorcery is the clear and patient mind. So Chrysom says. I am trying to be patient and clear-headed, for once in my life. But if the mage vanishes again with Meguet, I am liable to lose my temper and do something impulsive."

"My father says the heart of sorcery is the fire that forges the dragon's heart."

"He does."

"So he teaches."

"Moro's eyes. Just don't fight."

She summoned one of the tower pages, sent him running to the Holder's chambers to request a few moments' privacy. Then she vanished, reappeared in front of her startled attendants, picking jewels out of her hair. She changed quickly, packed a few oddments of her own. She felt for the amber at her ear lobe, and tossed everything——earring and key and cloak, comb and little jewelled mirror, a few dried herbs——into an ivory ball so tiny it seemed invisible in her pocket. The key, now that she understood it, had consented, to her relief, to fit itself inside the ball.

She didn't bother with stairs and towers; she simply appeared in front of her mother. The Holder had dismissed her attendants and was pacing; seeing Nyx she barely changed expression, as if what she frowned at were only an extension of her thoughts. She said,

"Where is Meguet?"

"I believe, in a land called Saphier."

"Where is that?"

"I have no idea. It's not on any map I can find."

The Holder was silent. Her arms were folded tightly; she seemed too disturbed even to throw hairpins. "You said the mage would return for the key."

"So I thought," Nyx said.

"Then where is he?"

"I don't know."

"I have told the Holding Council that Meguet is guarding you, and that
you are guarding Ro House against the return of the mage. Rumors are already——" She stopped, touched her eyes. "Rumors."

"They follow me, don't they?" Nyx said softly. "The bog-witch alone in
the tower with a bird . . ." Her own arms were folded; she was frowning, reflecting her mother, but pensively, at the problem itself. "The mage slowed
time and fought me for that key. It seemed most reasonable to think he
would return for it."

"Then where is he? Surely he didn't find Meguet an adequate substitute!"

"I think——" Nyx hesitated, received the full brunt of the Holder's troubled, angry gaze. Her brows lifted a little; she said patiently, "If you are going to shout at me, shout. I'll listen."

"What I think," the Holder said tersely, "is that my youngest daughter
and heir stays alone in that ancient, magic-riddled tower with a dangerous
bird, waiting for the return of a very dangerous mage, and that my niece is
lost in a country that exists on no map, and at the mercy of that mage.
Shouting would hardly satisfy. Reducing the hearthstones to rubble with a
poker might. Now. Tell me what you think."

"I think I can find my way to Saphier."

The Holder shouted, "What?"

"And I think I know why the mage has not returned."

"You are not going to Saphier."

"I might have to search for Meguet."

"No. Absolutely not."

"Mother, I may have no choice. From what Brand has said, Saphier is not
the most hospitable place in the world. It sounds fierce, violent, power-
ridden. The mage may be the least of Meguet's problems."

The Holder's tight grip of herself loosened suddenly; she pulled a net of
gold thread and emeralds from her hair, flung it to the floor. She stared at
Nyx, hair tumbling around her shoulders, her eyes night-dark, lined with
pain. She said harshly, "I forbid you to leave this house. You said the mage

will return. Wait for him. I will not lose both you and Meguet to some barbaric land beyond Ro Holding. Meguet is resourceful; she may be able to find her way back—"

"No." She gazed at her mother, her throat tight. Her face had lost color. "I won't let you sacrifice Meguet for me."

"You sacrificed her for a key."

"I—" She swallowed, unable to speak, then steadied her voice. "I make mistakes. Yes."

The Holder closed her eyes. "I'm sorry."

"I was careless." Nyx spoke carefully, her eyes wide, colorless as cloud. "But I'm not entirely without resources myself. Meguet fought for me. I owe her. I think I can find a way into Saphier."

"But why?" The Holder's voice rose again, dangerously. "Why must you go there if you expect the mage to come here?"

"I think he can't."

"Can't what?"

"Return. I think he was injured by the firebird."

"Moro's eyes," the Holder breathed. "Badly?"

"It's not a question of degree—"

"Do you think he's dead?"

"I have no idea."

"You saw him before he disappeared. What had the bird done to him?"

"It was enough," Nyx said slowly, "that the bird had done anything at all to him. If he had made the firebird, with all his formidable power he should have been able to control it. He never tried to harm it; it was trying to kill him. It drew blood; it lost a talon. That may have been enough to kill the mage."

"A bird claw? I don't understand."

"The spell itself. The sorcery that transformed the firebird. It might have been deadly to the mage."

The Holder stared at her. "I thought it was his spell."

"So did I, until I saw him wounded. I think Meguet may be somewhere in Saphier with an injured mage on her hands."

The Holder was silent. She turned abruptly, found the nearest chair and sat. "Then whose spell is it? Are we to expect yet another mage who won't bother to use the gate?"

"I don't—" Nyx's voice shook suddenly with worry. "I don't know what to expect next." She leaned against the massive fireplace, gazing down at her mother, and finding some comfort from the solid stones. "I've never asked your permission to leave the house before."

"I know."

"I've rarely even told you where I was going. I'm your heir, yes, but I'm also all you've got for a mage, and I must be free to work. Though I realize I've hardly given you much, these past months, to have faith in." The Holder shifted, gestured wordlessly, her ringed hands flashing, falling. "All you've seen me do here is turn the Hold Signs back into embroidery and silence a bird, which rumor already told you I could do."

"Nyx—"

"All I seem to do with the firebird in the tower is to fail. It does seem a simple thing to do: change a bird back into a man, something any mage could do."

"It must," the Holder said, "be a very subtle sorcery."

"Oh, it is. Very subtle. And so stubborn, it seems to me at times that Brand himself cast the spell, masked himself behind the firebird, and refuses to relinquish it."

The Holder made a noise, staring at her daughter. "He enchanted himself?"

"I don't think so. But I am beginning to think he has some very powerful reasons to avoid becoming himself again. And I think the truth of the matter lies in Saphier. He cannot return on his own; the time-paths on his wrists have been damaged. I must take him."

"I don't like this," the Holder said. "A ruler's son, ensorcelled and exiled—it sounds dangerous. It's not your business to solve Saphier's problems."

"No. But Brand has given me no reason to believe his father won't want him back. If I were missing in a strange land, you would be grateful if someone brought me home."

"Yes, but—"

"Also, there is Meguet. I can't leave her there."

"No. But—"

"But, why me? Because you have no one else who can do these things."

"You are my heir."

"I am your mage. This is what mages do."

"I don't like it." The Holder rose abruptly to pace again, down a woven path of flowers and ivy to its edge and then back again. "You are too much like me," she said abruptly. "Strong-willed and prone to wander. What if I lose you to Saphier? Where will I go to look for you? You can't even tell me where this land is, assuming it exists now, at this moment and not some other, which occurs to me to wonder about since it doesn't exist on any map."

"The problem," Nyx said carefully, wondering herself, "may not exist either. It's not something to worry about until we must."

"That," the Holder said explosively, "is the kind of muddy thinking that has led you into trouble before."

"Perhaps. But I've always found my way home. Somehow." She put her hand on her mother's arm. "Please," she said softly. "I didn't run away nine years for nothing. I am a sorceress. Let me do some sorcery."

The Holder came with her to the tower. The midnight bells had not yet rung; Brand, whirling mid-pace as the door opened, was still human. Nyx cast a glance around the room; he answered her unspoken question.

"No one came. No one that I could see."

"All right," she said tautly. "We'll go there." She turned, looked at the Holder a moment, wordlessly. She said with wonder, "I've never said good-bye to you before."

"Don't say it now," the Holder said fiercely. She touched an errant strand of Nyx's hair, then dropped her hand, stepped back. "Just go. Return Brand to his father, find Meguet, and come home. Nothing more complicated than that. Promise me."

"I'll come back as soon as I can." She drew the ivory ball out of her pocket, gazed into it. She could see the key floating in the dark; she touched it with her mind. Pages turned, time-paths wandered through them, through her thoughts, into the room itself. She was vaguely aware that Brand had knelt at the Holder's feet. He said something, rose again through a misty net of silver. Something else happened as he stepped to Nyx's side and the room itself wavered, dreamlike, beyond the widening silver filigree: There were un-expected sounds, sudden movements. A door opened; faces appeared, then faded into a soft darkness that grew so deep it swallowed even the bright stars of candlelight. Nyx, paths rushing everywhere around her, struggled a mo-ment to remember the faces. Not Meguet, though one had her hair. Not the mage. She was aware of Brand with her, a presence and a name, though he had moved behind her. *Saphier,* she said, and all the glowing paths around them froze and vanished. All but one . . . She stepped onto it; it began to move. As she shifted the path to form the pattern that led to Saphier, elusive sounds, faces, drew urgently at her attention, demanding to be named. She pushed them away, concentrating, intent on accurately shaping the whorls and crooks of time and distance so that the path would end in Saphier and not in the middle of some sea. It was not until she had formed the final turn and some-thing vast began to shape itself beyond the dark, that she relinquished her at-tention to memory, and the sounds, the faces, came suddenly clear.

A knock . . . The Holder turned, and the bells began to ring. The door opened . . . The Gatekeeper, his face hard, white, as it was when he swallowed fear whole and tried to hide it in some private place . . . The face beside him was so unexpected that for a moment she felt only amazement: dark-skinned, pale-haired, eyes as dark as the first night of the world. It was Meguet's kin, her unlikely shadow, as powerful and as powerless, standing under a roof that was not stars or light. And then she saw the warning in his eyes.

She felt the blood startle out of her face. The darkness ebbed, revealing a quiet, shadowy hall, a house at night, some time after, she guessed, the midnight bells had rung.

The firebird flew ahead of her toward a moving circle of light.

TEN

MEGUET picked her way across a dragon's spine. It pushed itself in a sharp, uneven ridge of red stone out of dry, weathered earth; it was not high, but too long to walk around and almost too steep to climb. Nothing grew on it. On the other side of it lay more of what she had already crossed: the Luxour with no perceptible horizon, shimmering with heat or with air disturbed by the flicker of dragon wings.

She had left Rad's village at dawn, sitting beside a young, straw-haired man on his cart. He was going to cut salt blocks, he had told her when she stopped him. There was a place he knew in the desert, a white pool of salt. She needed to get to Draken Saphier's court, she said. He looked surprised, but offered her a ride as far as the first wall of stone.

"I go due north," he said, "to the dragon's backbone. Then I go west along that to the end, and there's the salt pond. You'll want to keep going north." He eyed her askance as she climbed onto the cart seat; an answer presented itself. "You'll be a mage, too, then. We were all wondering. Only mages cross the Luxour on foot."

"How do others get across?" she asked. He urged his donkeys forward.

"They ride. Mostly they go around to the east, then follow the river. Others come in caravans, on carts, well-supplied. Those who hunger after dragons. Most buy a heart and go home again." He ticked at the donkeys; his voice was good-humored, unhurried. "Some stay along the river, spend their lives looking for crystal bones. A handful stay on the Luxour itself."

"In the desert?" she said, startled.

"A half-dozen, maybe, I've seen; there must be others. They find their places in the rocks, their underground streams. They see their private dreams of dragons to live near—a shape of stone, a hot spring, an odd configuration of shadows at sunset—and there they stay. They find me or they find the salt, eventually. That's how I know them."

She looked at him, at the crook of his mouth, his eyes that expected no surprises. "You don't believe in the dragons."

He shook his head, surprised again. "But I love the desert. It's enough for me, just the way it is, without suppositions. Most born around here never leave. Or like Rad, they come back. He never stays long, though. He believes in dragons, Rad. He's seen them since we were small, running barefoot into the desert after lizards. 'Look,' he'd say, 'look.' But I'd never see. So I wasn't surprised when he left for Draken Saphier's court. All mages go there. Is that where you were born?"

"No."

He waited, then flicked the reins idly. "I thought maybe so, because you came with him and you're going back there. But they say the mages come from all over Saphier, to Draken Saphier's court."

She opened her mouth to ask a question, closed it again. Mages, she thought, and wondered if they were all as powerful as Nyx. She felt a familiar, terrible impatience, wanting to be there instead of here with a desert to find her way across, at least until urgency loosed her powers, pleated time and desert to take her where she was needed. Whether or not Rad Ilex would search for her after he took the key from Nyx, she had no idea. She could do nothing for Ro Holding, staying in that village at the edge of nowhere. Nyx, she had reasoned starkly, would not sit still in Chrysom's tower wondering where Meguet was, if she could find her way to Saphier. And if she came, she would not bother with a desert; she would go straight to Draken Saphier . . .

"There," the young man beside her said. "The dragon's backbone."

The sun had risen above the distant blue mountains, begun its arc across the sky. It peeled shadow away from the dragon bone, left a low, jagged ridge cutting across the landscape, beginning and ending nowhere. He pointed.

"Salt's there, at that end." He looked at her a moment, silently; perhaps, Meguet thought, he did not believe in mages either, and saw only a woman, unprotected and ignorant, about to wander into a place abandoned by everything but light. He said only, "Rad's doings taught me never to question mages; not even their answers make much sense. If you need me again for something, I'll be at the west end for two days."

At the top of the ridge, she could still see his cart, lumbering and patient as a beetle, crawling along the bone. She rested a moment. Ahead lay the odd, crazed towers and palaces and dragons' wings of stone. Wind roused suddenly, pushed at her hard; she smelled sulphur, and a darker, sweeter scent, as if in some deep, moldering cave something huge had shifted, disturbing earth. She started down the slope.

Sometime later, she walked along shallow furrows, straight lines raked long ago across the ground as if by some giant claw. The scars had weathered, but never closed. She glanced up uneasily, wondering at the size of such a thing. A fierce, golden eye left an imprint of fire in hers. She looked down, blinking, and continued doggedly, wondering if she would become like the desert dwellers, seeing dragons everywhere. Her shadow fluttered like black fire in the wind: the loose, flowing garments she had taken from Rad. He had worked some magic into her velvet shoes, during one of his waking moments, so she could walk, he said, if she got restless while he mended himself. Wearing them, she would feel neither heat nor cold nor water nor stone; she would walk on air. Dust did not cling to them either, she noticed, though dust clung to her sweating face and wove itself into her hair. She carried a water skin and a pouch with some bread and fruit and goat cheese. She would find lizards when she ran out of food. She would find the water that the desert dwellers drank. She would cross the desert somehow; even the Luxour came to an end eventually.

Her shadow shrank; the eye overhead blazed at her. She felt even her bones shrink under its cruel gaze, as if the weight of light pouring down over her pushed her closer to the earth. She reached one of the strange ruins, steep upthrusts of stone that had weathered and sheared pieces of itself away. From a distance it had doors, broken towers, and fallen walls, empty windows framing sky. Close, it was simply a pile of rock, within which she found shade, a resting place. She ate and drank sparingly, then leaned against a slab of warm stone and closed her eyes.

She woke with a start at a sound, and found a woman watching her.

"Are you mage?" the woman asked. "Or dragon?" Her eyes were blue desert sky, split with streaks of silver lightning; she peered at Meguet, blinking. Her long hair was white, her hands slender and delicate. She wore a black robe and magic shoes; there was no dust on them. "I hear you breathing. I cannot see so clearly now; everything breathes now, everything has wings. Which are you?"

"Neither," Meguet said. She straightened slowly, stiff. The woman, perched on stone like a butterfly sunning, smiled, her smooth brown face breaking suddenly into a spider web of wrinkles.

"A riddle!"

"No. Only a woman crossing a desert."

"You are not a mage."

"No."

"Then," the woman said, "you have a chance of getting out."

Meguet was silent, puzzled. She found her water skin, drank a mouthful, and held it out. "Are you thirsty?"

"No. But thank you. I have learned to smell clean water, after so many years here. I never go thirsty."

"Years." Meguet swallowed, staring at the ancient, beautiful, half-blind face. "How many years?"

"I can't remember. I only remember how old I was when I got lost here; after I decided to stay I started counting dragons instead of years." She smiled again. "In dragon years, I might be five. Or a thousand. Or I may not even be born. They are that elusive. . . ."

"Are you a mage?"

"I was. Maybe I still am. I never think about it."

"I thought that's all mages thought about."

"Being mages?" She nodded, her hair drifting in the wind, a long cobweb cloak. "You've been around them, to know that."

"A couple of them. But how did you get lost? All you have to do is follow the sun or cross it, to find your directions."

"Mages," the woman said, "tend to get distracted in the Luxour. There's such a tangled magic here. It lures you this way, that. It tantalizes, it whispers." She put her hand on a jagged tower of rock. "It lies. It says: *Once I was this, search me, find who built me.* So you search, and once you begin to see one fine, lost palace, you begin to see entire kingdoms lost; you wander from ruin to ruin, trying to find a memory."

"A memory of what?"

"Of those who might have lived here among the dragons. Or, dragon-born, built them." She patted the stone fondly. "Oh, they're like the dragons, these old stones. They never say yes or no, but always maybe. *Maybe I'm stone. Maybe more than stone.*"

"Then why did you never turn your back on them and leave?"

"Because by then you yourself live within the ruined palaces; you have inherited the forgotten kingdoms." She stood up on the rock, let her hair flow on the wild currents. She held out her hand. There was a blood-red jewel on her forefinger: a dragon's eye. "Come with me. I'll show you where I live, among the lizards and the sand beetles and the blue-eyed snakes. There's a well of water beneath the rocks, so deep I never touch the bottom when I bathe in it. A dragon sleeps at the bottom of the well. Sometimes at noon when sunlight pours between the rocks, I glimpse it, coiled, golden as the light. Come. I'll show you."

"I cannot," Meguet said gently. "I must cross the Luxour. I dare not be distracted by it."

"So I felt, when I was much younger. That a hundred reasons compelled me across the desert. But after a time, I realized there was no reason for me not to stay. No reason at all. What compels you?"

"I must get to Draken Saphier's court."

"Draken Saphier." The woman's face smoothed, as if she barely remembered the name. Then she gave a sudden laugh. It held memory, ambiguity, a touch of rue. "The Dragon of Saphier. I was in Saphier when his mother ruled." She was silent a little, her silver-blue eyes looking inward. "Perhaps that's why I lost myself in the Luxour so long ago. I, too, wanted the dragon's child. But——" She tossed her hands lightly, freeing memory. "I could never find the dragon. If you stay long enough, Draken Saphier will come here. The Luxour will call him home." She waited; when Meguet did not answer, she turned, slipped away among the ruins, as swiftly and easily as a desert animal. Her voice drifted back. "The world beyond the Luxour is the dream. Stay here."

Meguet rose. As she stepped out of shadow, light pressed down at her again, trying to melt her, reshape her into something shrunken and flat that huddled close against the earth. She drew long scarves around her face, her head, and marked a path from stone to stone, shadow to shadow. Water, the desert-mage had said. A well. Deep water. But perhaps that was also a dream, for nothing grew out of the ground but rocks. Still, she remembered the ice cave, the dragon's cold breath. The memory itself cooled her until she reached another shadow. *Stay,* the desert said. *Sit. Wait. There is no end to me, I am everywhere, and you will never find your way beyond me. There is no path out of me. Stop here. Stay. Rest.* But she refused to listen, even when the light pressed her head down, her eyelids closed as she walked. The light was dragon's breath; the Dragon hunted the Cygnet . . . She walked across the face of the sun itself, and she told the desert: *I have fought the sun and lived.* She stumbled into shadow and back into endless fire, and again into shadow until both sun and shadow weighed her down, and time and the sun seemed to have stopped.

Finally the hot black cooled; the sun loosed its grip of the desert. A lavender sky began to darken, reveal the first faint stars. She heard water bubbling around her, smelled sulphur. Her mouth felt stuffed with sand, her body worn like old stone. She sat, felt for the water skin, took a few sips of warm water. Her eyes burned suddenly, though she had nothing left for tears; her body shook in a sudden, noiseless sob of fear and despair. She calmed herself, watching the night deepen, the stars grow huge, impossibly close. She saw no shimmering wings, no shadows unfolding to block the stars. Perhaps all she had ever seen were Rad Ilex's dreams. The vast, warm dark, the star-shot silence comforted her. *Others have been lost here and lived,* she thought. *And I'm not lost yet.* She ate fruit that had fermented in the heat, cheese that would not last another day. She lay back again, above the ground along a ledge of stone, feeling the stone pull at her bones as if to draw her into itself. *Tomorrow,* she thought, *I'll walk before dawn.* Just before she fell asleep, she saw the stars flow together against the dark, shape themselves into the dragon's face.

The next day she walked into the dragon's heart.

It was vast, golden, seething with hidden fires that blazed within stone, sand, shadow. Plumes of steam blurred the landscape, were snatched up and shredded by winds that blasted from the dragon's mouth. Mud bubbled and belched; the ground hissed. Even the air she breathed burned, rank and fiery with steam. Sometimes she could barely see to cross the sun's path; other times sun was everywhere, glowing in water, leaping out of raw crystals or dragon's eyes. Steam or dragon's breath trailed through the ruins, shaped ghostly faces where windows might have been. The ruins gave some shelter from the light, and the hot, stinging winds, but even their shadows burned. She made some attempt to capture lizards, shards of sun or shadow that scattered at her footfall and darted among the rocks. But they were too quick, and she couldn't remember which Rad had told her not to eat. She ate dried, crumbled bread, a withering apple. Her eyes closed. She forced herself to rise, find her direction. She could barely see the dragon's backbone pointing east and west behind her; the great towers, the roiling steam, half-hid it. At least it was still behind her; she hadn't begun drifting in circles. The broken fragments of the lost kingdom rose everywhere in front of her. She could only sketch a path from one shadow to the next, and hope they did not shift themselves from place to place, stones and memories of stone, like some moving labyrinth, to trap her there. She walked until she turned gold with dust, and her thoughts under the violent heat were distilled to vapor, blown away before she could grasp them. Finally, a dragon-claw of light raked through her eyes, into her mind, and, between one step and another, she fell into her shadow.

She tasted water, impossibly sweet and cold. She tried to speak and choked. A hand cradled her head, raised it. She opened her eyes, trying again to speak, and saw a stranger turned away from her as he set the water skin down. Behind him stood a great dragon the color of twilight. Its eyes were stars, its wings, opening, spread purple-grey across the sky. She tried to rise, managed to lift one hand. The stranger turned to her. The dragon breathed; night swirled around her, a blinding dark without a star.

When she woke again, a vast, silvery tide had swept across the sky. The dragon, looming against the night, was a shadow limned by stars. One star had fallen near her, giving out a soft, unwavering glow in spite of the restless winds. The stranger sat outside the circle of its light; she saw his loose, pale desert garb straying in the wind. He might have been dreaming or watching dragons, but he sensed her waking. She saw a flash of silver beneath his sleeve as he reached out to touch the fallen star. It burned brighter, sent its soft light washing over her face; his was still in shadow.

She asked, "Is the dragon yours?" Her voice sounded thin, far-away, as if she were dreaming it. But he heard her; he had risen suddenly, noiselessly, to scan the dark.

"What dragon?"

"The one there against the stars."

He saw it; she heard his breath. Then he settled himself again. "It's stone." His voice was low, dispassionate. "Sometimes I think these great stones change shape at night, wander where they will. . . ." He passed her the water skin. "Hungry?"

"No."

"You will be." He passed her another skin, of honey wine. She drank a little, and closed her eyes. She saw dragon wings, sheer and delicate as moth wings, dusted with stars. She remembered then where she was going and why, and dragged her eyes open.

"I must go." But she could barely lift her head. He took something out of a pouch, began peeling it; the wind brought her the impossible scent of oranges. He passed her a section, ate one himself. "It's easy to get lost at night, even for a mage."

The desert, it seemed, abounded with mages. "How many dragon years have you been here?"

He was silent; she felt him study her. "Not long enough," he said at last, "to be unsurprised by everything. Have you taken to dwelling in the desert?"

"No."

"Then you came to see dragons."

"No."

He handed her another piece of orange. "Then why are you walking through the heart of the Luxour?"

"I'm travelling north."

"From where?"

She did not, she realized, even know the name of Rad's village. "South."

"Most people," he commented after a moment, "would have followed the river around the desert."

"I'm in a hurry."

"The Luxour slows time for those who hurry; it elongates itself. It hides itself from the curious; it shows itself to the innocent, and the unwary. It works its own magic." His voice sounded detached, as if his attention were roaming the desert around them, peering into moon-shadows, listening to the winds. "It is a place of enormous power, and when you reach for that power, it slips away to return when you have stopped looking for it."

Scanning the night for intimations of such power, she saw only a great, sinuous spiral of stars following the moon's path, that reminded her of Rad's white dragon. She thought of him, drugged by some deep, healing sleep, and of the white dragon in Chrysom's tower, and then of Nyx, finding the key in Ro Holding that would unleash the dragons of Saphier, and she moved abruptly, murmuring in frustration, blinking dust out of her eyes.

"Do these winds never stop?"

"Never," he answered. "They are dragons' breath, fire and ice."

"I saw the ice-dragon."

He leaned forward slightly, his voice less distant. "Did you."

"Not the dragon itself—"

"No."

"But the cave where it sleeps. Like a hole in the night."

"Yes."

"I heard it breathe."

"And what else have you seen?"

"A shadow. But nothing that cast the shadow."

He said, "Ah," very softly. "And what else?"

"Nothing more. A heart, maybe. A bone. The mage I saw yesterday said there was a golden dragon at the bottom of a well. A dragon of light."

"Mage." His voice went flat on the single word; she sensed all his attention then, pulled back out of the night to focus on her.

"The one who lives among the rocks."

"Does this mage have a name?"

"I didn't ask. She is quite old and somewhat blind."

He made a soft sound; his attention strayed again. "She may see better, then, on the Luxour, where nothing is quite as it seems."

"She had lost, she said, all interest in magic long ago. How is that possible? To stop being a mage?"

"To stop being compelled," he answered; his face was turned away from her again, to the dark, singing distances. He added after a moment, "I don't know if that in itself is possible."

"She seemed compelled by dragons."

"On the Luxour everyone is compelled by dragons."

She was silent: A dragon had compelled her into the hot, unbearable eye of the sun. She said, "It was kind of you to help me."

"You're not the first I've found overwhelmed by the Luxour," he said. "It happens. People come looking for wonders, for the dragon's claw, the dragon's fire. They never stop to think that they might find what they are looking for. They see crystal bones, a piece of petrified fire, fragments of some long forgotten age. They never see the living fire that breathes over them out of a passing moment. I find them and they wake and tell me they were struck by sun. Then they stumble to the nearest village and buy a dragon heart and go home, never knowing they have worn dragon's fire, they have stood within the dragon's eye."

She was silent, compelled, by something in his voice, to search the winds and stars for their reflections. "I thought it was the sun myself," she admitted.

"I thought you must be a mage when I saw you," he said a little drily. "With enchanted shoes and no food. No one has less common sense than a mage on the Luxour. But I didn't recognize you, and I know all the mages of Saphier."

"I'm not a mage," she said. "A mage I met put the spell into my shoes."

"Yes." His voice went soft, very thin; he might have been listening to the sound of a shadow shifting across sand. "I recognized his spell. Mages leave fingerprints that the skilled can read. How well do you know him?"

She was silent, thinking of Rad with a dragon across his doorway, telling her what to fear. "Not well," she said finally.

"Is he in his village now?"

"I don't know," she said truthfully. "He comes and goes." He moved. The mage-light flashed suddenly in her eyes. She winced, catching dust again, her vision blurring.

"I know those river villages," he said. "Everyone knows everyone and everything."

"It's true." She wiped tears from her eyes, shielding her face from the light. "I've lost track of time, here. It seems so long ago, now, that I walked out of the village. I don't even know where I am; how can I know where a mage might be? Mages—except you—don't pay attention to you unless they need you."

"And did he?"

"Did he what?"

"Need you?"

She looked at him, her eyes finally clear, wondering at this stranger pushing her gently, question by question, into lies, and why she felt compelled to hide the sleeping mage within her thoughts. In the wider cast of light she finally saw his face.

She remembered to breathe after a time. It was the firebird's face, older, passionate, controlled. She recognized the black brows slashing over cobalt eyes, the hard, clean-lined warrior's face, weathered by experience. His long hair was varying shades of black and smoke and ash, tied back with braided ribbons of leather. The flash of silver at his wrists were the woven strands of time.

She swallowed drily. He said curiously, "You know me. I don't know you."

"You wouldn't," she said. She felt her body trying to grow small, push into the ground away from his eyes. "You wouldn't," she said again, desperately. "I'm just another face in those river villages you know."

He held her eyes for a long time until it seemed she began to hear the secret voices of his dragons, and to see their wings moving in his eyes. Then his expression changed, lines deepening between his brows, beside his mouth. He said, "Rad Ilex sent you into the Luxour leaving the track of his sorcery in every step you take. Are you running away from him? You won't elude him wearing those. He put some thought into your shoes, but into little else." She did not answer. He touched the light again; it dimmed, throwing a welcome shadow over her eyes. "You are protecting him." His voice was suddenly husky, edged with pain, his face so like Brand's it startled her. "It doesn't matter. I will find him."

"Why?" she whispered. He set the pouch near her, along with skins of water and wine. He sat still again, as she had first seen him, but his hands were tightly closed, his face taut.

"He injured my son." His hands opened, closed again; he stared into the mage-light. "Brand," he whispered. "My only child. He is lost somewhere in time, crying fire like a dragon, unable to speak anything but strange, jewelled spells. Rad forced him out of Saphier, and destroyed his only path back."

"Why?" The word hurt, coming out, as if it were a strange, hard jewel.

"I don't know. They had been friends. Rad Ilex had discovered something, I think, something of enormous power, dangerous to Saphier. Brand tried to warn me, Rad silenced him. I have been searching for them both. I have sent my mages searching for them. But Rad Ilex is elusive and my son is—anywhere. You have been with Rad in his village. Is he there, still? You do not know. He comes and goes. So he came and went in my son's life and twisted him out of shape, and tore time itself apart to fling him beyond Saphier. Beyond even my sight." He paused; she saw him swallow. "I taught Rad to do those things."

She started to speak, couldn't. She heard Rad's voice: *The Dragon of Saphier will test you and test you until you can't call your own bones private* . . . The dragon of night and stars had been on Rad's own threshold, had filled his own doorway. It was Rad who searched for the key, Rad whom the firebird attacked, Rad who had tested her himself . . . Rad who lay helpless against Draken Saphier, alone and dreaming, recovering from Brand's fury.

Or was he? Had he lied to her, gone in secret to Ro Holding to trade her warnings for a key? Was he on the desert now, coming to find her, or had he sent her on an impossible journey to Draken Saphier's court, simply to lose her and her suspicions to the Luxour?

"I can't help you." Her voice trembled badly, torn as she was between truth and lie, recognizing neither. She felt something like wind glide over her feet, and Draken Saphier rose, holding her shoes.

"You can help me," he said simply. "You can stay here until Rad follows the path of his sorcery to you. Not even the whims of the Luxour can hide your steps from him. When he finds you, I will find him." She stared at him, stunned. "Keep the food and water," he said. "I'll take the light." He added, "Don't try to walk in the dark. Things that are afraid of light, that bury themselves against the heat by day, dig out at night to feed. They are small, vicious, and can feel the vibrations of a falling pebble. As long as you stay still, you'll be safe. And I'll be here, watching."

The light went out. He was silent. He had, she realized, faded into the desert: a dark streak of wind, a thinking stone. She lay still, scarcely daring to breathe, trying to remember why, in another time, in another country, she had not picked up a sword instead of a rose.

ELEVEN

NYX sat in a white room, contemplating three black leaves floating in a bowl of water. The bowl was white; the table it stood on was white. Thin white curtains caught light before it spilled a hint of color across the white floor. Nyx wore a fine, flowing, complex assortment of garments, all of white silk. In the entire room, only her eyes had color, the lavender in them so deep it seemed, when she caught her reflection, a comment on her surroundings.

She was alone in the small chamber, whatever alone meant in a house full of mages. She had been treated with impeccable courtesy from the moment she appeared: a sorceress from a strange land walking a path of time into a ruler's house, with a firebird she claimed was his missing son. This she explained to more mages than she had ever counted even among the dead in the history of Ro Holding. There was not a shadow of disbelief in their expressions, as the firebird cried noiselessly, constantly overhead. Of course this was Draken Saphier's son, this wild bird trying impotently to turn them all into jewelled trees. Unfortunately, Draken Saphier was not there to thank her himself. Neither were Rad Ilex and Meguet, her eye told her, among this grave and attentive gathering. She must wait, of course, for Draken Saphier's return. She had, she explained, urgent business elsewhere. No, they persuaded her, she must wait. Draken Saphier would want to question her more fully about his son's enchantment, perhaps seek her advice. This, she had to admit, seemed reasonable, considering the state in which his son had returned. Draken Saphier's arrival, they told her, was imminent.

It remained imminent. She had been given pristine quarters, three leaves in a bowl to contemplate, attendants of exquisite tact and skill who were all, she realized, mages of varying degree. Draken Saphier had not yet returned, but would soon. Soon became three days, and in three days she had been shown extraordinary things in the vast, white, light-filled palace. But she had seen nothing of the firebird.

She kept an eye out for him, as mages led her through the palace. It seemed an irregular assortment of cubes piled at varying heights, the whole house formed around a great square which was separated into formal gardens, and, at the center, a broad square of red and white stone. From the highest windows in the house she could see the pattern in the stones: the emblem of Saphier, an intricate, stylized weave of lines coiling, locking, parting, meeting. She wondered, if she walked that path, where it would end. It held, she realized after a time, the only curved lines in the palace. The palace had no round towers, no turrets, no spirals or circles, only a series of arched windows now and then, open to air and light, overlooking the gardens. The chambers and halls, corridors, stairways, all carried continuous straight lines from angle to angle as the palace turned at the corners of the square. Nothing was jumbled, labyrinthine, untidy with past. Past had been relegated to memory, or it was framed in orderly fashion within the present. For a house full of mages of varying powers the space and pale walls and light would be calming, and the strict lines the eye perceived might order the mind. So much Nyx conjectured, though, within those lines, she was shown fascinating deviations.

"This wall is very old," a very old mage named Magior Ilel, who was Brand's great-aunt, told her. She was quite tall and thin, with hands that seemed all bone, translucent with age, and eyes as dark and still as the new moon. The wall, a great slab of pale wood at one end of a white room, was so completely and intricately carved with tiny figures that it seemed to move. It was a battle, Nyx realized, taking a closer look, depicted with ruthless and startling detail: Not even the cart horses seemed exempt from slaughter. Only birds, picking out an eye or a bloody heart, eluded arrow, spear, fire, club, stone. The carving of the devastation was elegant, skilled. She studied it, curiously; such fury seemed remote in the peaceful house.

"Where are the mages?" she asked, turning to Magior. She surprised a fleeting expression on the ancient, composed face.

"A mage witnessed it," she answered. "He carved it, as an example of power he thought beyond the control even of sorcery. There were few mages then, and magic seemed a force as raw and random as lightning."

"Then he didn't connect sorcery with savagery," Nyx commented. She turned away from the silent, frozen carnage, to a more tranquil tapestry hanging on a side wall. At first glance it seemed a tree full of birds and flowers, bright, varied blooms growing along the same bough, with small, vivid birds fluttering among the leaves. As she gazed at it, odd dark shapes intruded: broken pieces of shadow, faces, perhaps, half-revealed behind the leaves, or even within a flower, as if some other work were embroidering itself through this one. She looked closer, intrigued, trying to piece the darkness together, but it remained elusive.

"It makes me want to frighten the birds out of the tapestry, part the leaves," she said, "to see what the tree is hiding." She looked at Magior. "What is it? What do you see?"

"I am too old," Magior said in her slow, dry voice, "to see anything. Flower and shadow, dark and light, in the end they are what they are. There is no resolution. You are unconvinced. What do you see?"

"A mystery," Nyx answered simply. "What I would like to see, unless you have some objection, is the firebird." Magior looked at her silently; she added, "It flew to me for help. I've grown—accustomed to it. To Brand. I've left work unfinished, which worries me, and will worry me until I see it completed. Or has he remembered everything? Is the spell broken?"

Lines moved across the aged face, undecipherable expressions. "The firebird is resting. It has several—roosts, I suppose we must call them. We thought it best to surround him with familiar faces, so that he could more easily remember his past. The past he remembers with you is intricately bound with the spell."

"I see."

"Please do not be offended."

"No."

"If he looks at you, he will only remember himself as the firebird, needing help."

"And is he remembering himself?"

"It is," Magior said after a pause, "an exasperating piece of sorcery." Her face worked again. "When we follow his memories back, there is a point at which all we find, inevitably, is the bird's face. The bird's silent cry."

"You go into his mind?" Nyx asked, startled.

"You didn't?"

"Only to find the bird's mind. And that was like entering some hard, polished jewel, where every part is like every other part. And yet Brand kept insisting that all he lost of time and memory could be found in that enchanted bird."

Magior nodded. "So he still insists," she murmured. "All we can do is wait for Draken Saphier." She paused again, her eyes on Nyx's face. "We wondered," she said at last, "what you did with the bird's fire and its voice."

"I trapped them outside of the bird. I didn't want to dodge its fire while I worked, and I couldn't bear hearing its cry. No one in the house could. Have you heard it?"

"Once." Magior closed her eyes briefly. "In the middle of the night. Its first cry. Before it vanished. A terrible, terrible sound."

"The spell was cast here, then."

"Yes. By a mage who also vanished."

"Brand remembered something of that . . . He was afraid the mage had deceived his father, and was still here."

"No," Magior said a trifle harshly. "He has not been seen here since. He would not dare return."

"I see." Nyx kept her face and her voice calm, but still the dark eyes lifted, at some disturbance her impatience caused in the air between them. She asked quickly. "Something I wondered about: the time paths on Brand's wrists. How did they get so black?"

"We assume the mage destroyed them, when Brand tried to escape him."

"Would that be simple to do?"

"No. It would take enormous power. The paths are nearly indestructible. They must be so, or people might be left stranded in odd places, in strange times."

"Who made them?"

"Draken. He fashioned all the paths of time."

Nyx watched, the next day, the household guard gather in the stone square and perform a complex series of movements. They were very old, the young mage with her explained. Developed by the first mage-ruler of Saphier, for far different purposes. Now, despite the blades, it was more an exercise, a dance. The movements were slow, but Nyx recognized the whirling blades, the deadly rhythms of Brand's attack on Rad Ilex. There seemed guards enough for every window and every mouse hole in the house, all wearing the path of time that lay under their feet, emblazoned in red across their breasts. They also wore the familiar silver on their wrists. The thought of such an army marching the spiralling paths of time disturbed Nyx profoundly. Yet all she saw of martial art was relegated to a dance, and all she saw of magic was the complete disappearance of the firebird.

The mage with her, Parnet, a sturdy young woman from north Saphier, with a fat braid of red hair and a milky, freckled face, said when the guard dispersed, "Perhaps you would like to see the lemon garden. The fruit is ripe now and the trees are beautiful."

"I would rather see Brand Saphier," Nyx said. She added, infected by the constant courtesy. "Please."

"The firebird is resting," Parnet said slowly. "I don't know where in the house it might be."

"I thought you were trained to read minds."

"Oh, no," Parnet said, her complacency shaken. "I mean, yes, we are, but not without careful regulations, and not ordinarily without permission. It's punishable, though experiments are always made, among the younger mages. You can see such rules prevent a good deal of confusion, as well as animosity. Some mages are inclined to temperament."

"I see," Nyx said temperately. "Perhaps, then, at moonrise?"

"I'll ask Magior for you."

Nyx was silent, swallowing frustration. They had drifted to a stop beside an immense bowl of black marble, containing water. Above the water hung a huge tapestry of a man in a plain black robe, sitting on a floor of brilliant tiles, in front of a great black bowl of water. He studied it with interest, though it held, as far as Nyx could see, only a couple of threadbare patches.

"Who is that?" she asked. Parnet answered without a hint of judgment.

"No one. It is a question."

"The man?"

"No. What you see: the real bowl, the tapestry bowl, the water, the man. It is all a question about you."

"Me."

"Few pass here without speaking. What you say about this tells something about you. Even those who say nothing tell something. It is one of the ways of grouping beginning mages; according to their perceptions of what is most important. You chose the man. Some ask what he sees in the water; others what relationship the real bowl has to the bowl of thread. I suppose that, in a land full of strangers' faces, you would see the unknown face first."

Nyx opened her mouth, hesitated. The house came alive around her suddenly, puzzle-pieces everywhere, springing out of what she had considered background. "The bowl in my room," she said suddenly. "The color. Or rather the lack of it . . . This entire house is full of questions."

"Yes."

"How fascinating." She gazed into the water, saw the color deepen in her eyes. "And there are no answers. Only responses. Some must find all that white in my chamber peaceful."

"Yes."

"And the walls of battle-scenes?"

"Some find them absorbing," Parnet answered simply. "Most of them become the warrior-mages."

"Is Brand a warrior-mage?"

"Brand is a warrior. He has no gifts for sorcery."

"Yet he can walk the path of time on his wrists."

"That is common here, for warriors," Parnet answered, with a touch of surprise in her voice. Nyx frowned down at the water. She let one hand fall to her side, touch the tiny ivory ball that held Chrysom's key. She saw Parnet's reflection, her expression open, waiting, calm. She asked abruptly,

"And is the firebird itself a question? Or do you have a few answers for that here?"

Water rippled for no reason, obscuring both their reflections. Nyx turned her head, found Parnet still looking into the water. Her brows were raised slightly, worriedly: her face hid nothing. She said very softly.

"They have been trying, as you tried. All we can do is wait for Draken Saphier."

"Who will return soon."

"Soon."

Nyx sat that evening after supper, gazing into the white bowl of water in her chamber, watching the black leaves turn and turn, fashioning, out of water and air, some mysterious path of their own. Thoughts as dark were beginning to shape their own patterns in her mind. She barely gave them form, or language, for in that house apparently not even memory was private. One black leaf had Draken Saphier's name, one Rad Ilex's, and the third the name of an unknown mage who had entered Draken Saphier's house, ensorcelled his son, cast the blame on Rad Ilex, and vanished—or who had been taught by Draken Saphier, had learned far too well, and who, having fashioned the firebird and driven Rad Ilex away, still lived in the house, free and unsuspected. That mage would be among those working with the firebird now, to guard the spell. Someone close to Brand, who had flung him out of his world, destroyed the path back to it, and never expected to see him again.

Until I brought him back, she thought. *Along my private path*. The mage could destroy that, too, if Chrysom's key were found.

But who? And why? And what had Brand witnessed that he had been so ruthlessly reshaped, and even human, had only the firebird's cry to speak of it?

She reached out, turned a leaf over between thoughts, as if it were the page of a book. Its underside was gold. She watched it awhile, thinking of the silver paths, and Draken Saphier, who had a power like Chrysom's, to fashion bridges across time. How expansive was that power? she wondered. And why did one of those patterns lead to Ro Holding? Or had the bird simply gotten lost in the strands of time, fleeing down a path that was being consumed by sorcery?

She turned another leaf idly; it was deep blue. Blue, gold, black . . . What would the third color be? Did the colors have significance, or was it another of the house's questions? If she did not turn it, it would be any color she imagined . . . She could find the firebird in the house, open Chrysom's book and walk the path to the Luxour. The bird would follow. They would escape this house of puzzles, its bewildering courtesies and maddening equivocations. At least the desert would not equivocate: earth, stone, light, did not lie. Or did they? There were ancient magics in the Luxour, Brand had said, complexities even there. But Draken Saphier could be found, to free Brand from the firebird. Only for that, it would be worth some subterfuge to find Brand and leave. But if she fled with the firebird down one path, just as Draken Saphier returned by another, he would be mystified and justifiably outraged. She might put herself in danger, no one knew her here but Brand, no one could speak for her but a man whose memories of her might in their eyes be hidden within the firebird's cry. She had already taken its defense, its voice; they might wonder what else she had done to it.

She shifted restlessly, touched the third leaf gently to still herself. Meguet . . . where in Saphier was she, if not in Draken Saphier's court? With a mage hiding from Draken? Where would he hide?

The Luxour. Where the magic was unpredictable, and not even a mage could find a mage. And he knew the desert. He had been born there, Brand said, among the rumors of dragons. . . .

She turned the third leaf. The door opened behind her; she turned her head, saw Magior Ilel and a strange mage in the doorway.

Magior said, "Brand will see you now."

She rose, then turned back silently, looked into the bowl. Red as blood, as dragon's fire, the third leaf . . .

"Is it a question?" she asked.

"You chose the colors," Magior said without a flicker of expression. "It is an answer."

They led Nyx through endless airy corridors, toward chambers in an unfamiliar wing. Opening her mind a little, she sensed an enormous power, like a silent cataract. She barely touched it, a hand-brush against thundering, pounding water.

"Is this where the mages are trained?" she asked, and Magior cast a startled glance at her.

"Still your mind," she instructed.

"It has been suggested before," Nyx said tranquilly after a moment. "To no one's satisfaction."

"I do not mean to offend," Magior said stiffly. "You are a stranger in Draken Saphier's house. Your own powers are unknown to us."

Nyx glanced at the shadow beside her, flung forward by the angle of light, of the nameless mage who walked noiselessly behind her. He wore the emblem of Saphier across his chest; he would know, she guessed, the deadly movements of the dance. She swallowed a sharp comment, concentrating on her surroundings. They had moved into a corridor of rich dark wood, carved with ancient scenes, she guessed, of Saphier's history. A great bronze dragon clung to double doors at the end of the corridor. Warrior-mages guarded the doors. At a sign from Magior, they split the dragon in two, and through the open doors Nyx saw Brand.

The room was full of dragons, carved in wood, in red stone, in amber, painted, embroidered on tapestry, limned in ink on the margins and frontispieces of old books on stands and shelves. The chair Brand sat in had dragons' faces lifting out of the arms, and dragons' claws for feet.

"You wished to see me," he said to Nyx. The politeness in his voice chilled her until she saw that his face was as rigid as his courtesy. The firebird's cry of fury and despair, she guessed, was so close to the surface of his thoughts that it took all his patience to keep it from cutting to the heart of language. He glanced at the warrior-mage, and then at Magior, before Nyx could answer. "Why is Han here?"

"Only a precaution——" Magior began. Brand rose abruptly, his mouth tightening.

"No one set such guards on me in Ro Holding."

"My lord, you were a bird. Nyx Ro is an unknown quantity."

"I know her. Dismiss him."

Expression rippled across Magior's face, a mingling of worry and doubt. The warrior-mage inclined his head, disappeared into thin air.

Nyx said carefully, "I haven't seen you since we came here. I wondered how you were, if returning home had altered the spell at all."

"No," Brand said tersely. He paced among the dragons, touching an eye here, a claw there.

"It is a spell," Magior said fulsomely, "of unusual complexity and power."

"My father will help me," Brand said. "There's no more powerful mage in Saphier."

"Where is he?" Nyx asked baldly, expecting a straight answer at least from him; his reply overrode Magior's equivocation.

"He is expected back very soon."

"Dragon-hunting," Brand said, "in the Luxour." He stopped pacing, to gaze at a jet-black dragon painted on what looked like some kind of leather shield. The dragon's eyes were tiny, malevolent, red as garnet. "So I was told. He is drawn there sometimes, to search, he says, for his heart. Or he may be looking for Rad Ilex."

"You expected Rad Ilex to be here."

"I thought he might be."

"Rad Ilex has not been seen in this court since you vanished," Magior said. "He would have been killed, that night, had he lingered a moment longer. So your father said. Only one moment."

Nyx opened her mouth, closed it, swallowing a smoldering cinder of impatience. Brand said abruptly to her, "Then why are you still here? I thought you would have gone."

"I was asked to stay," Nyx said calmly, "to speak to Draken Saphier. It seemed a reasonable request. Everyone, it seems, expects him soon."

Brand's brows pulled together hard. He was silent a moment, his eyes on her, as if he had heard, even beneath the turmoil and frustration of the firebird's cry, the equivocation in her voice. He said finally, "The Luxour is full of voices. So the mages say. The desert speaks. The stones and the silence speak. So they say. I doubt if I would hear much. But that makes it difficult for the mages to call my father home. And finding him, if he does not wish to be found, would be impossible. So I am told. It's hard for me to wait patiently. The most I can manage at moonrise is just to wait. It would be kind of you to wait with me, at least while I'm human. The mages have tried to work with me; they get no farther than you did. I don't think anyone can help me but my father, and I have very, very little patience left for mage-work. So. Keep me company. Walk with me, in the gardens."

"I think," Magior murmured, "we should keep working. Such enchantments might be unravelled quite unexpectedly."

"Perhaps the moonlight will unravel it," Brand said, "since no mage in

this house can." His face was strained, taut; Nyx heard the noiseless cry ema-
nating from him so strongly, she wondered that the dragons around them did
not turn into spellbound jewels. His great-aunt heard it too, apparently; she
bowed her head in acquiescence.

"Perhaps you are right," she said. "I will wait for you here."

He did not speak for a while; he took Nyx's arm, his grip tight, as if he
expected the moon to toy with her shape, too. They left the house, walked on
wide paths of white stone that wandered among the rose-trees. Nyx, unused
to such formal progression through a garden, found it bewildering, for a
mage and a man about to fly away. She laid her free hand on his hand, reminding him that she was there, and said,

"I think——"

"Not here," he breathed, and she was silent again until they passed
through the courtyard of roses into a tiny walled garden full of lemon trees,
soft paths of moss between fountains and moon-bright streams. He closed
the gate behind them; his grip eased finally.

"It is my father's meditation garden," he said softly. "No one else
comes here."

"There is little hope of privacy in a house full of mages," she pointed out.

"Perhaps. But I'm used to being private with you. No one told me you
were still here. I thought you would have gone to look for Meguet."

"All they knew of me is that I brought you here. They couldn't have assumed you cared. Did you ask after me?"

"No."

"Then why are we here, whispering?"

"Because," he said restively, "your face looks changed. Wary. It wasn't
only you studying me, in that tower. I had nothing else to watch but you. You
do what you want, say what you think; you listen to reason, but not without
arguing. Here, you pick your way from thought to thought as if you are
afraid. No. Not afraid. But in danger. In my father's house. Why?"

"I'm alone in a strange land, surrounded by mages of indeterminate
power, and more warriors than I've seen in all of Ro Holding. It seems expe-
dient for me to be somewhat wary. If you have one enemy, you might have
two, and one of them under this roof."

He stared at her, amazed. "Me?"

"You said yourself you can't remember why Rad Ilex turned you into a
firebird. Conceivably to guard himself against something you saw, something
you know."

"A conspiracy? In my father's house?"

She sighed noiselessly. "I can only guess. You tell me. You brought me here. And I can't imagine even this place being completely private. Those goldfish are probably trained to eat whatever words fall like crumbs on the water."

"No one speaks in here," he said absently. His brows were drawn again; he glanced at the moon, then down at a little fish like an orange flame rising to the surface of the water. "The guard changes at midnight. I listen for that." His fists clenched. "I can't remember," he said tightly, "how it feels to stand in sunlight. To fall asleep in a bed. To know where I was at noon yesterday. If my father does not come soon, I'll go to the Luxour myself and find him."

"Would the bird fly there?" Nyx asked curiously. He looked at her, his eyes shadowed, haunted.

"It flew to you," he said slowly. "And here it sits in this house with you, waiting, though I assume that if it could find you in Ro Holding, it could find my father in the Luxour."

"Why Ro Holding? If your father made the paths on your wrists, why would he have fashioned one to Ro Holding?"

He shook his head, disinterested. "I don't know. He didn't create the patterns out of time and space. He only forged the paths, and I don't think even he knows where they all go. I think the firebird found Ro Holding by chance, though your power drew it, once it came there. Why? Is it important?"

"Perhaps," she said evenly, thinking of the flashing blades of the ritual dance, the silver paths blazing on every wrist. Brand was silent, watching the occasional moonlit glint of color in the dark water.

He said very softly, "You could take me to the Luxour. The bird would follow you."

"If your father doesn't return soon?"

"Now."

She looked at him, startled. "Why not Magior, or one of the other mages?"

"The bird follows you." He paused; his face loosened slightly. "I follow you. I'm here with you in my father's garden, where no one else is permitted. I trust you."

"You might," she said slowly, "but there's little reason for anyone else to trust a mage who absconds with you into the desert. If you vanish twice, they will be heart-struck. They are doing their best for you."

"And their best is no better than what you did for me in that tower." His voice sounded dangerously thin. "If I have to spend one more day covered with feathers and eating mice, and wake to myself again without seeing my father, I will walk out of this house and keep walking south, and no one will know where I am. You yourself want to go to the Luxour. Rad Ilex will be hiding there. It's the only place in Saphier where he can hide from my father. And it's the place to look for Meguet."

"Let me go," she pleaded. "By myself. That way you'll be here, if your father is on his way back now. If not, I can look for him, and for Meguet."

"No." His hands closed suddenly on her arms; she felt the tension in his grip. "No. I will not wait here. I'll walk out now. I know my father's private passage from this garden out of the house. You can stay here and explain to Magior where I've gone."

"Brand—"

"Now. Before midnight. I'm not a mage. If I tell Magior, and she thinks I'm unwise, she'll keep me here. She'll find ways. I can't stop her. I am unwise, but if I don't see my father soon, if this spell stays on me much longer, I will find a new voice for the firebird, and it will cry day and night without ceasing and no one in this house, not even you, will stop it."

"All right." She touched him gently, swallowing drily. "All right. I'll take you there. Now. And I won't walk. I think I have a path to the Luxour."

"Where?" he asked, amazed.

"In my pocket." She drew out the ivory ball. "Chrysom's book."

TWELVE

MEGUET waited a night and a day and a night for Rad Ilex. After staring down the moon and then the stars, listening for night-hunters, she finally fell asleep as the sky lightened, showing her broken airy palaces that would turn to stone at sunrise. She woke to light pounding down at her, ground shimmering with heat. She caught up the skins and pouch, and burned her feet running to shelter among the nearest stones. There she sat, shifting as the shadow shifted, her thoughts as formless and furious as the maddening heat. When night fell, she found a slab of rock to crawl onto, away, she hoped, from whatever small ferocious things might consider her supper. The first tiny lizard that slipped out of a crevice and ran over her nearly sent her tumbling to the ground. After that, she shared the stone with them, shaking them away with little more attention than she would give a fly. The inactivity was as maddening as the heat. If Rad Ilex did not bother coming for her, she assumed Draken Saphier would let the desert have her, a ghost to haunt the dream-castles. Dying alone in the middle of a desert in a strange land seemed preposterous. But if Draken Saphier told the truth, and she had helped the wrong mage, he had little reason to care what happened to her.

He might not even bother telling her if he caught Rad; he might just leave her anyway. That thought kept her awake the second night, listening for voices, for mage-work. In the darkest hour before dawn, when even the winds drifted gently, spent, she heard a pebble on the ground below her shift.

She tensed, thinking of the small, toothed animals. A lizard skittered across her hand. She flung it away, gasping. The lizard said as it fell,

"Meguet."

She peered over the edge of stone, saw nothing. She had to wait for it to work its way up the rock again, and then, in deep shadow, it changed. Rad whispered,

"I know Draken is here. I want you to run from me. Now."

She was silent, trying to pick out his face in the dark; it might as well have been the pocked and weathered stone speaking. "Are you trying to kill me?"

"What?"

"You want me eaten by the night-hunters."

"What night-hunters?"

"The ones who can feel your running steps."

"What are you talking about?" His voice, cobweb thin, took on slightly more substance. "There's nothing but lizards in this part of the desert. And you've been sleeping with them."

She was silent, her mouth tight, controlling a flash of temper as black as the sky. She said between her teeth, "Draken Saphier says they exist. You say they don't. He told me not to move among them. You tell me to run."

"Then believe him." There was no anger in his voice, almost no sound but a taut urgency trembling between them. "Yes, there are terrible night-hunters. Yes, I want to kill you. So run from me, Meguet, quickly, because they will show you more mercy than I will. Run. Now. Run."

She hesitated a moment, still trying to see his face. Then she slid off the ledge and ran across the cool, hard ground, blind until a light exploded behind her like the fallen star suddenly showering its pale fire across the sleeping desert. She tripped on a stone, came down hard, and heard, above her panting, Rad Ilex's sudden, twisted cry. She caught her own cry behind her hand, feeling tears sting her eyes. There was another flash. She pushed her face against her arms, felt the ground shake a little, as if, deep beneath it, the dragons stirred, disturbed.

The night was still again. She heard a step. And then Draken Saphier's voice: "You're safe, now. I have him."

She rose, trembling; she sensed only one shadowy presence in the dark. "Where? Did you kill him?"

"No. I need him alive to take the spell from my son."

She brushed hair and dirt out of her face, tried to speak with dignity, though her voice shook. "Will you give me back my shoes now? I'll walk home."

He was silent. A thin, white light snapped through the air, hit the ground near her foot. She glimpsed something small, many-legged, trying to bite the blade of light impaling it. She froze, speechless, and then felt the black anger again, as if she were truly blind, and teased and teased by voices, light touches, questions without answers, without end: *Who am I, Meguet? Who am I now? And now?*

"Please." Her voice trembled badly. "Give me my shoes and let me go."

"Come." He took her arm. "You want to go north; I'll take you. You're barely fit to walk, and I owe you something for helping me, though until you ran from Rad, I was not certain you believed me." She opened her mouth, closed it, speechless again. "Come to my court." His grip was not tight, but she suspected he would not let her go. "Wherever you are going, my palace must be closer to it than the Luxour."

She answered finally, wearily, using herself again as bait to lure truth, for her own hidden face only called forth other shifting faces. "It's where I am going. The court of Draken Saphier."

His voice sharpened. "You were walking to my house across the desert?"

"I'm a stranger in your land. My name is Meguet Vervaine. Rad Ilex pulled me out of the house of the Holders of Ro Holding, into the middle of the Luxour. He took me to his village from there. He was hurt; he hadn't the strength to take me back to Ro Holding. I recognized you because your son is in Ro Holding, in the care of my cousin, Nyx Ro, who is a very capable mage." He was absolutely motionless; she spoke to nothing, to the night. "Rad had told me certain things that made me wary of you. And you tell me things that make me wary of Rad. Whatever is between you is far too complicated for me to sort out. Perhaps Brand himself, when he is no longer imprisoned by the firebird, can make things clear."

"Ro Holding."

"Saphier is on none of our maps."

"I have heard of Ro Holding."

She was silent, aware of words scattered to a stranger's winds, like birds flying out of her mouth that could never be caught. She felt ancient, uneasy stirrings, not from the Luxour, but within her, a faint flurry of voices through the ages: *Meguet, what are you, are you doing, are you doing?* I am blind, she told them fiercely, desperately. *I am trying to see.*

The night shifted, as if it, too, had caught an echo of her past. She said quickly, "Then you will know where to go to get your son. If not how."

"Yes." She saw, finally, in the slow ebb of dark, a line or two of his face. "The mage Chrysom was born in Ro Holding. It seemed he liked to travel.

He left his name in the air of Saphier's past." She felt his hand again, tighter now; his voice was imperative, impatient of distances. "Come."

Stars blossomed from the dark, shot in streaks of silver past them and back again, winding, weaving, circling, until it seemed they stood in a web of silver that was at once rushing away from them and frozen still. Draken spoke; the paths blurred together, silver into dark, except for one. He led her onto it.

They were met, in a great, orderly hall, by a turmoil. Meguet, blinking at noise made by dozens of people, brightly dressed at that hour of the morning, at the bronze lamps and mage-lights burning everywhere, realized she had walked barefoot into the house of Draken Saphier. Her hair was loose, tangled, her clothes sweat-stained and dusty, her hands scratched. Draken, seen for once in light, was frowning at the chaos. Something seemed to drag at him; there were taut, weary lines beside his mouth, between his brows. Rad, she guessed, weighed heavily, wherever he was.

Draken said nothing. He picked up a mage-light from a ledge, held it aloft. Red, smoky, sinuous lines of light whirled out of it, took shape in the air above the crowd. A dragon floated above them, wings spread, neck arched, glaring down at the gathering. It hissed suddenly; the air chilled; lamps flickered. Draken tossed the mage-light; it hung in midair, illumining silent, upturned faces. The dragon reached for the star, held it between its claws, stared into it.

"It is a question," Draken said obscurely to the soundless crowd. "Contemplate it." Then he added, "Magior."

A tall, graceful woman with a still, seamed face came to him. She bowed her head. "My lord."

"What is this unseemly behavior from my household, my mages?"

"My lord—" She touched her eyes wearily. "Your son has disappeared."

"Magior—" His voice caught. Meguet wondered blankly if the silvery path had led them backward in time instead of forward. "What—"

"I mean, my lord, again. He has been here for three days."

"Here!" He looked stunned, and then suddenly harried, his attention drawn to his restive prisoner. He asked incredulously when he was able to speak again, "Is the spell broken?"

"No, my lord. He was brought here by a mage from some peculiar country where mages, apparently, are neither trained nor disciplined. We worked with the spell, and at her insistence finally permitted Brand to speak to her. They were last seen entering your meditation garden. Before midnight, last night. Neither has been seen since. We have searched ruthlessly, my lord. They are gone."

"Where?" Draken whispered. *Nyx*, Meguet thought. The name turned her cold as stone, as if it were a spell. Nyx in Saphier.

"I believe she intended no harm," Magior was saying. "Brand insisted that no one could help him but you. She apparently has some knowledge of the time-paths within Saphier, which is perplexing because she had never even heard of Saphier before the firebird flew into Ro Holding—"

"The Luxour." Draken said, his face taut, dark with care. Then he stopped breathing, stopped thinking, it seemed. It was something Meguet had seen Nyx do: grow so still she might have been painted on the air. "And that," he said very softly, evenly, as if he were recounting the ending of a tale, "is why Rad Ilex went to Ro Holding."

"Following the firebird, my lord?" Magior asked. His eyes went back to her.

"No doubt. For whatever his purposes. But Brand—was he well? What did he say? Does he remember anything? How could he speak at all?"

"Before he encountered Nyx Ro, he said that he could not even remember his name, where he was born, or when. The spell permits him to speak only at moonrise, until midnight."

"Strange," he breathed. "And this mage helped him remember?"

"Enough so that she was able to bring him here. But he still does not remember the exact circumstances of the spell, and he still changes; he is a bird, my lord, except for those scant hours." She shook her head. "It is an impossible piece of mage-work. We did our best with it. He was becoming extremely impatient, waiting for you. I'm sure that's where they have gone: to search the Luxour for you."

"Yes." The lines were deepening on his face again: He still wore the dust of the Luxour, he had an unruly mage in his pocket, it seemed, and now a firebird to find among the dragons. He looked at Meguet. "Your cousin, Nyx Ro—is it likely she would have been so impulsive?"

"Oh, yes," Meguet sighed. "But only to help Brand. She would never harm him. I watched her working with that spell in Chrysom's tower. She may not be disciplined—she trained herself—but she is fascinated by what she can't do, what she doesn't know. If Brand told her anything at all about the Luxour, she would have felt compelled by more than the firebird to go there."

"I see," he said, unsurprised, and Meguet realized what she herself had conjured in his mind: a kindred spirit.

She added, "Nyx must have come also to look for me. I vanished with Rad Ilex; Brand would have told her to look for him in Saphier."

"My lord?" Magior said abruptly, startled, staring at Meguet. "Is this another mage from Ro Holding?"

"She says she is not a mage," Draken said, though his eyes held Meguet's a moment before he answered, and there was the faintest thread of curiosity in his voice. "What we have here is the mage's cousin, Meguet Vervaine. I found her wandering across the Luxour: She had been pulled into Saphier by Rad Ilex."

Magior's brows rose. "How terrible," she said blankly. "But, my lord, why?"

"It's complex," Meguet answered, trying to keep a straight course, in this land of tangled paths and shifting landscapes, toward essentials. "What I need to do above all is to find Nyx and go home. She is heir to Ro Holding, and the Holder will not sleep until she returns."

"And we have kept her three days," Magior said worriedly. "And now she is in the Luxour. My lord—"

"I'll find her," Draken said. "Even in the Luxour, I can find my own son." He paused, thinking with an effort; he closed his eyes briefly, concentrating on a spell, or measuring his own weariness. He had been awake at night, listening for Rad's footfall, as well as Meguet.

She said, "I will come."

"There's no need."

"I need to come."

He shook his head. "You'll slow me," he said inarguably. "You have no conception of the difficulties of the Luxour. Even mages can rarely find one another. The great stones seem to deflect power, or attract it, draw it in. The land changes spells as it changes its face."

"You found Rad Ilex," she reminded him, and felt concentration crumbling all over the silent hall. He said, lifting a hand to catch the mage-light as it fell from the dragon's claws.

"I fought the Luxour for him and won. With your help."

"My lord—" Magior whispered.

"Yes," he said tautly. "I have brought Rad Ilex with me. And now I must go back and find Brand. Magior, see that Meguet Vervaine is treated with utmost courtesy."

"But what will you do with Rad Ilex?" she breathed. "What will contain him while you are gone?"

"Where is he?" Meguet asked, expecting no answer, but the entire hall waited, without a sound, for his response.

"I trapped him," Draken said, "in a time-path I made. I tricked him into running down it, and then closed the path upon itself. It has no beginning and no end. I can hold him there, while I am away," he added to Magior. "It will be draining, but not impossible."

"My lord, take the mages to help you—at least a few!"

"No. We'll only confuse one another. I need to find Brand and Nyx Ro quickly." He handed Magior the mage-light; she stood gazing at him, an old woman with a star between her hands. "Keep the house orderly, and do not trouble Meguet Vervaine with details. Show her the gardens. Let her rest. Ask her no questions beyond what is customary to reveal the status of a stranger in the house. Do you understand me?"

"Yes, my lord."

"I will answer everything else when I return."

He vanished; so did the dragon above their heads. Meguet, sagging suddenly on her feet, was grateful for Magior's firm hold, as well as her silence, as she led Meguet through a thicket of curious gazes. Exhausted as she was, she saw the silver enclosing every wrist; everyone, it seemed, was imprisoned in the delicate weaves of time, on its never-ending paths. She made nothing more of it then, barely aware of washing, eating, in a chamber so full of light it seemed made entirely of gold. The light hardened into the golden face of the Luxour just before she fell asleep.

She woke hours later at dusk, to a vision of silver. She almost cried out, but she had no strength even for that. The tangle of silver floated, glowing, in midair, its lines blurred in the soft shadows. Rad Ilex, standing in the midst of endless layers of paths, put his finger to his lips. Half his face was masked in blood, the other half gilded with the dust of the Luxour.

He whispered, "Meguet." His voice seemed to come from unexpected, ghostly places. She swallowed, felt the blood beating through her. "Where is he? Where did he go?"

"To find Brand," she answered finally. "And Nyx. They went looking for him."

"Nyx."

"She came here."

"To Saphier?" He moved slowly, as if caught in hard, rushing currents. He changed, she saw with horrified fascination, in unpredictable ways: He grew smaller, he lost perspective, a limb would disappear around an invisible corner, reappear. "Where is he?" he repeated.

"In the desert."

He said, "Ah," very slowly; the sound died on an ebbing wave. "The desert distracted him."

"What?"

"He has lost hold of me a little. So I came looking for you. I need help."

"I won't argue that," she whispered, still amazed. "But why me? I'm no mage. And the last I saw of you, you tried to kill me."

"I was trying to save you. If you hadn't run, Draken would have attacked us both—"

"You lied to me. You said there was nothing more dangerous than lizards in the night."

"I didn't lie."

"Draken killed something. With teeth. Beside my bare foot."

She heard him sigh. "Meguet. Would you rather be in here with me? I would have said anything to make you run. Besides, I didn't lie. Draken lied. He made that thing, then killed it. I know how his mind works. Can you get your own mind off small details for the moment?"

She put her hands to her eyes, still saw him floating in the dark behind her eyelids. "I was awake for two nights, terrified of those small details. Of such details are great lies formed. What do you want from me? Draken will bring Nyx back with him, and she and I will leave. If there is a threat to Ro Holding, we will face it there."

"Of course there's a threat. You've been in this house. Armed mages wear the paths of time on their wrists, and one of those paths, as the firebird has shown, leads to Ro Holding."

Her hands slid down slowly to her mouth. The blood drained out of her face; the room darkened a little, a shadow forming against the dusk: the dragon, hunting. "But why?" she whispered.

"Saphier breeds warriors. War is our history, our heritage. You saw Brand fight me. The movements of his attack are as old as Saphier. Draken is a double-edged sword: the warrior-mage. His eye turned to Ro Holding when he found Chrysom's writings here. I showed—" He stopped abruptly; she heard his voice shake. "I showed him the path to Ro Holding."

"You what?"

"Inadvertently. He discovered from Brand that I used to visit Chrysom. That I was searching for that key. That the key held in it paths of time beyond Draken's knowledge. He wants conquest, even through time, and he wants the dragons' power to make himself invincible."

"He wouldn't need much," she said numbly, "in Ro Holding."

"He wants that key. Does Nyx have it here in Saphier?"

"I have no idea."

"If she does, and Draken realizes that, she is in terrible danger."

"That key." She felt again the sudden, blind anger at the confusion, tangled as the winds on the Luxour blowing from every direction, into which he inevitably led her. "Always that key. Draken never mentioned it. You want it. You told me that I would be in terrible danger from Draken. That he would sense my odd powers and take my bones apart to analyze them. All he did in the desert was take away my shoes. All he's done to me here is give me a bed to sleep on instead of a stone."

"He's like that. He'll bide his time. And then he'll attack. Meguet," he said urgently, at her silence. "You must help me. You can help me escape this. There's not a mage in this house who would dare raise a finger against Draken Saphier. But you would never attract his attention. You must help me, set me free to help Nyx."

"Help her!" Her voice nearly rose above a whisper. "All you and Nyx do is fight. I won't free you to go and steal that key and leave her wandering alone in a desert—"

"She knows the path to Ro Holding. She got herself here."

"I don't know how she got here. You tell me this, you tell me that—and then you tell me that I know what you have told me!"

"You know the firebird." He was breathing quickly, the time-paths blurring around him. "Its face is the true face of Saphier, and its cry the only truth. Meguet." His face darkened; he seemed to flatten, an upright shadow. "Think. Help me. I'll come back when I can. If I can." The paths vanished, swallowed in Saphier's night. Only his voice lingered, urgent, imperative, to become her own voice as his faded. "Choose."

Thirteen

NYX stood with the firebird in the Luxour.

The firebird had perched above Nyx's shoulder on a ledge of rock. It watched a splash of milky silver spilling into the sky above the distant mountains. Its beak opened; a sapphire dropped. It cried jewels now and then instead of fire: a single blood-red garnet, an emerald. It left, to Nyx's bemused eye, a gleaming trail across the desert, as if it marked a path for Draken Saphier to follow.

She sensed power everywhere, as if the entire desert were under a spell, and its winds and piles of stone and vast stretches of nothing might change, at moonrise, into something completely different. It seemed always on the verge of changing. Stones shifted beyond eyesight; shadows tumbled across the ground, wind-blown, attached to nothing. Not even the ground felt solid; it seemed pocketed with echoing chambers, where things stirred, breathed, dreamed. Odd smells streaked the winds: sulphur, damp earth, even water, or some ancient memory of water. In the light of the rising moon the great piles of stone here and there took shape: They were dragon-bones and palaces; they reared, spread their wings; doors opened, windows filled with light.

The firebird cried a blue topaz. The moon slid free of the dark, jagged line of mountains. Nyx, watching, saw the bird seized, pulled almost into something else at the moment of transformation. Its eye narrowed, became slitted; its feathers froze into hard, smooth scales. And then Brand slid down off the rocks to her side, unsurprised, by now, at where he found himself under any risen moon.

"Did you feel that?" Nyx asked, amazed at the random, mindless power that had stopped for a moment to toy with a spell no one else could even grasp.

"Feel what?" Brand asked. He scanned the dark, looking for mage-fires, for his father to step out from behind a rock.

"Something emerged between the firebird and you. Only for a moment."

He looked startled, torn between hope and alarm. "What?"

"Almost like a—" She paused, trying to remember what it was almost like: the tapering head, the hard, tight skin. The word caught. "Dragon."

He was silent, staring at her. Then he turned, impatient, frustrated. "Where is my father? I hoped the firebird would find him, fly to him the way it flew to you."

"I doubt if even the firebird—whatever powers it has that you don't— could isolate one mage in this windstorm of power."

He shook his head a little, still searching. "I just see desert," he murmured. "Rocks. The wind feels like wind. It smells like dragons' breath. That must be the hot springs." He looked at her. "Now what? Do we just walk?"

"I'm thinking," she said absently, wondering if the whole of the Luxour were on the verge of turning itself into a dragon. In the next moment, it would become; but this moment, in terms of its own time, had begun before Ro Holding had a name, and might last until its name was forgotten. "No wonder Chrysom came here. . . . He must have loved this place." She drew the ivory ball out of her pocket, opened Chrysom's book. Many of its paths, she found, began and ended in the Luxour; it seemed riddled with secrets. "Yes," she said finally, choosing one. "We just walk."

The path brought them to the springs. The water churned and steamed in the dark; mud bubbled and snorted. Wind dragged steam over them, blew it away as quickly when they began to cough. Beneath the noise of water and the exuberant wind, Nyx was aware of something deep and constant, a heartbeat within the earth, so low she felt rather than heard it. She touched Brand.

"Do you feel that?"

"What?" he asked, wary again. "Am I changing?"

"No. It's like a heartbeat."

He listened. "No." He roamed, peering into moonlit crevices, studying pale crystals that crusted the edges of the pools. He came back to her.

"Nyx," he pleaded, and she heard the urgency in his voice. Time, for him, would not slow even in the Luxour.

"Yes," she said, but the wind brought her a breath of winter out of nowhere, and, wondering, she followed the chill.

Brand heard the heartbeat then; it came out of a hole in the night, a place so cold it was rimed with ice. For a moment, he forgot the firebird. "Is it a dragon?" he whispered, as if in his excitement he might wake it.

"I don't know."

"What else could turn desert into ice?"

"I thought they breathed fire. . . . I wonder if Chrysom mentions it." She opened the book again; pages riffled quickly, stopping to show her what was on her mind: *The Ice-Dragon . . . It exists,* Chrysom had written, *in a time accessible but not recommended. It is very cold, and the dragon, roused, is fearsome, a monster with night-black scales and white eyes. It will follow the time-path if you do not close it behind you.*

"What does he say?" Brand asked.

"He saw the dragon." The book misted away in her mind. "He made a time-path to it. I wonder if all his paths through the Luxour lead to dragons. . . ."

"If you free a dragon, that would get my father's attention."

"And what will I do with the dragon?"

"My father could deal with it. He always wanted to see a dragon."

"Your father might well be annoyed if I set a dragon loose into Saphier. Chrysom left them alone."

"It's not like you to be so cautious," Brand commented.

"It's not like you to be so impulsive."

She saw him smile unexpectedly in the moonlight; the Luxour was working its odd magic on him. "My grandfather was a dragon," he reminded her. "So they say. My father says the heart of power—"

"—is a dragon's heart."

"So perhaps we should look for my grandfather. See if he's in the mage's book. A dragon who could take the shape of a man. My grandmother didn't find him fearsome. If you find that dragon, my father would be in your debt. He always wanted to know his father."

She was silent, thinking of the smell of winter and the timeless dark of the ice-dragon's cave. Could it do such things beyond its own world? she wondered. Breathe a perpetual winter over a land, imprison it in ice? A *monster,* Chrysom had written. What might the other dragons do if they were loosed? She drew an uneasy breath, beginning to understand what she had dropped into her pocket, and carried so carelessly into a land ruled by a dragon's son who could forge the time-paths but not the patterns. To find dragons, he would need the patterns she had found. . . .

But it was Rad Ilex searching for the key, not Draken Saphier.

"Nyx?" Brand's voice pleaded again, this time for dragons.

"All right," she said slowly. "I'll see if Chrysom wrote of a dragon he didn't find fearsome."

She found several, after perusing the book for so long that Brand had vanished by the time she finished. She looked around, startled, for the fire-bird, and found Brand finally, standing inside the ice-cave, shivering, listening to the heart of power.

The path she chose ended in one of the massive tumbles of stone. The winds smelled hot and dry there, as if they were about to burst into flame. She felt no heartbeat, but an odd, shifting underfoot as if the earth were falling away like sand in an hourglass. The stones trembled a little. Nyx looked up, gripping Brand, in case she had to open a door into thin air and leave before a boulder flattened them. The bulky jumble resolved, as her eye travelled upward, into high, airy walls, half-broken turrets, moonlit windows.

"It's a palace," she breathed.

"It's just stones," Brand said. His voice was tense again; the moon was continuing its inexorable climb toward midnight. "What does Chrysom say about this dragon?"

"It is red as flame and breathes flame. However, when it understood him to be harmless, it ceased its baleful attack and permitted him to come close. Its eye, Chrysom said, seemed a portal through which he might walk."

"What does that mean?"

"It's enormous."

"What else? Did it speak?"

"It lies within a ring of fire."

"Did it speak?"

"The point is: You can't survive attack by fire."

"Chrysom did."

"Chrysom was a mage."

"Did it speak?" he asked again, patiently, and she sighed.

"It made, Chrysom said, overtures of interest in a language he found fascinating but obscure."

"Meaning what?"

"I'm not sure."

"It could be my grandfather," Brand said hopefully. "If it saw one human, it would have known what my grandmother was, when it saw her centuries later."

"How did she find it?" Nyx asked, puzzled. "Or did it find her? Did it walk its own path of time into Saphier out of some peculiar longing for a human heir to its powers?"

"No one knows," Brand said. "She was a warrior-mage, like my father, very powerful, though she did not train mages. She must have come looking for dragons; the dragon may have let her find it. But I wonder why."

"Perhaps, like Chrysom, it was very powerful and very curious. Perhaps it liked to travel. It had seen humans before, and it approached your grandmother in that shape so not to frighten her." She shook her head. "It doesn't sound like this dragon. This one likes sleeping in the hearth fire; it doesn't travel."

"More dragons than my grandmother's must have travelled," Brand pointed out. "Legends of dragons have come out of the Luxour for centuries. You saw my father's dragon-room. Some of the things are very old."

"How many dragons would it take to produce a legend?"

He hesitated. "None," he admitted. "Some say the only dragon ever seen was by a mage having a bad dream on the Luxour. But they're here," he said softly, fiercely. "Even I can feel them. Chrysom saw them."

"Yes."

"Then find another. One I can see with you. It may recognize my grandmother in me. She had long black hair and blue eyes." His hand closed lightly on her arm. "Please. I'm in no shape to worry about risks."

She opened the book again.

The next path ended under the earth. They stood in a starless black, surrounded by thunder. Nyx, casting a mage-light so Brand could see, found water everywhere, dark rivers and cataracts tearing at the reflection of her light. The mage-light hollowed a vast cavern around them; its walls and ceiling receded into shadows. Brand, his face teared with water from a misty, roaring waterfall, asked incredulously,

"Are we still in the desert?"

"Chrysom says so." She looked around, her hair shining with jewels of water. "How strange . . . It's as if the dragons create their own small worlds within the Luxour."

Drawn to the plunging water, he missed a step in the shadows; she heard him splash. "What does he say about this one?"

She consulted the book again. "This dragon is white as bone, with eyes like blue water. It recognized the human form. It is a shape-changer, an imitator, capable of taking any form——" Brand opened his mouth; she held up her hand. "It is quite old and transforms slowly, with much effort now. It breathes a kind of incandescence that shrouds it as it sleeps. The mist itself is a form of power. It seems to be a subtle labyrinth, a time-trap in which the unwary might easily become lost, if the dragon does not wish to be disturbed. Apparently Chrysom chanced on it at the right time."

"Does it speak?"

"It has, Chrysom says, the power of communication."

"Then let's communicate with it," Brand said tersely. Nyx looked past the book in her hand, at his set, tense face. "It may know my grandfather, at least."

"Well," she said after a moment, "I suppose it's pointless to be cautious now."

"It also takes up time."

"At least, if we're both trapped, I won't have to explain to your father what happened to you."

"Chrysom wasn't cautious," he reminded her. "And he lived to write the book."

"True," she said, but did nothing.

"Are you afraid of dragons?" he asked. "I didn't think you were afraid of anything."

"I seem to have grown cautious," she admitted. "There was a time when, like Chrysom, I would have taken every path to every dragon, for no reason but to see them in all their power. Then, I supposed I had no one but myself to think of, and the acquisition of knowledge of any kind seemed more important than returning home in one piece."

"I'm not in one piece," Brand said starkly. But he was listening; his eyes were on her face. He stood with his arms folded, motionless, while the dark water poured endlessly behind him.

"This is not my land," she said. "You belong to Saphier. I've brought you this far, and I am responsible for you on the Luxour. If I lose you to time, Saphier will mourn you and curse me, and if I lose us both——"

"Ro Holding will lose its heir."

"I'm not accustomed," she said apologetically, "to being this reasonable. But I have already lost Meguet somewhere in Saphier through my own willfulness, and I don't dare lose you. I can't go through my life scattering people into various bog-pools of time from which they might never return. I'm not afraid of much. But I am a little afraid of myself. And I am terrified of harming you."

He stood silently, still motionless, his brows drawn, a peculiar expression in his eyes. Then he blinked, and the expression faded. "That's odd," he said.

"What is?"

"That's all I thought I was to you: a puzzle to be solved. And so that's all I thought you were: a mage with a puzzle to solve. Now—" He hesitated.

"Now?"

"Now I wonder who you would be if I were not a man lost within a spell. Instead of dreading midnight, feeling time pass like this black water rushing away from me, I might ask you questions. For a change."

She was silent, seeing him differently now, as if for a moment, in that place beyond the world, his face was no longer haunted by the firebird within. It belonged only to him, and she knew him and didn't know him. She said tentatively, "What questions?"

"Anything. Why you're always walking out of your shoes."

"I find shoes distracting when I'm trying to think."

"Or how you knew you were a mage when you were young, and there was no one in your house to tell you what you were."

"I had Chrysom," she said. She was motionless herself, caught in his odd stillness, the little ivory ball in one hand, the mage-light at her feet. Water misted over them both, luminous in the light: the dragon's iridescent time-trap. She watched the light move in his eyes, the flick of cobalt beneath his dark, slanted brows.

"Chrysom is dead."

"Chrysom brought us here."

"Did you always follow his teachings?"

"No."

"My father's mages rarely question him. But the firebird follows you. As if you understand something more than power." He moved: his face grew clearer, chiselled out of light and shadow, the water flecked and gleaming along his cheekbones. "What do you think the firebird knows?"

"That it might be safe with me."

He blinked. "Are you saying—"

"No. Just that it couldn't fly home to safety. So it flew to me." She paused, her lips parted, remembering. "An odd choice, considering."

"Why?"

"Not so long ago, I was learning sorcery in a bog. I burned birds in my fires and read the future from their bones."

"You did."

"I thought—a mage should know everything, no matter what the knowledge entailed. So I tried to learn everything."

"Did you?"

"I learned to leave the birds in the trees."

He smiled a little, his face losing its·lean, feral cast, becoming, to her entranced eye, again a stranger's face: someone who, in his forgotten past, had learned to laugh, who had been loved. "Except the firebird." He moved again, step by step closing the distance between them. Light shifted over him, caught in the folds of cloth across his chest, traced the straight line of his shoulders. "Except the firebird. Your eyes have so much color now. What causes them to change like that?"

"When I work a spell." She paused, scarcely hearing herself, wanting to reach out, touch a star of water at the hollow of his throat. "When I'm angry. When I find something—something of overwhelming interest."

"And which is it now?"

"Probably not anger."

He swallowed; the star moved. "Probably," he said huskily, "you are casting a spell."

She shook her head a little. "I'm not doing it."

"You're changing shape."

"Am I?"

"You used to look like a mage."

"What does a mage look like?"

"Like a closed book full of strange and marvellous things. Like the closed door to a room full of peculiar noises, lights that seep out under the door. Like a beautiful jar made of thick, colored glass that holds something glowing inside that you can't quite see, no matter how you turn the jar."

"And now?" she whispered. He came close; the light at their feet cast hollows of shadow across his eyes, drew the precise lines of his mouth clear.

"Now," he said softly, "you aren't closed. You're letting me see."

He slid his hand beneath her hair, around her neck. She watched light tremble in a drop of water near the corner of his mouth. He bent his head. The light leaped from star to star across his face, and then vanished. She closed her eyes and he was gone: Her own hand shaped air, her face lifted to a dream. She heard his cry deep in her mind: the firebird's voice torn free. She heard her own cry and opened her eyes. A jewel fell at her feet.

She looked at the firebird, her eyes as colorless as bone. It spread its wings, crying noiselessly as it swooped into the shadows, found stone rising everywhere, no way out. It circled furiously as she turned helplessly to watch it; its wild flight slowed, spiralled inward around her turning, and finally the light caught it, pale and fiery, masked even to itself, trying to change the dark, rushing water into gold. It settled at her feet. She knelt beside it, touched its breast lightly with her fingertips. Then she rose and opened a path back into midnight.

FOURTEEN

MEGUET stood gazing at a waterfall that came out of a solid wall and vanished into stone. The water flowed noiselessly, ceaselessly, a thin, even wash that gradually fanned so wide it broke into graceful, shining threads before it disappeared. Mage-work, she decided, trying not to yawn. She had slept poorly after the sight of Rad Ilex in his prison; her dreams were fleeting, but seemed full of portents, urgent warnings that she could not quite understand. She hoped, when Magior appeared at mid-morning, to be taken to some peaceful place and allowed to contemplate grass. But Magior seemed to think she needed exercise, though she felt bruised in every bone from walking on fire, sleeping on stone.

"Is it real?" she asked, for Magior seemed to invite comment. "May I touch it?"

"You may," Magior answered. Meguet touched one thread of water gently. It separated instantly, formed a double strand. She put her finger to her mouth thoughtlessly, then flushed.

"I beg your pardon. I must have thought I was still in the desert. I am very tired."

Magior, oblivious to suggestion, moved down the hall. They were on some floor, in some wing of the vast house; Meguet had no idea how far they had gone. The long, pale corridors, the light-filled rooms, seemed never to vary. She remembered Nyx's odd house in the swamp, which seemed to ramble forever in and out of memory. She asked,

"Is the house real?"

Magior looked at her, astonished. "No one has ever asked before."

"It seems we might be walking down a single hallway, through a few rooms; only the things in them change. There's a timelessness about this place. As if it were constantly being made." She added apologetically, at Magior's silence, "My mind is still wandering in the Luxour, seeing odd things everywhere."

"Yes," Magior said vaguely. She led Meguet into a room full of gold.

It was stunning: a priceless collection of goblets and urns, vases, plates, sconces, baskets woven of flattened strands of gold, tiny, ornate tables, even a head molded out of gold, small statues of birds, lamps, a bouquet of golden flowers. As Meguet stared, the gold took on the hues of the Luxour: dust and light so rich it could not possibly fall for free. She followed Magior across the room; Magior stopped in front of a round gold table standing on three legs. On top of it stood a simple bowl carved of black wood.

Meguet looked at it, aware of Magior watching her silently. "There must be a land," she commented finally, "where wood is more important than gold. But somehow I do not think it's Saphier. What is this? Some kind of test?"

"In a way," Magior said calmly. "There are no answers. Only responses. Some see the wood more valuable than the gold. Others find its presence troubling, want it removed."

"Do you always test your guests?"

"No."

"Then why me? Because I am a stranger from another land? Is my presence troubling?"

"No." Magior said quickly. "Only the circumstances which brought you here."

"You mean Rad Ilex."

"I mean Brand Saphier. Rad Ilex is no longer a question; he exists only in Draken Saphier's mind. I know you are tired and need to rest. May I show you one more room? And then, I promise I will take you into the gardens." She moved without waiting for an answer. Meguet, bewildered, followed her down an interminable hallway, up a staircase or two, down another corridor until she thought her feet would simply stop, plant themselves in the floor, and she would become one of the house's ambiguities, for other guests to find troubling and wish removed.

A dragon reared in front of her; she paused mid-step, blinking. It was attached to doors, which armed guards opened, breaking the dragon in two. The inner room was full of dragons. She stopped in the center, turning slowly, for she had never imagined them in such vivid colors, with varying expressions and forms. They were woven on banners, tapestries, sculpted of bronze and clay, painted on wood, on silk, carved into chairs, screens, boxes. She tried to see them all, tried to look everywhere at once, until her eye was caught by one and it drew all her attention.

It was painted on a shield: a dragon black as shadow, with wings of shadow, and blood-red eyes of such malignity that, staring at it, she felt her heartbeat. Behind her, Magior was so still she might have vanished.

"Is it real?" she asked finally; her voice sounded thin, tense.

"Why that one?" Magior asked abruptly. "Why not others of far more beauty, far more mystery?"

"This one is terrifying. What terrifies also fascinates."

"So does beauty fascinate. Why do you fear this? It is only imagined: None of them is real. Why choose this, as the one truth in the room?"

Meguet turned. She closed her eyes briefly, felt the weariness in them, hot and dry as dust. "I don't mean to offend," she said. But the old woman frowned.

"You are more than just a stranger. If I had to place you, I could not be sure . . . But you felt the power, as we walked down the hall?"

"What?" Meguet shook her head, perplexed. "I don't understand."

"The mage's power. Your cousin felt it."

"I'm not a mage."

"Perhaps not. But Draken was right to ask me to question you. Your responses, even allowing for your unfamiliar surroundings, are not innocent."

"Innocent of what?"

"Experience," Magior said. She read the expression in Meguet's eyes; the lines moved on her face.

"Draken asked you to do this?" Meguet breathed.

"He is curious about you. You are in his house. He is always curious about those within his house." She turned. "Come. I promised to end this. I am sorry it has upset you. It was not Draken's intention."

"What was his intention?"

"To see if you possess power. Sometimes those who are gifted don't know it. Come with me. I'll take you to a more tranquil place. One without dragons."

Meguet walked alone among rose-trees. The vast house met her eye whichever direction she turned: a world enclosed, constantly looking inward toward the path of time at its heart. She could not stop her restless movements, though they led nowhere. In the distance, through the roses, she could see the movements of the household guard, a bright army wielding spinning shafts of light as they performed their ancient ritual. "Ritual" was the word Magior had given her: It was, she explained, little more than a meditation exercise. The meditators outnumbered all the inhabitants of Ro House. And that number, she had been told, did not include the warrior-mages.

She watched them as she paced, guessing that she herself was watched by someone, somewhere. It did not, she admitted to herself, take extraordinary subtlety to weigh the dangers of one mage, however powerful, against an army trained to march through time. The dragon, red-eyed and malevolent, loomed in her mind: destroyer, death-giver. That dragon she had recognized, of all those Magior had shown her.

The Dragon hunts the Cygnet.

But which dragon? Draken Saphier? Or the dragons of the Luxour which Rad Ilex wanted so badly to see?

Draken wanted the key, too. So Rad had said. Better, she thought coldly, to let the mage loose the dragons into Saphier against that army, than to watch its bloody dance across Ro Holding. Rad had been in the Luxour looking for dragons; Draken had been searching for the mage who had ensorcelled his son. Draken had saved her life, even knowing she protected his enemy. Still, he did not trust her: He had had Magior question her. How far, Meguet wondered uneasily, would he permit his curiosity to go?

The Dragon hunts the Cygnet.

Draken Saphier was in the Luxour, looking for his son. Who was with Nyx.

Rad, not Draken, had come to Ro Holding to steal a key. Rad had named Draken Saphier as the threat to Ro Holding, yet he himself dreamed dragons on the Luxour, longed to set them free. Draken, he said, wanted Chrysom's key. Yet Rad had ensorcelled an entire court to obtain it. So he had ensorcelled Brand Saphier, both Brand and Draken insisted, and his own spell was not strong enough to contain Brand's rage within the firebird. But it was the firebird's magic that had wounded Rad: It had been made, he said, to kill.

She sank down wearily on a stone bench. Did Nyx have the key with her? she wondered. She might have brought it to bargain with Rad for Meguet. Or she might have simply dropped it into her pocket and forgotten it was there. Was Draken only searching for his son? It was Rad who had talked of the key, of dragons; Draken had spoken most passionately of his son.

But he knew of Chrysom, of Ro Holding. He had brought Meguet into his house, and for all Meguet could see, every door was guarded. He would find Nyx, bring her back with him. And then what would he do?

The Dragon hunts the Cygnet.

She pushed her fingers against her eyes, blocking light, and the dragon rode the dark behind her eyes. She smelled roses. The dark became her shadow, with a red rose lying in it. *Choose,* the mage had said. *The rose or the sword.*

Choose, the colorful, motionless dragons around her had said, and she had found the face she had been warned to fear.

She stood abruptly, the images growing clear in her mind. The red rose. The black dragon. She drew breath, feeling her hands grow icy with terror, for she had made her choice about Rad Ilex before she ever learned his name. In Chrysom's tower she had wielded his rose against a dragon of thread; he would have the key now, if he had not paused to protect her from his own sorcery. If she had picked up the sword, he would not have recognized her in that brief, tense moment; he would have loosed the dragon, distracting Nyx, then taken the key and fled, leaving Nyx frustrated but safe in Ro Holding, never knowing what Rad had stolen.

If she had picked up the sword.

The rose had cost them all. But the mage was still asking her to choose between the sword and the rose, for if she refused to help him, he would be at Draken Saphier's mercy. There had been no mercy in the firebird.

The red rose. The black dragon.

The Dragon hunts the Cygnet.

She had seen the dragon's face.

Rad Ilex had left a rose in her mind. Draken Saphier had left a dragon, and it was not one of the Luxour's half-dreams, entrancing in their mystery, floating between worlds. A dark and killing thing, she carried in her mind: It had, of all the dragons in Draken Saphier's house, come alive within her heart and spoken.

The Dragon hunts the Cygnet.

She was in the dragon's house.

Magior took her back to the mages' wing that evening. She recognized the long, dark hallway, the great bronze dragon at the end of it. She asked, trying to keep her voice calm, controlled, "Is Draken Saphier back?"

"No." Magior said, as the dragon doors were opened for them. "I am taking you to supper with the warrior-mages." Meguet felt her face whiten. Around her the dragons seemed to come alive; their golden, glaring eyes, their brilliant wings, their breaths of fire burned the air with color. Magior glanced at her, as if she felt the sudden chill in Meguet's mind. "It is considered an honor."

"Then," Meguet said numbly, "I am honored."

"They will treat you with all due courtesy. There is no need to fear them."

"I'm hardly used to the company of mages. Nyx is the only mage I know." And Rad Ilex, she remembered, growing cold again at the thought that he might appear, bloody and helpless, floating above the mages as they ate. Guards opened tall red doors on the other side of the dragon-room; murmuring voices, the smell of food spilled into the air. Meguet walked blindly forward into a sudden silence, as faces turned curiously toward her, the stranger from the land at the end of one twisted strand of silver around their wrists.

"This is Meguet Vervaine, of the court of Ro Holding," Magior said, leading Meguet to a chair. Even the long tables were placed in a square; what seemed a hundred mages faced the intricate spirals and coils of Saphier's emblem patterned in the floor. They wore the emblem. Meguet saw, on their breasts, each path colored by a different thread. "She is," Magior continued as they sat, "quite weary from her ordeal with Rad Ilex in the Luxour and is not to be overly troubled with questions. Those of you who saw her at Draken Saphier's brief return know already that she is not a mage, though she is kin to the mage Nyx Ro. She is, however, by the standards of Ro Holding, a warrior, and has shown interest in the movements of the warriors' ritual."

Food, borne by a hand and a sleeve, appeared on Meguet's plate; she stared at it, wondering what she could possibly be expected to do with it. The mage sitting on her left, a woman with white-gold hair and a hawk's restless, hooded eyes, said kindly, "The movements of the warriors' dance are quite old. I take it you have no such tradition among your warriors in Ro Holding?"

We barely have warriors, Meguet thought starkly, then stilled her thoughts, lest the mage forget her manners and listen. She said, trying to find her usual composure, as if she had not fallen out of the sky into this elegant and dangerous land, "No. Only games and exercises involving appropriate weapons." She hesitated; the hawk's eyes watched her, waited for the trembling in the grass, the revealing word. "You call it ritual. In Ro Holding, while Brand Saphier was with Nyx, I saw him use that ritual to try to kill."

Again there was silence, even from the far table; the still eyes gazing at her reminded her of the dragons. Magior asked, her voice dry, precise, "Whom? No one of Ro Holding, I hope."

"Rad Ilex."

"Brand's father teaches him many things," the strange mage answered smoothly. "He is extraordinarily skilled and proficient. As tired as you are, I am sure it would be as tedious for you to listen to an account of a warrior's training in Saphier, as it would be for you to disclose your own warriors' training. In battle, as you know, everything becomes a weapon."

"You must eat," Magior murmured. "How will you recover your strength?"

Meguet picked up her fork, ate a tasteless mouthful. A man at a side table, with the stamp of Draken Saphier in the bones of his face and his black hair, commented, "The ritual originally involved ceremonial blades carved of bone. Since they could be played, it is assumed that the dance was performed to music."

"Perhaps a hunting ritual," someone else suggested, and the ensuing argument, tossed back and forth across the tables, brought to light an endless list of ancient and startlingly named battles.

"Much of the music in Saphier," the mage beside Meguet said, "originated in the battlefield, or the training field. In the Battle of Toad Stone, whistles made of raven bones were blown, to scare the scavenger birds from the dead."

"Toad Stone?"

"Two clan families fought over a great stone that resembled a toad. They revered the toad as kin to the dragon, a link between worlds, a messenger, perhaps. The dragon, in Saphier, is the symbol of all power: the power of magic, of battle, of art, of birth. I would imagine it means the same in Ro Holding."

"There are no dragons in Ro Holding."

"Some say there are none in Saphier. I meant in tales."

"There are no tales of dragons," Meguet said reluctantly, as if the mage might deduce from this no standing army, no fleet of warships, no revered toads and almost no mages.

The hooded eyes widened a little. "How curious. What, in Ro Holding, symbolizes power?"

The Cygnet, Meguet thought, and wondered if she would survive that supper to breathe under its familiar stars again. "In ancient tales," she said, "the sun symbolized the fury of war."

"And now?" the mage pressed, her gaze, intense and curious, searching for what Meguet strove to hide.

"Now it just grows crops."

"But under what symbol do you fight now?"

"Another ancient symbol," she said desperately. "A random grouping of stars. Is it the dragon you carry into battle? Or is it the symbol on the floor, there and within the square: the patterns that your warriors dance?"

The golden eyes flickered slightly. "The symbol," she said vaguely, "is not at all ancient, unlike the ritual. If you were stronger, I could show you one or two of the exercises the warrior-mages are taught. They are quite simple."

"I'm not—"

"So you say. Magior seems less certain. The exercises are designed to wake dormant power through physical movement, and then to channel that power, focus it, and release it as a weapon. The waking and release of power occasionally surprises those who think they have no such gifts. Magior rarely makes mistakes about those with potential for power."

The room was silent again, as if, Meguet thought, the mages' attention were tuned, beneath their lively conversation, to her voice. She said more calmly than she thought possible, "I have no such power. And I have no interest in it. My place in the Holder's house is bound by ancient traditions; I have no desire to trouble those traditions by changing my ways, even if it were possible. You understand tradition in this house, I know."

Magior moved her cup an inch, found no argument beneath it. "Perhaps," she said slowly, "you should consider the matter. In a day or two, if Draken has not returned, and you are stronger, we will broach the subject again. Tradition has its uses, and its limits. It ceases to be useful when it stands in the way of knowledge."

"I would not want," Meguet sighed, "to cease to be useful to the Holder."

"No. But—Enough. You have scarcely eaten. We will trouble you no more with such matters tonight."

In bed at last, exhausted with fear, she could not sleep. She lay staring into the dark, wondering if she could get out of the house without being seen, find her way back to the Luxour before the mages began to pick her apart. But if Draken returned with Nyx, if Meguet abandoned Nyx, if Draken found Meguet vanished . . . She tossed answerless questions in her mind for so long that the blood-stained face appearing behind its glowing silver prison seemed another dire portent.

"Meguet."

She was sitting bolt-upright, she realized, with both hands over her mouth. She dropped them. He could not seem to find her; he looked here and there as through shifting layers of time.

"Meguet. Help me."

She swung out of bed, stood in front of the floating, luminous weave. "Rad," she breathed, and tried to touch it; her cold fingers closed on air. His voice sounded weak, distant; still he could not see her. "Rad." Her voice shook. "I'm here."

He saw her finally. "You're so far away," he said. "Down a stairwell, at the end of a long hall. I'm getting lost, here. You must help me. Please."

"Yes."

"Please. Quickly. You must listen to me, you must believe me."

"I do."

"If you don't, I'm dead, and you will have Draken Saphier with his army in Ro Holding searching for that key. You're in his house, you must have seen something to make you doubt that his intentions are as peaceful as Ro Holding's heartland. He will burn across those fields of sheep and wheat until peace is a charred memory, and there is a warrior-mage in every Hold, and a dragon coiled around Chrysom's tower."

"Rad." She tried to grip the weave again, pull him closer. "Can you hear me?"

"Of course."

"Then why aren't you listening to me?"

"I'm trying to tell you—"

"Rad. I have seen that dragon. It is black as night, and its eyes are fire. Please. Help me."

He was silent, gazing at her, one eye out of dust, the other out of blood. He was trembling, she saw; the desert and the time-prison, as well as the firebird, had drained him. He said very softly. "Did they question you?"

"They have begun to. I don't want Nyx in this house. Help me find her in the Luxour. I'll set you free—tell me what to do before you disappear again." She slid her hands over the air, groping for a single thread of silver, as if she could pull the weave apart.

"Meguet. You need a time-path."

"Yes," she said quickly. "How do I get one?"

"There is a guard outside your door." She nodded; there was a guard at every door. "Open the door. Let the guard see me. I'm enough to amaze anyone for a split second. I don't have much strength in here, but I can disarm a guard who is not a mage. If he feels it, Draken will only think I am testing his power. Let's hope the guard is not a mage. Open the door."

She opened the door with shaking hands, gasped something unintelligible at the young man who stood there. He whirled into the room, a movement out of ritual, and stopped himself dead mid-step at the sight of Rad's face. Meguet swung the door shut with one foot, grabbed a bowl of water with three leaves floating in it, since the guard had nothing obvious in the dim, silvery light, by way of arms, and broke it over his head. He fell to the floor in a pool of water, a leaf clinging to his hair.

Meguet tossed the pieces of the bowl on the bed, checked the motionless body. "Not even a knife," she said, frustrated. "What in Moro's name do they use for arms in Saphier?"

"That is a mage," Rad said tersely. She stared at him, then began to move again, dressing quickly in the light, silken garments they had given her. She bent over the guard, touched the paths on one wrist. "You can't remove the time-paths," Rad said. "Just hold one. I'll open a path for you. Any warrior is taught this—it takes no power. You must walk down the path to me. Draken won't sense anything until you reach me. The path will end inside his trap. Don't enter; I'll be able to walk your path out. When I'm free, he'll know it. But I'll open another path to the Luxour, then; we won't return here."

"What about the mage?" she asked.

"What about the mage?"

"He'll wake," she said, holding the silver tightly, as if mage and time might disappear together. "He'll tell Magior—"

"Meguet. He'll tell the entire house. It will take them just long enough to find breath to say 'Luxour' before they know where we have gone. They'll come looking for us, they'll come fast, and they will be the warrior-mages. But they'll have to search the Luxour for us, and a hundred mages on the Luxour will confuse even Draken. For a while."

He was shaping time as he spoke, weaving a pattern around them, silver smoke in the dark; she could not tell if the path lay before her, or behind her eyes, within her mind.

"Trust me," she heard Rad say. The guard stirred a little under her hand. She heard Rad say something else—in her mind or beyond it—and she rose. *Come,* the path said, the frozen shining stream at her feet, and she followed it into Draken Saphier's tangled weave.

FIFTEEN

NYX sat outside a ruined palace, listening to the dry shift and stir of dragon wings. Earlier, the palace had been a pile of stones; twilight had reshaped it, given it depth, subtle colors, ghosts. She had been reading Chrysom's book, searching for Brand's grandfather, since his father had either left the Luxour or been swallowed by it. The firebird had flown somewhere within the rocks, dropping darkly gleaming garnets like a trail of blood through the shadows. Nyx drew her mind out of dragon-paths long enough to make a mage-light so that Brand could find her when he changed. Then she wandered back with Chrysom underground, within still water, up cold barren peaks, into magical rings of mist and gold and fire. Some part of her, listening for Brand, was aware of the gently changing hues of blue above the mountains where the moon would rise. She refused to look, for that might slow the moon. She refused to let her thoughts stray, for then she would find Brand's cobalt eyes looking back at her through every page she turned. The moon took its time, leaving her adrift among the dragons until a footfall brought her out of dragons' time into her own, and she closed the book in her mind.

The moon had not yet risen, but the man who stepped into her mage-light was so like Brand that she almost said his name. And then she saw the white in his long dark hair, the lines beside his mouth. He looked at her silently, out of Brand's eyes. She rose slowly, making no ambiguous movements, for she sensed an enormous power in him, as if in his dragon's blood he had inherited something of the Luxour. He stood motionlessly, taking in what she revealed to the inward and the outward eye, before he spoke.

"You are Nyx Ro."

"Yes."

"I know all the mages of great power in Saphier, and therefore you are not of Saphier. You know my face, therefore you know my son." He paused; she saw his eyes follow the glittering path of garnet into the stones. His lips moved soundlessly. He turned abruptly, disappeared for a few moments among the caves and crevices; Nyx waited. He returned without the firebird. "It's sleeping," he said. "On a high ledge, with its face toward the moon." She saw him swallow. "I think he can get down."

"He says he's grown used to finding himself in odd places when the bird changes."

"Where did you find him in Ro Holding?"

"He flew over the walls of Ro House, and started turning cart horses into trees with diamond leaves. Cobblestones into glass. He changed my cousin into a rose-tree. He was very nearly shot. His cries were terrible."

"Yes," he said huskily. "I heard him—it—cry before he vanished from Saphier. And then what? You calmed him. You call the bird him."

She nodded a little wearily. "Brand and I have argued over this. He insists the bird is sorcery, that it has nothing to do with him. But I think he is the man and he is the firebird, and the bird cries of all the things the man can't remember, in the only language he will permit himself to use."

She heard his breath. He moved closer to her, leaning against the stones between her and the firebird's trail of jewels. He studied her silently again. Mage-light catching in his eyes revealed fine rays, like dragon's gold, across the cobalt. "You are perceptive," he commented, "for so young a mage."

"I've seen his face," she answered grimly, "when as a man he hides from memory. It's like a man flinching from fire." His own face changed, as if he had felt the sear of memory; for an instant he wore Brand's expression. "What is it?" she whispered, shaken. "What is it he will not remember? Do you know?"

He looked away from her, down at a single jewel. "I heard Brand cry out," he said tautly. "And then I saw the firebird, and the mage who had ensorcelled him. I heard the firebird's cry before it disappeared. No one else had been with them, to witness what had happened between them. No one in my court could give me the shadow of an explanation why the most gifted mage

I have ever trained had cast a spell over my son. No one. I questioned every-one, often, and in every way I could, with and without language." He paused: the lines along his mouth deepened. He met her eyes again. "They had been close. That's all anyone could tell me."

"Yes." Her voice caught. "So he said."

His expression did not change, but she felt the sudden shock within his thoughts, as if it had disturbed the air between them. "He remembered?"

"A few things. The mage's name. That once he loved him and now he wants to kill him. Even the firebird recognizes the mage."

"And what more does he remember?"

"Saphier. You. That's why we came here: to search for you. He is con-vinced you can remove the spell because you are the most powerful mage in Saphier."

"The mage who made the spell will unmake it," he said harshly. "I have him."

She made an abrupt, uncalculated movement; her body peeled itself away from the stones, stiffening. "You have Rad Ilex?"

"I trapped him on the Luxour two nights ago."

She reached out to touch him, did not. "Please." She felt herself tremble, windblown. "Was there a woman with him? He pulled my cousin out of Ro Holding; I came to Saphier to search for her—"

"You followed Rad Ilex out of Ro Holding?"

"No, I came later. She is tall, with long pale hair—"

He was nodding. "Meguet Vervaine," he said, and for an instant she saw gold rays of dragon-light burn in his eyes. "I found her half-dead, alone in the Luxour." Nyx tried to speak, put her hand over her mouth. "I was suspi-cious of her at first. She tried to protect Rad Ilex, she lied about herself and him. But I persuaded her to help me trap him. She did, and so I took her with me to my court, where she is safe, cared for by my mages. She knows that you are here in Saphier, and that I am searching for you."

"Thank you." She closed her eyes, felt a burning like hot, dry winds, the merciless sun, behind them. She said again, numbly. "Thank you. I would have blamed myself forever if she had died here, alone and lost in a strange land."

"Blaming Rad Ilex seems more to the point. He brought her here. Under duress, you say. Then why would she have tried to protect him from me?"

"I don't know." She eased back against the stones, considered the ques-tion blankly. "Falling headlong into another world, perhaps she trusted no one. One mage had already terrified her; perhaps you frightened her even more. She isn't used to mages."

"I fed her, spoke gently to her. She recognized me as Brand's father and as Saphier's ruler. Still she tried——" He lifted a hand, let it fall. "It isn't important. I have you all now: Brand and Rad Ilex, your cousin and you. As you said, I must have frightened her, and it is sometimes difficult to think clearly in the Luxour."

"But where was Rad Ilex?" she wondered, puzzled. "Why was she alone? If she ran into the desert to escape him, why would she try to protect him?"

"People do strange things when they are confused by circumstance. She said, when she finally told me her name, that she was walking to my court."

"Across the desert? On foot?"

"So she said."

"But if she was running away from Rad Ilex to your court, then why was she afraid of you, and trying to protect Rad at the same time?"

"I thought," he said patiently, "you might explain that."

She brooded, her brows knit. "It makes no sense. Meguet usually makes more sense than that."

"Is she a mage?" he asked abruptly. She transferred her brooding from the ground to him.

"No," she said, surprised. "Why ask me? You recognized what I am the moment you saw me. You were with Meguet; if you were curious, you would have answered that question, one way or another."

"At first I thought not. And then I saw . . ." He hesitated. "A shadow. Perhaps it was only the Luxour."

She was silent, gazing at him, trying to put pieces together: Meguet protecting Rad Ilex from Brand's father, Meguet trying to walk alone and powerless across a desert to get to Draken Saphier's court, Meguet casting a shadow of power when she no longer had the strength to move. "It makes no sense," she said again, baffled. "If Rad Ilex left her in the desert to die, then why would she—and if he didn't, then what was she doing there? She has more intelligence than to try to cross a wasteland like this on foot."

"One or two other things I found puzzling also. Why did Rad Ilex go to Ro Holding? And how did you get from Ro Holding to my court, and then from my court to the Luxour? Rad Ilex wears the time-paths I forged for him, and so does my son. But Brand's were destroyed. So. You must have walked paths of your own making."

She opened her mouth to answer, and hesitated, unwilling, without knowing why, to open the marvels of Chrysom's book to Draken Saphier. As the answer hung in the air between them, she saw his eyes change, and she realized that he had known the answers to those questions even before he had found her on the Luxour. His eyes caught mage-light, turned gold. Dragon's eyes, she thought, frozen under the strange, inhuman gaze, and then: Meguet was born knowing what to fear.

She remembered the figures standing in the doorway of Chrysom's library, as the time-paths slowly misted the world with silver: the young man with Meguet's hair, and her heritage, with the warning to the Cygnet in his eyes. . . .

The stones and shadows were misting around her now, washed with gold; the pale mage-light burned gold. The key floated in a dark, secret place in her mind. But the dragon-eyes permitted no secrets; the key might as well have been in her open hand. It turned slowly in her mind, as if touched by invisible hands, that could not, for the moment, break through its mystery to open it.

Then the dragon closed his eyes; the gold melted into shadow and stone and light. Nyx blinked, saw Draken frowning deeply, concentrating, but not on her. She took a step away from him, another. He did not notice, lost in some private, harrowing moment. At her third step, his eyes opened. The taut lines of his face loosened; he sagged against the stones, spent and amazed.

"I've lost him," he breathed. "How could he escape a time-path looped back into itself?" He was silent, working out an answer; so did Nyx, in case the knowledge came in handy. But it only mystified her. "He had help," Draken said flatly, and Nyx felt herself grow cold with fear.

"No," she said quickly. "Not—"

"No one in my house would have helped him. No one else."

"She wouldn't have. She couldn't have. She has no power."

He shook his head impatiently. "She wouldn't need power for that. She'll be with him now."

"No."

He pondered, his eyes human again. "The Luxour," he said at last. "They'll come here. It's the only place in all Saphier where he can breathe a moment or two longer, though he is dead now, as he runs." Then a ghost of memory haunted his face; he whispered, "Brand." He turned away from Nyx, slumped against the wall, his face hidden in one upraised arm.

She heard a sound: stones shifting, dragon-claws scraping over them. It was Brand, she realized, climbing down from the firebird's roost. The garnets had vanished. Standing within the dragon's golden eyes, she had not seen the milky rising of the moon. Draken lifted his head, listening as Brand followed the path of the mage-light through the stones to Nyx.

He stopped when he reached the light; she saw him rock on his feet, as if a wind had pushed him. Then he made a sound, a broken word, and slid to his knees at his father's feet. Draken bent to pull him up, then knelt himself, as if even he could not bear the weight of all the bird's enchantments, and drew Brand into his arms.

Brand, lifting his face from Draken's shoulder, found Nyx, and stretched one hand out to her. Draken's shadow lay between them; she could not bring herself to move. Draken said, bringing Brand to his feet.

"Nyx Ro said she found you in Ro Holding."

"The firebird found her." His eyes clung to her a moment longer, and then returned to his father. His hold on Draken's arms tightened a little. "She gave me the only hope in the world of finding you again."

"Yes. I did not know how or when or where I would see you again, since your time-paths were destroyed."

"Nyx has a book. The ancient mage Chrysom of Ro Holding fashioned time-paths all through the Luxour. I made her bring me here to search for you. When we could not find you, I made her search for dragons. For my grandfather."

Draken looked at her, his expression unfathomable. "And did you," he asked, "find dragons?"

"No."

"Nyx decided that, even for a desperate man in the shape of a firebird, the dragons were too dangerous."

"That was wise of her." He touched his son's hair lightly, let his hand drop to Brand's shoulder. "What a strange thing to find in Ro Holding: the paths to the dragons of the Luxour."

"And equally strange," Nyx said tightly, "to find on a warrior's wrist the path from Saphier to Ro Holding."

They both looked at her as she stood alone, the mage-light casting her shadow wide and dark across the stones behind her. Draken seemed only thoughtful, but Brand, troubled, left his father abruptly.

"Nyx." He put his hands on her shoulders, frowning, then kissed her, as if to change the expression on her face. He succeeded only in changing his father's expression. "How can you believe that my father will be anything but grateful to you, to your house, to Ro Holding, for caring for me?"

"How could I?" she wondered.

He held her a moment longer, searching her eyes, tuned to the undercurrents in her voice, but not understanding them. He turned to his father again, said tautly. "Help me. Please. Nyx tried to remove the spell, Magior has tried—I can barely remember day, and I am beginning to hate the night. It's like drowning, every midnight, night after night after night. Only Nyx has made it bearable."

"I see."

"You can remove the spell. You taught Rad Ilex everything."

"Rad." Draken's mouth tightened. "For a day or two I had him trapped."

"You found him?" Brand said sharply. "Where?"

"Here in the desert. But he managed to escape." He touched his eyes. "I am sorry."

"Free me." For a moment Nyx, used to all Brand's expressions, barely recognized him: He wore the cold, intent, merciless face of a warrior of Saphier. "We'll both find him."

Meguet, she thought, chilled, and a stranger's eyes flicked at her, as if responding to her fear, yet hardly seeing her.

"He must be here still," Brand added. "Where else could he go without leaving Saphier? Unless he went back to Ro Holding. But he wants Chrysom's key, and Nyx has it here. He must have known she would come here to find Meguet."

Nyx closed her eyes, heard Draken say, "Chrysom's key."

"His book. The key is the book. Father—I am only human by moonlight, only until—"

"Listen to me." Nyx, wondering if she could fray into wind before either of them noticed, opened her eyes at the urgency in Draken's voice. He took Brand's face between his hands. "Listen to me," he said again. "I will try to help you. But I may fail."

"No."

"Listen. I know Rad's power. The Luxour shaped it. Before he could speak, he understood the language of these winds, the stones; he heard the dragons breathe before he knew the word for dragon. I don't know what of all this vast and unpredictable power around us went into the making of that spell—"

"Why?" Brand whispered. He was trembling; Nyx saw a streak of silver run down his face. "Why did he do this to me? I can't remember."

Draken shook his head. "I never knew," he said bitterly. "I only saw you after you had changed. When your human cry became the firebird's cry. You will remember. Look at me."

They were both silent. Nyx, sensing all Draken's attention on his son, was caught in the spell of the Luxour as its magic responded to Draken's making and unmaking. Their shadows, etched lean and black across the ground, changed shape: A great dragon spanned the circle of light, its black wings closed, its long neck bent toward the thing it held mesmerized beneath its gaze. The shadow of the firebird lay beyond Brand; winds shifted it, colored it yellow, red, peacock-blue. Then the dragon's wings lifted, opened, folded around the gaudy shadow, swallowed it into blackness. Nyx, staring, raised her head abruptly, startled by a movement above her head. Something shifted in the night: A head as bright as blood rose clear against the moon. Fire streamed out of it, washed red across the stars. The great head disappeared. Nyx found Brand again; spells flowed over and away from him like tattered rags: an owl wing, a lizard claw, a lion's face, his father's face, a dragon's misty, glittering breath.

Then the magic flowed elsewhere, left their shadows intact, shifting, as Draken's hands fell from Brand's face, and Brand, white, tearless, took a step back from him.

"I'm sorry," Nyx heard Draken whisper. And then she opened Chrysom's book, chose a dragon at random, and ran.

Whether Draken tried to follow her or not, she was unsure: What leaped at her like a great wind, nearly tangling the strands of the path in her mind might easily have been the raw power sweeping across the Luxour, forming its own spells around anything magical. She found herself in the deep caves, among the roaring waterfalls where Brand had forgotten, so briefly, the memories that constantly reshaped him. Her own memories threatened to distract her; she felt the sudden loss of him like a hollow in the air beside her, a silence where his voice belonged, stone where her eyes expected his face. But she had no time for such unusual feelings; she had no idea whether Draken would pursue her or Rad Ilex first, and she had to reach Meguet before he did.

She turned another page, opened another path. This one ended among the stones and dream-palaces, too close to where Draken had found her. She opened another path instantly, and fell into a place so black she thought she had reached the ice-dragon's hole torn out of the night between the stars. But the air was warm, tranquil; she caught her breath a moment, reading a phrase or two about the dragon hidden within this shadow.

. . . *a small and exquisite creature, with scales like gold leaf and shining copper . . . its eyes are azure. By temperament elusive but not unfriendly . . .*

She opened its path back into the Luxour, and came face to face with a warrior-mage.

He carried ritual blades; they and the time-paths on his wrists glittered like frost in the moonlight. His black garments flowed on the wind; odd colors seemed to flame and break free from them, then fade into night. With mages' sight, they recognized one another.

"Nyx Ro."

She stopped herself from vanishing before he attacked; he sounded only surprised.

"Yes," she said tersely.

"Draken Saphier is looking for you and his son. Where is Brand?"

"He flew ahead," she said, hoping it was somewhere near midnight. The mage looked disturbed.

"Rad Ilex is loose in the Luxour. It's not safe for the firebird to wander."

"How—"

"Meguet Vervaine is with him," the mage said without expression. "Your kinswoman. The warrior-mages are searching the Luxour."

"She was obviously under duress," Nyx said quickly. "He ensorcelled her."

"Most likely," the mage agreed politely.

"How many of the warrior-mages are out here?"

"All of them." He shook his head a little, fretfully. "Magic blows like sand in your eyes, here. It's hard to distinguish minds, even faces, from the lies the desert tells. Even those of us searching together got separated. You must not lose the firebird."

"No," she said, and he vanished, leaving a shining, faceless ghost of himself imprinted on the wild winds. She opened a path hurriedly to anywhere, and nearly scalded herself in steam from a boiling pool.

She backed away from the heat and cloying smell, and found a slightly cooler place where she could think. Surrounded by the bubbling pools, the mists, she felt hidden for the moment. She wiped steam-slick hair out of her face, and wondered starkly how, in a desert full of wild magic and mages who could barely find each other, she could possibly locate the two who had fled there to hide.

The Luxour itself had shaped Rad's power. So Draken had said, and if Rad could wear the faces of the desert, stones and dragon-dreams and shadows, and empty his mind of all but the constantly shifting winds of power, then even Draken with his dragon's eyes and relentless mind would have trouble picking him out of the air. But how Rad could hide Meguet, Nyx was unsure. Rad might transform her into a moon-shadow, but not even he could hide her thoughts. Nyx would be on her mind, Ro Holding, the Cygnet; words foreign to Saphier would drift into Draken's mind. If the warrior-mages did not find Meguet first. Like Draken, they would search for her to find Rad. Would Rad, knowing that, abandon Meguet to plead coercion and duress to Draken Saphier? Meguet would more likely fight what would be the shortest battle in her life. And if Draken didn't kill her, he would use her to force Nyx out of hiding.

And to yield the key. She stirred, remembering her own danger, and made herself as transparent as the steam billowing around her. But what, she wondered, would he do about Brand? Rad Ilex, she was certain, had not cast that spell. If not even he could remove it, Brand would wrench the firebird's voice out of the Cygnet's labyrinth, and its fire from Nyx's hold, and sear the burning desert itself with his despair.

But the firebird had attacked Rad. Brand had named him the maker of the spell.

Meguet had tried to protect Rad from Draken.

Rad knew who had cast the spell. He had been there.

She felt her body shocked into visibility: even in the steam, her skin was cold.

No witnesses, Draken had said. No one else saw, but he and his son and Rad.

Three leaves. One blue as Brand's eyes. One gold as the Luxour. One as red as the black war-dragon's eyes.

She whispered, "Draken."

As if she had summoned him, he began to shape himself out of the mists in front of her.

She ran before he had a face. But his mind's eye saw her and the random path she had pulled from Chrysom's book. He pursued her, a single burning dragon's eye in the dark, a force like night-wind at her heels. He could, she remembered with horror, forge his own paths, not from place to place perhaps, but from here to nowhere. As quickly as she shaped Chrysom's path, he reshaped it, cutting through her weave of silver, leaving her on an edge of nothing, or turning her own path back on itself, until she lost all sense of Chrysom's design, and guessed that the path she fled down would loop through itself to lead her inevitably, strand by shifted, twisted strand, to the Dragon of Saphier.

In desperation she opened another path, and then another, flowing away from that. She shaped a third, a fourth, flinging them into the dark, and running without knowing what dragons waited at their endings. She opened others, sending filaments of silver like crazed nets to catch a drifting moment and open it. She gave Draken no time to alter them before she spun another, sent it branching away into the unknown. Finally, she opened two that, by some luck, were so close they seemed almost indistinguishable. She fled down one, leaving Draken to snarl the other until he wove it through itself and then found he had trapped nothing.

So she hoped. The path she followed remained true to Chrysom's pattern. She had no idea where it led; there could be no worse, she reasoned, than the dragon hunting her. When the path ended, she closed it behind her, let it fade back into possibility, and then into a dream that only Chrysom's key would bring to life. Stranded on some island of time within the Luxour, she turned to face the dragon.

At first she thought she was alone. She stood at the mouth of a cave so massive even her mage's eye could not find walls or ceiling. But she smelled earth, wet stone, heard the slow drip and trickle of water. She took a step forward, sensed something where her eye saw only air. Tentatively, she let her thoughts flow around it: It might have been the ghost of stone that had once filled the cave. As she had with Chrysom's tiny jars, she let her mind drop into it.

She seemed, for an instant, made of light, as if the sun burned behind her eyes, and all her bones were lucent and bright as fire. She could not speak or think; she was as formless and bright as air at noon in the Luxour. Then the sun blinked, and she felt cold stone beneath her face, her body, and realized she had fallen. She pulled herself up, shaking, stunned, blind, waiting for the pain to begin, the punishment for touching fire. But she felt only the cool breath of the cave. She opened her eyes finally, and saw the dragon.

Its shadow had been burned into her mind, it seemed; her eye shaped a darkness against the dark. The heavy bulk of its head loomed above her; it could have swallowed her and scarcely noticed. Its huge eyes glittered faintly, flecks of light as colorless as stars. Its voice filled the cave or her head, slow, ancient, dry, dust blowing across dust.

"Who are you?"

Her own voice sounded small, trembling in the vastness. "I'm sorry—"

"Answer."

"Nyx Ro. A mage. I came—I was running—I didn't see you. I didn't mean to disturb you."

She heard its breath, long and endless. "Nyx Ro. Running. From where? To where? Answer."

"I was running away. From another mage."

"What mage?"

"Draken Saphier."

She had no idea what those words might mean to it: The act of running would not occur to it, and she could not imagine anything it would be compelled to run from. A great nostril, vague and colorless, expanded slightly; she heard a hiss from it. "When humans run, they run from the greater to the lesser fear. They do not run down the spider webs of time where unknown dragons wait. How did you find me? Answer."

"I have a book of paths—"

"You did not make them."

"No."

"I eat paths of the makers I dislike." It seemed to shift. A hollow echo rolled through the cave; light sparked as its scales dragged across stone. Still she could not see its color. She swallowed.

"You eat power."

"I dislike minor annoyances."

She made a movement, half a step. "I won't disturb—" Black moons sculpted out of the dark descended behind her, slid together and locked. She stood ringed by dragon-claws, and wondered if some of the minor annoyances it ate were human. She said carefully, "I would not make much of a meal. You have already terrified me. Your power is like the Luxour's, ancient and unimaginable. You don't need to threaten me, any more than the sun needs to threaten. I must get back to the Luxour. Those I love are in terrible danger. If there is a price I must pay for disturbing you, just tell me."

It made another sound, a faint, distant rumble. "Who disturbs the Luxour? Answer."

"Draken Saphier. And his mages."

An eyelid descended; stars vanished, reappeared. "A dust storm. A random shift of rock. The Luxour will survive that."

"Yes." Her voice shook again. "But Brand Saphier may not. And Ro Holding may not—"

"Human names. Human dreams."

"That's all I know. That's what I am. I have no dragons' time for loving. While I stand here in your hold I am disturbing you, and those I love might cease to exist. Please let me go. Tell me what I must do. I will leave you in peace; you'll never see me again. Please."

"You woke me. Nyx Ro. Weaving my secret path out of mages' fire."

"Destroy the path behind me," she said desperately. "I don't have the power to make such things, only to follow them.

"Who does make them? Answer."

"He is dead."

"Who else?"

"No one."

"Why have you come here? What petty breath of storm across the Luxour sends humans running in fear beyond time? Answer."

She drew breath, held it, feeling as if its thoughts had looped back through themselves, trapping her within some answerless question. There was no place where she could hide herself from its bright, relentless eye. It would burn the leaves of Chrysom's book inside her mind; it could turn her bones to gold and hoard them until trees grew on the Luxour. She searched for an answer it had not already heard, and remembered at last the word for what she fought.

"The dragon's son," she said.

The dragon was silent. She waited a moment or two, listening, before she realized that the black around her held no more subtle shades of dark, nor did the stillness hold more questions. She turned, trembling again, and opened Chrysom's book to fashion a simpler path back to the Luxour.

SIXTEEN

RAD Ilex took one step onto the Luxour from his time-path and vanished. Meguet, looking for him wildly in the moonlight, saw winds, shimmering veils of dark and silver, swirl around her. She closed her eyes and heard Rad's voice.

"Meguet."

"What?" she said tersely. She opened her eyes, saw nothing now but the vast, wind-swept desert.

"I've made you invisible." For a moment, she was afraid to move; she stared rigidly ahead, lest she look down and find she stood on nothing. "Don't be afraid," he added. "You can see yourself. I can see you."

"I can't see you."

"Wait."

Slowly he shaped himself out of air and night; she saw the strange winds glide over him. He said softly when his face became more than a blank shadow, "I'm using the power of the Luxour to do this. It's a turbulent force all across the desert. Draken will have trouble isolating me from it."

"What causes it?"

"The dragons, I think. They breathe power; they dream it; it escapes from all their private worlds into the desert. I can disguise myself in it. But hiding you will be more difficult. Look."

She looked down and saw a moon-shadow the strange power had shaped, that clung to her invisible heel: a black swan, its wings outstretched. She swallowed drily. The shadow peeled away, flew into the wind.

"Will he see—"

"I don't know. The magic creates itself constantly, especially when it responds to other sources of power." She stopped searching the night for the shadow of the Cygnet, and met his eyes. "I can hide from Draken Saphier. Perhaps I can hide you. But you cannot hide from the Luxour."

He was worried, she realized, and with reason; she felt the ground drop away again, as if she stood on nothing. "It's a power," she heard herself say, "that rouses only in defense of the Cygnet. When Ro Holding itself is in grave danger."

She saw his grim face tighten. "Now?" he demanded incredulously. "In the middle of the Luxour with a hundred mages and Draken Saphier alert for any hint of power?"

"If Draken threatens Ro Holding, or Nyx in such a way that Ro Holding itself is threatened, then by my heritage I must fight for the Cygnet. Even on the Luxour. Even against a hundred mages."

Another shadow formed, broke away from her: a black rose. She heard his breath. "How were you trained? And by whom?"

"No one," she said simply. "I was born. I am the Cygnet's eye, its hand. At such times. Now, I'm only a woman in a desert in the dead of night, facing danger without even a sword."

"A sword. You saw how much use that was to you in Chrysom's tower."

"I know. But it would make me feel better."

"If I could risk it, I would make you a hundred swords. But if you raise a weapon against the warrior-mages bearing the ritual blades, they will fight back. They are fast, ruthless, efficient. You saw what Brand could do. And he's not even a mage."

She nodded, her eyes wide. "They lied to me."

"Who?"

"The warrior-mages. They said the dance was only ritual. I didn't believe them and they knew it."

"They are preparing for war. They don't care where. They want to experiment with an attack through time: an army of mages and warriors and dragons that can appear and disappear seemingly out of nowhere. Ro Holding is as good a place as any to begin."

She stared blindly at the ground, trying to think. "We must find Nyx."

"And that key, before Draken does. I can hide it forever from him among the dragons."

"They will still have time-paths," she said starkly. "Who will hide Ro Holding?"

He shook his head, scanning the desert. She saw nothing move in the moonlight but dust; they might have been the only people on the Luxour. "I'll do what I can."

"Can you find some water? With your face like that, you look already dead."

"Oh." He touched it; the dark mask of blood and dust vanished. His own face, taut with weariness and pain, was no more comforting. He stood silently, letting his mind wander, she guessed, for a long time. He seemed to draw strength from the desert's power, calm from the ancient, unchanging mountains; his face eased a little as he contemplated the thing he loved. He stirred finally; she said,

"Now what?"

"There are a dozen mages prowling nearby, but neither Draken nor Nyx."

"I don't see anything," she said, shaken. "Can they see us?"

"I can't see them either. But I can tell the difference between a warrior-mage's power, and the Luxour's. That's what keeps me safe. To them, I am another random thought of the Luxour."

"And what am I?"

"In danger," he said. "Let's search among the stones and pools; it would be easier for her to hide there than out here."

They emerged from another silver path onto the banks of a steaming waterfall that poured down steps it had carved in stone washed with all the colors of opal. Rad was silent, searching again, Meguet guessed, while the damp, cloying mist billowed around them and away, finding nothing of them to cling to. She heard Rad breathe finally,

"I think she's here. . . ." Then he vanished again within his thoughts. Meguet watched the colors in the water swirl, form a reflection of her face. The reflection slid leaflike down the steps before it broke apart. A warrior-mage appeared out of nowhere, stared into the water. He turned abruptly, searched the mist. Meguet, not daring to breathe, turned her thoughts to steam, stone, crystal. Then the mist itself leaped at him, poured, burning, into his mouth as he drew breath to scream. He fell backward into the scalding water and followed Meguet's reflection into deeper water. Meguet saw a silver path begin to form in the air above him, break apart as he sank. One of his ritual blades spun out of the water, snagged on the crystals along the bank. She eyed it, but seemed oddly incapable of moving.

She heard Rad's whisper close to her ear, and started. "I found Brand. The firebird. But I can't find Draken."

She allowed herself to move finally, tried to touch him. "Let's find Nyx. She must go home. She won't leave until she knows where I am."

"She won't leave without you," he said, startled.

"I must stay. I can't hide behind the walls of Ro House and wait for Draken Saphier to bring his war there. If I must fight, I must fight here."

"You'll die," he said incredulously.

"Either here, or in Ro Holding. As I would have died defending Chrysom's tower, if Draken Saphier had come to steal that key instead of you. It's my heritage."

"It's ridiculous," he snapped, but no more, for the mists, snatching at Meguet's thoughts, whirled into a high white tower covered with what, at first glance, seemed to be red roses, but which changed, to Meguet's horror, into the black dragon's malevolent, flame-red eyes. They looked everywhere, the eyes of Draken Saphier; they saw through mist, through Rad's spell, through her mind into the Cygnet's eye.... "Come," Rad said, gripping her. She could not move. He pulled her roughly away from the image, and down another silver path.

Here they were surrounded by bubbling pools; even the mud spoke. Meguet could scarcely see the wall of yellow rock rising above the mud-pools, which she might have touched with the point of a broadsword. She waited while Rad searched the place; his thoughts came back to her.

"You must leave," he breathed. "You'll kill us both."

"Then leave me."

"No."

"Were they real?" she asked. "The dragon-eyes?"

"One might have been. Draken knows how to play with the Luxour's power. But only as a man with one finger knows how to play a flute. I still can't find him. Finding him will be dangerous enough, but it's far more dangerous not knowing where he is."

"Hide," she suggested after a moment. "I'll bring him to you."

He looked at her darkly, but said only, "You'll do that soon enough as it is. I want the key first. And then you and Nyx Ro out of Saphier. Then I want Draken Saphier. In that order."

She did not bother to answer. She saw something move in the solid wall of yellow stone. Mist, she thought, a trickle of water. But something made her reach out to grip Rad, warn him silent. Her fingers closed on nothing; he had vanished even to her eye. The dark shifting became a crack in the stone.

The crack widened as she stared. Then the face of the rock tore like paper and a dozen warrior-mages emerged.

She was surrounded in an instant; their whirling blades spun, plunged into the ground around her, elongating into a high, deadly cage so tight she cut her forearm, turning. The teasing desert gave one blade swans on its hilt, down its blade; she reached for it desperately. It snapped silver light, numbing her hand. She stumbled back, cut her shoulder on another blade. She caught her balance desperately, stood trembling while the mages appeared and disappeared into the mists, searching for Rad Ilex.

The ground around her turned to boiling mud. It swallowed the mages' blades, along with one mage who, leaping for Meguet, turned visible in midair as a wave of mud flung itself up and shaped him before it slapped him down. Steam blew everywhere, glittered with fine grains of silver and gold. Meguet, feeling a hand close on her wrist, pulled against it. It pulled harder; the silver grains snaked into a pattern around them. The pattern shattered like glass. She heard Rad cry out; the grip on her wrist slackened, tightened again. Light flashed, bright and painful as a flashing mirror; the island she stood on melted beneath her. She had no time to scream before she was dragged into mud. Like the mist, it found nothing of her to grasp. Silver wove in the murk; she could see again suddenly, as the mud pool faded. Still Rad remained invisible. Or was it Rad? she wondered suddenly, panicked. Was it Draken Saphier instead, leading her down the time-path? She pulled free abruptly; a flock of tiny swans formed themselves out of the silver path, soared upward, flew in a ring around her. She stopped, tense, her eyes wide, searching nothing.

"Meguet."

It was Nyx. The swans scattered at the word, turned back into silver. Nyx appeared a moment later, pale, and dishevelled, her eyes full of color, but, to Meguet's eye, unharmed. Nyx took a deep breath, closed her eyes. "Meguet," she said again. "What a place to find you in. A lake of boiling mud."

"Nyx." She felt, saying the name, as helpless as she had ever been in her life, finding the heir to Ro Holding underground in a strange country, while a deadly storm of magic raged above their heads. "Do you have any idea what kind of danger you're in?"

Nyx nodded. "I know exactly what kind of danger I'm in. And so are you and so is Ro Holding." Her voice sounded composed, but as she touched Meguet's bleeding forearm, Meguet saw her hand shake. "You're hurt."

Meguet ripped a length of silk loose from her torn sleeve impatiently.

"Nyx, listen to me—" She stopped abruptly, searching the soundless dark beyond the time-path. "Where's Rad Ilex?"

"Still battling mages." She took the silk, wound it methodically around Meguet's arm. "I thought he would be safer without you."

"He said so, too. But he wouldn't leave me."

"You might as well be carrying a blazing torch, the way power is escaping you."

"I can't help it. Rad complained, too." Nyx checked her shoulder. Meguet shrugged away. "Nyx, listen."

Nyx folded her arms, stood quietly, her eyes colorless again. "I'm listening."

"I want you to give me that key and go back to Ro Holding before we take another step in the Luxour."

Nyx raised an eyebrow. "You do. While you do what? Battle the warrior-mages of Saphier with your good intentions? Don't be preposterous."

"Then give the key to Rad and go home. He can find the dragons, bring them to the Luxour to fight Draken."

Nyx was silent a moment, her fingers tight on her arms. Her eyes slid away from Meguet's, the expression in them unfathomable. "Does he imagine them to be so obliging? To rouse themselves to fight for or against Draken, at the whim of whichever human reaches them first? They are very dangerous."

"I don't know." Meguet rubbed her eyes wearily. "I don't know what he thinks, except that this is what he wants. He takes power from the Luxour, he says. Maybe that would persuade them. At least he could hide the key from Draken. Or you could. Hide it on some path and go." Nyx remained unmoved; Meguet's voice rose. "Nyx, you are heir to Ro Holding!"

"I might as well be heir to the moon if we can't stop Draken here and now. I know what he wants. I'd go home only to sit in Ro House and wait for him and his army of mages and dragons to knock at the gate. I saw your kinsman with his corn-silk hair appear in Chrysom's tower just as I left with Brand. He came to warn me."

"Then why did you leave? Nyx, what possessed you to come here?"

"What possessed you to think you could cross the Luxour on foot to Draken Saphier's court?"

"I had to find the danger—I couldn't see it sitting safely in Rad's village."

Nyx shrugged slightly. "And I couldn't see what the firebird saw, by sitting safely in Chrysom's tower. Nor could I find you. A minor point to you, perhaps, but it seemed important to my mother. What was the warning you were given?"

"I saw a dragon of night and stars across Rad's doorway, in the morning light. At first I thought Rad was the danger—he knew too much—and Draken, when he found me in the desert, was persuasive. I didn't know—I was confused—"

"With reason."

Meguet paused, remembering the dragon, her hand straying to her shoulder. "I doubt that Corleu even knew the word for what he was compelled to warn you of. The Dragon hunts the Cygnet. That is the warning."

"I thought as much." Nyx gazed at nothing, wandering a tangled path of magic or memory, while Meguet contemplated their dubious fates grimly. "Brand," Nyx said softly. The color washed into her eyes at the name. "He might stop Draken."

"Why should he?"

"It's complicated," Nyx said, and nothing more, seeming, for once, at loss for words. Meguet, looking at her, found the unspoken words in her eyes.

"Nyx Ro," she said incredulously, the blood startling through her. "He's a warrior!"

"So? You love a Gatekeeper."

"At least he is part of Ro Holding." Meguet laid a hand on her forehead, where the headache was beginning, and added crossly, "Moro's name. Brand himself barely knows who he is. Other than the son of a ruler who wants to scorch the four Holds of Ro Holding with dragon-fire. Is he Saphier's heir?"

"I forgot to ask."

"Oh, Nyx, really."

"Such things are unimportant in Ro Holding. You know that. I never knew my own father's name."

"That's because your mother fell in love discreetly and in private, and not, I would imagine, in the middle of a strange land with a man who spends most of his day in a tree." She was holding her shoulder as she spoke, frowning at the nagging pain. "You love him for the color of his eyes."

"Most likely," Nyx said temperately. She drew the ivory ball out of her pocket, opened it, and extracted something that looked like a brown, withered hand.

"What is that?"

"Olem root. From Berg Hold." She applied it gently to Meguet's shoulder. A numbness washed across the pain; the scent of cloves and earth and mint seemed to quiet even the flickering ache behind her eyes. "Country magic. It will cling there until the bleeding stops, and then it will drop away and wither again. A trifle gruesome, but it works."

"Yes," Meguet sighed. "Thank you. So. Brand will stop his father from destroying Ro Holding for your sake?"

"Not exactly for my sake," Nyx said, but did not elaborate, nor did she allow expression into her eyes. She took the amber earring from the ivory, hung it from her ear. Gold fire shimmered across it, faded. "As you say, we hardly know each other. But," she added on a breath, "he knows his father even less."

"What—"

"We must find the firebird now. Quickly."

"Draken will be with him."

"Draken was alone, when I saw him last. I'm hoping the Luxour separated them."

"What about Rad?" Meguet asked anxiously, as Nyx shaped the silver pattern into their future. "Should we leave him on his own?"

"He would only distract the firebird. I want all of Brand's attention." She listened a moment, for what Meguet could only imagine: dragon's breath, the silent voices of the mages, the footsteps of the dragon-lord. "Come."

Winds, desert, stars, spilled around them at the path's end. Meguet saw the broken palaces rising up against the night. The transparent, elusive colors in a dragonfly's wing illumined windows, flickered away. In the next moment, the palaces were only stones.

"Should we hide?" she whispered to Nyx. "Are we invisible?"

Nyx shook her head. The wind tossed her hair into dark, tangled paths; for an instant her eyes reflected moonlight. "I want the firebird to find me."

"What if the mages find you first?"

"That's a risk I'll have to take. Meguet—" she breathed, as stars sparked in the ground around Meguet, shifted to form a familiar constellation. "Will you stop that?"

The Cygnet rose above their heads, star-fire marking its wings, its cold bright eye, until the winds picked the stars apart and they fell like fading embers into the dark. "It's the Luxour," Meguet said a little wildly. "I can't control it."

"I can't either."

"What do you want me to do? Should I hide?"

"Go wait among those stones. Maybe their power will disguise yours."

Meguet left her alone, barely more than a shadow in the desert, using a power at once simpler and far more complex than any mage's power to call the firebird. Turning as she entered the nearest mass of stones, she saw tiny black swans form and fly out of her footprints in the dust. Appalled, she moved deeper into the stones.

Moonlight pulled her own shadow from the dark; she looked up and saw again the haunting shift from jumbled stones to the sagging walls and broken towers of a great ruined palace. Her mind wandered down an imaginary time-path and found the palace again, in a moment so close to the Luxour's time that the two worlds of desert and palaces, made unstable by enormous, random powers, were constantly overlapping. The moonlight in the high windows grew filmy with butterfly colors. The colors washed away; the cold light poured down stone. She heard Nyx's voice.

She walked soundlessly to the opening in the stones, looked out. The firebird had come to Nyx; as it spiralled around her, she coaxed it down. It came to rest finally in front of her. It gazed at her a moment, motionless, crying neither sorrow nor fire. And then it changed.

He is free, Meguet thought, with wonder and then, as the stones around her shifted, he changed under her eye: She saw the broader, more powerful line of his shoulders, the white in his hair. She felt something flash out of her entire body; the winds took her fear and shaped it into the dragon's shadow.

Nyx vanished. Draken simply turned his head, looked at the stones where Meguet was hiding, and Nyx appeared again.

"No," she said sharply.

"Then give me what I want."

"Where is Brand?"

"Where I left him. Give me the key. Then I will set you and Meguet on the path to Ro Holding. You can go home."

"And wait for you." Her voice shook with anger. Draken said very softly. "Yes."

Meguet felt her body flash again. This time her own rage shaped the shadow that flew, soundless and dark as night, with its coldly burning eye on Draken Saphier. She flew and did not fly; she felt the power gather in her again, as the black swan neared him. Blue light flickered along its wings. He must have heard the winds part for it; he spun suddenly, flung up his hand. The black dragon formed against the moon and stars, its red eyes flaming. It opened its mouth, swung its long neck down and caught the black swan as it flew into Draken Saphier.

He cried out, as the blue flame rippled over him. Then the dragon broke the swan's neck and tossed it away. Meguet, still caught in it, felt herself grow limp and thoughtless with its death, falling farther and farther away from a point of light that grew small, so small she could scarcely see it, though it seemed, as she fell, the only important thing left to do.

Then the hard ground shaped under her again; someone gripped her, shook her. "Meguet!" She opened her eyes. The world was still black, but she recognized Rad's voice. She lifted her head, saw Draken rising. She heard a strange noise beside her; Draken, hearing it also, vanished just before the mage-light struck.

So had Nyx; the light snaked across the air where she had been, and picked one of the warrior-mages out of nothing. Her ritual blades and time-paths caught the light, flared brighter than the moon. Then she seemed to lose all light, become a piece of nothing darker than the night. She fell without a sound. Another mage appeared beside her; power snapped back at Rad. The stones shook around them; a shard flicked across Meguet's cheek. She flinched, heard Rad breathe something.

"Stay here," he said, and vanished. She stumbled to her feet, gripping stones to keep her balance, and looked out.

She saw a calm and empty desert. Then both Rad and Nyx seemed to waver in and out of the air, as if they were being pulled into eyesight and constantly pulling themselves back. As the silent struggle gradually and relentlessly worked them visible, the warrior-mages appeared around them, still as monoliths in the moonlight.

Draken saw her. He was an eye in her mind instantly, blood-red and unblinking, staring everywhere she fled, forcing her finally into a maze where she took every wrong turn she could make, and every wall that stopped her turned into the dragon's eye and forced her on. Once she turned and stood in its glare, refusing to move. The eye turned to fire in her head; from some far place she heard her own voice. She ran.

Abruptly, she could see again. She was on her knees, clinging to stone, trembling as if she had been running for her life through the maze of palaces on the Luxour. Draken had turned away from her to watch the firebird come.

It flew fast, and it flew straight to Rad Ilex.

He could not seem to move; he could only watch it, his head uplifted. He tried to speak; he could not. The bird's silver claws shone like ritual blades; they were open, curved, and dropping toward his heart. Nyx's face was turned toward the bird; she too struggled to speak. Meguet, freed from Draken's attention, walked the maze in her mind to what the dragon had sought: the eye of the Cygnet.

Nyx, she said, from that secret place, and Nyx met her eyes.

Power swept through her, from the Cygnet to the Cygnet's heir. Nyx shook free of the web of minds that held her, and cried to the firebird,

"Brand! Not Rad! It's your father's spell! Remember!"

The firebird faltered above Rad. It tore its voice out of Ro Holding and screamed, falling as if it had been shot. Brand, his face rigid with the fire-bird's fury, rolled to his feet and leaped in a single unbroken movement, at his father. Draken, startled, nearly unleashed mage-fire; he pulled it back quickly as Brand's body struck him. He staggered, regained his balance and gripped Brand. The back of his hand, coupled with the weight of time-paths, whipped across Brand's face. He fell like the firebird had out of the air, and lay still.

A few of the warrior-mages stirred; Meguet heard an indrawn breath. Draken met their eyes, said calmly, "It was necessary. He will understand." He looked at Nyx. "The key."

Her eyes flicked at Meguet, leaning drained and helpless against the stones. She bowed her head. Something small, burnished with amber fire dropped into her hand. Draken, his eyes on it, stepped toward her. She flung the amber at his feet.

It exploded with all the firebird's beautiful enchantments. For a moment Draken vanished among them: a scattering of garnet roses, a diamond snow-fall. But as he picked himself out of the spell he had made, the mages held Nyx, shaped her back into the waning moonlight as she tried to vanish. Draken, shaking gold leaves out of his hair, stepped across Brand's body to her.

"Perhaps," he said, "you will give me something to fight after all in your peaceful kingdom. You and your cousin who is not a mage."

He held her eyes and held out his hand. After a long time, during which she stood like the warrior-mages, a standing stone beneath the setting moon, she reached into her pocket for the key to all the dreaming worlds.

SEVENTEEN

THE first of the dragons appeared at dawn. Nyx watched the line of light above the mountains turn fiery with sunrise, and listened to Brand breathe. He might have been the firebird still, his bruised face empty, his thoughts hidden from her. Twice she had heard him try to speak in the night, then stop. He sat beside her on bare ground. The mages had tied his hands behind his back, while his father roamed the time-paths. They did not, Nyx guessed, want to use power against Draken Saphier's powerless son. Rad slumped against a rock near him. A web of power, spun from mage to mage across the circle, trapped him in its intricate strands; Nyx caught a glimpse of it in the dawn, fine-spun and dangerous, each tendril clinging to Rad, trembling a warning at his every breath. It vanished from eyesight, then; the mages hid it from the light of day. She felt no such elaborate constraints on her; they knew she would not leave Meguet or Brand. The mages had left Meguet free; they watched with cold curiosity the odd enchantments the Luxour pulled out of her. She was mage and not mage. Nyx they understood; they might not, Nyx feared, let Meguet return home. Meguet sat near Rad, leaning against the same rock. She watched the sunrise absently, frowning a little; Nyx wondered if Meguet saw, instead of the rising sun, the great shining prism hidden within time, which was the Cygnet's power and its eye.

She heard Brand's breath catch. An eye had opened in the distant mountains: a second sun, red-gold, flaming through the harsh, barren crags. A crag unfolded, extended itself upward in a broad sweep of gold. Another eye opened. The true sun rose above them. Shadows scattered away from the mountainside as the dragon's face emerged. A second crag broke away, moved upward into the sky, to catch the wind. The dragon shrugged itself out of the mountain, soared upward, light sliding like molten gold across its bright scales. In that moment Nyx felt the slackening of the mages' guard. It did not matter; as they watched the dragon burn across the morning, no one could have moved.

It came straight to them; its vast shadow, flung forward, reached them first. It seemed, as the earth darkened beneath its broad underbelly, to have swallowed the sun. Then it veered, loosed the sun from beneath its wing. It settled on top of the steep ruin of stones near them. It stretched its wings in the light; gold shook into their eyes. Then it faded into itself among the rocks, its brilliant, craggy profile to the light. One eye stared down at them, wide and ruthless as the sun.

Nyx felt a touch, and started. Brand had shifted closer; his shoulder brushed hers. She looked at him; the dragon had wakened something in him besides the firebird's silent, endless cry.

"My father——" His voice caught. He began again, softly, but Nyx sensed the mages' attention riveted on them. "He won't stop this, until he finds his own father. The dragon-mage."

"I know."

"Such monsters will make a wasteland out of Ro Holding." He closed his eyes, his face twisting. "Why must he take Ro Holding? There is a land for him at the end of every path."

"He glimpsed the power in Meguet," Rad Ilex said wearily. "It's mysterious, beyond his control, beyond his experience. He will take apart Ro Holding to find the source." Meguet's eyes flicked to him. She turned her face away abruptly, her mouth tight. He reached out with some effort, as if he lifted stone instead of bone, and touched her. "I'm sorry. If I hadn't dragged you here with me——"

"If I had just let you take the key," Nyx said bitterly.

Meguet's head bowed. "If I had not picked up the rose."

"It's my father's fault," Brand said with savage lucidity. "None of yours. Any of you." He struggled impatiently with his bonds, and added dispassionately, "I would like to kill him."

Nyx asked tentatively, "Do you remember——"

"Everything." He stopped. He raised a shoulder, brushed it against his swollen cheek, where a few fragmented time-paths had imprinted themselves in blood. He looked at Rad finally and said again, "Everything. You told me this would happen. That you needed to leave Saphier to look for Chrysom's key, and you told me why. You had told my father, in all innocence, that it existed, and then you realized that all the innocence was yours. You knew he would kill you for the key. I didn't believe you. Then he came in and I saw his eyes. Dragon's eyes. You had already opened a path to Ro Holding. He— I—" He shook his head. "It becomes confused here. He tried to stop you— I tried to stop him—I don't know how I thought I could." He swallowed, added huskily, "He was no one I knew then. Not my father—No one. He had transformed himself. He was the dragon. And I became the firebird."

"He made the firebird to kill me," Rad said, and then was silent, as if words, like his hands, were fixed to the mages' web of power and had become too heavy. He lifted his head suddenly; Nyx, following his gaze, saw a piece of morning sky detach itself and fall. Against the gold-brown desert its shape became visible: a sky-blue dragon, smaller than the first, with eyes like cloud. It dropped onto another pile of stones, and vanished again; with difficulty she saw it settle itself, now stone-brown and grey, flecked with black, a rock-dragon hidden among the rocks. "I envy him," Rad whispered. "Seeing all their private worlds." Only Brand stared at the ground, seeing nothing. "Brand," Rad said, again with effort, and Brand turned his dark, empty stare at him. "He didn't know you either, then. You were someone for him to use. He would have used anyone."

"Don't defend him," Brand said fiercely. "Not to me."

"I'm not. He barely glimpsed then what he is bringing to the Luxour now, and if you hadn't been there, he would have turned himself into the firebird to stop me."

"I was there. And so were you. He had no mercy for either of us. It was cruel. And unforgivable."

"Yes. I'm only explaining why—"

"Power. I know my father that well at least." He made a sudden, furious attempt at the leather thongs binding his wrists. The mages watched impassively. Nyx, her throat aching suddenly, reached out to loosen them. Light charred the ground under her hand; the snap of air numbed her fingers. She started to rise, swallowing anger, to plead with the mages. Meguet's eyes caught her, wide, warning, and held her still.

"But why," Nyx asked Rad, when Brand had calmed himself, "did Brand become human again, those few hours every night? Why would Draken have done that?"

"I don't think Draken did," Rad said softly. They watched a crimson dragon, long and sinuous, flicker in and out of time, its scenting tongue bright and quick as lightning, burning and vanishing. The winds of the Luxour finally dragged it into shape; it took its place on another ruin. "Brand and I met in secret at moonrise. Draken transformed him into the firebird at midnight. I remember hearing the changing of the guard, how the familiar ritual noises frayed apart at the cry of the firebird. I think Brand broke his father's spell every night trying to remember the significance of moonrise, of midnight. Not even Draken could cast a spell more powerful than love, or rage, or grief."

Brand shook suddenly with a terrible, noiseless grief. He bowed his head, hid his face behind his hair; Nyx saw the tears fall on the barren ground like rain. She eased closer to him, slipped her arms around him. He dropped his face against her. Her hold tightened; she felt her own tears slide into his hair. The mages cast no spell to stop her. She held him until his trembling eased, and her own eyes were hot, heavy. She sat back; he raised his head, shook the hair out of his face. He leaned forward, kissed her; she tasted his tears. He said softly,

"And so the firebird found you."

"If the firebird had come to Ro Holding a month or two earlier, it would never have come to me." Her voice shook. "In some ways, I was as ruthless as your father. The small birds in the back swamps of the Delta know. Meguet knows."

He rested his face a moment longer against her dusty hair. "My father does not intend to war against swamp birds," he said wearily. "And whatever you did to Meguet, she still loves you and she is still alive."

Another dragon broke into the morning, this one building itself out of a line of stones half-buried in the ground. It was huge, as grey as smoke, with a flattened, predatory skull. Its eyes sparked light like diamonds; they looked as hard and cold. One of the mages whispered uneasily to another as it took to the air. Its shadow slid slowly over them; it circled and settled on a massive rise of stones as grey as itself. Something in the distance disturbed it, perhaps an image drifting out of the winds. Its jaws opened; a colorless light flashed out of it. One of the piles of stone exploded, left a ghostly image of ruins where it had stood. The shock of boulders hitting the ground rocked the mages on their feet.

"Moro's name," Meguet whispered. Nyx watched her tensely, wondering if she were about to vanish to fight a dragon that made even the mages wary. Another appeared. This one Nyx recognized: A drifting wall of steam among the pools tore itself open to reveal an empty blackness, a hole in the shape of a dragon, with eyes like stars, and breath that froze the rocks it settled on. A few cracked; fragments rattled down. It curled and breathed; the hot morning light slid like white fire over the ice on the dark stones.

"How many more?" Meguet asked rigidly.

"I'm not sure."

"A dozen? Two?"

"Maybe. Not that a dozen more or less matters much."

"Draken can't control them all," Rad said. His head jerked, as if a strand of the mages' web had tightened around his throat. He swallowed, leaned back silently.

"He is looking for his father," Brand said. "His father will control them."

"I hope," Nyx murmured. Meguet turned her head, looked at Nyx without fear, without hope, simply recognizing the frail bonds of time and memory between them. With a shock deep in her, as if something named Ro Holding had suddenly ceased to exist, Nyx realized that the Luxour might hold the only moments they had left. All for a firebird, she thought numbly. All for a key. For a challenge to a mage on a warm summer day. She stared blindly at her eyeless shadow, felt sorrow, heavy, motionless, endless, begin to replace her bones.

More dragons became visible: one of air, translucent, its bones pale light, its wings faint shimmerings of heat; another, formed of twilight cloud, with scales of deep purple, blue-grey, violet. A white dragon, carved of ivory, it seemed, and as delicate, shaped itself out of steam and rode the wind to its distant perch. The stones were filling with dragons, watching the desert like birds of prey. A cobalt dragon flew out of the broken roof of one of the palaces, and then a black one with rust-red wings broke out of the palace's shadow, its great, ax-shaped head lowering on its long neck to study them as it passed.

And then Draken Saphier came out of a flash of silver.

He studied the dragons surrounding them, their heads and great winged bodies etched in vivid, powerful lines against the sky. He said to the mages, "There are others. I haven't found my father. He may be one hidden in a misty time-path with dangerous properties for the unwary. Have they been quiet?"

"The dragons, my lord?" With a start, Nyx recognized Magior.

"Our guests. What have I missed from Meguet?"

"A comment or two, my lord."

"I can imagine." He took a ritual blade from her, walked over to Brand.

His shadow fell over his son; Brand lifted his face. Whatever his eyes held made Draken toss the blade on the ground. He squatted in front of Brand, held his shoulders. "Listen to me—" He dodged spit, said again, patiently, "Listen." Brand gazed past him, motionless now. "I was aiming that spell at Rad Ilex. You flung yourself in the way, in some misguided attempt to protect him. You fled before I—"

"You," Brand said furiously, "destroyed my time-paths so that I could never return to Saphier! So that I could never speak the truth, never say that you had made the firebird out of me to kill Rad Ilex."

"That's not true," Draken said gravely.

"What's not true?"

"That I never wanted you to return. I would have searched for you in every world we conquered."

Brand's face flamed. He rolled so fast, his father barely had time to move; his sharp kick caught Draken Saphier in the chest, but only hard enough to stagger him. Brand, his hands tied, was off-balance as he rose. Draken spun around him, slid one arm between his wrists and jerked upward on the leather thongs. Brand gasped. Draken forced his rigid arms higher; the blood ran out of his face; his eyes closed.

"Listen to me," Draken said again, very patiently, and Nyx thought coldly: *Either here or in Ro Holding.* She flung power across the web and ducked into her own shadow. Meguet, moving faster than the eye could follow, was a blur, picking up the blade Draken had dropped. Nyx's power tangled in the web; it became visible for a second, a flaring crosshatch of light that dissipated just before it touched Draken. Meguet, nearly invisible, brought the ritual blade slashing down between Brand's wrists. It cut through the leather, but Draken misted away at its touch. Meguet vanished as he reappeared; the Cygnet, blown across the winds like black flame, marked the place where she had been.

Then a strange light sprang down out of nowhere, peeled layers of wind and power and time itself apart like paper to find her, force her, pale and shaking, back into eyesight, despite all the Cygnet's power. Nyx, stunned, dragged her eyes away from Meguet finally, traced the light through the air above their heads, through the bright morning sunlight, up stone and the shadow flung by stone, to its source: the dragon's mouth.

Around her no one moved. No one spoke. Even the mages were staring upward. Rad Ilex might have unbound himself from their loose and fraying concentration and slipped away, but his eyes too were on the dragon slowly rising on the stone pile above them, unfurling its wings to fly.

It had risen with the sun, Nyx remembered: the golden dragon with the red-gold eyes. It had perched up there all morning without a claw or a wingbone moving, its great eyes smoldering down at them, unblinking, until it had opened its jaws and caught Meguet with a flick of light as easily as a swamp toad catching a butterfly.

It dropped off the stones; the sky darkened as it flung its shadow over them all. It came down fast, for all its bulk; still no one moved, not even Draken, for it held them all with its fiery eyes. It could have landed on them, or scorched them all to ash, stray shreds of power for the winds to play with; no one could guess what it might do, and no one lifted a finger to stop it.

It vanished. So did the light holding Meguet. Nyx still searched the sky for it, her eyes bewildered by its absence, until movement among the motionless mages drew her attention back to earth.

A strange mage walked among them toward Draken. His hair was gold, his eyes were amber flecked with red. He wore a robe of dragon scales that drifted and glowed like the strange desert winds. His face was clean-lined, hard and powerful, like the desert itself, a thing so ancient it had been scoured by wind and sun and time of everything except its essence.

He stopped in front of Draken, studied him expressionlessly. Draken's face lost color in the light; Nyx saw him try to speak, falter. The dragon spoke first, his voice low, sinewy, harsh with unexpected inflections. "You are mine."

Draken's eyes burned, the dragon's gold in them reflecting light. "I am Ragah's son."

"She gave me no name," the dragon said indifferently. "She asked me to name her and I did. A word that means 'night-fall.' For her hair, and her powers that waxed by moonlight. She sent a message to the dreaming winds that she wanted a dragon-born child. I heard her dream in my dreams. She haunted the desert, she sent her wish on every wind, and I dreamed and dreamed until she roused me, drew me out of my world into this place. And I remembered the human-born, the human shape. And now you are here, Ragah's son, rousing dragons with your dreams."

"I was looking for you." Nyx heard the wonder in Draken's voice. "I didn't know I had already found you."

The dragon sighed, a long, slow, lizard's hiss. "You have found me." His burning, light-filled eyes moved to Brand, standing in Draken's shadow, and to Meguet, who still held Magior's ritual blade. He turned then; his slow, unblinking gaze swept around all the mages' faces. His hand opened. Nyx saw the mage-web become visible, shining, all its strands linked to Rad. The dragon's hand closed. The strands snapped in his grip, vanished. Rad gripped the rock, pulled himself to his feet, trembling with exhaustion, or with wonder. "You have dreamed," the dragon said to Draken, "of dragon-wars and found me."

"Teach me," Draken breathed. "Teach me. The heart of power is the dragon's heart. You have all the power of the Luxour in you, all the power of the dragon-worlds, all the power of time. You haunt my dreams, your shadow spans my life. I have looked for you since I was born."

"You woke me."

"Yes."

"And you brought me here."

"Yes."

"For this." His face tightened; deep, bitter lines formed. "For this." He looked at Nyx. His eyes were endless; they had seen forever, and they left her breathless, as if, meeting them, she had begun a slow fall off the world. They went to Brand again, who gave him only an expressionless, unyielding warrior's stare. The dragon sighed again. "What will you give me to teach you?"

"Anything."

"Your son?"

"Anything." The word flicked across Brand's face; he closed his eyes. "Everything."

"Seven years."

"Seven. Twelve. A lifetime."

"Seven I will take from you. In return, I will teach you what you need to know before I will permit you to call yourself my son."

"Yes," Draken breathed.

"If, in seven years, you have not learned what you must learn, I will kill you." Draken opened his mouth to answer, did not. "Answer," the dragon said. Nyx, staring at him, felt the cold silken touch of dread and wonder glide over her.

"Yes."

"So dragons treat their children. So I have learned from you, as I waited on that bright, high place, listening to your son. As I woke in my quiet dark to listen to the mage who, running for her life away from you, found herself faced with me. All these small, disturbing human voices. Because of you, I was wakened; because of you I listened, having nothing else to do. You taught me."

Draken was silent. He turned his head, looked at Nyx, as did Brand, Rad Ilex, and the entire circle of mages, everyone but Meguet, who had closed her

eyes at the thought of the Cygnet's heir running headlong into a dragon's lair.
"You? You found my father?"

"I didn't know," she whispered.

His attention moved to Brand. He seemed uncertain, suddenly, as if, not
seeing the firebird, he did not recognize his son. "Brand?" he said. The hard,
set face with Draken's hair, his eyes, gave him nothing.

"You wanted paths to find us," the dragon said. "You woke us, brought
us out to use us. To burn, to annihilate. There are those among us who crave
such work. Like you, they do not discriminate. They may begin here."

Draken moved a little, as if a wind had pushed him lightly. "In Saphier."

"You have brought us into your land." His slow, burning gaze swept the
mages again. "They could not begin to fight us."

Draken whispered, "You would not destroy Saphier." Something besides
the memories of his dead and blackened past touched Brand's face, altered
the white, stiff lines of it. His eyes glittered faintly, with a shock of hope or
horror, Nyx could not tell.

"It is a place," the dragon said indifferently, "to begin."

"No." The wind pushed harder, moved Draken back a pace. The mages'
voices murmured around him, shaken, protesting.

"You'll find another country. Take Ro Holding instead. What does it
matter where you rule, if you have conquered time?"

"It matters."

"Why?"

"Saphier is the dragon's face. The Luxour is its heart. Saphier's history is
my past, my future. The Luxour is my heart."

"You have no heart," the dragon said contemptuously. "This stone has
more heart. I should kill you now, let them burn Saphier to ash and rubble.
Shall I?" he asked Brand, who started under his sudden gaze. "Shall I? Answer."

Brand's hands clenched. His mouth tightened; his silence wore at Nyx as
she sat tensely, neither moving nor breathing, listening. It wore at Draken,
who seemed to hear in it, or in himself, something of the firebird's endless,
anguished cry. "He is your son," Brand said finally. His voice shook. "How
do dragons treat their children?"

Lines that were not bitter shifted unexpectedly across the ancient face.
"Who taught you to riddle with dragons? Your father? Does he know the answer to that riddle? Tell us the answer, Ragah's son. Guess if you do not
know. How do dragons treat their children? Answer."

Draken, his eyes on Brand's rigid face, started to answer, stopped. He
lifted one hand, hid his eyes from what he saw. "With lies," he said. "With

ruthless cruelty. They make their children love them, and then twist their love into hate, their trust into fury, their innocence into despair and grief. So dragons treat their children."

"No," the dragon said softly. "You are wrong. So humans treat their children."

The mages' voices fluttered like leaves in a treeless place. In the distance, the great, grey dragon rose on its rock pile, sent a flash of deadly light at whatever had annoyed it. The ground shook as the dragon-fire scarred the Luxour; stones whirled into the air. Draken watched them fall; they struck the earth like random heartbeats. He said, his voice sounding weary, almost as ancient as his father's, "I have nothing to give you for Saphier but my life."

"A poor price."

"All I have. Spare Saphier. I beg you."

"It made you. You are its past, its future."

"It made Rad Ilex. Something good must dream its way out of the minds of dragons into the Luxour, into the air of Saphier to shape the likes of Rad Ilex, who of all my mages defied me. And Saphier made my son. In spite of me."

"There is a price," the dragon said, "for Saphier."

"And all in it?"

"All."

"Take it," Draken said harshly, and bowed his head.

The air ignited with silver. Paths tangled with paths, melted, converged, tore, until it seemed to Nyx that they were all trapped in Chrysom's impossible black box, where all the threads of time led into one another, and no path opened beyond the chaos. The image of melted, burning threads of silver imprinted itself on the air for moments after the time-paths had vanished from every wrist.

"There are no more such paths anywhere in Saphier," the dragon said. "Except one." He held out his hand; the gold and ivory key lay in it. Again the hard lines of his face eased; he looked at Nyx. "The mage—what was his name? Chrysom. He was a gentle man. I dislike burning books."

Nyx's face shook. She put her hands over her mouth; the burning tears slid down between her fingers. Meguet, tearless, stunned, turned to her as at a touch, seeing what she saw: Time, nearly ended on the Luxour, was shaping its path again toward home.

"I will take the key," the dragon said. He added an afterthought, "And you, my twisted son. For seven years. And I will take the dragons back. But who," he wondered of the mages, "will watch these human dragons for me?" The mages, under his eye again, turned to stone. He lifted a finger, spun a thread of fire. It streaked through the air and caught Rad Ilex.

Rad, white, silent, ringed by fire, stared into the dragon's eyes. The winds died; time stilled on the Luxour. In an hour, or in the next breath, Rad moved again, turned to the mages of Saphier. The dragon-fire parted, looped around his wrist, burning gold and red and all hues between. He said nothing. He didn't have to, Nyx thought. Only he and the dragon knew what power had passed between them, and no one seemed likely to test him.

"In seven years," the dragon said, "Rad Ilex will come to me for Draken Saphier. Do not force him, by any intention or act, to find me sooner than that."

In the motionless ring of mages, someone moved: Magior stepped forward. "And who, my lord," she asked humbly, "will rule Saphier? It is best for Saphier if you choose."

"Who will rule in your place for seven years?" the dragon asked Draken Saphier. "Answer."

Draken was silent. An errant wind scattered a handful of dust at his feet; briefly, his noon shadow shaped the firebird. He swallowed something bitter, painful, the lines on his face running deep, before he lifted his head, held Brand's eyes.

"Brand Saphier will rule," he said. "Now and for the rest of his life. I know Saphier. I will not have it tear itself apart choosing between the dragon and the firebird." He added, so softly that even the Luxour stilled itself to hear, "If in seven years you have any desire at all to find me, look for me here. The Luxour seems the only thing that I have ever loved."

Brand's expression blurred, as if the magical winds had reshaped it briefly, and then shaped again the warrior's mask. The dragon said to him.

"Is human justice served between father and son? Are you content? Answer."

"No," Brand said huskily. His own hands clenched; expression shook again into his face, and, unexpectedly, into Draken's. "There is no justice for this. Nothing will ever quiet the firebird's cry."

Draken nodded wearily. "I hear it now," he said. He turned away from Brand, to his father.

"Come," the dragon said, and Draken vanished. A black dragon with eyes of cobalt and gold lifted itself into the winds above Brand. From the jumbled stones and palaces the dragons rose, soared into the air, shapes of fire and shadow, a progression across the bright sky as strange and gorgeous as the firebird's enchantments. As the dragon-mage led them back into their secret worlds, the Luxour sent a shadow after them, a memory in the wind: the Cygnet, with its wings of night, its starry eye, following dragons across an unfamiliar sky.

EIGHTEEN

NYX saw the face of the firebird one last time as the dragons disappeared: The cry filled Brand's eyes, then left them empty, searching the barren desert for something he had forgotten. She took a step toward him. His eyes found her then. He waited, drained, motionless, for her to come to him, the terrible emptiness in his eyes slowly filling again with memories, dragons, the magic of the Luxour. She put her arms around him, heard nothing for a long time but his breathing, his heartbeat. Finally she heard his voice.

"Can you stay?"

She shook her head against him, her own face colorless, expressionless. "I must go home."

"Then how will I see you again?"

"There is a way," she said, but for once she doubted herself. "There is always a way." She shifted to see his face; it was set, but more in determination than despair. He even smiled a little, crookedly.

"I have never made things easy for you."

"I never liked things easy." She held him again, tightly, aware this time, of all the silent, watching mages. "Will you be safe?" she asked him.

"The dragon rules Saphier," he said softly. "For seven years. Even the most powerful of the warrior-mages will be wary of that. I trust Magior.

And Rad. They will help me. Saphier's future has always been its past. I don't know how to change that. Perhaps only the threat of dragons can change Saphier's ways. The threat of something more dangerous than itself." He dropped his face against her lank, dusty hair, kissed it. "Some day," he whispered, "we will find that cave full of waterfalls and dragon-mist again."

"I'll find a way," she promised. Her throat ached. "Chrysom did it. I can do it."

"I can't. This time you will have to come to me."

She looked at him, saw his face, his father's face, even something of the dragon's hard, powerful face. "If Saphier's heart is the Luxour, and the Luxour is the dragon's heart, perhaps it is more your grandfather's heart. He found something of Ro Holding to value. Something of Ro Holding's peace."

"So have I," Brand whispered. He bent his head, found her lips, coaxed peace from them until the winds of the Luxour, hot and fuming and enchanted, swirling around them, seemed to her the winds of home. He raised his head finally; she felt him draw in air as if he would swallow all the magic in the winds.

She loosed him reluctantly. "Come to me," he said, and she nodded. He cast an eye over his mages then. Some were watching him, astonished; others dreamed across the distances, searching for a glint of dragon-wing. Most had clustered in small groups, to unravel the events that had so abruptly changed the path of Saphier's future. Nyx looked for Meguet. She stood beside Rad Ilex as he spoke with Magior; Nyx saw him lift one hand, draw it lightly down Meguet's hair. She stiffened slightly, then met Nyx's eyes. She looked too tired to stand; her face pleaded silently: *Home.*

"We must go," Nyx said to Rad Ilex as she joined them. Magior, her face seamed with fine, troubled lines, said to Nyx.

"Draken Saphier cast a spell, it seems, over his entire house, as well as his son. We were all ensorcelled by his vision. The dragon was wise to destroy the time-paths. It is still a very powerful vision."

"There are other visions," Nyx said wearily. "Perhaps the dragons of the Luxour will dream up something for the mages of Saphier to do besides war."

"Yes," Magior agreed, but doubtfully. "It will take some time to change. Saphier has always been"—she gestured toward a sudden feathery sweep of distant steam—"volatile."

"Saphier," Rad said grimly, "has a choice between inventing peace or ceasing to exist. A more merciful choice than you would have allowed Ro Holding."

"Yes." Magior cleared her throat. "I know. Force is its own justification. It exists primarily because it is capable of existing. Now that we are made powerless, I can find no justification for what we had contemplated. I thought I was too old to change. Too old to see Saphier in the light of anything but its own history. We will need help. Your ideas, Rad, and Brand's. Even Draken's. Perhaps, in seven years, he will be alive to advise us."

"You would trust him?" Rad asked sharply.

"I would trust his father," Magior said simply. "If he permits Draken to live, he will have changed the heart of Saphier itself." She paused, her eyes on Nyx. "Perhaps, with Brand, it is already changing."

"So will Ro Holding," Meguet murmured, "if you manage to find each other again."

"Across mountains and seas and endless wastes," Nyx said, seeing them spread across the distance between Ro Holding and Saphier, each mountain, each ocean, pushing them farther apart. "And worlds," she added speculatively. "And time." She put a hand to her eyes against the vision, felt Meguet's hand on her shoulder.

"There is always—"

"A way," Nyx finished. She looked at Rad, wondering how anyone so haggard and spent that he could scarcely cast his own shadow, could possibly be standing upright. "Is there a way home?" she asked him. "Will the dragon permit you to use Chrysom's time-path back to Ro Holding?"

He nodded, and held out his hand: What he had sought in Ro Holding lay in his palm. "One last time," he said with an effort. "Then I must return the key to him. Or he will come back to Saphier looking for it, and he will not be pleased. You'll have to help me open the paths. I can hardly open the book itself."

Nyx was silent, thinking of the key holding all the mysteries of the Luxour, all Chrysom's innocent, secret journeys. So was Rad; their minds touched inadvertently, holding the same key. They pulled back; their eyes met. Nyx said ruefully,

"Now I would be content for either one of us to keep it."

"Yes." He reached out to Meguet, held her wrist as he had when she had been pulled so precipitously into Saphier's history. "So," he said without looking at her, "I must return you to your Gatekeeper." She said nothing, did not move, until he finally raised his eyes. She said softly,

"I will never forget the dragons. Or the Luxour."

"Or the rose?"

She started to speak, then stopped. She smiled suddenly, and a little color came back into his drawn face. "Or the rose that got us into all this trouble."

"Now you know why I dropped it there."

"Now," she said, "I know why I picked it up."

He held her eyes, using her, Nyx realized, as his calm focal point of concentration. She turned abruptly, for one last glimpse of Brand standing in the Luxour, stones towering behind him in a tumbled jagged disorder that seemed to be always on the verge of order. In the next moment, in the next . . . Surrounded by mages, all their thoughts and ideas pulling at his attention, he detached himself for a moment, stood alone, saw only her. The Luxour slowly misted from gold to cobalt-blue to black, until the only clear thing in the world was the silver path to Ro Holding forming beneath their feet.

Chrysom's tower, building around them out of the mist, seemed, for a moment, another rising of stone at the moment of change. It did change into a palace and remained changed, though Nyx noted, with an instant of surprise, without the firebird. Her throat tightened. Rad's white dragon waited for him still; she freed it. It leaped gracefully to its place across Rad's heart. Together she and Rad fashioned a path back to the Luxour while he still had strength to think. Meguet had not even that left; Nyx found her a moment or two later, sunk deep into a leather chair and fast asleep.

She paced a step aimlessly, bewildered by the silence, some part of her still expecting to see the firebird. Her bones ached with exhaustion, but she could not bring herself to leave the tower. It seemed the only bridge between two worlds, and a broken one at that, but all she had. Memories crowded into her mind, far too many for the tower to hold; she had no other place to keep them. She touched her face, and still moving, found a tear on her fingers. Her hand shook, her whole body trembled. She looked at Meguet, who had escaped the world somehow; not even Nyx's tears brought her back. She was trapped, it seemed, like the firebird, by memory: impossible to go back, yet equally impossible to open the tower door, leave the past behind her. She forced herself still finally, stood in a drift of sunlight, her arms tightly folded to stop her trembling. Still she could shape no path, not even into the next moment.

The door opened abruptly. She caught a glimpse of her mother's face, chalk-white and delicately lined, before the Holder gripped her, shook her a little, and finally pulled her into an embrace that took her breath away. She blinked, vaguely aware that her mother was holding her upright; her bones preferred to spill onto the floor.

"What happened?" the Holder was demanding, her attention divided between Nyx's frozen face, her torn, dusty clothes, and Meguet, dressed in the same peculiar fashion, with blood on her sleeve and her face as pale and still as ivory. "What happened?"

"I fell in love," Nyx said.

Meguet woke out of a dream of dragons. A black dragon had been trying to tell her something: not the red-eyed dragon of war, nor the dragon with the human eyes that had been Draken Saphier, but one with a gentle voice, and eyes as cold and pure as stars. Or had it been a dragon? she wondered, in the moment between sleeping and waking. Something dark as night that flew . . . She opened her eyes then and found the night.

Memory returned slowly: She had fallen asleep in a chair in Chrysom's tower, not, as her bones felt, on the stone floor of a cave in the Luxour. Nyx was safe. Ro Holding was safe, time had been breached and sealed again. She gathered herself wearily, piecemeal, and stood. Nyx had left a candle lit for her. In the dark yard beyond the south window, she saw another flame. She moved toward it thoughtlessly, as if to walk to it on air, before her mind woke and told her what it was.

She turned and took the stairs instead.

She wondered, as she crossed the quiet yard, what time it was, what day it was. Midnight might have come and gone; there was no firebird to cry against it. There was still a Gatekeeper; she saw a taper flame, trembling in the sea air, rise to light his pipe. The flame vanished suddenly, as if he had dropped pipe and taper to stand, a dark figure against the torchlight at the top of the turret steps.

She did not see him come down. He was just there, with her in the yard, holding her face between his hands.

"Meguet," he said, and she felt his swift, fierce embrace, as if he could not bear even a shadow of night between them. She held him as tightly, feeling for the bone beneath his face, the bone beneath her hands, feeling for his heartbeat against hers. "I thought I lost you," he whispered.

She shook her head. "I came back." He said no more, turning his face, bone by bone, against hers to find her mouth. For a moment she wandered with him beyond time, beyond memory, beyond weariness and terror. A stray touch made her wince; she dropped back into time.

"You're hurt," he said, his hands sliding lightly down her arms, loosing her.

"Only a little." Draken's relentless eye tracked her suddenly as she ran down the secret paths in her mind; she hid her face against Hew's shoulder, added numbly, "I should be dead. And you should be trying to bar the gate against a hundred mages, and dragons of air and night and stone that could tear this house apart with a breath and toss it into the swamp. And the dragon-lord of Saphier. Brand's father, who caused all this trouble."

She felt him shudder. "There's been nothing at the gate lately but what's expected, familiar. All the odd enchantments went with you and Nyx. We had a warning. And then nothing, not even a lost swamp-bird. Blue sky and tranquil seas. And a Gatekeeper going blind trying to shape you out of thin air. You vanished out of the world with a mage who gave you a rose—"

She lifted her head, blinking. "I was dragged." She could see vague lines and shadows on his face in the torchlight; she could not see an expression. "Into a desert. Like no place I have ever been, not even in dreams. Dressed for supper in a hot, barren, nameless wasteland where there were dragons or maybe not, with a dying mage on my hands."

He made a sound, touched her again, gently. "Let's go up," he said, "where I can see your face."

They sat in the turret, a dragon's eye of a moon watching them from over the swamps while she told him where the rose had led her. She could see him clearly then, in the taper-light, the shadows beneath his eyes, the ghosts of worry and care still haunting his face as he listened, one hand linked in hers, so still she scarcely heard him breathe. When she had wakened herself again in the chair in Chrysom's tower, he moved finally. His lips parted; he didn't speak. One hand reached toward a taper, dropped. She said very softly.

"You opened the gate between Ro Holding and Saphier."

He met her eyes; still he didn't speak. Then she heard his breath, long and slow like tide.

"I am Gatekeeper," he said finally. "In the light of day or in the dark, in the end it's me, standing here, making a choice to open or not."

"Nyx said she was warned, just as she left with the firebird, that there would be danger to the Cygnet. You let her go."

He picked the taper out of its sconce then, lit his pipe. "I promised her I would."

"Even when—"

"She gave me a name. The place where you were lost, where she would go to find you if she found a way. I never saw the dragon's shadow behind the firebird, only the strange mage, and the firebird, who cried questions without answers here in Ro Holding. And only you, vanishing like that, dragged to anywhere by a mage who got past my eye."

"Did he? Or did you let him in, too?"

He shifted, putting the pipe down, and turned to her, grasping both her hands in his. "He found his own way in. As he had, you said yourself, many times before. Chrysom made this house, and its gate, and maybe left a door open somewhere, for the mage he liked. If I had stopped Nyx from going, then what? We would have had at least one dragon at our gate, and maybe we can move the house across Ro Holding, but not Ro Holding itself to a safe place. The Cygnet flies alone among the dangers of the night. It doesn't live quietly in some safe place. And neither, as you of all of us know best, does Nyx."

She opened her mouth, found herself wordless. The house, she decided, in that tangled moment, had its mysteries, and she was one of them and so was he. Mysteries, by their nature, behaved in mysterious ways. She settled back, calmer now. "Sometimes," she said, "I know you as well as yesterday. And sometimes not at all."

He watched her, his own face calmer, still holding her hands. He leaned toward her; she met him halfway. The moon disappeared between their faces, reappeared now and then, in various phases, until a step disturbed them, and as they drew apart, the full moon grew again between them.

Nyx stood at the top of the steps, looking tired but composed. "My mother sent me to find you," she said to Meguet. She held out a hand as Meguet straightened. "She doesn't need you yet. She only wanted to make sure you hadn't vanished again." Meguet eyed her narrowly. Nyx had dressed for supper in familiar fashion, but supper was long past, and small jewels flashed askew in her hair, and a button dangled by a thread.

"What have you been doing?"

"Trying to find Saphier." She tucked a strand of hair behind her ear. "What else?"

"How?"

"In books. And other places."

"What other places?"

"Odd places." Her eyes went to the Gatekeeper. "Hew—"

"What other places? That box of Chrysom's?"

Nyx drew breath, loosed it. She folded her arms, leaned against the stones. "Don't worry. I'm being careful. I've figured out how to come and go; I don't get lost inside the box and I don't go far down any of the paths. None of them," she added wearily, "are at all familiar. Hew——"

He was shaking his head, his brows crooked. "I'm sorry." he said gently. "You found your own path there before; I can't do that for you. All I do is open and close."

"Well." She pondered, her eyes on the stars, while the Gatekeeper shifted past Meguet in the tiny turret, came out to stand beside Nyx. He lit his pipe again. "Assuming it's on the same world, in Ro Holding's present, and not its past or future—which I can't entirely rule out—it must be somewhere. Not even Calyx can find it, and she's been searching records as old as the house."

"It's just as well," the Gatekeeper said, "from the sound of things, that the Dragon hasn't flown itself into the household records before now."

"I suppose." Nyx yawned; her eyes looked colorless and luminous as the moon. Meguet, watching her through the open turret arches, asked with some sympathy,

"What does your mother think of all this?"

"She seems unusually resigned. I suspect she hopes that I'll never find Saphier and that I'll forget about Brand. Perhaps. Anything is possible. But expecting me to forget Brand, and the Luxour, and the dragons of the Luxour, and the dragon-mage, and all that wild, unfocused power that shaped even the Cygnet out of our thoughts, is expecting too much. There is, I reminded her, a precedent. Chrysom also loved the Luxour."

"So did I," Meguet said softly. "For a few moments. When I saw it through Rad's eyes."

"You didn't tell me that," the Gatekeeper said. She met his eyes across the torch fire.

"No," she said, smiling a little. "I felt it was wrong of me, wanting to see dragons. Things that lay beyond the Cygnet's eye."

"How do you know they do?" he asked curiously. "Or do you know at all?"

She was silent, gazing back at him. "I don't," she said, and got to her feet abruptly. "None of us would have recognized a dragon before now. And perhaps I never saw the Cygnet among the stars only because I didn't expect it to fly anywhere in Saphier's sky."

She stepped outside the turret; Nyx was already searching the night sky. "The Dragon hunts the Cygnet," Nyx murmured. "Behind the constellation? Or above it? The black war-dragon with blood-red eyes."

"I saw it," Meguet said wonderingly. "The constellation in Rad's doorway. The dragon of night and stars. It never occurred to me it might be—"

"There," the gatekeeper said, pointing over the sea, "just on the horizon.
That red star. Two red stars. And look. One star its breast, one star the tip of
its outflung wing, those stars its claws, and those, that faint cloud of stars, its
breath of fire. And that star over there, perhaps its tail? Would that be it?"

"I see it," Nyx breathed. Her fingers, chilled, closed on Meguet's wrist.
"There. South and west above the sea."

"I see." Meguet was staring at the Gatekeeper.

"Is that what you saw, Meguet?"

"Yes."

"So Saphier lies somewhere beneath the dragon's eye. I can sail there—"

"Please," Meguet breathed.

"I'll send explorers," Nyx conceded. "Messengers. Even my mother would
approve of that. As much as she approves of any of this. I'll take Chrysom's
box to Rad Ilex; perhaps he can help me find a path between Ro Holding and
Saphier. A private path . . ." Her voice trailed into silence; she contemplated
the dragon's eyes a moment before she asked slowly, "How would a man born
in a swamp in the Delta in Ro Holding recognize a dragon?"

"I was wondering that myself," Meguet said. And then she felt all
thought fade away until she was barely air, barely night within the night. She
was touched, it seemed, by the light, flickering, changing winds of the Luxour. "Were you there?" she asked the Gatekeeper. His face was in shadow
again; she could not see his eyes. "On the Luxour? All those dark swans flying out of my night-shadow, all those winds stealing magic out of me. One
of those swans wasn't wind. One was real." He didn't answer. "Tell me," she
pleaded, her voice still spellbound, her bones shaped of stars now, at her elbow and ankle, throat and amazed eye. "Tell me that you saw the dragons.
That when I say dragon, that's what you will see: the flight of dragons across
the Luxour under the noon sun."

He started to speak, stopped. Then he shifted into light, and she saw
them in all their terrible grace and power flying through his eyes. He drew
her against him tightly, perhaps to hide what he had seen by day, perhaps in
memory of what he had fought by night. "Gatekeepers don't leave the gate,"
he said at last into her hair. "But what my heart does, flying out of me in
terror or wonder or love, only you can tell me, because it will follow only
you."

She felt his heart fly into her; her mind filled with dreams and memories of the soft touches of wings, the rustlings and night-murmurings of flight. Her hand brushed his wrist; his fingers opened, linked with hers. She whispered, "Then follow."

She led him down the turret steps. Behind them, Nyx stood in the moonlight, waiting as patiently as stone or time, for the slow dance of constellations to reveal a path by star and water into the Dragon's dawn.